WHAT A
MOTHER KNOWS

Praise for *What a Mother Knows*

"A missing daughter, a lost memory, and a desperate need to find the truth propel Lehr's achingly moving suspense drama. Dark and unsettling, but with a ray of hope like a splash of light, and a knockout ending you won't see coming."

—*Caroline Leavitt,* New York Times
bestselling author of Pictures of You

"Reminiscent of S. J. Watson's *Before I Go to Sleep,* Leslie Lehr's *What a Mother Knows* is a fast-paced and gripping exploration of a mother's love. A powerfully affecting novel."

—*Heather Gudenkauf,* New York Times *bestselling author of* The Weight of Silence *and* One Breath Away

"Leslie Lehr writes about a mother's devotion both intimately and insightfully, perfectly capturing its unique, all-consuming love. Her characters are so real I expect to bump into them whenever I walk outside. They'll stick with you long after the book ends."

—*Hope Edelman, author of* Motherless Daughters

"Imagine your worst nightmares coming true—a fatal accident, a missing daughter, a distant husband—and then finding out you might be at fault. In her provocative page-turner, Leslie Lehr illustrates how sometimes the right decisions can lead to unintended, life-altering consequences. *What a Mother Knows* is a poignant, powerful novel."

—*Jillian Medoff, bestselling author of*
I Couldn't Love You More *and* Hunger Point

"Leslie Lehr has crafted an insightful novel that gets at the heart of what it means to be a wife, a mother, a woman, in a world overrun by the expectations of pop culture."

—*Lisa Bloom,* New York Times *bestselling author of* Think: Straight Talk for Women to Stay Smart in a Dumbed-Down World

"The elements of Hollywood moviemaking and tabloid hedonism blend nicely with the desperate franticness of, say, S. J. Watson's *Before I Go to Sleep.*"

—*Booklist*

WHAT A
MOTHER KNOWS

LESLIE LEHR

sourcebooks
landmark

Published by Sourcebooks Landmark, an imprint of Sourcebooks, Inc.
P.O. Box 4410, Naperville, Illinois 60567-4410
(630) 961-3900
Fax: (630) 961-2168
www.sourcebooks.com

Library of Congress Cataloguing-in-Publication data is on file with the publisher.

Printed and bound in the United States of America.
BG 10 9 8 7 6 5 4 3 2 1

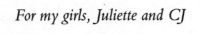

For my girls, Juliette and CJ

"If you run away," said his mother,
"I will run after you. For you are my little bunny."
—*The Runaway Bunny*
by Margaret Wise Brown

Prologue

No one saw the deadly crash in the canyon on that gray October morning. The weather was strange, an out-of-season sprinkle from the coastal fog drifting inland. Soggy hitchhikers huddling under the umbrella of an ancient oak tree were the last to see the black SUV as it hydroplaned past them into the Santa Monica Mountains. A muffled bass beat trailed as it climbed the winding lane, up and around the evergreen scrub, until it disappeared in the forest crowning the coastal range. A mile farther, at the lovers' lookout above the vast checkerboard of Valley streets, tire tracks puddled with mud were the only signs of human life.

As the headlights tunneled into the mist, no one noticed how the worn wipers flailed at the thrumming rain, how they blocked the bird's-eye view of the gorge that inspired the Tongva name "Topanga," a place above. No one could testify how the engine groaned as it climbed that ear-popping stretch of sacred land. Or how the vehicle veered around the dizzying curve, spraying water over the edge of the rocky cliff.

When a coyote streaked past to scale the hillside, the bumper dipped into a flooded pothole. Bright headlights bobbed across a plywood peace sign, then lit a tall pole flying a plaster pig toward heaven. A few yards farther, the beams flashed across the ruins of a legendary roadhouse like the spotlights of decades past. Echoes of Arlo Guthrie and Neil Young lingered in the air, but it was Jim Morrison's tribute that haunted the highway beyond. "Keep your eyes on the road, your hands upon the wheel...Let it roll, baby, roll."

The Explorer dove off the cliff. Airborne, the bass boomed louder and reverberated across the canyon, accompanying a chorus of screams. It crashed against a scrubby ledge, then spun through the shower of pine needles, shredded branches and shards of broken grill, hurtling down, down, down, ribs snapping against the steering wheel, head splitting on the dashboard, music still blaring until the SUV smashed against the rock wall, shearing off the side mirror, shattering the window, shooting out into the ravine where the chassis flipped. The car exploded into the creek bed, airbags popping, bones cracking, flesh tearing, as the two ton cage of steel folded like origami into the mud.

Raindrops fell.

When the sky cleared, the canyon Cub Scout troop began its weekly hike. They wandered out from the willows lining the flooded creek as the last plumes of smoke rose from the smoldering wreckage. Crows hidden in the hillside canopy flew out in a dark feathered cloud. A rabbit burrowed into his den beneath a steaming puddle of blood. Soon, sirens wailed in the distance.

By afternoon, the muddy canyon was clogged with emergency vehicles. The sky pulsed with the *thwack-thwack-thwack* of news helicopters circling for a story. Reporters soon pieced together the who, what, when, and where. But no one could explain the why. The only witness was trapped inside.

1

Eighteen Months Later

MICHELLE INHALED DEEPLY, INTOXICATED by the scent of orange blossoms infusing the spring air. She smiled at the sidewalk parade of baby strollers and couples holding hands as Drew drove slowly down their street. He braked for the children bicycling past, then pulled the car into the driveway. Their classic California ranch house rose up behind the picket fence like a mirage, glimmering in the last golden rays of the day.

Michelle fumbled to unbuckle her seat belt as her husband circled behind the silver Volvo and opened her door. She climbed out slowly, stiff from the long drive home from the hospital. When he gallantly offered his arm, she felt like a queen being escorted back to her castle. Her hungry eyes savored every inch of the yard until she felt dizzy and had to squeeze them shut. She opened them quickly to be sure she wasn't dreaming. No, she was awake. After all those grueling months learning to walk again, she yearned to dance barefoot in the lush grass. She was tempted to tear the petals off those crazy-big roses and toss them in the air like confetti. And she had never seen anything quite so wonderful as the name *Mason* spelled out on the mailbox. She was home.

When a Coldplay ringtone split the air, Drew pulled the phone from his jeans pocket and checked the number. He gave Michelle a quick kiss in apology, then handed her the cane that she rarely used anymore. Worn out from her last physical therapy session, she rested against it like a windblown palm tree.

She turned to admire her handsome husband as he spoke in the clipped tones of a work call. His hair had thinned to a halo and there were lines framing his face now, but she cherished every one. She was grateful that he had taken such good care of things while she was gone. He pulled a bandanna from his back pocket and wiped his face when he hung up, sighing with happiness or exhaustion, she couldn't tell which. Drew had always been full of mystery. That's what had attracted her when they first met, at a student film wrap party eighteen years ago. Or was it twenty now?

A car horn honked. Michelle turned to see a white Jetta pull to the curb. She hugged her bad arm out of habit and called to the young woman in periwinkle scrubs who was climbing out. "Hi, Lexi! I thought we lost you."

Lexi hung a nurse's case over her slim shoulder, then yanked her blond ponytail free of the strap. "Serves me right for finishing your discharge papers at rush hour. On a Friday, no less." When she opened the trunk, a bouquet of helium balloons burst out. She grabbed for the ribbons, but they were already rising high above her. The words *Good Luck* flashed until the balloons flew from sight. Lexi looked over with a pained expression.

Michelle laughed. She didn't need balloons to make this day special. She felt as if she were flying herself, nearly bursting with joy. She had dreamt of this day for as long as she could remember.

Lexi scooped up a large bakery box then shut the trunk with her elbow.

Drew waved. "Need help with the cake?"

A husky voice called from the front door. "Did someone say 'cake'?" Michelle smiled at her son, Tyler. After spending the last few weeks limited to cafeteria food between family sessions at the hospital, he could easily devour the rest of the cake in one sitting. Michelle would have to save a slice for his big sister, Nikki, who'd been away at school for months. She was due home in the morning, a mere twelve hours away. Nikki was the treat that Michelle craved most—she was starving for the very sight of her.

The bark of a dog drowned out whatever Tyler said next. Their St. Bernard barreled out of the house and headed directly for Michelle. Drew stepped in quickly to block the shaggy beast from knocking Michelle over.

"Bella!" Tyler called, but she kept jumping to get at Michelle. Tyler ran over and grabbed the dog's studded collar. "She missed you, Mom."

Michelle scratched behind Bella's ear. "I missed you too, Bella. Hard to believe you're the same pup I found licking hamburger wrappers on Sunset Boulevard." She looked up at Tyler. "What are you feeding her?"

"Hamburgers," Tyler admitted. His eyes were jade green, like his father's, and when he pulled his mother up for a hug, she saw that he was almost as tall. "And Easter candy, but don't worry, I saved you some." While his words were lighthearted, she could feel the longing in his embrace. She squeezed him back with her good arm to assure him that yes, she was still that person, still the one who loved stray dogs and chocolate—and him.

The front door banged open and a few friends leaned out to wave. "Welcome home!"

Michelle caught her breath and looked at Drew with her eyes brimming. He kissed her forehead and ushered her slowly inside. Before she knew it, Michelle had been swept right through the foyer into the living room, past the fireplace and French doors and over to the oak dining table. She was touched to see the spring bouquet and the boxed candle and the homemade lemon bars. There was even a bottle of bubbly wrapped with a red bow. But she took the most comfort from the sight of the table itself. The deep scratch in the center reminded her of that day early in their marriage when she and Drew had bought it at an after-earthquake sale. Since the accident, entire months were missing from her memory, so this fleeting glimpse of that moment inspired hope.

Julie, her wine-tasting buddy from across the street, gave her a tender hug. "Oh my god, Michelle, it's so good to have you home. You look fabulous! I never noticed how thin you were, wrapped in that hospital bathrobe."

Michelle looked down at her gaunt frame draped in cotton pants and a Velcro-tabbed top. "It's called the Coma Diet," she teased. "But I wouldn't recommend it." She took in Julie's curves, displayed to great effect in her fitted blouse and black pencil skirt. And after wearing slippers for so long, Michelle nearly drooled at the sight of Julie's burgundy pumps.

"Oh hush, it's been almost a year since you woke up. Didn't you get the case of Girl Scout cookies I dropped off at the hospital?"

"Sure, but aside from learning to talk and walk again, one of the first things I had to learn to do was share. The other patients in my ward finished them in a week."

"No worries," Julie said. "The gamine look becomes you. Like Audrey Hepburn." She pointed at Michelle's hair. "And how brave to go *au naturale*."

Michelle fingered her short gray locks. "I couldn't color it myself." She automatically looked down at her limp right arm, immobilized in a skin-colored compression sleeve from above her elbow down to her withered fingers.

"Of course not," Julie said quickly. "I'm just surprised they didn't have a salon in that place—your husband claimed it was state of the art."

"That hardly seems important," a woman's voice interjected. Cathy, the wife of Tyler's baseball coach, set plastic forks on the table, then joined them. "How are you feeling, Michelle?"

"Wonderful," Michelle said. Cathy was shorter, but her embrace was so warm and her sweater was so soft that Michelle was reluctant to let go.

"We're so glad to have you back," Cathy said, smoothing her sweater over her flowered skirt. She glanced at her husband, Kenny, who stood at the other end of the table speaking with Drew. Both men were circling forty, but Kenny still had a full head of brown hair. The stocky build beneath his Dodgers baseball jacket was a compliment to Cathy's cooking. "Want to sit down?"

Michelle wasn't sure if they'd seen her wobble or were just being polite, but her legs still throbbed from walking the hospital hallways long enough to prove herself competent to go home. She settled in the chair that Julie pulled out. "Join me?"

"I've been sitting all day," Julie said. "Plus, I like being taller than you."

Cathy refused as well. "We don't want to wear out our welcome. You must be exhausted. Can I get you anything to eat?"

"Thanks, but I had cake earlier. Or did I?" she called to Lexi, who laughed from a few feet away, where she was setting out slices on party plates. Michelle smiled at the others, who exchanged looks of concern. After a year of rehabilitation she was used to being prodded and poked, but not stared at. They were making her nervous. "That was a joke—I ate my piece and most of Lexi's. I do have memory problems, but I never forget dessert. Especially chocolate. Of course, now I'm forgetting my manners—have you two been introduced?"

"Oh, we're old friends by now," Cathy said. "Julie's daughter is in my Girl Scout troop this year. The girls are off at a cookie meeting with my co-leader."

"Goodness," Michelle said, looking at Julie. "Last time Nikki babysat your kids, Sophie was in Brownies." She rubbed her bad arm, wondering how much her own daughter had grown since she last saw her. She knew Nikki had visited in the hospital, but it was all so fuzzy. Straining to remember made the passage of time more real, and more painful.

Lexi noticed Michelle's distress and joined them. "Did someone say cookie meeting? Because I'd love another box of Thin Mints. I'm Lexi, by the way, Michelle's care manager."

Michelle relaxed when Lexi stepped to her side. "She's been torturing me since I came out of the coma."

"Almost a year now," Lexi agreed. "That may sound long, but most of my patients never make it out of Acute Care. They're either permanently disabled or…"

The women exchanged fretful looks. "Was Michelle's injury similar to that congresswoman in Arizona?"

"Yes, except with Michelle it was tons of steel crushing her instead of a bullet in her head. It's rare to recover from any traumatic brain injury, but Michelle is a fighter."

Julie shivered. "I've always hated driving through Topanga. It's pretty, but Sophie gets carsick around those curves. I'd rather sit in freeway traffic, especially in the rain. It's a miracle you made it."

Michelle put a finger to her lips. "Shhh! A miracle won't look good on Lexi's résumé." Lexi laughed.

Cathy spoke up. "So, Michelle, do you remember the accident at all?"

"Nothing. Last thing I remember is gift-wrapping a camera for Nikki's sweet sixteen a few weeks earlier. Weird, huh?"

"That's not atypical," Lexi explained to Cathy and Julie. "She remembers things before that. It's as if her brain is trying to protect her from the scary stuff so she can focus on feeling better. The mind-body connection is pretty amazing that way. Most of it will probably come back to her over time."

"Every once in a while I get a flash of something, but… it doesn't always make sense." Michelle lowered her voice and gestured to Julie's chest. "For instance, I don't remember you being so voluptuous."

"You remember right about that," Julie said, winking.

Cathy frowned and turned to Lexi. "So, at some point, it will all come back?"

"Hard to say," Lexi admitted. "Some TBI patients take a few months, some years; some never recover any memories at all."

"I'm not sure I'd want to remember," Julie said. "First all those surgeries—then being kept in a coma for all those months? What was that like?" Julie felt Cathy's glare. "I'm sorry, was that rude? I don't want to upset you."

"What could upset me now?" Michelle asked. "It's over. The coma felt like a long deep sleep. Then sort of an increasing aware-ness until one day…I woke up."

"Like Sleeping Beauty," Julie said.

Michelle glanced at Lexi, who smiled. "Once Michelle could speak comfortably, she started reading fairy tales to the patients who weren't functioning as well. They really responded to the fantasy aspect and the happy endings. It was brilliant."

Michelle interrupted. "I was bored. Newspapers and TV were off limits in our wing. They said we were anxious enough without outside stimulation."

7

"Don't pretend you didn't like it," Lexi argued. "Anyway, *Sleeping Beauty* was always a big hit."

"It's very romantic," Julie said. "But I'm glad you didn't have to sleep a hundred years for a prince to wake you with a kiss."

"Five months was long enough," Cathy agreed. She glanced at her husband, still deep in conversation with Drew. "You can miss a lot in five months."

"I didn't mind missing my fortieth birthday," Michelle said.

"I'll drink to that," Julie said. She picked up the bottle of champagne and read the card. "Who's Becca? And more importantly, will she mind if I open this?"

Michelle shook her head. "She's my best friend from film school. Sorry she's not here, but she's a party girl—wouldn't want it to go to waste."

When the cork popped, Tyler looked in through the French doors from the backyard. Cathy's son Cody, another strapping sixteen year old, wiped his hands on his grass-stained baseball pants and opened the door while Tyler held Bella back. They came inside and headed over.

"Don't even think about it," Cathy warned her son as he eyed the bottle.

Julie poured champagne into party cups and handed them out for a toast. Michelle sneezed, nearly spilling hers. "I think my drinking days are over. I could use a decent cup of coffee, though. Hospital coffee is like watered down mud."

"That's on purpose, my friend," Lexi said.

"Want us to go to the store?" Tyler offered. "I have my driver's permit."

Michelle nodded at Drew, who was devouring another lemon bar as he spoke with Cathy's husband. "Go ask your father." She watched them each grab a slice of cake on the way. "Lexi, could you wrap up a nice corner piece and hide it in the fridge for Nikki? I don't trust these boys."

Lexi chuckled and took a piece to the kitchen. Michelle looked up to see Cathy's puzzled expression.

"Nikki's back?"

"She will be tomorrow. Probably sleep all day after that long flight from Australia. You heard she's an exchange student, didn't you? Drew says the school in Sydney has a great photography program."

Cathy exchanged looks with Julie.

Michelle noticed. "I know it's on the other side of the world. But Drew shot a miniseries there and one of the crew knows the host family, so it's safe. What was she going to do, spend her senior year at my bedside?"

Cathy smiled. "You must be excited to see her."

"You have no idea—ten months of nothing but messages. Feels like forever." Michelle frowned at Lexi as she returned.

"The hospital doesn't allow Skype or cell phones because of the cameras. It's a privacy issue," Lexi explained. "Patients do have access to unit phones."

"Yes, but the time change is murder," Michelle said. "I always end up leaving voice mails. By the time Nikki calls back, I don't have the phone anymore. The messages the nurses passed along were short and sweet, but she seems happy."

"Probably because you're better," Cathy said.

"She did sound sad after the accident," Michelle said. "Visiting hours were so limited and I was pretty doped up. She sent me one of those voice-recorded greeting cards. I play it so often I worry the computer chip will break." Michelle felt the pinpricks of tears. She sipped her water and blinked them away, smiling. "Now she thinks postcards of the Sydney Opera House are enough."

"Teenagers," Julie replied.

Cathy nodded and looked over at Cody and Tyler, who had given up on borrowing the car and were licking frosting from their fingers. Lexi noticed and took them napkins. "It's nice to see the boys together."

Michelle agreed. "I'm sorry they don't see each other more. My mother got Tyler into that boarding school before I was well enough to protest."

"Be grateful, some of those East Coast schools have a direct pipeline to the Ivy League," Cathy said. "Our high school has been ruined by budget cuts. And it's impossible to get into UCLA anymore."

"Maybe Julie can help," Michelle offered. "She's in the English department."

Julie downed her champagne and poured more.

"Cody is more of a math and science kid," Cathy said, watching her son hang on Lexi's every word. "Maybe he'll be a doctor."

"Maybe," Michelle said, smiling. "But you might want to tell him that Lexi is already dating a doctor."

The doorbell rang. The boys went to the door and staggered back with an orchid plant so large that it seemed to erupt with white blossoms. The men came around to clear room on the table, where it dwarfed the spring bouquet. Cathy handed Michelle the gift card. "'With love, Victor,'" she read.

"Probably left over from a commercial shoot," Drew said, unimpressed.

Lexi plucked a fallen petal from the soil. "No, Michelle's boss sent orchids to the hospital every month. You would have noticed if she didn't give so many away to other patients."

"That's our Michelle. We're so glad to have you back," Kenny said, echoing Cathy's words. He leaned in for a light hug.

"Thanks, Coach. Did you find a player to replace Tyler?"

"We did. But as a matter of fact, our shortstop has the flu, so if you could spare your son on Tuesday, I'd like to have him play."

"I'm sure he'd love that, thanks."

Drew put his arm around Kenny's shoulder. "Kenny's been a real godsend. Handled all the legal work after your accident."

"All I did then was put the estate in order," Kenny said, wincing at the morbid implication. "The insurance company has their own attorney."

"Thank you," Michelle said.

"You're welcome. I was coasting on a fat contingency fee that fall. But now…" He looked at Drew, who raised his hand like a stop sign.

The doorbell rang again. "I'll get it," Julie said. "If it's more flowers, I'll be happy to take them off your hands." She came back leading a trim black man in a tailored suit. "Not flowers, but the same offer goes."

"Dr. Palmer," Lexi said. "When I invited you, I didn't think you would actually come."

"I missed the hospital gathering, so I wanted to drop this by." Dr. Palmer set a gift bag of French Roast coffee on the table and smiled at Michelle.

"How thoughtful," Michelle said, pushing herself up to stand before anyone could notice the blood rushing to her cheeks. "Drew, you remember Dr. Palmer, don't you? The one Lexi calls Dr. Frankenstein?"

"Of course," Drew said, shaking hands with the younger man.

"Dr. Palmer is my orthopedic therapist," Michelle explained to the others. "He tortured me twice a week, rain or shine."

"Nice work," Cathy said. "She seems good as new—except for the arm."

Dr. Palmer smoothed his silk tie. "That's a bit tricky. This may be the best we can do."

"I'm sorry," Cathy said. "I didn't mean to…"

"No, it's all right," he interrupted. "Believe me, I wish I could do more. Mrs. Mason, I have to head over the hill before the traffic gets ugly. I just wanted to say how much I've enjoyed working with you." He gave her shoulder a squeeze and waved good-bye to the others. Lexi walked him out.

"Thanks for the coffee," Michelle called, watching him go.

"You okay?" Julie asked.

"Just feels strange. He was around more than my husband."

Drew overheard. "Only because I was busy working to pay him," he said a little too sharply. The others exchanged looks.

"I know, honey," Michelle said. "I didn't mean anything by it. I'm just tired. And I missed you." She reached for his hand and squeezed it.

"Of course you did." Cathy checked her watch. "This is an awful lot of fuss all of a sudden. Why don't I take Tyler home with us tonight? I put a casserole in the fridge for you and Drew."

"Is that okay?" Tyler asked.

Michelle blushed at the idea of being alone with her husband. Tyler took that as a yes and kissed her cheek good-bye.

After the others left, Lexi asked to see the handicapped shower bar Drew had installed. As they disappeared down the hallway, it grew so quiet that Michelle could hear the hum of the refrigerator in the kitchen. She was used to the white noise of hospital activity, but now even Bella had stopped barking.

Michelle swiped chocolate frosting off the last clump of cake and licked it from her finger. She felt too frail to clean the mess of crumpled napkins and half-filled cups. She had been warned that fatigue could last for years, but that didn't explain her unease.

Certainly, her friends would watch her closely to make sure she was okay. But they seemed wary as well.

As she looked around the room, something else felt off. The very air smelled different, perhaps from dust. Michelle's senses had come alive during her recovery, as if compensating for the loss of sensation in her right arm. She loved the orchids, partly because they had no scent. The lavender candle from Julie was sealed well enough, but the whiff of lemon crumbs on Cathy's platter made her nose twitch.

Drew and Lexi's footsteps echoed down the hallway. "Time to say good-bye, my friend," Lexi called, meeting her in the foyer. She unzipped her case and pulled out the clipboard full of discharge papers. Michelle hesitated, feigning interest in the X she had made on the signature line—all she could manage left-handed. Despite months of anticipation, saying good-bye to Lexi was the moment she had dreaded most.

Lexi handed the clipboard to Drew. He flipped through the documents until he came to an outpatient referral form. "I thought she was done with Dr. Palmer."

"Yes, as far as the hospital is concerned," Lexi said. "But the physiatrist who coordinated her treatment always recommends outpatient care. Patients tend to slack off on home exercises. If she sees Dr. Palmer at his clinic, he'll bill your insurance directly. If she decides not to, he can sign the physician's release to complete the file. Oops, I forgot to include that. I'll drop it by in case you need it."

Drew saw the prescriptions clipped underneath. "More antidepressants?"

"No, that was short-term, typical for recovery patients. These are antianxiety meds, in case of adjustment issues. Some patients need them, some don't."

"Good idea," Drew said.

"Oh, please," Michelle said to Lexi. "The only adjustment I'll have is to you not being here." When she heard the words aloud, she burst into tears. Over the past year, friends and family had come and gone, but Lexi was there every day. She was the one Michelle could trust with each step on the treadmill, the one who refused to let her settle for less.

Lexi embraced Michelle. "I'm going to miss you, too. Everybody will—and now the nurses will have to read the fairy tales." They laughed together, triumphant and miserable. After a moment, Drew reached for Michelle, as if to reclaim her.

Lexi handed a tissue to Michelle. "You'll be fine, see? This big strong husband of yours will take good care of you." She reached in her case and pulled out the plastic bag of Michelle's personal items. The bag slipped, spilling treasures to the floor. Lexi apologized and crouched to retrieve the silver brush and a wooden nesting doll, then fretted over broken glass in the picture frame. She stood up to show Michelle that the family was still visible, posing at the beach on a sunny day. In the photo, Michelle had long brown hair, Drew had all of his, Tyler had a baby face, and Nikki was making bunny ears behind her little brother's head.

"Don't worry, it's a copy," Michelle said, pointing at the larger version hanging behind them on the wall.

Lexi admired the portrait. "Must feel good to be home."

Michelle wiped her tears and smiled. "Like a fairy tale."

2

AFTER A QUIET DINNER, Drew put his arm around Michelle and walked her down the bedroom hall. The first door on the left was closed, but since Nikki was out of town, that was to be expected. Drew reached to pull Tyler's door shut just as Michelle spied the sleeping bag on the bare floor. The empty room shouldn't have been a surprise since Tyler lived away at school, but Michelle had never stopped picturing him here.

Drew misunderstood her confusion. "He's not sick of you, honey, he's just being a teenager. He misses Cody. And this does give us a chance to catch up."

"Catch up?" Michelle asked.

"It's been a long time. A lot has happened."

"I may be behind on current events, Drew, but we haven't been alone in over a year. You really just want to 'catch up?'" Now it was Drew's turn to blush. Michelle smiled to herself, pleased at how easy it was to flirt again.

Drew's warm hand squeezed hers as they reached the open doorway of their bedroom. When he turned on the light, Michelle was comforted to see her antique dresser and vanity table, and especially their king-sized sleigh bed. She went right to her suitcase, already unzipped, on the chenille bedspread.

Drew stood by the footboard for a moment and cocked his head to listen. He went around the bed and opened the window. Then he pointed outside where the crickets sang. "Hear that? They're early this year. Usually don't hear them until the end of April."

Michelle smiled. Drew was an audio engineer, famous for dubbing cricket songs into the night scenes of every movie he worked on. He was expert at enhancing evenings, setting the stage for romance. Michelle tried to hear the opera he described, the chorus of males rubbing their wings together to attract females. Her hearing was more acute than it had been before the accident, but she still couldn't distinguish between the rhythmic chirps. She felt oddly jealous. She wanted Drew to forget about the crickets, to rub his wings together and rekindle their romance.

"Shall I get that fancy candle?" he asked, as if reading her thoughts.

Michelle nodded, and found herself hugging her bad arm. She had anticipated her first night with Drew for weeks now. It was almost comical, but after wearing nothing but a flimsy gown in front of doctors and nurses for months, tonight she felt shy about stripping down for her own husband. He hadn't seen her naked since before her horrible accident. What if he thought she looked like a freak?

"Do you mind if I take a few minutes?" she asked.

"Sure," he said with a trace of relief in his voice. "I'll walk Bella and check the score of the Lakers game."

Michelle admired his long legs as he left. "You'll come to bed after?"

Drew nodded, then whistled for the dog.

The moment Michelle heard the front door close and the house go quiet, she tiptoed into the master bath and locked the door. She flipped on the light switch and took a good, honest look at herself in the mirror. She tried not to cry. No wonder Julie had been so overwhelmed by her appearance. Her hair was a shock of gray, chopped short to make it easy to brush. Her skin, deprived of eighteen months of sunshine, was ghostly pale. She took a deep breath, slipped out of her top and kicked off the elastic-waist pants.

There was no denying that she had lost her figure. When Michelle used to complain about being a few pounds overweight, Drew insisted her shape was sexy. This, of course, worked to her advantage in male-dominated Hollywood. Now, with sharp cheekbones and jutting hips, she looked like the underfed actresses who surrounded him on the set every day—before they went to hair and makeup. Audrey Hepburn she was not. She tore open the Velcro seam of her compression sleeve and dropped it on the tile floor. If only she could hide the ribbon of scars on her chest and the bracelet of burn marks down her right arm, maybe her husband would forget how much time had passed. Michelle wasn't sure how much time had passed since they'd made love before the accident, either. This was a chance to start fresh.

Soon, cheers erupted from the TV and echoed down the hall. Michelle could make out Jack Nicholson's name as she struggled to wash her face and brush her teeth. She was determined to get the toothpaste out and the cap on and off without asking for help. But all she could think about was the Staples Center packed with screaming fans and all the beautiful women with long shiny hair. She used to be one of them.

Michelle opened the drawer where she kept her nightgowns, but it was empty. So was the lingerie drawer above it. She opened the dark closet, but it looked empty, too. She struggled to close it and fell off balance, then spotted her garment bag in the shadow at the far end. She nearly cried with relief. When she managed to open it, she found her power suits, her wrap dresses, and her precious Louboutin shoes. Best of all, she found the satin negligee that she used to wear for special occasions. Tonight would certainly qualify.

The spaghetti straps slipped on easily and the fabric felt like heaven against her hard, abraded skin. Sure, the fit was baggy, but it was short enough to be sexy and the ivory color was ideal. This was a far cry from the sheer black teddy that Drew had once bought her for Valentine's Day. Still, it suited her mood. She had no idea how much her husband had missed her or when he'd gotten used to her being gone. She only wanted to feel safe in his arms. To forget the aching chasm of time that had come between them.

Michelle turned off the light, climbed under the covers, and waited. She practiced a seductive pose. After a few minutes, she sat up, arranged her treasures on the bedside table, and brushed her hair. Then she reached over and picked up the Russian Matreshka doll painted like a ballerina that her mother had given to Nikki. It didn't belong in here, but feeling the grooves from Nikki teething on the outer doll made Michelle smile. She opened the drawer where Drew had put her mail and flipped past the postcards to find the voice-recorded get well card. When she heard Drew shouting at the TV, she put it back. By morning, she wouldn't need to listen to the canned sound of her daughter's voice. Nikki would be home.

Michelle got out of bed and called down the hall. "Drew?" When she heard his footsteps approach, her heart skipped a beat. She climbed back into bed, pinched each cheek, and fluffed out her hair.

Drew towered over the bed as he set the candle on the table. His phone rang, but he glanced at the number and turned the ringer off. Michelle watched him undress to his boxers and realized that he, too, had lost weight. Long ropey muscles had replaced the soft flesh from Sunday dinners. After he disappeared into the bathroom, she heard the buzz of his electric razor and smiled; he was making his chin smooth for her.

"Did you have enough to eat?" she asked.

"Plenty," he said from the doorway. "You?"

Michelle nodded. She was only hungry for her husband now, to be hugged and kissed and held in his arms. She looked at the candle.

"Let me light that for you." He pulled a lighter from the Marlboro pack in the pocket of his denim shirt.

Michelle sat up. "Does Tyler know you smoke? He asked me to stop the car once to tell a man at a bus stop that it was bad for his health."

"He pretends not to know, I think. See no evil. Truth is, I like to sneak a smoke when a director is up my ass. Gives me a minute to think." Drew lit the candle, then sat down on the bed. "I never claimed to be as honest as you, Michelle."

She watched the flame flicker. "You used to make fun of my candles, too. You said if I had to set the scene to feel romantic, then I didn't really want it."

"I was wrong. You should have what you want." He hesitated, then turned to face her. "I mean it, honey. You don't deserve this. Any of this." His voice was husky as his arms wrapped gently around her.

She clung to him until his arms tightened, then she pressed her lips against his, ignoring the sour taste of nicotine beneath his toothpaste. They exchanged a few shy kisses before she pulled away. "Do you remember this nightgown?" When he didn't answer, she giggled. "It never stayed on long." He laughed. She reached for him, but lost her balance and rolled back, triggering a spasm in her bad arm.

Drew hesitated, so she pretended it was nothing and braved the rub of tender scar tissue as he pulled her back up. He held her and kissed her on the cheek, but she wanted more. She scooched back and bent her knees for balance to rest on her right side. He tilted his head to gaze at her as he lay on his side, then touched his fingertips to her temples. Slowly, they slid down her neck to her collarbone, then around the strap of her nightgown to her waist.

"Don't stop," Michelle whispered.

"I don't want to hurt you."

"You won't. The doctor said it was okay." Drew slid his hands between her legs, then stopped abruptly. "Please, honey, it's just me." Her voice had dropped to a whimper.

"No, it's just—it's been a long time."

She inched closer. Her body was willing, but she could tell by his hesitation that it wasn't the body he remembered. "Do you still love me?"

"For better or worse."

"Can't get much worse," Michelle teased, but Drew didn't laugh. Michelle ached for her husband. She laid her palm on his cheek and wobbled. He put his right arm on her side to steady her. She followed his smooth pelt with her fingers, down to where his ribs gave way to his belly, but she couldn't reach any farther. She nudged him with her knee. Nothing. As if Drew was the one who'd been maimed in the accident. "Is your back hurting? What did you call it, the tall man's curse?"

"That's not it. I'm sorry."

"It's just me. Remember the bride who did you on the golf course in Maui? And behind the Hemingway House in Key West? And on top of the Empire State Building?"

He quieted her with a kiss, rolled her back, and kissed her again with lips as tender as her memories. Then his eyes drifted shut, and all at once he was on her, kissing so hard her lips were bruising. She blinked up at him, but his eyes were still closed.

Drew rubbed his hand down her side and cupped her bottom. He kissed her neck until her head fell back. There were cobwebs on the ceiling. She closed her eyes. Pressure grew against her thighs. His hand slipped between her legs until she could feel his fingertips. She startled, afraid for a moment, but then he kissed her again and shoved himself into her. He was panting now, pushing into her, raw and burning, until it hurt. She held on as the backboard hit the wall, *then she was flipping over and upside down and inside out, tumbling inside the SUV, dark with the music still pounding. Steel was groaning and lights were flashing in the darkness and she heard a scream.* Then it was over, and all was still.

Michelle felt the pressure lift around her, like a seat belt unbuckling, an airbag deflating. She caught her breath and let it go. What she wanted was to feel alive, connected, but all she felt was alone. Drew pulled the covers over her and let his hand linger on her hip. Then he rolled over.

She climbed out of bed slowly and went to the bathroom to clean up. The moon lit the room through the window so there was no need to turn on the light. In the silence, she heard the crickets sing. She wondered whether Drew could hear them from the bedroom, whether he recognized their call. When she got back to bed, he was snoring. She blew out the candle.

3

THE AROMA OF STRONG coffee woke Michelle the next morning. Confused, she opened her eyes, expecting to see long tubes of fluorescent light above her hospital bed. Instead, there was a smooth white ceiling. She basked in the warm sunshine streaming in over the headboard and considered the empty trough in the mattress beside her. She was sore from their reunion, but that was to be expected, wasn't it? Then she realized the bright room faced west. She must have slept late.

Michelle spotted her bathrobe draped over the chair of her vanity, where the spring bouquet now rested. She stood up slowly and inhaled the fresh perfume of the daisies before slipping on her robe. She ignored the cane leaning against the chair and headed down the hall to the kitchen. Drew was reading a newspaper at the dinette. A plate of sandwich crusts lay in front of him. "Good morning! What time is it?"

"Afternoon," he said. "Would you like some French Roast?"

"Definitely," Michelle said, sitting carefully. Drew circled a trash bag full of party debris, then poured her a fresh cup with far too much milk. She took a sip, then noticed that the orchid plant was here on the dinette.

"Looks like you've been busy. Sorry I wasn't up to help."

"Tyler helped. He's out walking the dog."

"Is Nikki with him?"

Drew shook his head. "Can I make you some toast?"

"No, thanks." She looked back down the hallway to Nikki's closed door. "Shall we wake her up? I can't wait any longer."

He bit his lip, but didn't answer.

Michelle hurried back through the foyer. "Nikki! Rise and shine, honey! It's me!" No answer. She knocked on the door.

"Don't, Michelle," Drew warned.

"Don't what?" Michelle asked. "Nikki! Come on, I'm dying to see you!"

She turned the doorknob. It was locked. She rattled it, then looked up. "Didn't you pick her up this morning? Is her flight late?"

"Not exactly." She turned to see Drew with his arms crossed over his chest.

"What's going on?"

He squeezed his eyes shut as if enduring unbearable pain. "She's not here."

"Did something happen in Australia?"

"She didn't go to Australia. I didn't want to upset you, so I made that up."

Michelle blanched as if she had been struck. "You what?" She rattled the knob again. "No. She told me about it last summer, right before she left."

"Her last visit was the December before that. After they induced the coma."

"No, I definitely saw her after I woke up." She pounded on the door.

"You must have imagined it."

Michelle stopped pounding. She imagined it? She envisioned her daughter's brown eyes, sparkling as she described her upcoming trip. Lexi had warned her about confusing memories with imagination. Michelle tried to sort the swirling fragments in her mind. "Are you sure?"

"You had plenty of visitors, Michelle—some you didn't recognize at first. But Nikki wasn't one of them."

"Then where is she?" She saw the dark look on Drew's face and screamed at the locked door. "Nikki?" Michelle burst into tears. "Nikki!"

"She's gone."

"Where?" Michelle was shaking so hard she could barely stand. Had Nikki been in the accident? Had she been—Michelle couldn't even say the word in her head. Maybe she was still asleep and this was a nightmare. Wake up, she told herself. But Drew was still there. And from the look on his face, she got the feeling that the nightmare was just beginning.

He put his arm around her. "Calm down."

"Calm down? What are you not telling me?"

"She ran away."

"No. Why are you saying that?" Michelle pressed her hand to the wall for support. He was making it up. And she had proof! She hurried to the bedroom.

Drew followed her. "It was after the accident," he said, following her. "She just…disappeared."

"No, she didn't!" Michelle yanked the drawer of her bedside table out so hard that it fell. Postcards went flying across the floor. She fell to her knees to collect them. "Look! The Sydney Opera House, the Harbour Bridge, Manly Beach…" She held one up to show him her handwriting in purple ink. "See? *Thinking of you. Love, Nikki.* She even made a flower dotting the *i*."

Drew reached to help her up, but she was too angry to accept his hand. He pointed at the smeared postmark.

Michelle blinked back her tears. "What? I can't read that tiny writing."

"It says Los Angeles. They all do. They were mailed from here."

Michelle squinted to decipher the print. It was true. She knocked it from his hand, then sunk to the edge of the bed while he gathered the rest. She glared at him through her tears. The liar. "Where is she, Drew? What are you doing to find her?"

Barking drowned out her voice as Bella dragged Tyler into the house. Michelle pushed herself up from the bed and shuffled to the doorway. "Tyler?" He peered down the hall, but looked past her to his father. He led the dog out of sight. The back door slammed shut and the barking grew faint.

Michelle started after him, but Drew caught her shoulders. He spun her around like a lifeguard saving a drowning swimmer, then steered her back to the bed. He shut the door, then went into the bathroom. She heard the faucet gurgle, then he returned holding a cup of water out to her left hand.

She took it, but she wasn't thirsty. "What did the police say? Could she have been kidnapped?"

"No. There was no ransom note. Hundreds of kids run away every month."

"Not my kids!" Michelle slammed the cup down. Water spilled on the quilt.

"Our kids," Drew said.

"You know what I meant. I read to her every night, took her to every checkup, scheduled extra driving lessons for freeways and canyons—"

"You're a good mother."

"Then why would she run away?" She felt as if someone had carved out her insides. And that someone was standing right in front of her. "How could you let this happen?"

Drew crossed his arms. "Don't put this on me."

"Did you put up fliers and freeway signs and post a reward on Facebook and everything? Are the police still looking?"

"Everyone is looking," Drew said.

Michelle pushed herself up. "So why are you just standing there!"

"I'm doing everything I can."

"What do you mean, everything? Nikki's not here! She could be lying in an alley off Hollywood Boulevard, for all we know, shooting up heroin on some urine-stained mattress. She could be selling her body for food!" She punched his shoulder, then felt a shooting pain across her shoulders, rippling down her back. She squeezed her eyes shut and shuddered, her whole body collapsing, until Drew caught her. She whispered her worst fear. "What if she's dead?"

Drew brushed the tears from her cheeks. "She's fine, Michelle."

"How do you know that?" She opened her eyes and looked up at him. Drew's face settled into deep lines of pain. She clutched his pocket and pleaded. "Drew, talk to me. How can you say she's fine if you don't know where she is?"

"Because she calls. Every couple of months, I get a message. Short and sweet, like the ones you got."

The relief she felt wasn't enough to make her chest stop aching. "Call her now, tell her I'm home."

"I did. I left a message, but she hasn't called back. It's an Internet number, untraceable."

"Then how can you be sure she's all right?"

"Because I can't bear to think of her any other way!" Drew pulled free of her and pounded down the hallway.

Michelle looked back at the postcards, then spied the get well card half hidden by the bed. The front showed a bunny carrying a basket of daisies. She picked it up and pressed it to her chest.

Please, don't let it be a trick, she prayed. She opened it and listened closely to the familiar recording.

"Hello, Mother. I feel awful about what happened.
But I can't see you like this. I hope you understand.
Love, me."

Michelle sighed. That was Nikki's voice, all right. Who else called their mom such a formal name—besides Michelle? It had started as a joke and then it stuck.

The message was simple, but maybe it explained why she left. Michelle had looked awful after her surgeries, with all the tubes and machines that kept her alive. Nikki must have been so traumatized by the sight of her mother as a vegetable that she couldn't bear to see her. Michelle shut the card quickly, as if to keep her daughter safe.

She wondered about the postmark and went to ask Drew, but was winded by the time she reached the foyer. She leaned against the corner to catch her breath.

The afternoon sun blasted through the French doors, casting a harsh light across the living room. Without the crepe paper and cake, the room looked bigger than she remembered. She looked around, then realized that it wasn't bigger, it was emptier. The leather couch was gone, and the rest of the furniture had been rearranged so that the plaid armchairs flanked the fireplace. The coffee table was also missing, leaving faded squares of green carpet. Only the bookshelves looked the same, stuffed with files and photo albums and parenting books. Except, now there was a film of dust on them. The sight was upsetting.

She crossed the hall to the kitchen where Drew sat with his head in his hands. Her voice trembled. "Is that why the furniture is gone—the police are dusting for prints?"

"Not exactly," he said. "Remember the apartment I rented in New York for that miniseries? I've been working as a local for the past year."

"In New York?" Michelle tried to understand. "You're telling me that Nikki hasn't been here in over a year—and you're living it up in New York?"

Drew's voice rose in anger. "She's not the only one I have to take care of, Michelle. I need union hours to qualify for benefits. Your insurance was tapped out long ago. You've had the best care possible and I flew back to visit as often as I could. Should I have put you in a cheap convalescent center to waste away?"

"I just find it hard to believe there are no jobs in LA."

"There aren't enough that pay union," he explained. "Reality shows pay shit. You can't count on a series like you used to, the state film commission is broke, and locations are cheaper in Canada. Half the guys I know are on unemployment."

There was a knock on the French door. Michelle backed up and spied Tyler through the glass. "Is that the real reason why Tyler is in boarding school? To be close to you?"

"It wouldn't have done him any good to be close to you," Drew said, rising to go speak with Tyler.

Michelle sputtered from all the swear words that came to mind. She took deep breaths to calm down, but it was no use—she was furious. To think she'd felt so grateful that he'd taken such good care of things, when he hadn't at all. He had abandoned her. "Drew!"

He came back inside the living room.

She held up the get well card. "Where was this mailed from?"

He shrugged. "Someone at the hospital opened it. Every time we visited, there were more cards in your room. Clients and friends—"

Michelle remembered Nikki's words about feeling awful. "Oh my god, was it Nikki's fault? Was she driving?"

"No, honey. You were."

Michelle blinked, trying to remember. Her anger began to cool from the effort. "Right, that's what the lawyers kept asking about. Car insurance or something." She looked through the glass at her son playing with Bella, as if nothing had happened. Michelle had always feared that something *would* happen, as soon as they left her sight. Nikki would fall off the swing set onto cement, or Tyler would be struck in the head by a baseball, or a bomb would go off on a field trip. And sure enough, that time had come. How could she not have felt it, deep inside? "Does Tyler know?"

"Let's get you back to bed. Let Tyler be—this has been hard on him, too."

She pulled her hand away. "I can imagine. He had to lie to his mother for—oh, I don't know—almost a year?" She spied a napkin left on the floor beneath the dining room table. The thought of her friends at the party last night made her stomach clench. "Tyler wasn't the only one pretending, was he? Is that why Julie didn't know about Australia—because you forgot to tell her? Cathy was acting strangely, too."

"I'm sorry, honey. I really am."

"I don't understand. Why pretend at all?"

"You were already overwhelmed. Lexi dragged you from one rehabilitation room to the next all day long. I wanted to tell you, but every time I visited, you were too exhausted to have a serious conversation. And to be honest, I didn't want Lexi to know."

Michelle was relieved that at least one person hadn't betrayed her. "Why? Because she would have told me?"

"That, or she'd ask to be reassigned to avoid saying something that might hamper your progress. The doctors were adamant that we were not to let anything upset you. Anything."

Michelle heard Tyler coughing. Drew swore under his breath and stood up. "I need to run out and get him a new asthma inhaler. I'll fill your prescription while I'm there," he said. "How are you feeling?"

"Like I woke up in the Twilight Zone."

"You need rest. Let's get you back to bed."

Michelle let him help her back down the hall and into the bedroom. But one thing was certain. She was not staying in bed.

4

MICHELLE HAD LEARNED TO pick door locks with bobby pins long ago, but opening Nikki's lock was tricky using only one hand. She was tempted to ask Tyler to let her go through the adjoining bathroom, but his father had expressly ordered him to make sure Michelle got some rest. He had been caught between loyalties for long enough. Finally, Michelle felt the lock surrender. She dropped the flayed bobby pin into the pocket of her bathrobe, pushed the door open, and stepped inside Nikki's bedroom. It felt like a forgotten world.

Dim light filtered through the front window blinds. Stripes marked the bare mattress. Michelle flipped on the ceiling light. The bulb popped and went dark, but the buttercup walls still glowed. This pale yellow paint was the only thing she and Nikki had agreed on after they'd torn down the bunny wallpaper. Nikki's walls were bare of posters now, but her old blanket was folded on the end of the dusty trundle bed.

Michelle picked up the blanket and rubbed the frayed fabric against her cheek. It had been a gift from her film crew a few days before Nikki's birth. After staying home for twelve weeks, Michelle had hired a babysitter and packed her briefcase for a production job wrapping another movie. She ended up wrapping her baby in this blanket instead.

Growing up in the Midwest, Michelle had seen her share of tornadoes ushered in by green skies of warning. But when she awoke to the cacophony of furniture crashing to the floors, there was no mistaking the neon sign flashing in her head: earthquake.

Michelle scooped up the baby and staggered across floors that were bouncing up and down between walls that were moving side to side, like the rope bridge of a fun house. Just as suddenly, it all stopped. The power went out. Time slowed like an intravenous drip. In the eerie silence, she sat in the front hall, haunted by a high-pitched hum from the earth until the dogs howled and the house shuddered again. In the darkness, through endless aftershocks, Michelle kept Nikki wrapped in that blanket, safe in her arms.

At dawn, she carried her baby around the rubble and climbed over the upside down dresser back to her bed. That evening, when the sun hid behind the black smoke, Michelle nursed Nikki to sleep by candlelight. Then she lay, fully dressed and rigid with fear, as fire trucks blared past. No power, no plumbing, no phone service—and the baby didn't get so much as a cut from all the glass on the floor. The next day, Michelle found her briefcase and unpacked it. That show would go on, but without her.

Michelle turned to survey the room. A new crack rose from the corner of the window frame and spread a foot across the wall. The plaster buckled in spots, as if reluctant to let go. "Settling," the local realtors called it, a natural phenomenon that was as much of a surprise to new homeowners as the reality of parenthood was to new mothers. She gave up the long hours of production for a desk job close to home, but as Nikki grew, so did the job of protecting her. And now it seemed that everything Michelle had done was for nothing.

A few minutes passed, or maybe an hour. Michelle shook herself awake and surveyed the dusty room. It was like a magazine puzzle: what is wrong with this picture? Nikki's white dresser and desk were still here, but the drawers were empty. Storage boxes were stacked in the corner. Michelle stepped slowly across the room to find the seams of the top box taped shut. She backed against the wall and braced her feet to get leverage. She tugged at the tape with her left hand, but the box shifted. When she shoved it back with her shoulder, the box toppled to the floor and took her with it. She listened for a moment to be sure Tyler hadn't heard the crash from his room. Thank goodness for headphones.

Michelle spied Nikki's little bookshelf behind the door. She rolled over to her knees and crept closer. The particleboard was plastered with stickers ranging from My Little Pony to a Skull & Crossbones sneaker logo. A forgotten ball of knitting yarn was wedged behind the bottom shelf. Michelle used it to dust off the plastic snow globes Drew had brought home from location jobs, then the spines of books ranging from *The Tell-Tale Heart* to *The Runaway Bunny*. She pulled out the picture book and flipped through the scribbled-on pages. No matter how far the little bunny ran away, the mother vowed to find him. Michelle put the book back and wiped her eyes. "For you are my little bunny."

The top shelf was empty except for a jewelry box with a ballerina that twirled when she opened it. Inside, there were two pennies, a purple pen, and one dangling disco ball earring. Nikki always used purple ink, much to the consternation of certain English teachers. Michelle smiled at her daughter's independent streak, despite the trouble it caused. Her knees were getting stiff, so she took the earring and stood up. The tiny mirrors caught a shaft of light from the hallway and reflected sparkles on the walls. Michelle's eyes widened to take it all in—the room seemed to be alight with fireflies. That must be why Nikki had kept it. She wasn't big on jewelry.

Michelle wanted more sparkles, more fireflies, more of Nikki, so she pulled the drawstring to open the blinds. Beneath the window, she spotted one of Nikki's posters jammed between the bed and the wall. Michelle couldn't lean very far without losing her balance, so when she grabbed it, the corner ripped off. The rest of the shiny paper slipped from sight. Michelle held up the corner, but could only read part of the band's name: house. Playhouse? Dollhouse? Michelle had been quite the rocker in her day, but gave up when it came to the kids' music. Tyler was into hip-hop, but Nikki preferred obscure indie bands she found on the Internet. This must have been one of them. It seemed vaguely familiar, but then, everything did.

Headlights lit the window as Drew pulled up. She closed the blinds. A few minutes later, he leaned in the doorway. "I saw you."

"I wasn't hiding. It's my house, too." Her nose twitched at the reek of cigarette smoke, but she let it go. "Will you open those boxes for me?"

"Not today. I picked up your Xanax. Take one and get some rest."

Michelle shook her head. "It just doesn't make sense, Drew. I left her a message last week that I was leaving the hospital and couldn't wait to see her. There's no reason for her to be upset anymore."

"You hungry?" Drew asked. "I got three flavors of applesauce."

"Stop changing the subject. I've been eating solid food for months—and I can smell the burgers you brought home."

"Your discharge papers say to go easy on the digestion. Those are Animal Style with extra dressing and onions—a far cry from hospital food. Want me to go back for a plain one?"

"No, stay." Tyler was coughing in the other room. Drew went to the door. "Wait, I still don't get why she didn't come home." He didn't turn around. "If it's not about my injuries, what else could it be? People have car accidents all the time—and Topanga is notorious for being dangerous. Nikki used to complain how long it took to drive the ten miles to the beach. I know I'm foggy on the details, but..."

Drew turned around slowly. Too slowly.

She was beginning to feel nauseous.

"There was more to the accident than you know," he admitted.

"What are you talking about?"

"You might want to sit down." Drew pointed to Nikki's trundle bed.

Michelle held her ground.

Drew took a deep breath. "The accident happened after one of Tyler's games. There was a boy in the car with you. He was killed."

Michelle froze. This couldn't be true. Why was he looking at her like that? A boy was dead? She tasted bile and swallowed it down. She reached out to Drew and her whole body jerked with pain. Wrong arm. "No," she wailed. The room started to spin.

He helped her to the trundle bed and sat beside her. When the stars cleared, she thought of all the times she had driven boys home. Michelle hardly understood what it meant for anyone's life to end, but for someone so young…"Who was it? A teammate?"

Drew shook his head. "Noah Butler."

She thought for a minute, then remembered the lanky college student. "Tyler's pitching coach?" He nodded.

"Oh my god."

A few minutes ago, she'd feared the worst for her daughter and it was unbearable. Now this—it was hard to comprehend. She took a deep breath and tried to connect the pieces. "Could this have anything to do with Nikki running away?"

Drew shrugged. "There was some innuendo that might have embarrassed her."

"Innuendo?"

"I was out of town, so—you might have been lonely. And you were an attractive woman in a car alone with a nineteen-year-old, a good-looking college kid with a band." He stood up and crossed his arms.

"Are you out of your mind?"

"No."

"But you believe that?"

"No, but things had been strained between us, so it was awkward. And some people blame you for Noah's death."

"Because I was driving?"

"Yes."

Michelle couldn't fathom Nikki's embarrassment. "Does Lexi know?"

"How could she not? It was in all the newspapers."

Michelle covered her face with her hand. "That explains why we were so cloistered at the hospital. But…"

Drew's phone rang. He checked the number, but didn't answer. When the screen went dark, so did the room.

"This light needs a new bulb."

Drew tested the switch. "Forget it. Moping around in here will only upset you."

"Right. Nikki is missing and Tyler's pitching coach is dead, but an empty room will upset me." She stood up, fueled by anger.

"See what I mean?"

Michelle kicked the dented corner of the fallen box. "Do we have scissors?"

Drew heaved the box back on the stack in the corner, then rubbed his lower back. "Forget it. I've been through her things. Who do you think packed these?"

"But why? What if she comes home?"

"That's why I kept the bed. But it was creepy seeing her T-shirts piled on the floor where she left them."

Michelle leaned against him. He put his arm around her.

Tyler coughed again.

"I need to give him the inhaler," Drew said, walking her out.

He took the bags he'd left on the hall table into the kitchen, where Tyler had the refrigerator door open.

He held up the plastic-wrapped piece of cake saved for Nikki. "Okay if I eat this?"

"No," Michelle snapped.

Tyler eyed his father and put it back. "Dad, can I go to Cody's? I need to practice for the game—and his mom's making stroganoff. I can walk over."

Michelle felt bad. "I'm sorry, Tyler, I didn't mean…"

"Go ahead," Drew interrupted, tearing open the pharmacy bag. "I don't blame you for being sick of burgers. Take this with you."

"Thanks," Tyler said. He pocketed the inhaler, kissed Michelle, and started heading out.

Michelle followed him to the foyer. "But, don't you want to have a family dinner?" She winced at how lame that sounded, especially with Nikki missing. And someone dead. *Noah Butler dead.* It was a long time ago now, though, and she wondered how Tyler felt about it. Was he over it? Did he blame her? She was afraid to ask and risk upsetting him. She wanted to say something, to hold him and make it better, but she didn't know how to do that, or if it was even possible. She hated feeling so helpless.

"Be home by ten," Drew told him.

Tyler's phone buzzed. He read the text before walking out and closing the front door behind him.

Michelle wondered what happened to her own phone. Was it lost in the wreckage with her wallet? And her wedding ring? When Drew took the other bag to the counter, she noticed that his hand was bare, too. "What happened to your ring?"

"Got caught on scaffolding when I was hanging mikes. Nearly ripped off my finger."

"Ouch," Michelle said.

He glanced at her withered right hand and shrugged. Then he put the last grocery bag away. She watched him, conscious of every movement, as if they were acting in a play, reading lines someone else had written. He brought paper plates to the table with the In-N-Out bag, then set out the prescription bottle like a condiment. "Want Tyler's shake?"

She sat back down at the dinette while he grabbed a beer from the fridge. He pushed the vanilla shake toward her, then unwrapped his double burger and dumped a haystack of fries beside it. The shake reminded her too much of the protein drinks that she'd grown to hate at the rehab center. She stole a french fry, which tasted a lot saltier than she remembered. She consoled herself that this was like a second date with her husband—if only she were in the mood. All the hope she had yesterday was gone. She could say words out loud and swallow bits of potato, but all the while, a dead boy hovered in her thoughts. Maybe he always would.

She eyed the prescription bottle. The promise of relief was tempting. She had no idea what had happened, and even if she did, she could never bring Noah back. But she could try to find her daughter. And she needed to be clearheaded to do that.

She took a deep breath and pulled the dangling disco ball earring from her pocket. The mirrors reflected sparkling light across Drew's hamburger.

"What's that?"

Michelle hesitated, surprised that he didn't recognize it. "An earring from Nikki's jewelry box. It doesn't look familiar?"

"She didn't wear earrings," Drew said. "Remember how mad she was when I gave her the sapphire studs? You said it was the September birthstone."

"It is," Michelle said, toying with the clip. "But she was so proud about being natural—no pierced ears, no tattoos. She was disappointed you didn't notice. If she were here, she'd be eating a cheeseburger without the burger. Hold the lettuce and tomato."

"Right. A vegetarian who doesn't like vegetables. Except in the form of ketchup." Drew squeezed a packet of red goop over his fries.

"Remember the night she announced it?" Michelle said, pleased to reminisce. "We were having your favorite Sunday dinner, pork chops and mashed potatoes, and you complained that she didn't appreciate it. Then she fell off her chair."

Drew frowned. "She did that on purpose, to change the subject."

"No, she didn't. She'd get so excited talking about something and she'd be swinging her leg and—boom. On the floor." Michelle nearly smiled. "Always cracked Tyler up."

"Maybe that's why she did it. For attention."

"No." Michelle shook her head. He had it all wrong. Nikki was shy, always had been. Even at preschool, when Michelle dropped Nikki off at the gate, she hung back from the children shouting hello. The Greta Garbo of the play yard, her teacher teased. No wonder Drew hadn't found Nikki—he was out of town so much that he hardly knew her. In a way, that gave Michelle hope. She clipped the disco ball earring on a tall orchid branch.

"Where is the filing cabinet? Maybe there's something in her old class rosters. Or her debit card statements."

Drew cut her off. "There's not. I left the house files here, but everything else is in New York." His eyes met hers, as if in apology. For a moment, they let the sadness surround them.

Michelle held the look, wishing he would put his arms around her. Instead, he plucked *Variety* off the stack of trade magazines he'd bought at the store. "You mind?"

"Can I look, too? I went from flash cards to large print books, as if the outside world didn't exist. But don't you read the news online?"

"There's no Internet service here."

"No wonder Tyler doesn't want to stick around. Will you order it?"

"You don't need it, Michelle. Rest and do your exercises."

"I will, but Nikki's high school directory was online. And kids she knew on Facebook." She tried to sound calm, but it was impossible.

"Private detectives did all that."

"So, I'll do it again," Michelle said. "She's just a name to them. Please, Drew. The Internet company will want a credit card and I don't even have a purse!"

Drew's phone rang. He got up and fetched another beer while answering, as if relieved to get a break from her questions. "Hey Tyler. No, you have to sleep here. I need a ride to LAX in the morning." He hung up. When he shut the refrigerator door, he saw Michelle's frown and swore under his breath.

"You're kidding, right? Don't you dare say you're leaving."

"I'm sorry, Michelle. I have to go back to New York. I meant to tell you."

"Like you meant to tell me my daughter is missing?"

"Our daughter."

"Is that how you justify lying about her? And poor Noah? When were you going to tell me about leaving, Drew? In a postcard?"

"Calm down, honey. I blew off two commercials to be here when you got home, but this is a feature. My assistant has done most of the prep, but if I don't set the sound cues myself, they'll replace me and I'll be out months of work."

Michelle hugged her bad arm. "I just got home. We've barely had any time together. The director will understand!"

"No, he's a prick. Won't even pay my kit rental. But he works a lot and I'm his first call." Drew chugged the rest of his beer. "Don't worry, your mother is flying in to take care of you."

Michelle gave him a dirty look, already dreading the heavy perfume that clogged the air during her mother's hospital visits. All that time, Elyse must have known the truth, and she didn't say a word.

"I know you two have issues, but she means well," Drew said. "And I hired Lexi to come by every week to help."

"I don't need help. I need you."

He tossed his beer in the trash and took her hand. "We need this job, honey. I took out a second mortgage to pay your hospital bills. You want to lose the house?"

"No, of course not, but…What about Nikki?"

"Michelle, when I said everyone has been out looking for her, I meant it."

"That doesn't mean we should stop." She poked at the mirrored ball hanging from the orchid until the reflections spun like Drew's words in her head. Then she yanked it free and threw the earring across the room. She burst into tears. Drew touched her cheek, but she stumbled to the hallway to get away from him, away from the truth that he had known all along.

Bella whined outside the French doors when he saw her across the room. Dizzy, Michelle leaned against the wall in the foyer and looked at the family portrait. Drew had hated the idea of family portraits, found it hopelessly bourgeois. But he'd grinned like a good sport that day on the beach, with his arm around Michelle's shoulders. Tyler's white polo shirt was already dirty, but his smile was goofy and sweet. In this larger version, Nikki's fingers had been airbrushed from where she made bunny ears over her brother's head. She smiled with her lips closed over her braces, but her brown eyes were as wide as could be.

Michelle was drawn to those gold-flecked eyes, as if they were her own and she was looking in the mirror. She slid down until she was sitting on the floor. She no longer heard the dog, or her husband calling her name. She used to remind herself not to confide in her daughter when she was lonely, and yet Nikki always seemed to read her mind, as if Michelle's life had imprinted on her before she was born. Michelle read once that females are born with all the eggs they'll ever make, and the notion had resonated with her—it confirmed how she felt. Nikki had always been part of her. At this moment, curled up on the cold tile, Michelle felt bereft of more than flesh and blood; she had lost her very essence. Who was she without her daughter?

She buried her face in her arm and began to moan. After working so hard to get better, counting the weeks to come home, she felt more pain now than ever. For the slimmest of seconds, she wished she had never woken up.

After a few minutes passed, Michelle's moaning turned into a whimper. She felt the warmth of Drew's arm around her shoulders and his lips pressed against her head. When she opened her eyes, he offered her the pill bottle. She held out her hand.

5

$\mathcal{T}$HE SCREAM STUNG MICHELLE'S ears. She struggled to shout at someone, to make it stop, but she was unable to form the words. As the sound faded to a hum, she floated until the wave washed over her, pushing her back down into the numbing calm. But soon there was muffled noise on the surface, luring her back.

Tyler's voice. "Bella, no!"

Michelle opened her eyes.

The morning light was hazy through the bedroom curtains, but Drew's side of the bed was already empty. She heard banging in the kitchen and remembered that he was leaving today. A pain shot like electricity through her bad arm. Wincing, she paused until it passed and she could breathe again. If Drew was cooking for Tyler, she could take her time. The boy ate a lot.

She slipped on her hospital bathrobe without bothering to maneuver her bad arm into a sleeve, and managed to snap the front closed enough to cover her wrinkled nightgown. Then she headed down the hall. As she approached the foyer, she smelled Chanel No. 5 and stopped short.

Michelle peeked around the corner to the front hall. Sure enough, a Louis Vuitton tote rested by the entrance table next to a matching cosmetics case engraved with the name *Elyse Deveraux*.

"*Bonjour!*" Elyse called. Her dancer's posture was silhouetted in the kitchen doorway where she stood, impossibly chic in a knit St. John suit despite the dawn flight from Columbus. She wrapped her arms around Michelle and hugged her close before kissing her smack on each cheek. Michelle felt the creamy lipstick prints and pulled away. Elyse wiped them off with a graceful swipe of her manicured fingers, then adjusted the silk flower pinned to her silver chignon.

"Hello, Mother. You look as beautiful as ever."

"Ah, *ma chérie*. I wish I could say the same for you." Elyse straightened Michelle's bathrobe then tapped her chin as a reminder to stand up straight.

Michelle couldn't help marvel that her mother's idea of a warm homecoming was to revert back to her habit of critiquing her only child. At least some things hadn't changed.

"How are you feeling?" Elyse asked, as she glided back toward the sound of gurgling coffee.

Michelle followed her mother into the kitchen where the blessed scent of coffee overpowered the perfume. The counter was covered by breakfast takeout cartons. Michelle sniffed at the bacon staining one of them. "How could you not tell me about Nikki?"

"I know it's horrible, but we couldn't risk your recovery."

"I might have recovered faster had I known there was an emergency."

"You were the only emergency we knew how to handle." Elyse poured a cup of French Roast. "Our Nicole is more of a mystery. Try to understand."

Michelle reached for the cup.

"Non, *ma chérie,* I made this for your husband."

"It's not too strong, if that's your concern. Dr. Palmer gave it to me."

"How kind." She pointed to a tub of oatmeal. "But no caffeine this morning. You must eat your fiber and return to bed."

"No, thanks. I'm going to the police department."

"Absolutely not. You need to rest."

"I'm not a child," Michelle said. She followed her mother's gaze out the window to where Drew was pacing in the driveway.

Elyse unbuckled the purse that lay atop her Burberry raincoat and pulled out a Chanel lipstick. Then she attacked Michelle's chapped lips. Stop, Michelle tried to say, but she was trapped between the refrigerator and her mother's iron grip. She finally pushed her away with her left hand.

Elyse scrutinized Michelle's face. "Better. And I see your good arm is compensating nicely for the damaged one. That charming doctor of yours was right. *Mais alors*, I owe your husband a dollar."

"You bet against me?" Michelle asked.

"No, I bet against him." Elyse redrew her pout in the glass window of the oven door. "How are things with Drew? He's a good man, Michelle. He's missed you terribly. You have a lot of making up to do, if you know what I mean."

"Now you're an expert on relationships?" Michelle eyed the tan line on her mother's left ring finger. "What happened to fiancé number three?"

"Be nice to your husband. That's all I'm saying." Elyse pulled a brochure from her purse and set it on the dinette. She tapped it with her pink talon.

Michelle looked at the new brochure. *Elyse Deveraux School of Dance* was printed in florid script across the cover photo, a glossy reprint of a young Elyse dancing in the classic blue costume of Giselle.

When she glanced up, her mother was waving to Drew, who was still on the phone. He barely noticed the neighbors walking their dogs or strolling past in church clothes.

"It's a work call, Mother. Producers don't respect Sundays—I never did."

"His breakfast is getting cold."

Michelle was tempted to mention that it was only takeout, but even that was better than she could provide. She sat down at the dinette and pushed the trade papers away. "May I borrow your glasses?"

She waited for Elyse to unfold them, then gave her full attention to all the glorious things her mother had written about herself. The back copy described Elyse's early training at the Paris Opera, her star turn with the Bolshoi, her performances in San Francisco, Chicago, and her last role as the prima ballerina of the Columbus Ballet. Michelle opened it to the schedule of classes printed inside. At least the background montage of baby ballerinas was adorable, with all of them playing dress-up in matching blue tutus. She pressed the brochure closed.

Elyse smoothed her chignon in the reflection of the upper oven, then raised her eyebrows as much as her Botoxed forehead allowed. "Did you get a good look?"

"*Très élégant*, Mother." Michelle was about to ask why the brochure glossed over the reason for Elyse's fall from grace, how she was seduced and abandoned too late to do anything except have her unwanted baby and drop lower and lower on the ladder of dance until she landed in Ohio. But it wasn't the brochure that upset her.

"No need to lie if you hate it," Elyse said with a sigh. "Throw it away; I don't care."

"I don't lie as easily as you, Mother. And I don't hate it. But it looks expensive." Michelle's eyes went to her mother's bare ring finger. "Did you sell your diamond ring?"

"That's not your concern. Advertising is important."

Michelle took off her mother's glasses and got up to open the nearest cupboard. It was empty. She slammed the cupboard shut.

"You could pretend to be happy to see me, you know. That's what Frank does when I visit him in Key West."

Michelle resisted the urge to say that was because her stepbrother never actually lived with her. She opened another cupboard instead.

"Did you know I was Queen of the Conch Festival this year?" Elyse stuffed the brochure back in her purse. "What are you looking for?"

"Coffee mugs. I've lost my daughter, a year and a half of my life, and all memory of my kitchen."

Elyse shook her head. "*Non, ma chérie*, I reorganized." She opened the cupboard above the coffee maker and took out one of the few remaining mugs. "Perhaps some green tea before your nap."

Michelle picked up the mug and read the faded print, *World's Best Mom.*

"Let me help," Elyse said, reaching for the mug.

Michelle pulled it away and went to the refrigerator, looking for juice. She pointed at the bare door. "Where are my magnets?"

"Those tacky things? They're around here somewhere. I meant to throw them away, but..." Elyse put food cartons in the microwave to reheat.

Michelle began a new search. She opened drawer after empty drawer. The next one contained silverware and the clip-on earring that Michelle had thrown across the room. Nikki used to accuse Michelle of being a control freak and maybe she was; she liked things to run smoothly. But now, everything was out of her control, even her kitchen. Where were those magnets?

She opened the floor cabinet where the trash can used to be and found a grocery bag full of expired coupons from the junk drawer. She gripped the top and lifted it up to the counter. Then she fished in the bag with her left hand and pulled out the first thing she touched, a photo of Tyler at bat, framed by a magnetic mock-up of a Wheaties box. Delighted, she stuck it up on the refrigerator and reached in the bag for more.

Her hand closed around the plaster turtle she'd bought in Maui the year the kids found airline tickets from Santa in their stockings. She rubbed her thumb against the moss-colored magnet, a souvenir of their snorkel trip. She could picture those enormous green turtles swimming beneath the glass bottom boat when it stopped at Turtle Town. The children had been giddy at the sight of the creatures gliding below, with their fins flapping like underwater wings. Once the turtles had safely passed, the boat motored to the lip of Molokini Crater. Everyone latched on life jackets and snorkeled around the reef. A lone sea turtle spotted Nikki and flapped behind her like a long lost friend.

The microwave dinged. Startled, Michelle dropped the magnet. The green shell cracked into shards on the floor. Michelle stuck a green fin back on the fridge, then reached back into the grocery bag.

When she pulled her hand out, a red line bled from a slice on her finger. She sucked on it, then grabbed the folded paper that had cut her. She recognized the elegant cursive of Elyse's Parker Penmanship on the outside. The words looked fuzzy, but when she squinted, she could read her name. *Michelle Deveraux Mason*, it read. *Daughter of prima ballerina Elyse Deveraux*. A line was scratched out, then: *Executive Producer of Golden Hour Productions. She is survived by…*" Michelle dropped the paper. Dread shrouded her like a cloud of smoke. Her mother had written her obituary.

Elyse returned and saw Michelle's stricken face. She snatched the paper from the floor. "Try to understand, Michelle. You were not expected to…You were not…What is the word? Viable."

"You gave up on me?"

"*Non!*" Elyse folded the paper to hide her writing.

Michelle couldn't bear to look at her mother any longer. Her eyes dropped to the paper. There was a fuzzy image from a cheap printer on the back. "What's that?"

"It's scratch paper," Elyse said.

Michelle grabbed it. The picture showed Michelle and Tyler embracing Nikki, who wore a bulky coat and a birthday crown. She held a muffin topped with a candle shaped like the number sixteen. Nikki's lips were spread, but not enough to be a smile. There was a smudge of ink on her cheek. "This must be from Nikki's birthday. September 19."

Elyse nodded. "I sent that lovely sheepskin coat."

"Yes, because it's so important to have a winter coat in California."

"Don't be rude," Elyse said. "It was on sale and Nikki adored it. When I called to make sure she received it, you put her on the phone, remember? I could barely hear her over that horrible music."

Michelle looked back at the image. She had researched cameras for weeks before Nikki's birthday. The lens had to be better than the one on her phone, or why bother? This one also had the timer that was so easy to set. It looked like Nikki had put the camera on the counter to shoot it, then printed it out on her old inkjet. Michelle peered at the circles beneath Nikki's ears. She dug the disco ball earring from her pocket and matched it to the picture.

"A gift from Frank," Elyse guessed. "Those tacky souvenirs are as popular as key lime pie down there."

"So her birthday was two weeks or three weeks before the accident? I keep forgetting the date. What happened?"

Elyse poured her own coffee. "It was October 8. Your husband called, of course. I flew in as you came out of surgery. Then you took a turn for the worse, and there was more surgery in November, which you did not come out of so well. By December, doctors had

49

induced the coma to avoid permanent damage from your brain swelling." She offered the juice, then gave up. "It's too horrible to discuss. There were so many forms to sign: liability releases and health directives and the legal conservatorship. Then five months later, you started to wake up—and I reorganized the kitchen."

Michelle shook the obituary at her mother. "How long after the accident did you write this? Was Nikki still here?"

"I don't remember. I found it in the drawer and used it as scratch paper during one of my visits." Elyse sipped her coffee. "That's the thing about memory. It has a way of being exactly what you want it to be, *mais oui?*"

Michelle wondered if her mother had planted the idea of Nikki's hospital visit to keep her from knowing she was gone. Or was Drew right about it being wishful thinking? But there was no reason to pick a fight over it; there were more important things to do.

Elyse noticed the prescription bottle, then poured juice for Michelle. "Now drink up and get some rest. Would you like pharmaceutical help?"

"No, would you?" Michelle scowled at her mother. "I'm not ready to write my daughter's obituary. I'm going to the police."

"All in good time, *ma chérie*. No one is going to help if you barge in wearing hospital clothes. You'll need proper attire."

"Aren't my suits in that garment bag in my closet?"

"*Bien sûr*, for charity. You were a bit more, shall we say, *zaftig* then."

"A few extra pounds are not the same as fat, Mother. I ran three times a week."

Elyse rubbed her own svelte hip. "In any case, your suits won't fit you now. And black is no good. No need to look like you're going to a funeral. Or like you missed one." She raised a penciled-in eyebrow.

Michelle sipped her juice. "Point taken, mother. But I work in Hollywood—everyone wears black."

"*D'accord*, but no one has gray hair." She turned Michelle gently toward the oven until she could see her homely reflection in the glass window. "Go blond. The roots will barely show." She tapped the small scar on Michelle's forehead. "And you can cut your bangs to cover this scar."

Michelle pushed her mother's hand away to feel the now-familiar scar from the accident. "I'll ask Sasha, my old stylist, to come by. She can color my hair in the sink. May I borrow your phone?"

"*Non*, I've made you an appointment for later this week at a spa in Beverly Hills: facial, mani-pedi, the works." She pressed the loose skin on Michelle's face. "Your eyes are hollow and your lips have thinned, but fillers can fix that."

Michelle scoffed. "I'm not going to a spa while my daughter is missing."

Elyse continued, undeterred, and reached into her purse for a silk drawstring bag. "Let's start with these." She pulled a strand of pearls from the bag and hooked it around Michelle's long neck.

Michelle rubbed her fingertips over them. "Were you planning to donate these or sell them?"

"I was saving them for Nikki. They're of little value."

"*Au contraire*, Mother," Michelle said, spying Drew in the doorway.

He stepped inside and kissed her on the head. "I gave you those for our first anniversary," he confirmed. "Good morning, ladies. How is everything?"

"*Bon*," Elyse said. "If you don't count the breakfast." She set his plate of eggs in the microwave and pressed Start.

Drew was already eating when Tyler burst through the front

door with Bella. He locked her in the backyard, then returned for a stack of pancakes.

Drew downed the last of his black coffee at the sink. "Be quick. Security at LAX is a bitch."

Elyse took Drew's empty mug. "I don't like my grandson driving in LA traffic."

"Not much traffic on Sunday. He'll be fine," Drew said, rubbing his lower back. He gave her a hug and slipped the copy of *Variety* under his arm.

Michelle blocked Drew's path out of the kitchen. "Please don't go."

"Oh, honey. I'm doing this for you." Drew kissed her cheek, then saw her tap her lips. "Sorry, I didn't want to wreck your lipstick."

Michelle glanced at her mother, then clutched his denim sleeve. "We need to talk."

"I'll call you," he said as she walked him to the door. He pulled a petty cash envelope from his wallet and fanned it to show her the $50 and $100 bills inside.

Michelle shoved it in her bathrobe pocket. She used to pass out per diems in the same kind of envelope during production. "Do I have to sign a receipt, too?"

He chuckled and pulled on his jacket. "I'll send you a debit card, but first you need a new ID to prove you exist."

Michelle raised her eyes to his. "What do I need to convince *you* I exist?"

"Please, Michelle. Don't make this harder than it already is."

"You're right," Michelle said. Embarrassed, she dropped her eyes to the *Variety* pinned beneath his arm. Then she tilted her head to see the photo of the woman on the cover. The headline screamed about a three-picture deal at Paramount. "Is that Becca? We used to make up headlines like that in film school! I can't believe she didn't mention this when she visited me in the hospital. She did visit me, right? I didn't make that up?" When he nodded, she smiled. "Let's call her. She'll give you a job."

"I already have a job, Michelle." He opened the door.

"You know what I mean." She clung to him, but he peeled her off like Velcro. "At least let me call Victor—I need to thank him for the orchids."

"Get some rest," he said, leaning down for a real kiss. She sighed into his lips. This was how she wanted it to be. She wanted to forget about yesterday, to remember the good times, the soft kisses, like this.

"Be nice to your mother," Drew said, zipping his jacket. "She talked the rabbi out of performing last rites."

"Last rites?"

"Whatever they call it in Jewish." He meant it as a joke, but she could tell by the way his eyes darted past her that it was true. He pulled her into his arms. "Promise you'll go back to bed and rest."

Michelle nodded. She would promise him anything right now. She didn't even mind the stench of tobacco imbedded in his jacket. She could live with that, with anything, if only he'd stay. "I'll miss you. I've been missing you forever."

"Me, too, honey." He blew her a kiss and left.

Michelle ran her hand through her hair, then saw the gray strand caught between her fingers. She hurried outside to the porch and waved to him frantically. When the passenger window rolled down, she called out. "How would you like me as a blond?"

Drew smiled and rolled the window up as the Volvo backed out of the driveway. The tires bumped over the curb.

6

TYLER HAD BEEN HOME from the airport for over an hour before Michelle could shoo Elyse to the mall. Although the Van Nuys Police Station was open twenty-four hours, Saks closed early on Sunday. There was no time to waste.

Michelle gazed out the window as they crested the on-ramp to the Ventura Freeway. From here, she could see the San Fernando Valley, lush and green and teeming with life. The mountains rimming the north side looked close enough to touch, with gray peaks edging the sky like knives. Michelle's Hollywood coworkers used to make fun of her Valley life, but where else could you find sidewalks for skateboarding, public schools that won Academic Decathlons, and pristine baseball fields? Without winter? And yet none of that mattered now; all she could see was the grid of red traffic signals, like the flashing lights of an ambulance. Nikki could be strapped inside one, breathing her last breath.

"You all right, Mom?" Tyler asked. "You look sort of pale."

Michelle smiled at the irony. "Remind me to get a spray tan."

Tyler laughed. He had been so quiet when they started out that Michelle thought he was simply focusing on the road. But now she realized that this was the first time they had been alone since the accident. She had missed him so much that the air was awkward between them.

His phone buzzed and he checked the number. "Cody. I forgot his dad wants you to call him."

"Please tell him I don't have a phone yet. And I already said you could play—my memory may be spotty, but it was only two days ago." So much had changed in such a short time. She didn't want to think about it. "Tell me more about your new school, honey. Any favorite teachers? Girlfriends?" Tyler began filling Michelle in on his life at Rutgers Prep. She cherished every word, every intonation, every moment of his attention.

Michelle smiled and caught his eyes as he checked the right-hand mirror to exit the freeway. She marveled at their color—the same opaque green as his father's. It reminded her of the algae-rich quarry she used to swim in when she was a little girl. Cool and refreshing, but there was no telling what swam below. Tyler's thoughts were more transparent as he navigated the parking lot at the police station. He'd always been easier to read than his father.

"Mrs. Mason, hundreds of runaways end up in Los Angeles every month—and that's the half we know about." Detective Alvarez, a portly man with silver hair stretched like telephone wires across his head, opened the drawer of his scarred wooden desk and took a hit of Mylanta.

Michelle scanned the bullpen, where cops interviewing witnesses and processing suspects created a mighty din. She raised her voice. "I didn't come here for a lecture, Detective. I need you to find my daughter."

"We may be close to Hollywood, ma'am, but this isn't a TV

show with an entire squad assigned to one case." He tapped a stack of folders cluttering his desk. "These are from the last twenty-four hours."

"How many Nicole Deveraux Masons could there be?"

"None, according to our records." He tilted the computer screen toward her, revealing columns of names.

"Please, it has to be there. My husband said her calls couldn't be traced."

"Could be misfiled, misspelled, or just plain lost. We have twenty-five thousand cases on a public database you can search online. The only thing more I could try is to look up the report log. What was the date?"

"Year before last. Late November, I think."

"You don't know?" He appraised Michelle, from the gray hair against the Burberry collar framing her pearls, down to the flip-flops peeking from her hospital pants. He took another swig of Mylanta.

Michelle dug her bad arm deeper in her pocket. Maybe she should have taken more time to dress. She called over to Tyler, who was sitting on a bench across the room. Tyler pulled one of his earbuds out, but not because he heard her. He was saying something to the man next to him, a stringy rocker type in a black T-shirt with a red *R* on it. Something tugged at Michelle's memory until her view of him was blocked by a hug from a friend who looked exhausted, as if he'd spent the night in jail.

Giggling erupted as a few teenage prostitutes in trashy lingerie surrounded Tyler. Detective Alvarez whistled sharply and the whole room stopped cold. A female officer clucked over and hustled the girls to a holding pen farther down past the rows of detectives' desks. The youngest girl pulled down her tube top and flashed Tyler before being yanked away.

Tyler hurried over to Michelle, his cheeks flushed with blood. "Mom, remember when you pointed out those girls walking to Nikki's school with bare bellies and you said they'd end up pregnant and working at McDonald's all their lives?"

Michelle nodded. She used to think that was the worst thing that could happen, to have Nikki end up working at McDonald's.

Tyler laughed nervously. "I thought it meant they'd get free french fries."

Michelle longed to tousle his hair and kiss his cheek, but he was on her right side. She introduced him to the detective. "Tyler, do you remember when the missing persons report was filed? We need a date."

Tyler shrugged.

"That's okay. Why don't you go see if the snack cart has fries? I'll be out in a minute." Michelle doubted that, but she wanted to spare him the nightmare of envisioning his sister as one of those giggling girls. As he left, she could hear the girls reciting their names, Dot and Taffy and Sugarbaby. A cop tossed over a handful of condom packets and the girls fought over them like candy at a piñata party. She turned back to the detective.

"If we don't find her file can we start a new one?"

"You said she was sixteen when she disappeared."

"A young sixteen. Not like them," she said, nodding toward the girls.

"But she'll be eighteen by the end of the year, no longer a child. Unless there's a warrant out or new evidence of foul play…" The desk phone rang. He answered it and grumbled in Spanish.

Michelle saw the portrait of a cherubic teenager on the desk. The girl smiled like a princess in a white gown with sleeves shaped like puffy clouds. It was typical for a *Quinceañera,* the Latina version of a debutante party. Michelle wondered whether a party would have made a difference for Nikki. She pointed at the photo. "Is this sweet girl yours?"

"Granddaughter," he said, beaming as he covered the phone. "I bought the gown."

"How would you feel if you never got to see her in it?"

"I hear you, ma'am. But in twenty years behind this desk, I've learned a few things. These kids don't take off for no reason. Usually they're being abused or—"

"Excuse me?"

"Nobody leaves a warm bed and food on the table unless something's going down. It ain't called 'running to.' It's 'running away.' Half of 'em end up in County." He lowered his voice. "And between you and me—I'd rather my granddaughter be on the streets than in County. Too many of them end up in the morgue with slit wrists." He resumed his phone conversation.

Michelle looked at the photo again, trying to picture Nikki in that fluffy gown flitting about at a party. She couldn't. During preschool, Nikki cried when her classmates ran to the gate to greet her. At Brownies, she'd spent every meeting hiding under a desk playing with plastic unicorns. She was never picked for plays or invited to slumber parties, and puberty hit so hard she punched holes in the wall. If only slit wrists weren't so easy to imagine.

Detective Alvarez pointed to his business cards.

Michelle stood up slowly, so straight and tall that even her mother would be proud. She put her left hand on his phone. "Pardon me, but I don't have Internet service. Do you mind giving me a few more minutes' worth of my tax dollars to check the database again?"

Her crippled right arm swung out of the pocket. She pulled it back, but not before he cringed at the sight of the scar tissue wrapping her right hand.

"You're not on the dole yourself?"

"The what?" Michelle asked.

"Disability." He pointed at her limp arm.

Surprised, she looked down and saw where her power lay. She had thought of herself as injured, not disabled. It hurt to think that's how others saw her now. But if it helped her find Nikki, she would use it to her advantage. She cleared her throat. "Detective Alvarez, are you discriminating against the handicapped?"

The room quieted as others turned to look. He saw them and ended his phone conversation. He put his hands on the keyboard. "Name?"

"I gave you her name. Can you try different spellings?"

"Let's start with the correct one." He gestured to the chair.

Michelle spelled out Nikki's name. She estimated Nikki's height to be the same as hers, five foot eight, and her weight at 130. She had mousy brown hair, brown eyes, the gazelle-like gait of her *grand-mére*, and a wee bit of her father's Irish pallor. The detective promised to do what he could, but now she understood. He couldn't do much.

Outside, Michelle scanned the quadrant of dead grass between the courthouse and the county offices, then spotted Tyler at the food truck.

"Get any answers?" Tyler called, waving a half-eaten churro.

"Just more questions," Michelle said, spotting a cigarette butt on the sidewalk. She tossed it in the trash and wondered if Drew's plane had landed. She wanted to call him, but he had already refused to talk about this today. She could try tomorrow, but how would it help to interrupt his first day of preproduction meetings? She knew firsthand how hectic that could be.

They walked to the car. Michelle wished she had brought her cane, but at least she had Tyler to lean on. If only he didn't walk so quickly. She watched him take another sugary bite. It was satisfying to watch him eat—must be the Jewish mother in her. She hoped he didn't have to go back to school anytime soon. "Are you on Spring Break?"

"Not for a couple of weeks. But this is an excused absence. The attendance lady loves me."

Who wouldn't? Michelle thought. Then she realized that Nikki's school had an attendance office, too. If she could find out the first day Nikki missed school, Detective Alvarez might have a better chance of tracking down that file from the report log. Michelle was reluctant to get her son more involved, but she didn't see a way around it.

She couldn't imagine how hard the whole thing must have been for him. Aside from the usual problems of puberty, with his voice breaking up and his face breaking out, his entire life had been turned upside down. One day, he was playing baseball and all he wanted to do was pitch. The next day, his pitching coach was dead, his mother was gravely injured, his sister had disappeared, and he had to leave the only home he'd ever known to attend school clear across the country.

When they reached the car, he opened the passenger door for her. She gave him a kiss before getting in. "I'm so sorry, Tyler."

"For what?"

"For putting you through all this."

He shrugged and helped her with the seat belt. "It's not your fault, Mom."

She nodded, but it didn't make her feel any better.

7

THE NEXT MORNING, MICHELLE looked out the kitchen window at the children swinging their lunchboxes on their way to school. She used to love sending her kids off with peanut butter sandwiches cut in the shape of a heart. She and Drew had given up their apartment close to the beach and moved to the Valley because it was supposed to be the best place to raise children. Now, she wasn't so sure.

A car horn honked and the pace quickened as parents hurried their children to the playground before the first bell rang. Michelle was eager to get going too, but Elyse was still playing show-and-tell, matching each new sleeveless shift to a cardigan that would disguise her scarred arm.

"The actress from that HBO show bought this beige sheath in bright red. Poor thing had to duck the photographers outside of Saks, but the dress is classic."

"It's lovely," Michelle said, running out of polite adjectives. She followed her mother to the bedroom, where Elyse spread a navy ensemble on the bed.

As soon as Elyse left to give her privacy, Michelle shoved the sliding closet door open and found a garment bag. She pulled down the zipper, relieved to find her old uniform of black blazers and little black dresses, armor for the daily battles she'd fought in Hollywood. The suit hangers were too heavy for her left hand, so she yanked off the closest jacket and hoped the notched lapel was still in style. She struggled to slip the sleeve over her left arm only to see that her mother was right. She looked like a little gray-haired girl playing dress-up. Or worse: a little old lady.

By the time Tyler returned from walking the dog, Michelle was dressed in the navy shift and ballerina flats as if she was going to a Junior League luncheon. Her mother was thrilled, and frankly, Michelle didn't care anymore. She gave her blessing to her mother's plan to buy makeup and waited for the taxi to leave. Then she hurried Tyler to the car.

Michelle tried to relax and enjoy the scenery en route to the high school. She used to dream of living here, back when she shoveled gray slush from her mother's driveway in Ohio. Whenever the Buckeyes played in the Rose Bowl, she'd put on another sweater and watch the lollipop palms wave from the blue sky on the television screen. When Nikki learned in California History class that they weren't native, Michelle was disappointed. Michelle wasn't native either, yet she had dug her toes in the sand. She prayed to the palms in the blue sky now: let Nikki be okay. She didn't have to cure cancer or fly to the moon. Let her just be okay enough to go to college and get married and have a normal life. Let her be happy. Was that too much to ask?

At the stop sign, Tyler pulled out his inhaler and sucked on the plastic spout. Michelle was looking out the window at the lost cat flier stapled to a telephone pole. His words came out in a rush. "Dad calls those coyote menus."

Michelle patted his knee. "I remember. They come down from

the hills to hunt on hot summer nights. Had to take your baseball bat on walks when Bella was a pup." She looked at Tyler. "Did you post fliers when your sister disappeared? Was there a reward?"

Tyler steered the car onto the busy main street. "That's the first thing we did—in the mall, at school, all over the neighborhood."

"What about the private detective? How long before your dad gave up?"

"He didn't give up; he just stopped looking for her. At least, that's what he told me. He said it was his job to worry, not mine. Then he did it all by phone."

"What do you mean?" Michelle looked at him.

"When we went back to New York, he put me on the train and told me to focus on school. They don't play baseball year-round there, so I signed up for basketball." He put his arm up and tipped his wrist as if shooting a ball. "I suck."

"Two hands on the wheel," Michelle commanded. "What do you mean, *back* to New York?"

"We went for the holidays that year. You bought plane tickets way early, remember? You wanted us to have a white Christmas? After you were, you know, asleep, Dad said it would be good for us to go."

"Was it?" she asked, imagining them riding a snow-covered horse-drawn carriage through Central Park without her. Tyler nodded. Of course it was—they ended up moving east, didn't they? But that was temporary. Now that they were visiting the high school, Michelle would ask about transferring him back.

A neon scrawl on the sign above the school entrance announced the upcoming Spring Dance, SAT tests, and sporting events. Tyler braked, then jockeyed to park the Volvo between a dented Kia pickup and a gleaming black Mercedes. This was Michelle's place in the order of parents who believed enough in democracy to put their children's education on the line in public school. Either that, or they couldn't afford private school, either.

She looked across the cement courtyard and empty planters in front of the low brick building. When Tyler pulled on his Rutgers Prep letter jacket, she wondered if Elyse was helping with his tuition. That might also explain why Drew had refinanced the house to pay her medical bills instead of asking her mother for a loan. Michelle smoothed her dress to her knees and tried to feel grateful for the new clothes. The shift was a respectable length and the sweater hid her arm. If only the flats didn't pinch her toes.

Inside the glass doors of the main corridor, the blue floor was waxed to a blinding gloss and there wasn't a speck of trash in sight. In fact, there was no one in sight; only a trophy case, the bell schedule for short Fridays, and a sign-up for reality show auditions. As soon as Tyler signed in with the security guard in the front hall, a bell clanged as if he'd given the wrong answer on a quiz show. Michelle covered her left ear while classroom doors banged open and a multicolored stream of students flooded the hall.

A sea of sweatshirts and jeans, midriffs and miniskirts, surrounded them. Enormous boys bopped to exotic beats and shouted across the crowd in Spanish, Farsi, Vietnamese, and English. With four thousand students, somebody must know something about Nikki. It was strange to picture her shy little girl among these rowdy teenagers. They parted around Michelle as if she was a rock in a rushing stream. She squeezed her arm to her side, but no one even nudged her. She was a parent, invisible.

Tyler, however, was not.

"Hey, Mason, is that you?" A tall boy high-fived Tyler and dashed off, pausing to make some sort of hand signal from atop the stairs. Tyler understood the language. He understood the language of girls, too, purposely ignoring the cheerleaders giggling past, then glancing back to check them out. Just as quickly, the students vanished, leaving a trail of body odor and trashcans overflowing with notepaper.

They found the office for the dean in charge of the eight hundred students with last names from *K* to *R*, then squeezed past a dozen students making origami with hall passes as they waited in a line against the wall to see her. Michelle perused the colorful display of pamphlets warning about the evils of drugs. While Tyler studied a poster for the PTA silent auction featuring autographed electric guitars and Emmy-winning television scripts, she snatched a copy of each pamphlet.

When the door finally opened, the Dean's red glasses peeked out. "Excuse me, do you have an appointment? These students have been waiting."

"It'll only take a minute—it's an emergency," Michelle said. She stepped quickly inside, beckoning for Tyler to follow. Dean Valentine sat down behind her massive desk. "Thank you," Michelle said. "I'm Nicole Mason's mother. She used to be a student here?"

Dean Valentine tucked a loose thread back into the sleeve of her peasant blouse. "And?"

Michelle glanced at Tyler, but he was studying his cuticles as if they held the mystery of the universe. She dropped the pamphlets in her lap and folded her good hand around her bad one, hiding her arm beneath the navy sweater. Why was she so nervous? Her children didn't even attend this school anymore.

"I'd like a copy of her attendance records. *M-A-S-O-N*. She'd be in the current senior class. With the fall birthday, we should have held her back, but when it was time to decide about kindergarten she was excited and I was working full time, so…" Michelle caught herself rambling and shut up.

The Dean clicked the keyboard on her aging computer and read the screen. "Nicole Mason dropped out shortly after being suspended."

"Wrong Nicole."

"Mother is Michelle, father is Andrew, middle name Deveraux. We may have four thousand students, but we keep accurate records. Apparently she slammed the metal door of a PE locker in another girl's face." She printed out a copy.

Michelle looked back for moral support from Tyler, but now he was pretending to be invisible. Now she understood: this woman was scary. "Of course, but I don't remember any locker accident."

"I don't believe in accidents, Mrs. Mason."

Michelle nodded. Her mother used to say that.

"We have a zero tolerance policy for assault. That's why we suspended Nicole."

Michelle looked at Tyler for confirmation, but he just shrugged. "When did this happen?"

"November. The year before last. We sent a note home."

"I was in the hospital."

"Regardless, you're lucky the Levines didn't sue when their daughter required rhinoplasty. They asked only that we hold her place on the cheerleading squad." She studied Nikki's attendance report. "Nicole was readmitted the following week, but only attended class for a few days before going truant. After thirty days, we confiscated the contraband found in her gym locker."

"Contraband?"

"As her legal guardian, it's your property. May I see your ID?"

Michelle forced a smile. "Sorry, I...forgot my purse."

The dean appraised Tyler. "Weren't you in Little League with my son?"

"Yeah, but I heard he quit for surf team." Dean Valentine nodded. Tyler stood up. "I'm gonna hit the john," he said and escaped.

The dean looked back at Michelle. "We generally don't hold confiscated goods beyond the school year, so you can sign a release for it. However, if Nicole wishes to re-enroll, you'll need to petition the district." She circled Michelle and went out to the main office, leaving the door ajar.

Michelle tried to read the attendance slip upside down while she waited, but the ringing phones and shouting teenagers outside the door made her nervous. She scanned Dean Valentine's degree certificates and autographed celebrity photos until an Abba ringtone drew her attention to the patchwork purse on the shelf behind the desk. Beside it was a photo of three towheaded boys with surfboards and a mug identical to Michelle's that read, *World's Best Mom.*

Dean Valentine returned and opened the clasp of the bulging envelope while Michelle scrawled the *X* that passed as her left-handed signature. She peered inside, then pulled out a baggie and opened it, spilling several dusty white pills onto the desk. Then she pumped antiseptic cleaner from the desk dispenser and washed her hands.

Michelle put her hand on her heart to steady herself, then picked up one of the pills, hoping it was only Midol. Stamped on the side was a word she couldn't read. She could, however, squint enough to decipher the first letter: *V.* The white tablets were familiar now. They were Vicodin, the painkillers Drew used to take for his back. "She probably brought this for the girl who got hurt. Misguided, of course, but well intentioned."

"Mrs. Mason, are you familiar with our antidrug policy?"

"'Just say no?'"

Dean Valentine opened Nikki's folder and held up a card with Michelle's old signature. It wasn't as elegant as her mother's, but it was better than an *X.*

"Perhaps you'd remember it better had you read it before signing."

Michelle waved the antidrug pamphlets. "I read everything, Dean Valentine, which is how I know Vicodin is not a gateway drug."

"No, but it is illegal without a prescription. Students who require medication during school hours must have a physician's note on file."

Tyler slipped back in. "Yes, I recall the red tape for Tyler's asthma inhaler. But I'll bet you still don't have a registered nurse here every day."

"Our parent volunteers are fully capable. How you parent your children at home is none of my concern, but when it affects my students, it is. Perhaps you would benefit from our seminar series on Practical Parenting for Teens."

Michelle slapped the pamphlets on the desk but kept her voice under control. "Maybe if you spent more money on the students, and less on seminars, you wouldn't be so paranoid."

"I don't control the budget, Mrs. Mason."

"You don't control much of anything, do you? You get your kicks from terrorizing kids. The last time my daughter got in trouble, it was for reading a poetry book during biology lab. How dare you enforce such bullshit?"

Tyler gasped.

"I beg your pardon." Dean Valentine stood up.

"Nikki is a good girl!"

"Every child is at risk." A commotion rose in the hall, then there was a knock on the door and Dean Valentine hurried out.

Michelle hesitated. Zero tolerance? She had zero tolerance for being in this office another moment. But she wanted Nikki's report. She heard the dean shouting in the hallway and decided not to wait. She handed the bulky envelope to Tyler, then snatched the attendance sheet. Michelle led Tyler down the hall past students craning their necks to see a fight, then race-walked down the corridor.

Tyler caught up as she slowed by the security guard at the entrance. "Did you just steal that?" he whispered.

"Shhh," Michelle said as he held the front door open. A few steps into the windy courtyard, the attendance report slipped from her hand, paragliding across the pavement to the curb where the Volvo was parked. Tyler shoved the fat envelope beneath Michelle's arm and chased after the paper.

When she reached the car and looked around, Tyler was ten yards behind her, chatting with a group of athletes in varsity warm-ups. The bell clanged, and the jocks ran to the gymnasium entrance, leaving him with two pompom girls in pleated skirts.

Michelle waved for him to hurry, but he was lapping up the attention of the older girls holding their long hair back from the wind. If he were a puppy, his tail would be wagging.

The ear-splitting squeal of brakes filled the air. Michelle looked up to see a school bus, as long and yellow as caution tape, lumbering toward her. A bus just like the one that had pulled up there on Nikki's birthday.

The bus driver honked the horn for Michelle to move the car, but Nikki refused to get out. She complained that her teeth were sore after having her braces removed, but it was more than that. Tyler kicked the front seat in frustration, late for school. Students shouted from the bus windows, and Nikki shoved her birthday cupcakes to the floor. When Michelle pleaded, Nikki stumbled out to the pavement. She melted onto the sidewalk, her tears streaking red rivers down her pale cheeks, her new purple sneakers glued to the cement. The bus lumbered past.

Michelle called for backup. By some miracle, Drew answered his cell. "Let her go home and eat cupcakes, for chrissakes," he said. "Everyone needs a mental health day now and then."

Michelle leaned back against the car, waiting for Tyler to finish chatting with the girls. She tried to picture Nikki in one of those pleated skirts. If she had kept up with dance, or done some other activities, maybe she would have felt more like she belonged. Instead Nikki spent her weekends at home, reading poetry and switching between kid shows on the Disney Channel and cult films like *Donnie Darko*. At the time, Michelle was proud that her daughter was unique. She hadn't minded that Nikki was younger than the other kids in her class. It just meant she got to hold on to her little girl a bit longer. But no wonder Nikki didn't want to go to school on her sweet sixteen—there wasn't much to celebrate.

"Mom!" Tyler called.

"Ready to go?" Michelle asked, then looked back where the girls posed, all shiny and pert, as the athletes from a rival school hopped off the bus behind them.

Tyler stepped closer. "Mom, this is Kelsey and Ashlyn."

Michelle hid her arm beneath her sweater and smiled. "Hello. Do you girls know Tyler's sister?"

Their mascara-draped eyes darted at each other. "Give me a minute," Tyler told them. He guided Michelle back toward the Volvo.

"Wait, honey, I need to ask if they've heard anything. Maybe they were friends."

Tyler stopped at the curb. "Mom, Ashlyn's the one who had to get a nose job. Nikki shut the locker in her face. For real."

Michelle looked back. Sure enough, Ashlyn's nose was perfect. "She probably didn't know Ashlyn was standing there. It was a misunderstanding between friends."

"Mom to Earth? Nikki didn't have any friends." He spread his fingers into an *L*. "She was a loser. If I was her age, I wouldn't have hung with her, either."

Michelle felt a shooting pain, but this time it was in her heart. "How can you say that about your own sister?"

"Ty, are you coming?" Kelsey called.

He offered Michelle the report. "I'll get a ride home, okay?"

"No, Tyler, I need to talk to you."

"You want me to like it here, right?"

"I can't drive myself."

"Please, Mom, you used to drive one-handed all the time, before talking on the phone was against the law."

"That's beside the point. Why didn't you tell me any of this about Nikki?"

Tyler's face was red with frustration. "Because I wasn't supposed to upset you, duh!"

The girls called out one last time. "Ty, we have to go. See you later?"

Tyler waved at them in defeat, then opened the passenger door for Michelle. Once she was seated, he dropped the report in her lap and kicked the door shut.

8

TYLER WAS SEETHING AS he sped away from the school. Michelle struggled to buckle the seat belt with her left hand, wishing he would slow down, but she bit her lip to avoid playing the mom card again. The shock of going from no mother to a bossy one was reflected by the speedometer, going from zero to sixty in a matter of seconds. Still, all she needed was another accident.

Michelle's stomach dropped. For a blessed few minutes, she had forgotten about the boy who'd died in her car. The thought made her shiver. A police car approached and Tyler slowed, causing the old key chain, a beaded row of their names, to click as it swung back and forth. Nikki had made it for her mother in another lifetime: Before. This was After. Their lives were officially split into two.

Michelle sighed and dumped the contents of the school envelope on her lap as they drove though the suburbs. There was a moldy stick of Teen Spirit Deodorant, a pair of cotton, turtle-print panties from Target, and a crumpled black T-shirt that Michelle didn't recognize. The attendance report would have to wait until her hands stopped shaking.

A motorcycle cop waved them toward a detour past a street packed with white equipment trucks. After recognizing the camera truck and rented star trailers, Michelle searched for familiar faces among the film crew. She wished they were breaking for lunch, but the only ones visible were busy holding up shiny boards and aiming overhead mikes. She pointed toward a man with a walkie-talkie. "That looks like Aziz, the AD from Budweiser. I should call him."

Tyler drove another block before he finally burst. "Dad's not coming back!"

Michelle looked at him. "I wasn't going to call for your father's sake. But it does prove there are jobs here." She waited, but Tyler said no more. "What are you not telling me?"

Tyler focused on steering through the busy intersection.

"Come on," Michelle said. "You knew Nikki had been in trouble, I could tell. I felt like an idiot in there."

"You have an excuse," he said.

"Maybe, but you don't." Michelle picked up the turtle-print panties that Nikki used to love. "Remember the meltdown she had on her birthday?"

"How could I forget? I could have been class treasurer if she hadn't pitched a fit and made me late for elections. She didn't want to go to PE or something."

Michelle looked at the panties and realized that, at sixteen, Ashlyn and Kelsey were probably wearing lacy thongs. "I'll bet that's what the locker fuss was about. Nikki wouldn't hurt anyone—she was too shy. Those girls must have teased her about the panties until she couldn't take it anymore."

"Whatever." Tyler replied. He turned the radio on to a hip-hop station.

"How about something with a melody?"

He switched to a classic rock station, but Michelle's head still hurt. She unlatched the glove box filled with fast-food napkins, hospital parking stubs, and a bent pair of readers. "No Tylenol?"

"Dad took it. Want water? You used to make us drink it for headaches."

"I didn't want you to get in the habit of using drugs."

Tyler snorted. "All your classic rock is stoner music: Clapton, Jagger—" The Beatles tune on the radio segued into the Doors. "My English lit teacher said the Doors got their name from the Aldous Huxley book *Doors of Perception*. He and Poe and Blake—all those dudes were total druggies."

"Your school curriculum is impressive," Michelle said.

"Seriously, Mom. You ever see Jim Morrison live?"

She swatted him. "I'm not that old, Tyler! But my friend, Becca, won a Morrison film scholarship at UCLA. He wasn't much of a filmmaker, evidently, but he was quite the poet."

"Like Noah. Must be why he was so obsessed with the dude."

"Noah Butler? The one who was…your pitching coach?"

"Sucks, huh? He was a cool guy," Tyler said. He pulled the visor down to block the sun and braked to avoid rear-ending a UPS truck. A BMW honked past.

"Hands on the wheel," Michelle reminded him.

The song on the radio echoed: "hands on the wheel." They smiled at the coincidence, then Michelle listened more closely. The percussion was off. "Wait—that's not the Doors."

She reached for the volume, just as Tyler reached to change the channel. He banged into Michelle, throwing her off balance. "Fuck me," he said.

"Tyler!" Michelle glanced at him. The DJ was announcing a Roadhouse concert at the Wiltern. Michelle recognized the name but couldn't place it.

The DJ continued, "Took their name from the Doors' song, 'Road House Blues,' about driving to the nightclub in Topanga Canyon called the Cellar, where Neil Young used to—"

Tyler turned it down. "Idiot. Everyone knows it was called the Corral."

Michelle didn't, nor did she care. But that would explain why she recognized the name of the band—that song was a classic. And the burned-out ruins of the club were still there. Michelle used to notice them every time she drove through the Canyon. Then it hit her. "Roadhouse was Noah Butler's band, wasn't it?"

"Still is. I mean, they still play without him." He shrugged. "I just wanted a chance to pitch, that's all. Or I wouldn't have begged you to help."

Michelle's head was pounding now. "Help?"

"You produced the video for him in exchange for pitching lessons." He adjusted the rearview mirror and swore. "Dad's gonna kill me for telling you."

"No, he won't. It makes sense," Michelle said. When her boss used to complain that he wanted to make a movie, she urged him to update his director's reel. He had a few CLIO-winning commercials, but he needed something creative, like a music video. "That's what I do for a living. Did, anyway. And it might explain why he was in my car. But it doesn't make it your fault."

She looked down at the black T-shirt in her lap. She spread it out as much as she could with one hand, tugging at the safety pins holding the sides together. The front was painted with red triangles forming the letter *R*. "So why was this in Nikki's locker? Was she a fan? Like that guy at the police station yesterday—he wore a shirt like this." Tyler didn't answer. "Tyler, no more secrets!"

"She was more than a fan, Mom. She was in the video."

Michelle nearly laughed. She looked to see if he was teasing, but he wouldn't meet her gaze. She took note of his smartphone. "Pull over."

He slowed past a sushi restaurant and a swimsuit store but found only No Parking signs. "I'll show you when we get home."

"Now."

He maneuvered over to the curb, then turned on the next side street and parked in the red zone. Tyler tapped on the screen of his phone a few times, then held it up sideways. He pressed Play.

Michelle watched the title screen cut to a wide shot of four boys standing with their instruments in front of a plain backdrop. The low-budget style was a throwback to early Beatles videos, grainy and soft, so different than the sharp edges of digital images. Victor had taken advantage of the malleability of film. The blacks were saturated, and the shadows were velvety warm.

The musicians looked like any other amateurs, a bunch of scruffy kids in black T-shirts hand-screened with the red *R*. The shots were long, lingering on fingers plucking guitar strings and bouncing along with the drums, catching a laugh between the boys when the bass player slipped on a lick. It was less a performance and more an invitation to join them, to sing along. "Let it roll, baby roll, all night long." Tyler clicked up the volume of the tiny speaker until they heard laughter in the background, the chuckle of the chubby bass player as the drummer beat an extra roll. There was no reverb, no echo, only a shouted chorus mellowed by the tenor of Noah's voice.

The camera swung to him, the pretty boy at the mike, crooning with the charisma of Frank Sinatra. He glanced behind him where a shadow swayed—a dancer, Michelle guessed. Victor's camera panned the other boys' faces, but they were stealing glances off camera, at Noah.

On screen, Noah held out his arm and drew the girl close. She looked like a typical groupie in ghoulish makeup, a bit on the thin side, with a black Roadhouse T-shirt pinned together at the side.

When the camera cut to a close-up, she winked her false eyelashes, raised her black-penciled brows, and stared right into the camera lens. Her eyes were round and deep, like marbles made of Tiger's Eye.

Michelle could hear her heart beat. She held up her hand to make it stop, but searing pain shot up her arm. Wrong hand. She cried out and cradled her arm.

"You okay?" Tyler asked. He hit Pause.

She nodded, pretending the Earth had not just shifted off its axis. She opened the glove compartment, grabbed the bent glasses, and shoved them on quickly. When Tyler hit the Play button, she leaned in for a clearer look.

On-screen, Nikki resumed her swaying dance. The camera pulled back to reveal the entire the band, then panned back to Noah, who strummed the last chord and looked over at Nikki. She was laughing as her hand reached up into the frame. Her bitten nails were painted black, and she spread two fingers apart into her trademark sign. The image froze, then the screen went dark.

Michelle found her voice. "She looks so different. If it weren't for the bunny ears…"

Tyler half-smiled. "Nobody gets that. They think it's a peace sign, like she's so hip."

Michelle smiled at him. No one knew Nikki like they did. She wasn't a truant or some hippie chick. She was their girl. "You think this had something to do with her running away?"

"I don't know, but after it went viral, she sure got popular all of a sudden. Then, boom, Noah was gone. You both were."

"Then maybe I was wrong about her being teased."

"No, she was still teased. But not about underwear." He avoided her eyes and cranked the key so far the engine screamed.

Michelle put her hand on his leg. "Did you ever get to pitch?"

He shook his head and drove home.

9

MICHELLE THOUGHT SHE WAS dreaming again, swimming through darkness in search of some light. Round, racking sobs filled her head, water slipped through her fingers, and her lungs strained for air. She fought to pull out of it, to keep from drowning beneath the weight of her tears. Then she unclenched her hand from the bed sheet to wipe her eyes. They were dry.

Someone else was crying. Michelle fumbled to find the lamp on her bedside table, then gave up, leaping from the bed only to bang her bad shoulder into the wall. She ignored the pain and stumbled out the door into the dark. Another sob barreled down the hall like a cannonball. Michelle prayed it was her daughter. While Nikki's tears used to torment her, now the sobs were a symphony, the hiccups heaven-sent. Michelle could bear anything, even her baby's unhappiness, if only she could see her again.

Michelle pushed the door open. A figure lay beneath the knit blanket. Michelle tiptoed in. A car sped past, streaking light through the shutters and across the walls. The light gleamed against the woman's silver hair. It was Michelle's mother.

Elyse was quiet now. Whatever nightmare roused Michelle had ended. She backed slowly out of the room and sat down in the hallway. She crossed her legs and leaned back against the wall in a familiar position. This wasn't the first time her mother's tears had woken her.

Behind the locked door her mother was crying. She'd called Michelle to her room late at night. Wine-stained crystal goblets were lined up along her bedside table like wounded soldiers. Elyse's bloodshot eyes were smeared with mascara as she begged her little girl to go downstairs for more wine. She needed to take her Seconal, she cried, she was in so much pain.

Michelle saw the gold pill box cupped in her mother's hand and refused. Elyse slapped her.

Michelle felt the handprint rise like a hot brand on her cheek.

"Go away!" Elyse screamed.

Michelle stood frozen in fifth position until her mother swallowed the pills dry and pushed her out of the room. Michelle pounded against the door. There was no answer. She took a bobby pin from her pin curl and bit off the plastic tip. She jabbed the metal point in the keyhole until the lock clicked open. Then she pushed the door ajar and sat guard all night. The next night, Michelle waited until her mother went to bed, until she heard silence, then she picked the lock and crept inside. She put her hand to her mother's mouth to make sure she was breathing. Then she opened the pillbox and counted her pills.

Michelle leaned her head back and tried to make sense of things. Here she was, outside her mother's door again. But this was Nikki's room—Elyse was supposed to be at a hotel. As Michelle looked back at her mother's moonlit silhouette, she felt grateful that the door hadn't been locked.

She could hear the crickets now, their song rising until the repetition was painful. Michelle pulled herself up against the smooth white wall and limped to the kitchen to get an ice pack. She tiptoed around shopping bags that hadn't been there when she fell asleep, then noticed the stolen attendance report on the dinette. Elyse's cat-eye glasses lay on top. Michelle slipped them on.

The official record showed a week-long absence in October, a three-day suspension in November, and the semester ending with incompletes. Nikki could have run away any time after Thanksgiving.

Michelle turned the page and saw a spot of red. Another drop was on the table. For a moment, she feared her mother was hurt and felt that old familiar panic. Then she realized what she was looking at and flushed with anger. Michelle yanked the trash can open and saw the gleam of glass buried beneath crumpled napkins. She pulled out an empty bottle of Bordeaux.

Michelle strangled the wine bottle by the neck and stormed back into Nikki's room. She set the bottle down and shook her mother awake. Elyse pulled off her satin eye mask and sat up slowly.

Michelle held the bottle up. "Back to your old tricks, Mother?"

Elyse shook her head. "I had one glass and poured the rest out."

"I don't believe you. Did you cancel your hotel room, or just pass out?"

Elyse pulled her silk robe over her matching peignoir and followed Michelle into the kitchen. The morning sky was beginning to glow through the window. Elyse checked to be sure she had filled the coffee machine, then pressed the button to brew. "French Roast?"

"Oh, now it's okay?" Michelle asked.

"Anything to help you calm down."

"I heard you crying, Mother. Were you drunk?"

"*Non, ma chérie, je suis très fatiguée.* And I was upset."

"Upset that I'm no longer an invalid, so you can't tell me what to do?"

"Don't be rude," Elyse said. "I know you're tired, too, but—"

"If you only had one glass of wine, why didn't you just cork the bottle?"

"I didn't want to leave any temptation for Tyler."

"Right, because teenage boys have a real palate for Bordeaux." Michelle opened the wrong cupboard for a coffee mug.

"You're overreacting," Elyse said

"Am I? Nikki used to cry, too, you know. She got it from you."

"She was a teenage girl with raging hormones. That's perfectly normal."

Michelle slammed the cupboard. "She cried a lot more than normal, Mother. Her own brother called her a loser. And you know what she wanted to do on her birthday? Watch *Winnie the Pooh*."

"So?"

"She was sixteen."

"Everyone needs a break now and then."

"Everybody doesn't have a genetic predisposition for depression, Mother. And most kids don't refuse to go to school on their birthday. But I remember now. I took her home, but she just curled up in her bed and cried more. She put on those stupid disco earrings and got out her paintings of ponies and ripped them all up. People do things like that before killing themselves!"

"So, she felt bad about the trouble at school and decided to clean up her act."

"No, she was so miserable that I was afraid to leave her here alone. But I had to go to work. That must be why I brought her to the set. She had been crying all night, every night, for weeks. Just like you!" Michelle dissolved into tears. "What if she…"

Elyse wrapped her arms around Michelle. "Shhh. Nikki would never hurt herself. She's much stronger than I was."

Michelle broke free. "She'd better be. Because if anything happens to her, I'm blaming you."

Elyse held Michelle's glare. "It's you I'm worried about, *ma chérie*."

"Me?" Michelle grabbed a paper towel and dabbed at her eyes.

"You need to rest. Let me help you."

"I don't want your help," Michelle insisted. "I'm not a child."

"You've never been a child, that's the problem."

"Whose fault is that?" Michelle asked.

Elyse stiffened. "Don't make me say something we'll both regret."

"Then don't say anything at all. Just get the hell out!"

The coffee maker gurgled. Elyse yanked the carafe out, then dumped the steaming liquid in the sink. She opened the trashcan and dropped the carafe in. The glass shattered against the side.

Tyler entered, rubbing his eyes. Bella bounded in after him. "What's up?"

"I'm afraid I must go," Elyse said.

"Is something wrong?" Tyler asked.

"No," the women said in unison. Elyse pivoted and went to pack.

"Go back to sleep, honey," Michelle said. She heard them say their good-byes as she opened the window. Elyse was right that she needed rest, but exhausted or not, Michelle had meant what she said. She just shouldn't have said it aloud.

Michelle was still stewing when a taxi pulled up in the driveway. The driver, whose head was wrapped in a white turban, trudged to the porch. He saw her and shouted, "Does a Madame Deveraux live here?"

Michelle shook her head. "No, thank goodness, but she'll be out shortly."

The wheels of Elyse's suitcase rolled down the hall like an aftershock, getting louder as they approached. Elyse set another shopping bag in the kitchen. "Here are some other items you won't like. Feel free to return them—or give them to Lexi, for putting up with you. Also, Dr. Palmer's office called." She tapped a note pinned on the refrigerator beneath the green plaster fin, all that was left of the turtle magnet.

Michelle looked around. "You didn't happen to see an envelope from Nikki's school, did you? With clothes from her locker?"

Elyse pointed across the room at the laundry basket on the couch.

Michelle rushed over and dug through the folded pile for the hand-stenciled T-shirt that Nikki had worn in the Roadhouse video. She tossed Tyler's jeans aside and pulled out a black rag held together with safety pins. Sure enough, Elyse had washed it. Michelle held it to her face and sniffed, but her daughter's scent was gone. Michelle shook it in the air. "Mother!"

Elyse sighed. "A good deed never goes unpunished, *mais oui*?" The house was quiet as she slipped out, then Michelle heard laughter outside.

Michelle nearly tripped over a shopping bag on her way to the window. When she spied the beautiful leather purse inside, she felt a pang of guilt. She shook it off, then looked outside. Her mother was smiling, flirting with the driver as he lifted her luggage into the trunk. That was more like it, Michelle thought.

When the taxi backed out of the driveway, Michelle snatched the shrunken T-shirt to bring to Nikki's room. She turned and caught her reflection in the oven glass. The truth was, blaming her mother might make her feel better, but if anyone was responsible for something bad happening to Nikki, it was Michelle. For whatever reason, she wasn't there when her daughter needed her most.

10

MICHELLE WAS SORTING THE rest of the laundry when Tyler called out from the front door. "Coach is here! Are you decent?"

That was debatable, Michelle thought, now that the guilt from kicking her mother out had set in. "Let me get dressed!"

Kenny's voice barreled down the hall. "No need, Michelle, I'm due at the courthouse at eleven."

Michelle heard the front door shut and zipped up her hospital bathrobe. She took her cane, almost as an excuse for not being dressed. At least she still had her pearls on—it was impossible to take them off by herself.

Kenny looked different than usual as he looked up from chatting with Tyler in the foyer. "Hate to barge in like this, Michelle, but I've been trying to reach you."

"Sorry about that. Do I need to sign a permission slip for Tyler to play?"

"Nothing that simple," he said. "I need to file some documents. May I?"

As she followed him into the living room, Michelle realized what was different. Instead of his blue baseball jacket, he was wearing a suit. A stinging sensation overwhelmed her, as if a swarm of wasps was trapped beneath her clothes. It reminded her of the feeling you get after your foot falls asleep and the warm blood rushes in. Only this time she could feel the pins and needles all over. "Does this have to do with Nikki?"

"Ah, the million-dollar question." He pulled a chair out for her at the dining room table, then sat down at the end. "Make that fifty million."

"What are you talking about?"

He opened his briefcase and took out a legal pad. "Do you remember anything about the accident yet?"

"I don't remember who visited me at the hospital yet."

"Lexi said that'll be patchy for a while," Tyler said. "TBI patients can't have retrograde memory without autograde—the old stuff comes back first. It's like a rule."

Michelle smiled. "Remember my care manager from the party? She dropped off a medical release earlier. Tyler has a thing for older women," she teased, thinking of the cheerleaders.

Tyler blushed. "No, she just knows all this stuff from dating your physiatrist. He's the dude in charge of all the other doctors. "

Kenny nodded. "From what I gather, before you remember recent events, you have to recall much earlier experiences, correct?"

"But I do," Michelle said. "I remember so much from when the kids were little…" Her thoughts went to Nikki as a little girl, twirling in the front yard. She tried to picture Nikki the last time she'd seen her, with the braces off, but all she could think of was the video.

Kenny cleared his throat. "Memory is a tricky thing, Michelle. You'd be surprised how many witnesses identify the wrong suspect in police lineups. Compound the power of suggestion with a trauma-based amnesia and you'll understand why I asked Drew not to say anything he might have heard about the accident."

He pulled the rubber band from a thick file, then spread newspaper articles on the table.

Michelle looked at Tyler. "Could you please get those old reading glasses from the car?" While he ran outside, she read the headlines: "Fatal Crash in Topanga" and "Freeway Accidents Rise Over Rainy Weekend."

"Ah, yes," Michelle said. "*Force Majeure*. That's what the motion picture insurance companies call it when a production shuts down and they won't pay. An 'Act of God.'"

"Your insurance company has a similar philosophy," Kenny said, scowling. He unfolded a feature article.

Michelle spotted her professional headshot, but barely recognized the striking brunette in a dark blazer. The caption read, "Michelle Mason, Executive Producer of Golden Hour Productions." Noah was in the picture beside hers, with dark hair to his shoulders and eyelashes any girl would envy. The caption read, "Noah Butler, singer-songwriter, whose band, Roadhouse, signed with Sanddollar Records."

Kenny read the next line. "'Survived by his father, Guy Butler, CEO of Butler Music, of Malibu, and his mother, Laura Braunstein, MD, of Tarzana.' Says he was 'thrown clear of the wreckage.'"

Tyler came back in with the glasses, but she just toyed with them.

"So, I know it happened after a game. It was raining." She looked at Tyler. "And your father wasn't there."

"He was just back from location. He had to return mikes and submit receipts and stuff. We were late for warm-ups, and you didn't want to stop for gas, so you switched cars."

"How do you remember all that?" Michelle asked.

"I had to answer a bunch of questions when you were in the hospital."

86

Michelle looked sharply at Kenny. "A deposition? Drew allowed that?"

"It was necessary. You answered a few preliminary questions as well. Tried, anyway. But everyone is in agreement that you were driving the SUV."

Michelle leaned back from the table. "Then we must have been more than a few minutes late, because I hate that car—it rattles. Plus, I'm five foot eight, and I can barely see over the hood."

"Please don't repeat that to anyone; it implies you couldn't control the vehicle," Kenny said. He showed her a white postcard stamped with the Orrin Motor Company logo. "Do you remember getting a recall notice about a seat belt malfunction? Or whether the seat belts were working? It's part of our defense."

"Defense for what?" Michelle asked. "How could a seat belt cause a car crash? And why are we talking about the crash instead of Nikki?"

Kenny hesitated, then opened a file of legal documents. "There's no way to sugarcoat this, Michelle. Your husband mentioned that I helped out with the estate, but once you regained consciousness last year…Well, let's just say it became a whole new ballgame."

"Are you trying to be funny?"

"Nothing funny about it. The driver is responsible for the safe transport of passengers. Your insurance company dealt with the burial expenses, but once it was clear that you would survive, Noah's parents decided to file a civil suit. Noah Butler was thrown from the car. They believe you're liable for their son's death due to negligence."

Michelle tossed the glasses down. "I haven't gotten so much as a speeding ticket since college. What could they possibly gain by suing me?"

"Besides closure?" Kenny sighed. "Noah was more than just a

volunteer pitching coach. The band he started is extremely popular. When I checked Google this morning, there were twenty-five pages of related articles."

"What does that have to do with the lawsuit?"

"He wrote most of the original songs they play. And they had already recorded that first album before the accident."

"What first album?" she asked, then clapped her hand to her mouth. The cane clattered to the floor.

Kenny bent to retrieve it. "You remember something?"

"He told me he was making an album with his friends at UCLA. He had written all these songs and was using crowdsourcing funds to pay for the recording sessions—I had just been to an industry seminar about it, for financing independent features. Noah said his friends thought a video would help."

"Those friends are now millionaires. The boy was talented. He was nineteen, legally a man, but you know what I mean."

"I do. He was a sweet kid, too, or, I would have just paid him for extra pitching lessons." She looked at Tyler.

"Were you having an affair with him?" Kenny asked.

"Of course not! I'm a married woman."

"Take it as a compliment," Kenny said. "Tyler's not the only one who appreciates older women."

Tyler shrugged. "Some of the boys on the team used to call you a MILF."

"That's disgusting," Michelle said.

Kenny clicked his pen a few times while he studied her reaction. "Tyler, how about pouring me a cup of the coffee that smells so good?"

"I'm afraid we're fresh out," Michelle said. "Tyler, stay right here. This whole idea is ridiculous. And your father knows it."

Kenny put his pen down and pulled a laminated *National*

Enquirer article from his briefcase. The headline read: "Hollywood Producer in Fatal Crash with Young Lover?" The photo showed Michelle with her arm around Noah. Before Michelle could look closer, Kenny pulled out a yellowing page from *Us Magazine* that read: "Funeral for Roadhouse Rocker Held in Malibu."

"At least my picture's decent," Michelle said.

"This is no time for jokes," Kenny said. "You were an attractive woman in your prime with a husband who was out of town half the year—a typical 'location widow.' Right now, all we know for a fact is that you went to all the trouble of producing a music video for this boy. You have to admit it reads well."

"You believe everything you read?"

"Of course not." He pointed at the printed mailing label. "But my wife has been subscribing for years. And I've noticed that often where there's smoke, there's fire. Would you really put your company on the hook for tens of thousands of dollars for a couple of pitching lessons?"

"Oh please, it was a low-budget video. Noah could have shot it in his basement, if he had a camera."

"You remember?" Kenny asked.

"No, but I saw it." Michelle avoided looking at Tyler. The last thing she wanted to do was get him in trouble with his coach. "Victor probably shot it on leftover short ends of film with that old Arri he keeps in storage. We did a lot of public service announcements, so his crew often volunteered their time to stay in his good graces. And I could usually rustle up a little tabletop stage for half a day as a favor. Victor needed something besides commercials on his director's reel to get out of advertising. He wanted to do movies—why else work in Hollywood?"

Unless you have kids, she thought. Then someone has to stay close to home. She caught herself and smiled at Tyler.

Kenny made a note. "So this music video would help your career, too?"

"I suppose so," Michelle said. "Does that help?"

"Not really," Kenny said. He put the pictures away and tried another approach. "How about your daughter? Could she have been involved with the deceased?"

Michelle shook her head. "That's just as ridiculous. Didn't you ever see her on the field? Scrawny thing, with braces right up until her birthday. She was too shy to get out of the car at Tyler's games until we started knitting together on the sidelines."

Ken held up a still shot of Nikki from the video. "That's not how she looks here. And she wouldn't be the first to jumpstart an acting career this way."

"Not a chance. She was tagging along with me at work, and somebody probably talked her into dressing up to save us from paying an extra." She pulled the photo down. "I've always kept my kids as far from Hollywood as possible."

She rose to leave, but Kenny stopped her. "I'm not finished."

Michelle surveyed the clippings spread across the table. "I am. So far you've accused me of being an unfaithful wife and a bad mother. What does any of this have to do with being a negligent driver?"

"Just covering my bases," Kenny said. "Noah's parents filed separate lawsuits against you and Orrin Motors. You—meaning, the lawyer hired by your insurance company, Pacific Auto, to represent you—filed an answer to that, saying you were not liable for negligence, and a cross complaint against Orrin alleging product liability due to faulty seat belts. So naturally, Orrin filed a lawsuit against you. And if the jury finds that both you and Orrin Motors are liable to some extent, they want to be sure the judgment is split according to whatever percentage the responsibility is determined."

"I lost you at Noah's parents."

"We are saying that you did not drive improperly. Period. We're using the seat belt issue as one argument. No one in Detroit wants a class action suit about seat belts. Or controversy about the death of a rock star. And since Orrin sent notices to inspect and repair a potential seat belt malfunction to all owners of that vehicle model, they allege you were negligent in disregarding the notice and also in operating the vehicle. If I argue that there is no legal deadline as to how long a car owner has to address a recall, they'll want to convince the jury that you are known to be irresponsible or have some motive to drive improperly. If any evidence comes out that supports their allegation, it could get ugly. They'll be like pit bulls with a steak bone, trying to pin this all on you. Do you understand?"

"They want to make me the bad guy?"

He nodded.

"Then let them. I feel horrible about poor Noah, of course. But they can fight over the money all they want. All that happened a long time ago. Right now, my daughter is still out there. And I intend to find her."

Kenny nodded. "Here's the thing, Michelle. Attorneys representing the car manufacturer want to find her, too. They want Nikki to testify against you."

"Me? Why?"

"Because there are millions of dollars at stake, and she's the only one who hasn't been interviewed. She's the closest thing to a witness they have."

"She saw the accident?"

"No, but she may have seen you drive away. And she may have known about the recall. Your husband said you wouldn't allow her to drive the SUV."

"That car was huge. Practically a truck. She was just learning to drive!"

"In any case, she disappeared shortly after your doctor induced the coma, and the negligence claim was filed soon after you woke up. Believe me, they are sparing no expense to find her."

Michelle rubbed her bad arm. So that's what Drew meant when he said everyone was looking for her. He wasn't just talking about the police or the detective he hired. He meant the lawyers, too. "I'll find her."

Kenny sat up. "Why, is there a reason we need to find her first? Does she know something?" He gestured at the magazine articles on the table.

Furious, Michelle swept the articles off the table. "My daughter is missing!" She turned and headed back toward the bedroom.

Michelle could hear Tyler as she headed down the hallway. "Coach, can we finish this another time? Dad said she needs to rest, you know, and not get so upset."

"You're a good kid, Tyler," Kenny said. "Unfortunately, there isn't a lot of time. The judge has fast-tracked the case." He called down to Michelle. "The next deposition is coming right up, Michelle. We need to prep you. "

Michelle stormed into the bedroom and slammed the door. She climbed back in bed, but her mind was racing. She opened the get well card and listened to her daughter's message for the hundredth time. But instead of listening to her voice and cherishing every inflection, this time she focused on the words.

> *"Hello, Mother. I feel awful about what happened.*
> *But I can't see you like this. I hope you understand.*
> *Love, me."*

Now that Michelle knew more about the accident, she wondered what her daughter had meant. Initially, she'd assumed Nikki meant that she couldn't bear to see her mother injured. But maybe she was upset about more than that. Tyler said the video gave her a bit of notoriety at school—the accident would have put an end to that. If the cheerleaders had read those magazines, too, and teased Nikki about her mother having an affair with Noah, that would explain how she got angry enough to slam a locker door in someone's face. Either way, Nikki hoped her mother would understand. And of course Michelle wanted to, if only she had the chance.

When the sound of muffled coughing intruded on her thoughts, it was almost a relief. Michelle felt herself slip back into mom mode, when concern for her child outweighed everything else.

"Tyler, are you all right?" she called.

He opened her door. "Just the spring pollen. Coach said I can get a ride to the game with Cody's mom if I go early."

"Okay, but the ball field won't be any better for your allergies."

"Worth the hassle," Tyler said. "Will you be okay here alone?"

She nodded and reached for her son's hand, so he could help her sit up. When he leaned over, she kissed his cheek, grateful he still let her do that. His sister used to turn her head until Michelle's lips met her hair. Boys were so much easier, she thought, as he waved good-bye and left. What was it about mothers and daughters that felt so fragile?

She saw Nikki's card on the bedside table and considered showing it to Kenny. She felt bad about causing a scene when he had only been trying to help. But what if Kenny decided to keep the card? Michelle couldn't bear to give it up.

11

A FEW HOURS LATER, MICHELLE hiked past the West Valley playground where she used to push Nikki on the swings. She quickened her pace toward the manicured baseball diamond and spotted the blue team warming up. For once, she wished she had her cane. While the winter rye was as plush as shag carpet, Michelle's legs ached for a rest. But she was determined to get to the field before her son came to bat.

As Michelle approached the fence by the dugout, she spotted Kenny in the outfield. Tyler was nearby, throwing the ball to Cody.

A man stuffed into stretch pants in the dugout glanced up from his newspaper, then did a double take. He spit out a sunflower seed and stood up. "Well if it isn't Tyler's Mom."

Michelle relaxed a little. They were all called that, Somebody's Mom. That was the only title that mattered here.

"Howdy there, Michelle!" Kenny's wife, Cathy, approached in a T-shirt bedazzled with the words: Team Mom. Michelle was grateful to see her nod at the coach, who loped back to the third-base line. Cathy gave Michelle a warm hug. "Sorry I couldn't say anything about Nikki the other night. Drew insisted, and when you said she was coming home, I didn't know how to handle it." She released Michelle and looked around. "How did you get here?

Never mind. You look good," she said with a nod to the linen dress and ribbon-edged cardigan that Elyse had bought. "How are you feeling?"

"A little overwhelmed," Michelle said. "I'll feel better after I've spoken with Kenny again."

"Would you like to sit with me and Emily until he has a moment?" Cathy pointed toward the bleachers.

Michelle looked over. A coven of baseball moms perched on the first few rows strained their necks around the crowd to see her. Michelle waved. Some of them waved back halfheartedly before turning to chatter with each other. But from the way their eyes kept darting back to her, Michelle guessed that they read the gossip magazines, too. She hugged her right arm. "No thanks, I'll wait."

"Anything I can help with?" Cathy persisted.

"I want to apologize for this morning."

Cathy lowered her voice, but her tone hardened. "I didn't hear the whole story, but I do know one thing: my husband knows what he's doing."

Michelle heard the pride in her voice. "I don't mean to be ungrateful."

Cathy smiled. "Good, because I need to ask you a favor." Before she could explain, warm-ups ended and the boys ran into the dugout and onto the field. "Game's on." She marked the score chart, then offered a lemon bar from a Tupperware container. Michelle demurred.

"What's wrong? You used to rave about these. Did your taste buds change?"

"A little, but Drew is the one who loves those. I'm more of a chocolate person—otherwise, why waste the calories?" Michelle was teasing, but Cathy didn't laugh. Shouts erupted and fans behind them cheered. They looked up at the field as the shortstop caught a grounder and shot it to first base for the out.

"That's the way, boys!" Cathy shouted. She marked hieroglyphics on the score chart.

"What happened?" Michelle asked. "I can't seem to remember the plays."

"Can't blame the coma for that."

Michelle glanced back from the field. "Excuse me?"

"Since we're being honest, Michelle, admit it. Six years of baseball and you never took the time to learn how the game is played."

"I never had the time."

Cathy kept her eyes on the game. "Maybe because you were so busy with your BlackBerry and your *Variety* and your bills. It was sweet when Nikki started coming and the two of you would knit, but even then you had to ask me for the score."

"Sorry, but I thought it was enough to leave work early and fight traffic to be here." Michelle's voice rose along with her frustration.

"Dressed in designer suits and heels that poked holes in the grass."

"In Hollywood, you either go glam or go home."

"Oh, Michelle. Look at you. You went from a hospital gown straight to a designer dress that a celebrity wore on *Letterman* last night."

Michelle started to explain, but Cathy was on a roll. "And there was more than one complaint about how you flirted with the dads while your husband jet-setted around the world."

"He wasn't jet-setting, he was living out of a suitcase. And I wasn't flirting; I was trying to get help for Tyler. I was friendly to the moms, too!"

"Sure, to switch snack day. Seriously, polite is one thing; friendly is another. Forget it. From what Kenny says, you can't remember much, anyway. But this has been really hard on everyone, you know? Not just you."

Michelle tried to enjoy the game, but after a few minutes, she realized that Cathy was right. She had no idea what was happening on the field—nor did she care, unless Tyler was involved. But did that make her a bad person? She looked down at the Tupperware. "The truth is, I could never make lemon bars. I can't even do Slice and Bake cookies without burning them. I was never Team Mom or Captain of the Neighborhood Watch. Even if I stayed home, I could never be like you, with the homemade snacks and holiday decorations."

"What is this?" Cathy asked. "Mommy Wars?"

"Call it what you want. At least your kid didn't run away." Michelle turned toward the field, fighting back tears. She felt Cathy's hand on her arm. "Do you know anything about that? About Nikki?"

Cathy dropped her hand. "Can't go there."

"Please, Cathy, I'm begging you."

Two teenage boys in brown baseball jerseys ran up, interrupting them. "Aren't you Tyler Mason's mom?"

Michelle wiped her eyes and smiled. "Yes. He's in the bullpen if you want to say hello."

The taller boy shoved a Roadhouse CD in her face. "We want your autograph, Killer Mom!"

Michelle balked. She must have heard them wrong.

Cathy snatched the CD. "You boys should be ashamed of yourselves!"

"Hey, that's mine!" the boy said as the other kid dragged him away. "Fucking bitch!"

"I'm calling your mother!" Cathy called. She handed the CD to Michelle. "Look, I'm sorry about all this. I really am. You may think my family is perfect, but I count my lucky stars every day. Like that expression, 'There but for the grace of God, go I.'"

Michelle nodded. "Do people really call me that?"

"Just kids. Fans. You can throw that CD away if you want. I would."

"No, I'd like to hear it." Michelle looked up from Noah's sweet face on the cover and tried to shake off the spooky feeling. "Didn't you mention a favor?"

Cathy marked the score chart, then lowered her voice. "When your husband first called, I was against Kenny taking the case. I thought there was a conflict of interest, since he was the last one to see you."

"Here at the field?"

"Yes. I warned him about the rainy forecast, but he refused to cancel the game, because we needed the win to make playoffs. By the third inning, when the boys were soaking wet, some of the parents had already left. We took a bunch in the van, so you offered to take the banner in the SUV. That's the last I saw of you."

Neither spoke for a moment.

"Besides visiting a few times in the hospital, I mean. Which was almost impossible with such limited visiting hours. Anyway, around Thanksgiving, Kenny gave Drew a hand with the paperwork over a couple of beers. The auto claim was open and shut because you were in such bad shape. When they induced the coma, he set up a conservatorship with power of attorney and the living will and all that. Then, you pulled the Rip Van Winkle act and everybody started suing each other. Drew got a letter from Pacific Auto saying the case value might exceed the policy limits for personal liability, and you would be responsible for any judgment beyond that. So, in addition to the insurance lawyer, you needed a lawyer to protect your personal exposure. I think it's called Cumis counsel."

"And he hired Kenny?"

"Don't act so surprised."

"I'm sorry," Michelle said, shaking her head. "It's just—a lot to digest."

"Fair enough," Cathy said. "But just so you know, my husband has the highest record of wins in the Valley, probably most of LA. He's got the right kind of charm." She glanced over at her husband with pride, then marked the score chart.

"Since your health insurance maxed out, Pacific Auto kicked in up to the medical limit of your policy, but then Drew had to start paying out of pocket. Which made it impossible to pay Kenny. By then, we'd received so many new legal documents and subpoenas we had to get another filing cabinet. I begged Kenny to quit the case, but he didn't want to leave you in the lurch." Cathy sighed. "He's trying to work something out with the insurance company, but the whole thing is out of hand. I've been making Hamburger Helper for dinner three times a week. They have forty-some flavors, but they all taste the same. And Kenny had to let his secretary go, so I had to step down as PTA president to help."

"That's awful," Michelle said. "How can he still volunteer to coach?"

"It's the only thing that keeps him going. That and the hope that he'll get a ton of new business if he wins."

"Do you think he has a chance?" Michelle asked, watching him across the field.

"You tell me." Cathy lowered her voice. "When I was helping Drew pack, I found your love note from Noah."

Stunned, Michelle looked at Cathy.

"It said, 'LA woman, you're my woman.'"

Michelle relaxed. "That's a song lyric, isn't it? Tyler said Noah was a Doors freak." Michelle waited, but Cathy kept her eyes on the game. "Oh, please, you can't possibly think…"

Cathy interrupted. "Doesn't matter what I think. It didn't look good, so I threw it out."

"Thanks, I guess."

"You're welcome." Cathy paused to record a run on her chart. "But I didn't do it for you. I need this all to end. We're already dipping into Cody's college fund to pay the mortgage. Unless he gets a scholarship, he's looking at community college. With all the state cutbacks, it'll be years until he gets the classes he needs to transfer—and those baseball programs are a joke."

Michelle saw Kenny whispering in a boy's ear at third base. "No wonder you're so angry with me. I am so sorry, Cathy. But what can I do?"

"Kenny mentioned a release your nurse dropped off—a formal agreement to end medical care. Sign it. Drew's already on a payment plan, but with more expenses coming..."

"What if something else crops up?"

"Then open a new claim that you won't have to pay until after the trial. But your knitting days are over, right?" They both looked down at Michelle's useless arm.

Michelle tried to understand. "So Kenny would get paid sooner?"

"That's the idea. Do you want to talk to Drew about it?"

"No, I'm a big girl. Just tell me what you heard about Nikki. Please."

"You'll have to get that rehab doctor to sign the release, too."

"Deal. Tell me what you know."

Cathy looked up at the baseball field. "Kenny said not to upset you."

"That's what Drew said, too. As if nothing upsetting has happened so far."

"Men," Cathy said. They laughed together, but only for a moment.

"Please?" Michelle asked. "All I know is: it rained. Did I take Tyler and Noah home?"

"Noah wasn't at the game."

"You sure?" Michelle asked.

"He was mostly around at practices. And I would have noticed his Harley."

Michelle looked at her. "Hard to picture that skinny kid on a Harley-Davidson."

"This wasn't the big kind, not like Kenny had back in the day. Can you believe my husband had a 650? Looked like Russell Crowe riding that hog," Cathy sighed. "Traded it for the minivan, poor thing."

"Can you think of anything else?" Michelle asked.

Cathy shook her head and marked the scorecard.

"Which other parents should I talk to?"

"None! Please don't. They had to deal with the police and the news reporters. We forfeited the last game of the season to be at Noah's funeral. For most of these boys, it was their first one. And here you are, like the ghost of Christmas past, to stir it all up again."

Michelle was beginning to understand why she felt stares pelting her back. When she looked at the bleachers, a few faces turned away.

"Go home," Cathy pleaded. "Besides distracting the parents, there are too many teenagers here. Roadhouse is the biggest LA band since the Red Hot Chili Peppers." She pointed at a cluster of teenagers aiming their phones at them. "You're probably already on YouTube."

People were cheering again.

Cathy looked out at the field. "Drat. I've lost track."

Michelle spotted Tyler trotting to the far side of the outfield. "Fine, I'll go.

"Thanks. And keep that dress clean for the deposition—it's perfect."

Michelle looked at the beige linen. "Does it make me look innocent?"

"Aren't you?" Cathy asked.

12

THE NEXT MORNING, MICHELLE poked her head outside like a groundhog checking for spring. Her conversation with Drew last night hadn't gone well, but at least he promised to order her a phone. She used to handle all the house accounts—now her name wasn't even on them. After they hung up, she was so worn out that she got a decent night of sleep. All she wanted now was a little bit of fresh air while she figured out what to do next. She fastened the Velcro square of her hospital blouse, hooked Bella's leash on her collar, then opened the door wide. Before she could grab the leash again, Bella ran out.

"Tyler! Hurry!"

Her son bolted out of the bathroom, already dressed. "What?"

She pointed outside. Fortunately Bella was more interested in smelling every tree on the street than in stretching her furry legs. As the St. Bernard sniffed her way to the next yard, Michelle imagined how she must have suffered on the smoggy streets of New York City. Here, she could inhale information about the age and sex of every animal that had peed there in the past month. If only Nikki's trail was that clear.

"Will you please take her for a walk?"

Tyler ran out and grabbed the leash. "Can I do it later? I'm meeting friends for breakfast."

"Fine. Put her in the yard, and I'll give you money. But I need you to pick up my alterations, okay?"

He pulled the dog back in the house. She watched him track dirt as he crossed the living room carpet, then caught her reflection in the glass of the French doors. When he returned, they went in the kitchen, where she gave him cash from the envelope she had wedged under the orchid vase. "Leave your phone."

Tyler hesitated, then sent a quick text and handed it over. "This is not the part of having a mom that I missed."

"Well, get used to it, honey." She watched him go, then looked at the phone and sunk into a chair. She had no idea how to use it. She set the phone on the dinette and tapped in her old office number, one digit at a time.

A young woman answered. "Golden Hour."

Michelle recognized the voice of her former assistant. "Asia. It's Michelle Mason."

"No way! How are you?"

"Fine," Michelle said. Lying was easier than explaining. "Thank you for the orchids. Victor's name is on them, but I know how things work over there."

"You should," Asia said. "You taught me everything I know."

"True. So who's been running the place?"

"Me," Asia said.

Michelle chuckled. "Good for you. Then you know what's up with Victor's crew. I'm trying to get in touch with Sasha. Is she working?"

"Not for us," Asia said. "Last few times I tried to book her, she was unavailable."

"Bummer. Is Victor around? Maybe he'll know."

"He's shooting today. Shall I give him a message?"

"Please. Tell him thanks for the flowers. And can you give me the number for Paramount? I want to congratulate Becca on her production deal, but I can't find my address book."

Michelle memorized the number Asia gave her, then tapped each digit quickly, before she lost her nerve. Her old film school friend had jumped a dozen professional rungs above her while she was asleep. After repeating herself to a gauntlet of studio assistants, Michelle was finally transferred to Becca's cell.

"Oh my god, Chelle!" Becca exclaimed. "I'm just leaving Malibu. Stay where you are—I'll head right over."

Michelle hung up, pleased. Becca wouldn't care how awful she looked. She was one of the people Michelle remembered most from visiting hours at the hospital.

Forty minutes later, a black limo pulled up in front of the house. By the time Michelle shuffled to the foyer, Becca's snakeskin boots were already tapping a dance on the tile. When she saw Michelle, she hugged her with such ferocity that Michelle almost fell over. "Look at you!"

Michelle didn't want to cry, so she laughed. "What about you—gorgeous as ever in those leather pants."

"Sorry, it's just so good to see you home," Becca said. "Home, hell. Alive!"

"Then why did you miss my party?"

"I was in Vancouver. I called your cell, but a plumber has that number now. You got the champagne, right?"

"Yes, thanks," Michelle said, walking her to the kitchen. "Kudos on your three-picture deal, by the way. I can't believe you didn't mention it. Now I have to hate you."

"Why do you think I didn't mention it? You weren't in a position to compete. Not that you ever were."

"Hey, I was always the better producer. I rarely went over budget."

"Oh, Chelle. That's because you played it safe. I fought for this deal. You never had the balls. And I mean that in the nicest way."

Michelle laughed. "Well, I hate you in the nicest way."

Becca pulled a bag of Famous Amos cookies from her purse. "Will this make up for it? I would have brought fresh ones, but the shop by your office is long gone." She ripped open the bag and poured the cookies right on the dinette. They dove in.

"Yum," Michelle said, "but I still hate you. And there's a better way for you to make up for it. Get me a good hair stylist—I haven't been able to reach Sasha."

"Of course not," Becca said.

"What do you mean?"

Becca almost choked on her cookie. "I mean, last I heard, she was working back east. And there are better stylists who charge less."

"Victor's girlfriends always get top dollar," Michelle said, "until he dumps them. But I like Sasha. And she taught me to knit."

Becca got up and foraged the refrigerator. "That's not as trendy as it used to be. A lot has changed. Must be scary."

"It's scary just to look in the mirror. Know anyone who will do my hair for free?"

"You mean someone who wants to kiss my ass now that I've got studio backing?"

Michelle nodded. "Exactly. You still owe me for sleeping on my couch in film school."

"No way. That futon gave me so many back problems that my chiropractor bought a Mercedes. You're out of milk, by the way. Is that slice of cake from your party?"

Michelle got up and put the cake she'd saved for Nikki in the freezer. "What about when I got pregnant and gave you my job on the film in Turkey that ended up winning Sundance?"

"See what I mean about being a softie?" Becca said. "I'd send you to Lorenzo, but he only does red." She fluffed her short hair.

"I just want to go back to a nice, polished brown."

Becca poured a glass of tap water, then appraised Michelle. "Why? That was fine for a 'suit,' but you're not going back to work, are you?"

"Not until I find Nikki." Michelle sat back down at the table. She didn't have the strength to explain while standing up. "She's missing. She's not an exchange student, she's a runaway. Drew lied."

Becca looked at her water, as if she couldn't find the right words.

Michelle had rarely seen her friend so quiet, and the loss hit anew. She couldn't blink back the tears, so she wiped her face with her sleeve and closed her eyes, waiting for the lump in her throat to dissolve. She felt Becca's embrace.

"I'm so sorry, Chelle. What horrible news to come home to. Do you have any idea where she might be?"

Michelle opened her eyes. "No. But I'm going to find her."

Becca nodded and smoothed Michelle's hair from her face. "How?"

"I don't know. There are lawyers involved."

"I hate lawyers." Becca tilted her head to think and spotted something beneath the dinette. She reached down and scooped up a lipstick.

Relieved for the momentary distraction, Michelle pointed at the black-and-white Chanel logo. "My mother's. She thinks I should go blond."

Becca smiled. "How is Her Majesty? Or shall I ask her myself?"

"You missed her by a day," Michelle said. She laughed as

Becca held the back of her hand to her forehead, imitating Elyse's dramatic way of expressing concern. "You always did have good timing."

Becca opened the tube. "I bet she left this on purpose. She's been trying to get you to go pale for as long as I've known you." Becca sat down again. "Honestly, I wasn't sure you'd make it. And in the rehab center, you were really struggling. There were a lot of tears." She closed the lipstick. "You didn't recognize me until I started bringing cookies."

Michelle sniffed a cookie and teased her friend. "Hard to forget this smell. But I appreciate you hanging in there, Becca. It means a lot."

"I was happy just to flirt with your hot doctor. Told him I could get him on that *Doctors* TV show, but he wasn't interested. Nice change from the egotists I work with. Once I realized he was there twice a week, I had my assistant put it on my schedule." She chuckled, then heard her iPhone buzz. She pulled it from her pocket and clicked to read the message. "Speaking of which, I have to head back to the studio soon, so let's get down to work. You can get laser treatments for the scarring and an airbrush tan, but—blond? Sex appeal is not going to help you find Nikki."

"I just want to cover the gray."

"Oh, Chelle, you'll need to do more than that. You'll need to look the part."

"Is that your secret?"

"One of them," Becca admitted. She put her phone away. "So, tell me. If this were a movie, who would you be?"

Michelle toyed with her cookie. It had been a long time since they played this game. Now Becca did it for a living and Michelle was playing for real. "Sleeping Beauty?"

Becca scoffed. "All that princess did was wake up. She didn't have to reclaim the kingdom." She looked at Michelle. "And this is no fairy tale."

"Maybe not, but I could definitely use a fairy godmother."

They were both quiet as they thought of all the stylists they had ever known. Then Becca smiled. "I know who you need: the Wizard!"

Michelle pushed the cookies away. The woman known as the Wizard was a Hollywood legend behind the scenes. Not only could she turn a plain Jane extra into a red carpet femme fatale overnight, but she was famous for the glamorous return of a certain alcoholic has-been who went on to win an Oscar. "Is she still working?"

"Not officially—she must be eighty by now. But I bet I can find her."

"I bet she charges a fortune."

"This one's on me. The truth is, you're right—I do owe you. And I can't imagine how horrible it must be to come home to all this." They both rose and hugged good-bye. Silence filled the kitchen, as comforting as any words could possibly be.

"Okay, then," Michelle said, walking her out. "Off to see the Wizard."

Becca gave her an air kiss and hurried to her waiting limo. The uniformed driver closed the door behind her.

13

MICHELLE CLIMBED OUT OF the Volvo, then held the medical release form above her head to protect her new hairstyle from the drizzle. Cody came to the rescue from the back seat, his black umbrella already opened. "Thanks."

"Keep it," he said. "I only took it to school to get my mom off my back."

"Then tell Cathy thanks. I'll be out in ten minutes." She tiptoed around the puddles to protect the new boots the Wizard had chosen, then realized she'd forgotten the umbrella. When she glanced back, Cody was still there, shadowed by the high-rise across the street.

"Stop gawking and get in before I puke, dude," Tyler called from behind the wheel.

"Not my fault your old lady is smoking hot," Cody mumbled.

Michelle pretended not to have heard him and turned back toward the Palmer Clinic. She reminded herself to thank Becca as well. It had taken an entire day, but there was no doubt that the legendary stylist still had a magic touch. Michelle took a deep breath, raised her chin, and strutted past the mud-splattered luxury cars and the silver Prius with a *Star Trek* bumper sticker.

She had been afraid to do this, to get Dr. Palmer's signature and say good-bye for good. But as soon as he was formally dismissed, Drew could pay Kenny, Kenny would clean up the legal mess, and Michelle could focus on what really mattered: finding her daughter.

Michelle stomped her high heels on the sodden doormat, then hit the buzzer with her elbow. The door opened automatically, of course. It was designed to accommodate handicapped patients.

Inside the waiting room, a Jamaican nurse brushed her braids behind her shoulder and applauded as a muscular man signed in with his fiberglass arm. Once he disappeared behind the swinging door, she logged Michelle in, eyed her outfit, then set a starfish-printed patient gown on the counter. "I'm Bree," she said with a lilt. "Dressing rooms are down to the right. Need help?"

"No thanks, I won't be changing."

Bree pursed her plump lips. "Then I'll let Dr. Palmer know you're here." They heard a man humming to a jazz instrumental just inside the double doors. Bree laughed and pointed behind her. "He's eager to see you."

"Me?" Michelle asked.

"You're kind of famous around here."

Michelle scanned the magazines strewn on the table by the couch. "Not from the tabloids, I hope."

"No, from the *Medical Association Journal*. We hear of coma patients who make a full recovery from time to time, but it's always worthy of a case study." Bree removed Michelle's wet raincoat just as Dr. Palmer peeked over the swinging doors.

"Did she call?" he asked.

"She's here," Bree said.

Dr. Palmer looked around Michelle at the empty waiting room. Bree pointed at Michelle. His eyes widened and he cleared his throat. "Nice to see you again, Mrs. Mason. I didn't recognize you."

Bree laughed.

"Could you please turn the music down?" he asked Bree, while holding the door open for Michelle. In heels, she was almost as tall as he was, so she avoided his gaze by admiring the Lakers tie he wore under his lab coat.

Inside the cavernous treatment room, the clanging of weights echoed as the music dropped to a background buzz. Michelle looked past a row of exam tables and padded benches to the tall machines where a dozen patients struggled with steel plates and pulleys. She caught the eye of the burly man with a prosthetic arm who had dropped his stack of weights. One by one, all the men slowed their movements to look up.

"You all right, Sam?" Dr. Palmer called. The man grumbled something and turned back to his task. Dr. Palmer turned to Michelle. "Sorry about that."

"About what?"

"About—at the risk of ruining our doctor-patient relationship, Mrs. Mason, you do look quite nice."

Michelle studied her reflection in the mirrored wall by the weights. She tucked a chestnut-colored lock behind one ear to reveal her gold earring, and her red lips spread into a smile. Yes, she'd finally come back to life. If only Drew could see her. But Dr. Palmer was the one who was looking at her now, in a way that made her conscious of how close he stood.

"You've never seen me dressed," she said. Then she realized how that sounded. And worse, that it was true. He'd seen her, scars and all. Alarmed, she stepped away. "I mean, except for the hospital gown. But those days are over."

"Speaking of which, mind if I check your progress?"

Michelle shrugged. A final checkup seemed like a good way to officially close the case. She smoothed her clinging wrap dress over her hip and tried to convince herself it had nothing to do with the chiseled cut of his cheekbones. She followed him to a makeshift office at the back of the room, where he laid her coat across a door resting on cement blocks. When he plucked a clipboard from a plastic crate filled with files, Michelle shook her head. "This doesn't look much like a doctor's office."

"I apologize for any inconvenience," Dr. Palmer said. "But it's mostly a physical therapy facility, so I spend money where it counts. If my grant comes through I'll get a real desk, but I spend half my time at the hospital anyway."

The desk phone rang. He hesitated.

"Go ahead." Michelle wandered toward a pale blue wall lined with light boxes, then stopped at several display cases. Beneath the glass was an unusual display of hardware. She looked up as Dr. Palmer hung up and joined her.

Michelle pointed at the middle case. "I understand the medical equipment, but what makes this rusty hook more important than a real desk? Reminds me of my son's Captain Hook costume from Halloween."

Dr. Palmer chuckled. "It's crude, but it was popular a few centuries ago. Worked better than this." He pointed to a plastic baby doll arm attached to a sling.

"That reminds me of a horror movie," she said. She pointed at the shiny white tube of wires in the next case. "What's this?"

"That's a prototype of the prosthetic worn by the gentleman who dropped his weights."

Michelle looked across the room. "Robocop?"

"He is a cop, actually. Or was, before the shooting. The Utah 3 was an option for you as well, had we amputated."

Michelle hugged her arm. "Interesting work."

Dr. Palmer scowled. "I'm just a glorified mechanic—that's what pays the bills. But, want to see something really neat?"

"Neat?" she scoffed. He didn't wait for an answer, so she followed him, weaving between the examination tables to the gurgling aquariums against the back wall. Michelle studied the mounted posters above the tanks. She recognized Aron Ralston, the mountain climber who'd cut off his arm to save his life, and a faded photo of Bethany Hamilton surfing sometime after the shark ate her arm in Hawaii. Michelle had read about them in *People*, but she was too uncomfortable to see their movies. She certainly never imagined having anything in common. At least she still had her arm; for that she was grateful.

As she rounded a padded table, she stubbed the toe of her boots on a heavy box. A picture of Dr. Palmer graced the cover of the books stacked inside. The photograph didn't do his short hair and coffee-colored skin justice. She almost asked for his autograph, then remembered that she needed it elsewhere. She opened her purse for the release. It was stuck to the get well card she always carried.

"Mrs. Mason?" Dr. Palmer beckoned her to the first tank, labeled *Starfish Enterprise*.

Michelle didn't see anything moving inside the misty glass, but the algae smelled like Tyler's socks after a baseball game. When Dr. Palmer pointed inside, she scanned the seaweed for signs of life. Finally, she spotted a coral starfish with a missing arm. Then she spotted the stub growing from the scarred joint of the starfish. Equal parts fascinating and creepy. No, more creepy, she decided, following Dr. Palmer to the next tank. She spotted the salamander right away. There was something stuck to its side. She studied the growth until she recognized the shape: toes. She felt faint.

Dr. Palmer's thick forearm caught her waist just as her knees gave out. "Easy now. Little soon for high heels, isn't it?"

"No, but now I see why Lexi called you Dr. Frankenstein."

He chuckled. "More like the Reanimator. These sea creatures

are just a hobby. But regeneration research is big business. Burn centers are experimenting with spray-on liquid skin cells. And the Pentagon is funding projects to benefit veterans—prosthetic arms with synthetic impulses propelled by rocket fuel."

"Sounds like science fiction."

"So does being put in a coma to save your life. Look it up—a lot of money has been spent on 'pixie dust' made of genetic material."

"From stem cells?"

"From pigs, actually."

"Pigs?" Michelle smelled the clean scent of soap on his arm as he helped her to a bench.

"It works like a cellular scaffold—a hammock for fresh growth." He picked up her limp arm and twisted it slowly in each direction.

"Ouch. I don't understand."

"Neither do scientists, that's why it's such a compelling subject. I applied for a research grant to study it. That's why I wrote the book. I thought the publicity might help win funding."

"No, I meant what does pixie dust have to do with me?" Michelle asked.

He looked from her hair down to her stylish boots. "It does look a bit like someone waved a magic wand over you."

Michelle blushed. "Wish it could have fixed this useless arm."

"You think it's useless?"

"You're the one who said it's tricky. That's why I'm here—to get you to sign off. I'm one of those people who actually does the exercises on my own."

"Great. But tricky doesn't mean hopeless. We could try some alternative therapies." Dr. Palmer reached into his pocket and pulled out a handful of chocolate Kisses. "You like chocolate, right? My mama sent me these. Thirty-six Kisses for my thirty-sixth birthday."

"Happy birthday," Michelle said, swooning at the scent.

He unwrapped a Kiss and popped it in his mouth, closed his eyes, then swallowed. "Would you like one?" He unwrapped another and held it out to her limp right hand. "Oops, sorry."

Michelle slapped the release down on the table and snatched it with her left hand. "I think you like torturing people. Honestly, I don't know why they didn't just cut the damn thing off."

"As I recall, there was already one DOA in that crash. Maybe it was too risky." Dr. Palmer walked over to the fish tanks. He opened a vial of fish food.

After unwrapping the Kiss with one hand, Michelle savored the chocolate, feeling better already. "Since you have your own clinic, why aren't you treating professional athletes? If you signed on with a football team, you could be making millions." She followed him as he fed each creature.

"Hard to care about football players. As soon as you fix them up they rush back out to get hurt again." He looked across the room then lowered his voice. "Rehabilitation only goes so far. I'm more interested in regeneration. But without the research grant, I'm limited to these cold-blooded experiments."

Michelle looked back at the starfish. She didn't notice his hand on her shoulder until she flinched. "You want me to be one of your experiments?"

"The referral was to reinforce the progress you made in the hospital. But you are a viable prospect."

"How?"

"Your arm was a peripheral injury to the brain trauma. No connection at all. Do you think you might have reached across to the passenger side?"

"Maybe," Michelle said, straining to remember. "Don't all mothers reach out to protect the passenger?"

"No idea," Dr. Palmer answered. "My mama took us on the bus. But your arm is a separate injury, probably from reaching out and getting hurt during impact. Recovery might still be possible. When I touched your shoulder, you flinched."

"Of course I did, it's freezing cold in here," Michelle snapped.

Dr. Palmer went to the next tank, but Michelle didn't follow. He sat on the bench and tied the lace on his wingtip. Then he grasped her useless hand before she could stop him, so she had no choice but to sit down. When he kneaded her wrist, she cried out.

"So what if I flinched?"

"It was a muscle contraction. The nerves are atrophied, but they could regenerate." He showed her a small electrical meter with wires connecting to a switch that resembled a medieval torture device. "The idea is to wake up your nerves. To jumpstart the natural process of rebuilding muscle."

"Is that one of those ab stimulators that actors use to avoid sit-ups?" Michelle asked.

"Similar," Dr. Palmer said. "Insurance companies don't cover those either. It's like cognitive therapy: we know talk can rebuild neurological pathways, but it takes years. Why not take a pill and feel better right away?"

Michelle smiled. "Do you have a pill that will do that?"

"No." He poured alcohol on a swab. "Give it a test run. My treat."

The air filters gurgled, and the raindrops pinged against the roof. Michelle took a deep breath. She felt more comfortable here than she had anywhere else since she'd woken up. No one here knew what she'd been like before the accident. No one here cared how it happened. No one here was judging her. She felt a cocoon-like comfort just leaning against the table beside him.

"If it works, will I be able to knit again?"

"Doesn't knitting require lateral supination?" He moved his

hands to feign knitting, but it looked like he was dancing the Pony. He shook his head. "Probably not. But you might be able to crochet."

His cell phone rang, and Michelle recognized the *Star Trek* theme. "May the Force be with you," she teased.

"That's *Star Wars*, not *Star Trek*."

"Oh right, much cooler." She couldn't help but roll her eyes.

He turned it off. "Why is *Star Trek* so lame and *Star Wars* so cool?"

"Special effects?"

Michelle was tempted to brag that she lived within running distance of Spielberg Drive, the frontage road for the Motion Picture Hospital where her medical coverage maxed out a million dollars ago. Then she remembered that Spielberg didn't direct *Star Wars*, he directed *E.T.* "Phone home" was the line from that one. She noted the electrodes on the table. She needed to phone home as well, to ask Drew about this.

Dr. Palmer was justifying his affinity for science fiction. "In the morning, I used to get on the bus in Crenshaw, all ninety pounds of me. Then an hour later, boys from the nice neighborhood would pull me off and beat the daylights out of me. I used to close my eyes and ask Scotty to beam me up."

"Are you trying to tell me you were a geek?"

He split his hand into a Vulcan peace sign. "Still am, under the lab coat."

"No, this is what you men don't understand. Clothes don't hide who you are; they show who you are. I bet those little thugs are sorry now."

He laughed. "One of them is a mechanic at the gas station on the corner. He has to drive past here every day. My mama wanted me to autograph a book for him, too, but I said no, so she signed it herself."

"Your mother sounds fun," Michelle said. Then she remembered. "I can't even sign my own name."

He patted the seat beside him. "So practice. Or change your name to X."

"I can make a great X. And I can put on lipstick now," Michelle said.

Dr. Palmer rubbed her arm gently. "Good. The more you practice, the faster you'll regain coordination."

"You're assuming I was coordinated in the first place," Michelle joked.

"May I?" Dr. Palmer asked. When she nodded, he traced the scar on her shoulder until it disappeared under the fabric of her dress.

She tugged the fabric higher. "Ow!"

Dr. Palmer stood up. "You protect yourself with a thicker shell than my crustaceans." He went back to his desk and returned with a novelty pen complete with a tiny Starship *Enterprise* floating in the barrel. He sat down at a table and skimmed the release form before looking up. "Look, everybody else gave up on that arm a long time ago. Not Lexi, but nurses never get the respect they deserve. Her opinion doesn't carry a lot of weight."

"It does to me."

"That won't be enough for the insurance company. I'll sign the damn thing. But just so you know? I think you're stronger than you realize."

Michelle thought of Drew's second mortgage and Cathy's Hamburger Helper and all the trouble she had caused. "People are counting on me to end this."

"Are you afraid it will hurt?"

"Hurt? What's an arm compared to—" Michelle pressed her heart. She sunk to the bench beside him. "Do you know about my daughter? That she's missing?"

"Yes. And when you find her, won't it be nice to put both of your arms around her?"

Michelle tried not to cry. "You mean *if* I find her?"

Dr. Palmer laughed.

"What's so funny?" Michelle asked.

"The folks who want that release signed—they're right. The odds are against you. But they've been against you from the start, yet here you are. There's no doubt in my mind that you'll find your daughter."

Michelle took a deep breath. "I might need more of that chocolate."

Dr. Palmer set a Kiss out on the table, but he didn't unwrap it. Instead, he reached for her right arm and attached the electrodes to it. She picked up the chocolate with her left hand and fumbled to unwrap it. Then she popped the morsel in her mouth. Nirvana.

A car horn honked outside. Michelle swallowed. "My ride."

"What do you want to do?" Dr. Palmer asked.

She looked at the release again, wishing it would disappear. She could have Drew fax his signature and make the decision for her, but it was time to think for herself. This form was like a thank-you note for all the help she had been given. But every time she looked at her arm she would only see what was missing.

She took a deep breath. "Could you ask Bree to send them away?"

A few minutes later, the black arrow sprang to life on the meter box. Dr. Palmer twisted the dial until it moved slowly across the thin red lines. Electricity shot through Michelle's right arm, but she didn't feel a thing. Then Dr. Palmer put his hand on her other arm, and she did.

14

ALL THE ATTORNEYS LOOKED up as Michelle entered the sleek conference room in Beverly Hills. Apart from the platinum CDs lining the walls, the office was stark, as black-and-white as the law. Michelle hovered in the doorway as they exchanged looks over the smoked glass table. Then she took a step across the checkerboard floor, careful to land on a white square.

Mr. Greenburg, the host of today's party, straightened the French cuffs peeking from his Armani suit before rising to meet Michelle. His sun-kissed crown barely reached the shoulder of her chic black suit, but when he whispered hello, the others leaned forward to listen.

Kenny met her by the door. He pushed a lock of hair off his forehead, pulled a handkerchief from the pocket of his brown blazer, and quietly scolded her all the way around the table. "Wipe off that red lipstick. Where is your cane? And what happened to the other dress?"

"I don't do beige," Michelle whispered. "This jacket is bulletproof."

"Good, because Guy Butler hired the big guns. Greenburg himself is taking the deposition."

Michelle whispered to Kenny as they walked. "Don't be intimidated by the gold cuff links. If he's anything like the producers

I used to deal with, he has two ex-wives and an upside-down mortgage in Malibu Colony. My guess is, he'd give it all up for five more inches and your head of hair."

Kenny blotted his forehead. "We needed to rehearse last night. Where were you?"

"Took a bus home from Dr. Palmer's clinic on the west side. I had no idea it would take three hours."

"Did he sign the release?"

Michelle shook her head.

"Greedy bastard. He could string you along for years. You should have called the minute Tyler gave you my message."

Michelle scoffed. "You left a message with a teenager?"

Greenburg checked the time on his Rolex. Then he studied Michelle, his eyes like X-rays scanning for cracks in her armor. "Shall we begin?"

Kenny whispered to Michelle as he pulled out her chair. "Answer only what he asks. Don't do that mom thing and try to please everybody." Michelle wondered whether that was a compliment or an insult. Undecided, she tilted away from the freesia centerpiece infusing the air with a strong Fruit Loops scent.

Greenburg waited while Kenny introduced Ms. Leticia Rodriguez, the young attorney from Pacific Auto Insurance, who sat beside them. She pointed a fiery talon in the air and corrected his pronunciation. "*Let-i-ci-a*," she said.

Michelle nodded, picturing Nikki in her place. Nikki was smart enough to be a lawyer, and just as particular. She was always so sure about her opinions—yes or no, guilty or innocent. What would she make of this mess?

A young man in a vest opened the door and tapped on his earpiece. Greenburg excused himself and followed him out.

Ms. Rodriguez unbuttoned her ill-fitting blazer and turned to

Kenny. "I got your message about an advance, but Mrs. Mason's medical bills have already surpassed the limits of the auto policy." She slid financial statements across the glass to prove it.

"I'm familiar with your investment," Kenny said. Michelle wasn't. She squinted to add the numbers from West Hills Hospital, Valley Convalescent, and UCLA Acute Care, but there were far too many. "All reasonable expenditures."

"Agreed. After her health benefits ran out, we honored the difference up to the policy limit. And if Orrin is found to be liable, they'll be responsible. But we can't advance payment against a trial outcome.

Michelle turned to Kenny. "I'm sorry."

Kenny shrugged. "In for a penny, in for a pound."

Greenburg overheard them as he strode back in and sat down. "In for a penny, in for a hundred mil." His assistant sat beside him and set up a digital tape recorder.

A Beverly Hills blond of indeterminable age strutted in and set down a silver pitcher of water, then a stack of leather folders embossed with the firm's name. She cleared the platter and left, the men's eyes trailing behind her. Michelle noticed the red record light on the tape recorder and met Ms. Rodriguez's narrowed eyes.

Greenburg put his palms up. "Apologies. Let's push on."

He signaled the stenographer, an elderly woman in a peach-fuzz sweater, nearly hidden behind a small desk in the corner of the conference table. She began tapping the tiny keyboard on her stenotype machine as soon as Greenburg asked Michelle to state her name.

"Michelle Deveraux Mason."

"Driver's license?"

"I don't have one."

"She means with her," Kenny clarified. "Her wallet was destroyed in the accident." He nudged her under the table and wrote *DMV* on his pad with exclamation points. She nodded.

"Do you plan to drive once your new license is issued? With one hand?" Greenburg asked.

"I put these pantyhose on with one hand. Granted, it took twenty minutes, but I can certainly drive with one hand."

"Can we just get past the preliminaries here?" Kenny asked.

Greenburg spoke quietly. "With all due respect, Mr. Kazan, legal infractions tend to lend weight to testimony. Mrs. Mason's character is relevant."

"I assure you, Mrs. Mason is a law-abiding citizen with no prior record. She hasn't been well enough to go to the DMV." Kenny looked at Michelle. She played along, lifting her limp hand to the table.

"Shall we postpone until she's feeling better?" Greenburg asked. "We could try again in a few weeks." He tapped his iPhone calendar. "No, I'm in Cannes. We'd have to postpone our June trial date. Which is fine. The statute of limitations gives us until October—plenty of time to subpoena the witnesses again." He leveled his gaze at Kenny. "And let me be clear, sir: we will not hesitate to cite Mr. Mason in contempt of court. Or Mrs. Mason. We may need to call you back in as well."

Michelle turned to Kenny, eyebrows raised.

"It means, don't leave town." Kenny nodded to Greenburg. "Let's proceed. June it is."

"Excellent. Mrs. Mason, were you wearing a seat belt at the time of the accident?"

"Of course," Michelle answered.

The lawyers all sat up. "You recall the events?"

"No, but I always wear a seat belt. It's the law."

They sat back. "So you can't say for sure that you wore one that day?"

"I guess not." Michelle fanned the lapel of her jacket. Didn't anyone else notice how hot it was in this room?

Greenberg continued. "Then, can it be said that you also don't know if, on the morning in question, your passenger was wearing a seat belt?"

"That's ridiculous. What kind of mother drives kids around without seat belts?"

Kenny looked at the stenographer. "For the record, let it be known that the defendant is in the practice of wearing seat belts, and she has no history of transporting passengers in noncompliance; therefore, we can assume that all passengers in the car were in compliance."

"With all due respect," Mr. Greenburg replied, "this is not philosophy class. The law of syllogism carries no weight. Only the law of evidence." He pointed at the embossed folder in front of Kenny. "Evidence shows that the fatal injuries sustained by my nephew were inconsistent with the use of a seat belt."

Michelle's breath caught in her throat. Noah Butler was his nephew?

Kenny whispered to her before opening the folder. "Relax, this could work to our advantage. He's an entertainment lawyer—a deal maker, not a litigator. He's doing his brother a favor, probably hasn't been in a courtroom for years."

Beside them, Ms. Rodriguez gasped. They looked up and saw her staring at a photo in her open folder. Michelle reached for hers, but Kenny slapped his notepad on top of it.

Mr. Greenburg continued. "Please be aware, Mrs. Mason, that our suit against the driver is a claim for negligence in driving improperly or unsafely. Our suit against Orrin Motors is for product liability, which may or may not affect you as a responsible party. Do you understand?"

"I think so. Yes." She whispered to Kenny, "Didn't you say the car company is suing me?"

"Yes, a cross complaint for negligence. We filed an answer on your behalf. Didn't I explain that the other day?"

"I was a little distracted the other day," Michelle admitted.

"Doesn't matter. We're not going to complicate matters with two separate trials. You'll only have to go through all this once."

Greenburg cleared his throat. "As stated in the civil suit, we ask the responsible party or parties to cover loss of income based not only on album and concert sales for the last two years, but in perpetuity. We estimate that additional revenue streams will bring the total to approximately one hundred million dollars."

Michelle whispered to Kenny, "They're kidding, right? Who has that kind of money?"

The door banged open. A rotund man in three-piece pinstripes apologized profusely as he barreled across the room. Greenburg stood to shake his hand then addressed the group. "May I introduce Mr. Dillenger, from the Orrin Motor Company?"

"His stockholders have that kind of money," Kenny whispered. "Which is why Greenburg would rather they be found liable."

"Sorry I'm late," Dillenger said. "Flight delay. Weather can be a bitch, eh? Snow, sleet…rain in Topanga Canyon?" He zeroed in on Michelle. "Mrs. Mason, I presume?"

She nodded.

"What have I missed?" he asked, as the secretary served him coffee.

Greenburg spoke up. "We've established that while the rain may have contributed to the cause of the accident, the absence of a functioning seat belt may have contributed to the outcome." He nodded at the stenographer.

She scrolled back and read the last sentence. "'What kind of mother drives kids around without seat belts?'" They all looked at Michelle.

"Not me," Michelle said.

"Would you be willing to take a lie detector test?" Mr. Greenburg asked.

"Sure," Michelle said. Then she felt a pinch of doubt. What if she hadn't reminded him to wear it? Could she have forgotten this once?

Kenny saw her face flush. He took her left hand and gave it a squeeze. "There's no need for that, gentlemen. It won't hold up in court."

She smiled at Kenny, appreciating his faith in her, and relaxed. It was fear that had caused her to panic, not guilt. This wasn't her fault. She spoke up. "I always say 'seat belts' before I put the key in the ignition. Ask my kids. We used to sing the jingle, remember? 'Buckle up for safety, buckle up.'"

"Click-it or ticket," Mrs. Rodriguez added, quoting the freeway billboards.

"Click it or die," Mr. Greenburg said.

The stenographer's keys stopped clicking as silence engulfed the room.

Michelle shrugged. "Maybe the seat belt didn't work. Wasn't there some sort of recall?"

Kenny was still holding her hand. Now he held it so hard, it hurt.

"Indeed," Mr. Dillenger said. He smiled, his fangs just short of wolf-sized. He pulled a postcard emblazoned with the Orrin logo from his titanium briefcase. "This is a recall notice for a seat belt locking mechanism malfunction. Look familiar?"

Michelle nodded. "Yes."

"And what did you understand it to mean?"

"That there might be a problem with the seat belt and the manufacturer knew it." She smiled at Kenny, but he shook his head to quiet her.

"Isn't it true, Mrs. Mason, that you received this notice prior to the accident in October?" He leaned across the table to hand it to her. But with Kenny still squeezing her left hand, she couldn't take it. "How much prior, would you say?"

"I'll have to stop you there," Kenny interrupted. "My client has suffered a significant memory loss. Any answer she gives will be conjecture."

"Be that as it may, there is no record of compliance with the maintenance request."

"It was my husband's car. The notice was addressed to him."

"Under California law, any vehicle acquired after marriage is community property."

Michelle looked at Kenny. He was right: she should have let him coach her. And she should have worn the beige dress. She felt nauseous.

"Were you aware the inspection and potential repair were offered without cost?" Dillenger asked.

"What about the cost of my time—getting a ride to the dealer and picking it up? I had a full-time job with two kids to drive and shop and cook for. It was hard enough to maintain my own car, let alone one I never drove."

Greenburg's cell phone rang. He turned away to take it. A tapping noise punctuated his quiet conversation.

Michelle looked down to see Ms. Rodriguez stamping her navy pump on the marble floor beneath the table, as if to wake a sleeping foot. Michelle could see the ankle strap cutting into swollen flesh. She wondered what shoes Nikki was wearing now: bunny slippers, or plastic sandals, or the purple sneakers embroidered for her birthday? Were Nikki's ears buzzing from this ping-pong game of blame?

When Greenburg finished his call, he walked to one of the draped easels in the far corner. "The fact is, Mrs. Mason, you did drive the car." He pulled off the drape. Noah stared back at them. In the thumb-sized newspaper photo, he looked like a rag doll with pale skin and dark curly hair framing his light eyes. Here, he had the lanky ease of a frame not yet grown into, a frisky colt with clear blue eyes. Noah would always stay this way, young and pretty, like Dorian Gray.

As Michelle gazed into his eyes, fire consumed her belly and flared up until her chest burned. These eyes would follow her right into hell.

Kenny poured Michelle water from the crystal pitcher. "Take a sip every time they ask you a question," he whispered.

"Why?"

"So you have an excuse to keep quiet. And if you're not absolutely sure of the answer, just say you don't know. A little knowledge is a dangerous thing."

"So is a little bladder." Michelle pushed the water glass away.

"Ready?" Greenburg called.

"No," Michelle insisted. "Can we get back to the last part? Is it against the law to not do the inspection? Was there some time limit?" Nervous, she held her breath.

"Not that I'm aware of," Kenny offered.

"Good," Michelle said. "I'm sure Drew was planning to do it when he got back."

"Compliance is expected within a reasonable amount of time," Dillenger said.

"'Reasonable' is a bit of a gray area, is it not?" Greenburg asked.

"Not if it leads to a fatality," Dillenger argued.

Michelle saw Greenburg wince. She wondered how he was picturing his nephew now—on his first birthday, or at his Bar Mitzvah, or the last time he saw him alive? He caught her looking and averted his eyes.

She forced herself to focus. "Are you saying that Drew could be arrested for not fixing the car quickly enough?"

Mr. Dillenger nodded. "There is precedence, Mrs. Mason, stating that a responsible party aware of a mechanical malfunction that contributes to a fatality can be found at fault."

Michelle turned to Kenny. "Does that mean Drew could go to jail?"

Kenny watched the other men argue and spoke quietly. "It's possible, but this sounds more like due diligence. My guess is that Greenburg would prefer you not be found liable. If Dillenger's client is responsible, the damages will be much greater."

"Damages?" Michelle whispered back.

Kenny shushed her as the men finished their discussion. He wrote a note on his pad: *payment for their loss*. He underlined the last word, but Michelle understood. *Loss* was the four-letter word she was most familiar with. She looked out the window at the blue sky, imagining her daughter to be looking up at that same moment, at that same sky. She took a ragged breath and tried not to feel the hole in her heart.

Mr. Dillenger began anew. "Mrs. Mason, in the twenty-four-hour period preceding the car accident, had you consumed any alcohol, prescription, or nonprescription drugs?"

"Objection." Kenny pushed the water glass toward her as if he was being polite. "Mrs. Mason's medical records are available by subpoena."

"Noted. Mrs. Mason, we are aware that there is a family history of mental illness and that you underwent psychological counseling during your rehabilitation. Is it possible that, on this day, you experienced any depressive impulses?"

Kenny waited until Michelle drank some water. "Mr. Dillenger, with all due respect, there's no basis for this line of questioning. The weather report confirms hazardous driving conditions. Psychological profiling is standard for rehabilitation. And it's been established that my client has no memory of that day."

Dillenger held his hands up in mock surrender. "Damn shame about your memory." He twisted his pinky ring around his chubby finger. "Would you object to hypnosis?"

"No," Michelle said.

"Yes," Kenny said. "Remember the McMartin Preschool case? Couple of imaginative toddlers sent innocent teachers to jail. Hearsay is not admissible in California."

"I didn't intend to use it in court, only to aid her memory," Dillenger said. "Perhaps it would help to revisit the scene of the crime?"

"Objection. Assumes facts not yet in evidence and lacks foundation. No criminal charges have been filed yet."

Dillenger put his palm up in mock surrender. "No harm meant. Too many reruns of *Law and Order* on the plane." He looked at the court reporter, then back to Michelle. "Mrs. Mason, have you visited the three hundred block of Topanga Canyon Boulevard since the accident?"

The very idea gave Michelle goose bumps. Kenny refilled her water, but she ignored it. This one was easy. "No."

"What was your daughter's relationship with Noah Butler?"

She picked up the water and drank the whole glass. Kenny nodded as if to say: good girl. "I don't know. Did you ask the other boys in the band?"

"We haven't found teenagers to be a reliable source of information," Greenburg said, fixing a cuff link. Michelle couldn't help but smile at Kenny. When she looked up, Greenburg was addressing her. "Did you approve of the relationship?"

"What relationship?" Michelle asked.

"Objection," Kenny piped in. "Even if a relationship were to be established, what mother thinks anyone is good enough for her daughter?" The others exchanged knowing smiles and chuckles.

Dillenger waited until the room was quiet again. "Since we are unable to verify the precise nature of Nicole Mason's relationship with the deceased, perhaps, Mrs. Mason, you could enlighten us as to yours?"

"I was Tyler's mom," Michelle said. "He was Tyler's pitching coach."

"Why was he in your car on the day of the accident?"

"I don't know." Michelle strained to remember.

"Where were you going?"

"Good question." She felt Kenny's gaze. "I don't know."

"Isn't it true that you gave him his first big break?"

"I don't know." She reached for the water glass.

"I may be from out of town, Mrs. Mason, but we've all heard of the casting couch. Could it be that you offered the deceased this opportunity to star in his own video in exchange for sexual favors? Could this knowledge be why your daughter has eluded subpoena for well over a year now? Out of embarrassment? Or to avoid ruining your reputation?"

"No! Isn't it more likely she saw the recall card in the mail?"

"Conjecture," Kenny cried. "Please strike that from the record." He gave Michelle a scolding look.

"I'm sorry," Michelle said. "Can't we just apologize or give them money or whatever it is they want?"

One by one, they heard the sharp echo of her words. There was no more laughter, no more conversation, no one even looked in her direction. The clock tick-tick-ticked and stopped.

Kenny put his pen down. "They want their son back."

They all looked up at Noah's face. Greenburg's phone interrupted like a funeral dirge, but this time he didn't answer. Michelle stood up so fast that her chair toppled over. Her right arm sprang loose and knocked over her glass. Water dripped on Kenny's notepad. He picked it up and shook it, knocking the glossy folder to the floor. It landed open to the eight-by-ten photo. She looked down and saw blood and pulp and tufts of hair. The room started spinning, the walls were caving, and the ceiling was pressing against her head. She had to escape.

She ran to the door but couldn't budge it. She turned to shove it with her hip and saw the boy on the easel, the smile that was gone forever. The door opened as the secretary returned. Michelle stumbled out to the hallway. She heard the lawyers' buzz behind her, but not a word they said. She fled down the hall to the ladies' room, slammed into a stall, and locked the door. She didn't ever want to go back to that room, to those eyes, to the horror she had tried to forget.

After a few minutes, the bathroom door banged opened. The tap of heels rose as they crossed the tile floor. The latch of the next stall slid shut. Michelle looked down and recognized the ankle straps. She slunk out to the bank of washbowls. The water flowed automatically, then stopped, revealing another noise: retching. Michelle gagged at the acrid odor. The toilet flushed and Ms. Rodriguez emerged.

Michelle noted the bulge beneath her jacket. "When are you due?"

"September." She pulled a toothbrush from her purse and brushed.

The child would be a Virgo, like Nikki, Michelle thought. She wondered if Ms. Rodriguez would count baby teeth or billable hours. She was still young enough to believe that both were possible. Michelle used to believe that, too. She finished drying her hand. "Good luck to you."

Ms. Rodriguez fumbled to put her toothbrush away. "Thanks. I lost the first one. I wasn't even trying then." She put her hand on her belly and looked up at Michelle in the mirror. "I'd do anything to protect this baby."

Michelle smiled. "Welcome to the club."

Ms. Rodriquez smiled, then looked alarmed and left quickly.

Michelle looked in the mirror, disappointed. She had gone from friend to foe within the space of a sentence. Or was it during those weeks Michelle couldn't remember? Or the months that she didn't get the damn seat belt repaired? She could smell her armpits now, a blend of baby powder and fear.

Muffled voices seeped under the door. Kenny called, "Michelle? You okay?"

She shook her head at the question—she would never be okay again. But she could pretend. She pulled her sleeve down over her limp hand, smoothed a lock of hair over her scarred forehead, and marched out.

"Murderer!" The word hissed down the hallway.

"Keep walking," Kenny said, steering her past.

Michelle held her breath through the poisonous cloud. She averted her eyes from the man in mirrored shades outside the conference room until she realized it was Noah's father. When he turned away, the Harley-Davidson wings on his jacket resembled an angel rising from his back. He took the elbow of a woman walking slowly, in a daze. Like Michelle, she was wearing black, but her caftan was not remotely stylish. She was in mourning.

Michelle had avoiding thinking about Noah's mother, but here she was, painfully real. She stole a glance at the woman's glassy eyes and stumbled. She wanted to say she was sorry, but Kenny pulled her past. "They have to blame someone," he said.

Michelle nodded as he led her out to the lobby, but she couldn't get that word out of her head. *Murderer*, the man had called her. What if it was true?

15

WHEN KENNY DROPPED MICHELLE off, she was relieved to see the Volvo parked in her driveway. Tyler had been out late every night, so she suggested he stay home and get some rest. His company would be comforting.

The garage door began to grind slowly up the rusty tracks. Michelle stood in the driveway and cringed, wondering if Drew still kept the WD-40 in the laundry room. At least she knew Tyler was awake.

As the door rose, she spotted his gray sneakers circling like sharks around a tarp-covered mound. His cough rang out, then the tarp dropped in a heap to the cement floor. Michelle stopped short as the hulking form in front of her was revealed. It was a black Harley-Davidson motorcycle.

The garage door crashed at the end of the track above Tyler as he swung his leg over the leather seat. "Tyler?" Michelle hurried up the driveway. "Is that Noah's?"

He looked back, his eyes wide with surprise. "It's mine."

"Nice try. I'd never let you have a motorcycle. Too dangerous."

"That's what Dad said." He climbed off to face her.

Michelle almost smiled. "Why is it here?" She could hear the engine growl in her head. *Vroom, vroom.*

"Noah's mom said to keep it."

"But why is it here at all?"

"He left it here."

Michelle wasn't sure if she recognized the Harley or imagined it from Cathy's account. Either way, Cathy said it wasn't there the morning of the accident. Since the game was called on account of rain, he must have stopped by to see if Tyler had gotten a chance to pitch. "Was Noah waiting here when we got home from the game or did he come by later?"

"Beats me," Tyler said.

"I was probably giving him a ride home. Motorcycles are dangerous enough when the streets are dry." She felt a wave of relief that Noah was in her car for safety reasons. That she was being a good mother, like she said in the deposition.

"Come on, Mom, let me keep it."

"No. Doesn't Noah's father want it?"

"I dunno," he said. "They're divorced."

Michelle nodded, as if that explained everything. For Tyler, it did. For her, it simply explained why she'd given Noah a ride: she felt sorry for him.

"Please, Mom? Girls love motorcycles."

Michelle looked at her son more closely. From the look of that hickey on his neck, Tyler didn't need any help with girls. For the first time, she had a feeling that Noah didn't either. She had to find something to prove it. She would start in Nikki's room.

Tyler's phone rang before she could mention the hickey, so she pressed the button to close the garage door. He shouted something amid the earsplitting noise, but she missed it as she hurried inside.

Michelle kicked the tower of boxes in Nikki's room. Her stiletto heel jabbed a hole in the cardboard and caught, forcing her down to the wooden floor. "Goddamnit!" she cried. "Tyler!"

She looked out the window as the Volvo pulled out of the driveway. She suspected he needed a licensed driver with him, but it was too late to scold him now. He could get the proper California certificate when he took her to the DMV. Bella loped in and licked her. She held up her arm to protect whatever makeup remained after crying all the way home from Beverly Hills, then crawled back to the bed and pulled herself up to a stand. Then she stormed to the kitchen to scrounge for scissors.

The drawers were still empty, but the knife block was on the counter by the refrigerator. Apparently, the Costco set wasn't good enough for Drew to take to New York, but surely it would slice through cardboard. Michelle grabbed the butcher knife and head back through the foyer just as the doorbell rang. "Go away!" she called.

"It's me," Julie said, peeking inside. "Wow! You look scary."

Michelle put her hand up to her new bangs and nearly stabbed her eye.

"Not the makeover, Michelle, that's fabulous. But if you want folks to believe in Killer Mom, you're on the right track." She stepped inside with the mail.

"You've heard that, too?" Michelle scanned the street.

"Don't worry, the only one out there is the mailman. Remember Joe?" Julie shut the door and adjusted her clinging warm-ups. "He says welcome home. He missed your Christmas cookies."

Michelle half-smiled, then saw the box from Verizon that Julie set on the hall table. "Finally! It was a little awkward moaning to Drew on my lawyer's phone."

Julie leaned back as Michelle took aim at the top. "Shall I open the letter, or do you want to use your knife for that, too?"

Michelle recognized her mother's florid script on the return address. Elyse was famous for her ten-page diatribes and this would probably be the worst she'd ever received—an analysis of every word of their argument. "Neither. If Joe's still outside, tell him: Return to Sender."

"Too late. Seriously, Michelle, you look gorgeous, but what's with the Lizzie Borden act?"

"The deposition was today." Michelle marched back to Nikki's room, knife in hand. She hacked at the storage boxes, stabbing them like the killer in *Psycho*, over and over again. The blade cut jagged paths through the cardboard until bits of colored fabric poked out. Michelle stabbed the school mascot with her six-inch blade, until the dragon's stuffing fell in lumps around her, as if she was an island in a sea of puffy foam.

"Phone is charging," Julie called, before appearing in the doorway. "Maybe you need a few more weeks in the hospital."

"Guy Butler called me a murderer!" Michelle cried.

"That is the popular theory. Teddy bear shish kebab won't change that."

Michelle tried to catch her breath. "It was an accident, Julie, even though the car company is trying to pin it on me and Drew for not getting the damn seat belt fixed. But I need to focus on Nikki. Drew doesn't know a thing about girls' clothes or keepsakes. He had to have missed something. Help me, will you?"

"Okay," Julie said, easing the knife from Michelle's hand. "But let's sit down for a minute." She led her over to the bed and sat with her until Michelle caught her breath.

"So I guess you heard what happened with Nikki?" Michelle asked.

"Heard about it? I nearly lost custody of my children because of it."

"What are you talking about?"

"We're separated. I'm getting a divorce," Julie said.

"Oh, no. But you look fabulous. Are you happy about it?"

"No, being too stressed to eat is the only good thing about it. Asshole cheated on me."

"That's awful."

"I'm so sorry I couldn't say anything the night you got home. Drew asked us to avoid any serious conversation. It's nice that he's so protective. Not like Jack."

She set the knife on the windowsill, out of harm's way. A shadow shaped like a dragonfly fell across the street as a helicopter buzzed. Julie bit her lip as it flew over and began to circle, close enough to read the call letters of a local TV station. A white van slowed as it passed.

"Oh, crap," Julie said.

"What?" Michelle asked. Another helicopter was circling now, but it had the police emblem on the door. After a moment, they both nosed farther away.

"Probably a freeway accident," Michelle said.

"Thank goodness. Not that I want anyone to be hurt, but... After Noah Butler's funeral, things went nuts around here. Fans started camping outside your house, and reporters parked vans along the street. Maybe it was a slow news week, but it got so bad that I couldn't let Dylan outside to skateboard. These people are like a cult—they graffitied the side of your house and pushed your fence down. It's still a little tilted, if you don't believe me."

"I do, it's just so bizarre."

"Tell me about it. My soon-to-be ex's lawyer convinced the judge that our neighborhood was not a wholesome environment. Even after Sophie sold the most Girl Scout cookies in her troop. 'Course, she sold them to me to drop off at your hospital, which irked Cathy no end, but still. After working my rear off to be tenure track at UCLA, I had to reduce my schedule to part-time so the court sees that I'm home keeping my children safe."

"I am so sorry."

"It was just bad timing. And then our favorite babysitter ran away."

They surveyed the clothing strewn across the floor. "Julie, did Nikki ever talk about dating anyone?".

"If you mean Noah Butler, no. But she wasn't the kind of girl who talked much to grown-ups. I could ask the kids if you want. Why, do you think that's why she ran away?"

"What do you mean?"

Julie leaned past her to tug something up from behind the bed. It was the dust-covered Roadhouse poster with the corner torn off. She showed it to Michelle.

Michelle swore under her breath.

Julie crumpled it up and tossed it on a pile of white stuffing. Then she sat on the floor and gathered the fallen clothing into piles. "If it's any consolation, my kids thought she was the coolest babysitter ever. She showed us her new purple high-tops with those tiny black skulls and her name stitched on the back." Julie folded a bunny T-shirt from *Donnie Darko*, then held up a vintage Lucky Charms leprechaun top. "The picture she took of them in some of these T-shirts with their hair all funky is still on my fridge."

"When did she take it? She didn't have a decent camera until her birthday."

"Not sure. She sat for me when I taught a night class and Asshole was supposedly working. She was scheduled to come at seven the night of the crash so we could have a date night, but she didn't show. Her cell was off, so I figured she flaked. Teenagers, you know. Then I saw the police at your house the next day. She emailed the picture after that."

"You mean, after the accident? How long after?"

Julie shrugged. "I'd just found out about Asshole's girlfriend, so

I was in pretty bad shape. Nothing like you, of course," she added quickly. "We were all praying for you."

Michelle put her good hand on Julie's arm. Julie rose to her knees and gave her a hug. Michelle's shoulder hurt, but her heart felt better. It felt good to have a friend. She pulled away. "Do you have any idea of the date she, um…"

"Ran away? Must be hard to say out loud."

Michelle pushed past the lump in her throat. "The stupid police lost track of the missing persons report. I need to remember more. I seem to have forgotten all the important things." She sunk to the floor and leaned against the bed.

Julie noted the red soles of Michelle's shoes. "You haven't forgotten your sense of style. Louboutin, am I right?"

Michelle nodded. "EBay."

Julie picked up some jeans with a $200 price tag attached. "These too?"

"No. According to Tyler, Nikki was having a rough time with the girls in her PE class, so I bought her a new wardrobe for her birthday. Guess I was desperate."

"At least you weren't around to get the MasterCard bill." Julie held them up, eyeing Michelle's hips. "These might fit you. Try them on."

"I'd rather sell them—I could use the cash. I'm still seeing Dr. Palmer."

"That's just greedy. Two handsome men."

"For my arm. He has a book out, have you seen it?"

"I only have time for self-help: *Dating after Divorce*, *How to Not to Screw up Your Kids Forever*, that kind of thing," Julie said. "But I sure know what you mean about needing cash." She stood up and hung the jeans in the closet next to the shrunken Roadhouse T-shirt. "Is this what I think it is?"

"Used to be, before my mother washed it. Think it's worth anything?"

"Maybe, but it wouldn't look good to sell it." Julie pointed at the loose ball of yarn that had rolled from behind the bookcase. "Care to donate that to Troop 577?"

Michelle tossed the yarn to her. It unraveled and a matchbook fell out.

Julie looked at the neon palm tree logo on the cover. "Does Nikki smoke?"

"She better not. She didn't used to. Then again, neither did her father, or so I thought."

Julie read the cover. "Ever hear of the Venice Bistro?"

Michelle got up and went to her room. She came back with the CD Cathy had confiscated from the boys at the baseball game. The Bistro was listed above Victor in the credits. "That's where Noah's band played on Sundays."

Julie opened the matchbook and read, "'Hello, I Love You.' Cheesy line."

"That's a song title. 'Hello. I love you; won't you tell me your name?'" Michelle sang. "Evidently, that's how Noah expressed himself to everyone."

"Not very original," Julie said.

"No, but maybe it will stop Cathy from believing all those articles about my affair with him." She pulled herself to a stand by the bed.

"He did look a bit like Jim Morrison. Sensitive, with the long eyelashes."

An image flashed in Michelle's mind: Noah's eyes were alight as he hugged her, a little too long. She remembered his hard chest against hers in a way that was disturbing. She had been lonely and he had been grateful. Did she have an affair with Noah Butler?

Or was her memory playing tricks on her again? She heard Julie's voice and shook it off.

"What's wrong?"

"I'm scared." Michelle looked around at the mess, then back to the matchbook. "Feel like going out for a glass of wine? I bet there are lots of single men at this Venice Bistro."

"Can it wait until tomorrow?" Julie asked. "I have a date."

"Already?" The sound of Bella's bark distracted her, then she heard Tyler's voice as he came inside.

"Mom?"

They met him in the hallway. "What's up for dinner?"

"Let's go out," Michelle suggested. "When's the last time you saw the sunset over the ocean?"

Julie laughed and helped her up. "Thanks for the yarn."

"My pleasure. Hope you get lucky tonight."

Julie gave her back the matchbook. "You too."

16

As they strolled down the Venice boardwalk, Michelle watched the blazing sun drop to the line where the sky met the sea. The last surfers paddled in, their dark figures aflame against the brilliant backdrop. She thought of Nikki again, still, always. Was she watching the same sunset? Or was she on a different patch of the planet, where the day was done and the stars were winking down at her?

Tyler stopped to watch a half-naked man juggle chainsaws. With his sharp profile backlit by the sun, Tyler looked so much like his father, who'd sworn that Nikki was still alive. She was desperate to believe him.

As the twilight deepened, the wind rose. Michelle looked toward the pier and spotted the Bistro. The neon palm tree on the bar sign blazed like a beacon lighting her path. She waved to her son through the dwindling crowd of tourists sorting through water pipes and handcrafted jewelry. He headed toward her, momentarily distracted by a bikini-clad model posing for a photographer in the last golden light.

Michelle pointed out the bar a few doors down. "Ever hear of that place?"

He looked over at the patio, just starting to fill up with art students dining on dollar pizza. Painted on the wall above them were the words, *Break On Through Every Sunday*, then the hours for the weekly Doors tribute concert.

"No," Tyler said. "But I'm guessing you have or we could have gone straight through Topanga and stopped in Santa Monica."

"Smarty-pants." Michelle showed him the matches. "I found these in Nikki's room and thought it was worth checking out."

"Guess it'll be more fun than stapling 'missing' signs to telephone poles."

"Thanks, you're a good kid. Your father did a good job while I was gone."

Tyler said something that was drowned out by the hip-hop beat of a Rastafarian closing up a sunglasses booth. They waited for an elderly man to rollerblade past, then crossed the boardwalk to the Venice Bistro. On the patio, a greasy-haired hulk in a Gold's Gym tank sat on a barstool. Tyler held back, pointing at the "You Must Be 21" sign nailed to the gate.

The bouncer squinted at her suit, then down at her legs. Michelle dug her right hand into her pocket and flashed her friendliest smile. "Hey, handsome."

He glanced at Tyler's face. "Does he have ID?"

"No, but neither do I," Michelle said. "Can we use the bathroom?"

"Leave junior outside, darlin', and you can use whatever you like."

"Aren't you sweet. But he's with me." She winked and whipped out a fifty. He opened the gate.

Inside, a Dodgers game blasted from the TV mounted up by the security camera. Michelle pointed Tyler toward the empty counter beneath it. The bartender wore only a burgundy bra beneath her leather vest, but Tyler was more intrigued by the red Cheetos she was pouring into plastic tubs. Michelle spotted a wiry old man counting receipts in the archway lined with band photos.

He gave her the once-over as she approached.

"You the owner? I'm writing an article on bands who play Doors music."

"For real?"

"Why not?" She pointed at the photos. "Who was your most famous?"

"The Doors," he said. "Been here a while."

"No wonder. I'm interested in a tribute band called Roadhouse."

He pursed his lips. "They don't play here no more."

"That's too bad. You'd think they'd be more grateful."

"Damn straight." He cracked a roll of quarters over the change drawer.

"When they did, you ever notice a girl hanging around Noah Butler?" He chortled until he coughed a wad of phlegm. "I know, there were probably dozens. But rumor has it there was one girl in particular." She reached in her handbag and pulled out the folded paper with her mother's obituary on one side. She shook off the bad feeling and showed him the birthday image of Nikki with disco ball earrings.

"We don't serve minors."

"That so?" She pointed to Tyler, dumping his pocket change at the bar.

"He with you? Cuz I don't want any trouble."

"No trouble intended. I just want to know about Noah's girl." She put the picture back and pulled out her last fifty.

He held it up to the light, then pointed across the room where the bartender was setting a slice of pizza in front of Tyler. Michelle's stomach cramped, but not from the greasy smell. Aside from two Hells Angels playing pool in the corner, the bartender was the only girl in sight. She didn't look like Nikki, with that washboard belly and bleached hair, but who knew? No, Michelle knew: that was not her daughter. Tyler knew, too, or he would have called out instead of shoving the folded slice in his mouth.

Michelle burned at being taken for a fifty-dollar ride. She stepped over a mound of straw on the floor to reclaim her son, but something stuck to the red sole of her Louboutin. She wiped her heel against the metal rung of a barstool.

"You okay?" Tyler asked, wiping his mouth with his hand

The bartender handed them each a paper napkin. Michelle smiled thanks, wondering what Tyler made of her risqué outfit and the flowered tattoo winding around a skull and crossbones. The girl was too young to be a Deadhead. Michelle looked closer at the skull tattoo. She saw the blue eyes and the inscription below: *Noah R.I.P.* Michelle's mouth went dry. She turned to push her bad hand out of sight. "Thanks. I see you've met Tyler. I'm Michelle."

The bartender stared at her, then looked down at the wadded straw Michelle was brushing off her heel. "Sick shoes."

Judging from Tyler's grin, Michelle realized that meant they were nice. Which of course they were. "Sick arm."

"It's called a sleeve, Mom. But don't bother. Celeste doesn't know Nikki."

"Celeste. What a pretty name." Michelle couldn't help but kiss ass—there had to be a clue here somewhere. She studied the matchbook. "Do you have any coffee?"

"Just Kahlua," Celeste said, eyeing the matches. "Where'd you score those?"

"Don't you give them out?"

"Been a few years. No more smoking on the beach." She poured the Kahlua. When Michelle put the matches down, Celeste made a grab for them.

Michelle reached for them, too, but with the wrong arm. She cried out.

Celeste nodded. "I knew that was you. Got a tweet from the Roadhouse website. You were in Beverly Hills today, right?"

Alarmed, Michelle gulped down the liquor. "Just give them back and we'll go." She looked at Tyler, who took his last bite and stood up. "Please?"

Celeste read the lyric inside the flap. "No way. This is Noah's writing."

"How do you know?" Michelle asked.

"We were tight," she said, then turned to stack beer glasses.

Michelle shook her head for Tyler to sit back down.

"Don't you want to go?" Tyler whispered.

Michelle lowered her voice and leaned away from the bar. "Not if we can prove her story. Do you remember when Kenny asked if Noah was Nikki's boyfriend?"

"I get it. If he was Celeste's boyfriend instead, then he couldn't—"

"No, musicians aren't known to be exclusive, honey, but it would sure make it look like he went for a different type."

Tyler nodded. "So you wouldn't have motive to kill him in order to protect Nikki—that's what they'd say on *CSI*."

"No one is saying that here. But this could help deflect any gossip and keep the car company on the hot seat. They might even have to pay us."

"Could I get a car?"

Michelle smiled. Teenagers. She had forgotten how the world revolved around them. "We'll talk about that later. For now, just act impressed, okay? Maybe Celeste knows something about Nikki."

Tyler sat back down. "Celeste, that's so chill that Noah was your boyfriend."

"Don't bullshit me, kid. Your old lady wants the matches back."

Michelle shrugged. "I don't believe you. Why keep it a secret?"

"No secret. I told that dude from *Rolling Stone*, but he just wanted to fuck me. I gave him a phony name, and he cut me from the article. Prick."

Michelle ignored Tyler's look. "He probably didn't believe you, either."

"I do," Tyler argued.

"Oh, honey, you'll see. People lie all the time. Even under oath."

"Fuck you," Celeste said. "I'm no liar."

"She has a tattoo, Mom. What more proof do you need?"

"Anyone can get a tattoo." Michelle pushed the glass forward for another shot of Kahlua. When Celeste refilled it, she snatched the matches back. "How do you know this is his writing?"

Her eyes flashed. "I told you—we had a thing. He wrote me a note."

"Heard it before, Celeste."

Celeste hesitated, then crouched down behind the bar. After a moment, she stood up and set a macramé purse on the counter. She dug inside and pulled out a rumpled cocktail napkin. She spread it out to reveal the faded handwriting. Sure enough, it matched the lyric inside the matches. But it wasn't a love note, it was a playlist.

"Not exactly proof." Michelle spied the small blue rectangle that had fallen from the napkin. "What's that?"

"Just trash that fell out of his pocket when he took off his Levis."

Tyler blushed and looked at his mother, but she was thinking about the camera she'd bought for Nikki's birthday. She'd gift-wrapped the case with a 2 GB memory card. But the camera itself came with a test card. And that little blue piece of plastic could be it. Why would Noah have it? This was a long shot, but so was finding Celeste. "That reporter was a jerk not to believe you."

"Crazy, right? Like I wasn't good enough for him? Noah wasn't one of those dudes that slept with every chick who tossed her thong on the stage."

"Glad to hear it," Michelle said, smiling at Tyler. "That reporter will regret it when someone pays a ton of money for your story."

"Who would believe me?"

"Everyone, if you testify. Other reporters will be there, too. Just show up at the trial in June with that sleeve bared and tell the truth about you and Noah."

"You could even blog about it," Tyler said.

Celeste turned to the bar mirror. "Everybody on the Roadhouse fan site says they slept with him. Like friggin' Jesse James. But it's not true."

"You have evidence," Michelle agreed. "I'll tell my lawyer about the napkin. But I'll need to take the disk now."

"No way. It's sentimental."

Tyler interrupted. "Give her money, Mom."

Michelle was feeling woozy from her first alcohol in years. "Do you have any? I'm out. I'm sorry, I can't even pay for my drinks."

Celeste gave her the once over. "I'll trade for your shoes."

Horrified, Michelle looked down at her beloved black Louboutins. The memory card could turn out to be blank. But what if it wasn't? She sat on the sticky barstool and slipped off her shoes, one by one. "Deal."

Celeste came around the bar and offered her tattered boots in trade. Michelle shook her head. Celeste lifted her ragged jean hem and jammed her feet into the stilettos. She rose, not just in stature, but attitude. "How do they look?"

"Sick," Michelle said, watching her beloved shoes disappear around the bar.

The straw pricked her feet and poked runs in her pantyhose that rose quickly, as if trying to escape. It was time for Michelle's escape as well. She led Tyler out. Halfway across the room, Noah's voice began crooning from the speakers.

Celeste shouted from behind the beer tap. "Hey, Killer Mom! Am I going to be famous?"

Michelle looked back. "I hope so!"

17

"NUMBER ONE HUNDRED FORTY-FIVE," the tinny voice blared across the Department of Motor Vehicles. Michelle kneaded her pounding temple as she slouched in the second row of plastic chairs bolted to the bare cement. The good news was that her license was still valid. All she needed was a new picture and they'd replace the one that disintegrated in the accident. And despite the packed waiting areas circling the hub of clerks' windows, the system was impressively efficient. If only the police department was as efficient with their missing person files.

Tyler bopped his head to an unknown beat over in the main waiting area. Earbuds in place, he smiled as he texted who knows what to who knows whom on his phone. Michelle wished she'd brought the book Dr. Palmer gave her at her last appointment, but she'd only grabbed the mail before rushing out. For the last hour, she had ignored her mother's letter burning a hole in her purse by practicing her left-handed signature and programming her new phone.

There wasn't much left to do to break the boredom. Michelle was dying to listen to Nikki's get well card again but the voice recording was too soft to be heard over the hubbub. Michelle stood to find the ladies' room, then saw a preppy woman from the

PTA standing nearby. Michelle sat back down quickly, slumping behind the man in front of her. The last thing she wanted was to catch up with one of those moms whose kids were always on the honor roll.

"Number one hundred seventy-six," the Orwellian voice droned. The number on her application was 181. Michelle stretched her neck until she felt that familiar flicker of pain in her shoulder. There were no more excuses for stalling. She reached into her purse and pulled out her mother's missive. She'd expected a long letter documenting every misspoken word, every hurt feeling, every detail of how Michelle had gone wrong years before that argument. But this envelope felt mysteriously thin. Michelle was tempted by the trash can nearby, but the suspense was unbearable. The envelope was a time bomb ticking to explode.

Michelle counted to ten in French to calm her nerves. Then she unfurled the string closure that Elyse had so thoughtfully provided, and pulled out two pages of monogrammed stationery. She studied the elegant arcs of her mother's handwriting until the words leapt off the poisoned page.

> Ma chérie,
>
> It pains me to have left in your time of need. Mais alors,
> I had no choice. Perhaps if you come here to rest, I can
> help you through this unfortunate situation. You are not
> the only one who has suffered.
>
> Mother

A round-trip e-ticket from LAX to CMH was printed on the second page. Michelle looked up toward the heavens. Recover? The only way for Michelle to recover was to get her family home. The very idea of being back at her mother's house in Ohio and being lectured twenty-four hours a day made her more nauseous than any hangover.

"Number one hundred eighty-one," the loudspeaker droned.

Michelle marched to the line behind the window where her number was displayed. As she waited for her paperwork, she was distracted by the ticket stuffed back in her purse. How should she respond? If only "no, thank you" would suffice. Michelle got the form and filled each box with careful marks, as if it was tangible proof that she was a person of good character, not an ungrateful daughter or bad mother or—God forbid—a murderer. Her lawyer would be pleased.

That was it! Kenny was the perfect excuse to reject her mother's invitation. Michelle dug her phone out of her purse. It was three hours later in Ohio, so her mother would be in the studio teaching *pointe* to her advanced students. She found the number and hit Send. She took a deep breath while it rang, then Elyse's voice spoke over classical music. Michelle knew exactly what to say after the beep.

"Hello, Mother. Just got the mail and wanted to thank you for your generous invitation. My lawyer insists I stay in Los Angeles. He actually said, 'Don't leave town.' Shall I return the ticket so you can get a refund?"

By the time Michelle handed her documents to the snaggle-toothed man with the clip-on tie behind the counter, she was giddy with relief. She gave him such a dazzling smile that he checked out her bare left hand and asked her for a date. She thanked him politely and went to wait in line behind a Spandex-clad cyclist ranting on his Bluetooth. She realized she could make her own calls now and held up her phone. "Husband," she commanded. After a few rings, he answered.

"Hey, there you are. How's the new phone?"

"So far so good. I had to charge it, or I would have called you last night."

"That's all right. Are you feeling better today about the deposition?"

"I guess so." There was something nagging at Michelle, but she felt a jab in her shoulder. She looked behind her at a woman wielding a plastic hairbrush and moved up. She heard Drew calling her name. "Sorry, I'm at the DMV. But guess what I found in Nikki's room yesterday?"

"Michelle, I told you to let it go," he said. She could hear the edge to his voice, even three thousand miles away. "I'm worried about you. Your mother called, still upset that you asked her to leave."

"If I need a nurse, I'll call Lexi. Besides, Tyler is a great help," Michelle said, glad she hadn't mentioned the Venice Bistro.

"Kenny said you're making erratic decisions about medical treatment. Is that true?"

"No, there's nothing erratic about it. I want treatment."

"Michelle, I don't want you getting your hopes up."

"You'd rather I have no hope at all?" She remembered what was bothering her. "Oh! I have a question about something that came up in the deposition."

"Make it fast, I have to get back to the set."

Michelle stepped up in line. "Okay. One of the lawyers threatened to hold you in contempt of court if you prevented anyone from testifying. But since Tyler already gave a statement, who was he talking about?"

"He was talking about Nikki."

"How can they subpoena a missing person?" Michelle asked.

Voices shouted his name in the background. "I gotta go," he said.

"Wait! That detective couldn't find Nikki's file, but he said if we had the date it might help. When I couldn't get hold of you, Tyler and I went to the school."

"Michelle, I told you not to do this. It's too much activity, too soon. You need to take it easy."

"But Drew, we only learned when she dropped out, not when she ran away. How long did you wait before going to the police? What was the date of the report?"

"Forget about the report, Michelle," Drew said.

"How can I?"

"One hundred eighty-one?" the clerk's voice rang out.

Michelle looked up at the clerk, then back at the phone in her hand. Why didn't he care about learning whether the police had new leads? The clerk called her number again while she waited for Drew's answer. But still, he didn't speak.

"Hang on," she told Drew. She put the phone down to keep her arm hidden, then hurried to the X in front of the camera. She stood still and smiled—flash!—then stepped away.

The woman behind the camera rubbed her stiff neck. "Again, one hundred eighty-one, open your eyes!"

Michelle stepped back and waited for the next flash. Something did not add up. The camera flashed again. This time, her eyes were wide open. She put the phone back up to her ear. "Oh my god. You never submitted a report, did you?"

"Michelle…" He was pleading.

"You lied to me!" He hesitated a moment too long. "Where is she?" Michelle demanded.

"I don't know!"

"Are you lying now?"

"No! I was trying to protect you."

"From what? What else are you lying about?" Michelle asked. She felt a shove and moved aside to wait for her paperwork.

"There's a lot at stake here, Michelle."

She leaned against the wall. "Is this about money, you fucking asshole? Did you tell Tyler he could get a car if we won the case?"

"Number one hundred eighty-one! Need your signature!" The woman behind the camera called. People were staring at Michelle. She had been shouting. The clerk gestured to the hairbrush lady, already toeing the taped line.

Michelle couldn't keep the phone open and take the papers with one hand. Frustrated, she burst into tears. She dropped the phone into her backpack, wiped her eyes with her sleeve, and hurried back to the counter. "I'm sorry. My husband just lied to me!"

"Welcome to the real world." The clerk stamped her temporary license. "Next!"

Michelle headed toward the drinking fountain to splash her face and calm down enough to call Drew back. What was he afraid of? As Nikki's guardian, if he knew where she was, he'd be put in jail for obstructing justice. Maybe he didn't report her missing to keep the police detectives from finding her. He could have been afraid that Nikki's testimony about ignoring the recall might send him to jail, right? Maybe it still could.

A voice interrupted her thoughts. "Michelle? It's me, Colleen. How nice to see you. And looking so trim."

Michelle blinked at the woman locked arm in arm with her daughter in the plaid school uniform. She sounded sincere, as if she didn't know about the accident. How refreshing. Michelle cleared her throat. "I could say the same thing about you. Tennis, right?"

"Something like that." Colleen's smile was as polished as a china plate, her eyes just as flat. "You remember Natalie? She just passed her driver's test."

"Congratulations, Natalie. Wow, time flies. Tyler's around here somewhere. Remember him? You were in second grade together, I think."

The girl nodded politely while dabbing on lip gloss that reeked of watermelon, then pulled a comb from her mother's purse. Colleen nodded toward the restroom. "Go ahead, but come right back. Don't talk to strangers."

Michelle watched her trot off. "Adorable. And how is your son? Did he get that scholarship to Yale? Or was it Penn?"

Colleen's lips trembled. "Montana."

"Tennis camp?"

"Boot camp." Her eyes turned red, as if all the blood vessels burst at the same time. Then they flooded. "We had to kick him out. He was using…" She jabbed the inside of her elbow.

"Oh my god, Colleen, I am so sorry." Michelle had goose bumps.

Colleen rubbed her eyes. "I didn't know what to do."

"I'm sure you did the right thing," Michelle said. "If anyone is a good mother, it's you."

"Makes no difference," she said. Her eyes narrowed. "His dealer was a girl. From the Palisades, no less. Did you know that heroin is cheaper than pot?" She shook her head and pulled a tissue from her sleeve.

Michelle saw Natalie approach and lowered her voice. "How's Natalie?"

"Hard to tell. Her big brother hacked into her savings and stole it all."

"I am so sorry, Colleen." Michelle reached out to console her, but she reached with the wrong arm. Fiery pain burned down her arm.

"Mom, it's our turn." Natalie put the comb back in her mother's purse.

Colleen tucked her tissue away and slapped on a mask of good cheer.

"Good luck," Michelle called, as if luck had anything to do with it. Maybe it did, she thought, catching Tyler's wave from the test area. How ironic that a near stranger had confided in her, as if she had all the answers. Michelle didn't even know what questions to ask.

Tyler headed over with his paperwork, stopping by Natalie for a hug. Colleen looked back at Michelle, just as surprised. Michelle waited for him. "You remember Natalie?"

"From Facebook. She's a friend of Cody's."

"Tyler, you would never do drugs, right?"

"Mom, I'm not stupid. I'd get kicked off JV."

"Sorry," Michelle said. "What about your sister? She ever say anything about drugs?"

"Nope." He checked his phone "Can you drop me at Eric's? School's out early, so he's having a kickback."

"A party?"

"No. A bunch of kids kicking back."

"Not a party?" Michelle wasn't clear on the difference. When she was in school, *party* was a verb.

"Nope. I just asked Nat for a ride, but she has to drop her mom off."

"Okay, but let me call your dad first. I have a question about insurance coverage." Among other things, she thought. She found her phone and pounded redial until *husband* appeared on the display.

"No answer." She looked at Tyler.

"He must be busy. Text him, that's what I do." He looked at her limp hand. "That might be hard."

"Slow, anyway. Like my brain these days." She dropped the

phone back in her purse, wondering what would have happened to Tyler had his dad gone to jail. "Tyler, did your dad ever mention you moving in with Nana?"

"Sort of." He shoved the papers in his jeans pocket. "His hours are so long, I guess he thought I'd be better off in tights than shooting up in Times Square." He noticed her alarmed expression. "Kidding. I wouldn't wear tights, even for Nana." He laughed.

"What's so funny?" Michelle led him toward the exit doors.

"I was just thinking about that time we visited, and Nikki had to take her ballet class. Nikki wanted to wear a tutu, but Nana said it was only for recitals. She put on some goofy music, and all the girls were twirling like little dolls. But not Nikki—she just stood there. Nana got so mad, in front of the parents and everyone, but Nikki wouldn't twirl without her tutu."

"She just stood there, crying," Michelle said. "But how do you remember that? You were six."

"We were watching through that two-way glass. You gave me change to buy Milk Duds from the machine. You usually made me get a granola bar. Remember?"

Michelle nodded. She didn't remember the candy, but she'd never forget feeling so torn between her mother and her daughter.

Michelle rescued Nikki by leading her out of the dance studio. The car ride with Elyse back across the river and through miles of cornfields was stuffy with anger. Michelle grilled hot dogs and fresh corn cobs out on Elyse's wooden deck while watching the kids trawl the creek for crawdads. Mud spotted Nikki's tutu when she clambered up for dinner. Elyse rocked on the wooden glider without a word. As the sun slipped down and the fireflies lit up and the crickets began to sing, Nikki twirled. She spun across the dandelion-covered yard spreading the fluffy seeds like a fairy. Her smile grew as she twirled, faster and faster until she collapsed in a giggling heap, until even her grandmother laughed.

"She never did anything on demand," Tyler continued. "Wish I was more like that."

"You're perfect the way you are," Michelle said. "Though I think you'd look good in tights."

Tyler blushed. "Dad said I'd meet girls that way. But then I got into Rutgers Prep."

Michelle nodded. Drew had obviously never told Tyler that he might not have a choice about where to live. No need to scare him; one lost parent was enough. But it was one thing to lie to your child and another to lie to your wife. Michelle's temple throbbed. She stopped to dig in her purse for some Tylenol and felt the memory card in the pocket. Trust was a two-way street.

"Tyler, let's not tell your dad that I took you to a bar."

"Are you kidding? He'd kill me." He smiled at her in solidarity.

"Now all we need is a camera. When you helped your dad pack those boxes, did you see your sister's?"

"No, but that disk looked generic."

"Is my pocket camera around?"

"It's at school." Tyler looked outside the exit doors and pointed at the lone paparazzi loitering in the parking lot. "We could borrow his. Just kidding. Seriously, though, Celeste already posted about meeting you."

"Lovely. Shall we make a run for it?"

Tyler grinned. "You want to be Butch Cassidy or the Sundance Kid?"

"You know neither of them made it out alive, don't you?" She calculated the distance to the car. "Never mind. Besides, if people know I'm out of the hospital, Nikki must know, too. Why won't she come home?"

Tyler shrugged. "Maybe she's afraid."

"Of what?" she asked.

"Of you. Or of them." He pointed outside.

Michelle backed into the door until it swung open, ignoring the flash. "I'll drop you off at the kickback, but do me a favor. Tell all your Facebook friends to put the word out."

"What, a reward?" he asked, as they hurried through the busy parking lot.

"No, that funny phrase you shout during hide-and-seek. The one that means it's safe to come home."

"Ollie ollie oxen free?"

That was it, she nodded. But was it true?

18

THE CURTAINS OF THE director's cottage closed with such force that Michelle stopped short, amazed how little had changed in eighteen months. Here, yards from the back entrance of her old office on Sunset Boulevard, the scent of marijuana was so strong that she was afraid she might get high just by breathing. But she needed to borrow a camera and Victor had a closet full of them.

A piece of paper blew across the small courtyard in the wind. She put her boot down on it and saw the cartoon-type drawings that made up a storyboard. She glanced back at the cottage it had come from. They were just smoking weed, right? The cocaine years were long past, with those foil packets of powder fueling the thirty-hour beer shoots that put them so far over budget that only CLIO Awards kept clients coming back. Michelle had always been a "suit," but she'd done her share of partying before she had children. She wasn't proud of the double standard of her antidrug policy, but things were different now. The drugs were far more potent since they'd become medically prescribed. And those privileged enough to be in Victor's cottage were craftsmen at the top of their games. Old enough to fry a few brain cells, if they so chose.

She studied the illustration of Tarzan swinging over the sand, an image designed by some advertising genius to sell an energy drink. Michelle tried to guess the price, whether shot on location at Zuma Beach or on stage at Raleigh Studios. She used to come within 10 percent of the actual estimate, but after all this time away, she wasn't sure how to adjust for inflation. In the old days, if Victor really wanted the job, she would recommend the live location and cut the greens rental altogether. Executives from Chicago never noticed the lack of plants on the beach until they got there. By then, their director's chairs had been set out, their coconut shells were filled with piña coladas, and they were happy to pay extra for palm trees.

Michelle spied a cluster of nubile young women on the sidewalk adjusting black bustiers and fishnets. They were the same age as the working girls in the police department, the same age as her daughter. Nikki had been to Michelle's office, so it was unlikely she would work this corner even if she had taken to the streets, but Michelle couldn't help but scan their faces.

"Michelle, is that you?" Victor let the door of the cottage slam behind him. He shook his head of too-black hair and buttoned the bowling shirt over the threadbare jeans dragging on his leather flip-flops. Then he crushed her with the embrace of a man whose personal trainer was on speed dial. He smelled of second-hand smoke, but his eyes were bright. He raised his hands as if framing her in a camera lens. "You look even better than before the accident, if that's possible."

Michelle blushed and handed him the storyboard. "Looking good yourself."

High-pitched voices called from the curb. "Victor!" "Pick me!"

Michelle was relieved to see the girls waving glossy head shots, but noticed with a start that their costumes weren't far off from Nikki's outfit in the video.

Victor ignored them and popped a stick of gum in his mouth.

Cinnamon, by the smell of it. They strolled over to the main office, an architecturally acclaimed mid-century box. Music blasted when he opened the door. "Why didn't you call? I'd have cleared my day."

"I didn't think I was up to it until last night. No need to bother you and Sasha at home."

"Sasha? Ancient history. You don't remember doing the honors for me?"

Michelle racked her brain as they stepped inside the bullpen, a room with worktables lined up for the production crew. Victor pointed at the production coordinator, a twentysomething kid in a knit cap banging away on his laptop. "Fletch, call casting. Talent is still showing up."

Fletch pulled out his phone. The other production assistants, a plain girl in a pink Save the Ta-Ta's T-shirt and a guy in a Stones T-shirt that looked like it could walk home by itself sorted out receipts on the long tables. They all had dark circles under their eyes. Cheap labor, Michelle knew, because she used to cut their checks. Before that, she was one of them. They stole glances at Victor, as if God was opening the mini-fridge. He offered her a bottle of pomegranate-acai water.

Michelle declined the water and followed Victor down the hall to the front entrance. She took in the wall photos that had been moved downstairs from her office. In one of them, Michelle wore a gorgeous gown at the CLIO Awards with Victor; in an auto-graphed shot, a hot young actor kissed her after a car commercial. In the reception area, the classic movie stills Michelle had bought still lined the metal stairway leading up to her old office. She peered up the steep stairs, hoping little had changed there either, especially the existence of cameras hanging in the storage closet.

Victor picked up the new issues of *Ad Age* and *Variety* from the empty desk. "Did you hear Becca got a studio deal?" Michelle asked.

He nodded. "I have a project there."

"Wow. Everyone's doing so well, I'm jealous." Michelle said. "Might be awkward if you run into her at the commissary, though. She always bugged me to quit working with you and hang up my own shingle as an independent producer. What's the project?"

"A documentary." His eyes skimmed her arm, then he called upstairs. "Asia!" He turned to Michelle. "You're coming up to say hello, right?"

Michelle followed Victor to the stairs. "I already thanked her for the orchids. They're nicer than the ones I sent your girlfriends."

"You're worth more than any girlfriend," Victor said. "I saw pictures of the accident, you know." He shuddered. "Glad you made it out."

Michelle was touched. The railing was on her bad side, so he held her like a prom date and walked her up. "Did you hear about Nikki?"

He nodded. "Awful. Any word?"

Michelle shook her head and caught her breath at the top. "To be honest, I want to borrow a Nikon to see what's on this memory card." She pulled it out of her purse. He held the blue disk against his forehead as if trying to read the contents. She laughed. "If you're old enough to mimic Johnny Carson, you might as well stop dying your hair."

A young woman in a short black dress and a chopstick poking from her glossy bun popped her head out of the first doorway. She clapped a hand over her ruby lips and widened her eyes beneath a black slash of eyeliner. If it weren't for the dragon tattoo on her shoulder, Michelle wouldn't have recognized her old assistant without the combat boots and black nail polish. Asia had obviously taken Michelle's advice about dressing for the job she wanted. And just as Michelle had suspected, that job was hers.

Michelle brushed off the *All About Eve* moment as she stepped into her old office. The walls hummed with high-definition monitors, and Asia's assistant, sleek as a seal, murmured into a headset as he filed completed production binders in a cabinet in the corner. Asia shook hands hello, reaching to Michelle's left without hesitation. She was a quick study.

"Have a seat?" Asia straightened the printouts on the table under the window and pointed at the executive chair at her desk.

"No thanks," Michelle said, flattered by the VIP attention. She was nostalgic for the powerful position, but it was clear from all the clipboards hanging across the wall, one for each commercial job in the works, that she'd been nothing more than another body in that chair. "Looks like you're busier than ever, Victor."

"What can I say?"

Michelle saw the autographed Roadhouse print from the video shoot on the wall and blinked. Noah had given her that as a gift when his recording deal came through. That's when he had hugged her so tightly. Here was one thing she'd done that made a difference. She pointed at Victor. "You can say: thank you, Michelle, for talking me into doing that video for my reel."

When the PA looked up, Michelle explained. "He said pigs would fly before it helped him get a movie."

The PA chuckled on his way out.

"Thanks, doll. Asia, get this woman a camera. I have a meeting."

"Don't you want to have lunch?" Michelle asked. "I'm dying for sushi."

Victor tossed out his gum and unwrapped a new piece. "This is a 'meeting' meeting. Friends of Bill."

Michelle recognized the code word for AA. "Oh, good for you."

Asia disappeared into the closet, then emerged with a digital Nikon hanging from a thick shoulder strap. She also had a small Dolce & Gabbana box. She lifted out a pair of glasses with magenta frames. "They arrived after…you left."

"Thanks for saving them," Michelle said. She didn't remember ordering them, but when she put them on, voila! "All the better to see what's on Nikki's memory card."

"Nikki's?" Victor asked.

"I think so," Michelle said. "It's probably just ten shots of her birthday muffin, but I miss her so much, even that would be worth seeing. If you could give me a hand with the disk, I'll take a peek at the viewfinder and head out."

"Nonsense," Victor said, his hand trembling as he inserted the disk into the proper slot. "Asia will screen it on the monitor. Excuse me while I make a phone call. Sushi sounds good. I'll try to reschedule."

Michelle watched him go. "He seems shaky. How long has he been sober?" Asia shrugged, and connected a USB cable to the camera.

Fletch, the coordinator from downstairs, rapped on the open door, then loped in, his arms piled high with petty cash envelopes and a thick production binder. "This gets us current, except for the reshoot at Chaplin." When he set them on the desk, his eyes went to Michelle's arm.

She looked down to avoid making him uncomfortable. Her glasses made it easy to read the label on the production binder: "Untitled Noah Butler story." Michelle's breath caught. Rings of sweat burst through the silk blouse beneath her blazer. "What the hell is that?"

Asia noticed and pushed Fletch out the door. "I thought you knew."

"Are you fucking kidding me? Was there a secret code in the orchids? 'With Love from Victor,' my ass. The traitor."

"It's a documentary," Asia explained. "The making of the video, the singer's tragic end, and the band's phoenix-like rise from the ashes."

"You're exploiting his death, that's what you're doing. Victor!" She looked at the Nikon. What if Nikki brought her camera to the set before switching this test disk out for one with a bigger memory? If there were any images of Noah here, Victor would want to put them in the documentary. Michelle was not about to take that chance. She yanked the USB cord from the computer.

"What are you doing?'

"Leaving!" Michelle scooped her arm through the strap and slung it over her shoulder. She grabbed her purse and raced out of the office.

"You can't take the camera!" Asia lunged for it, but Michelle was already scrambling down the stairs. She took another step down, then stumbled. She held tight to the camera, but her right arm automatically braced for the fall. A familiar arrow of pain shot out from her right shoulder. She struck the railing, righted herself, and kept going.

"Are you okay?" Asia called. "What should I tell Victor?"

"Tell him to go to hell."

Michelle ran across the courtyard, panting as she passed the cottage and headed for the parking lot. A few other people were getting into their cars, so she slowed to a walk until she reached the Volvo. Chest heaving, she unlocked the door and climbed in. She couldn't wait any longer to see what was on the memory card. Maybe it was nothing. But what if it wasn't?

She pulled the camera from her shoulder and hunched over the viewfinder so that her left arm could reach the control button. Then she pressed it.

The first two frames were completely black. The third and forth showed a ceiling light and a blurry thumb. Michelle breathed a sigh of relief. Nikki didn't know how to work the camera. Maybe her fears were unfounded.

She clicked to the next frame and found a picture—the color version of the three-shot that Michelle had found in the kitchen with her obituary on the back. She found the zoom button and looked closer. Michelle and Tyler still flanked the birthday girl, but Nikki's disco ball earrings were sparkling, and the birthday candle on the muffin was purple. Something else was different, as well. The spot on Nikki's cheek was clearly not ink. It was a tear.

Michelle had to swallow hard to not start crying. She forwarded to the next frame, a close-up of a birthday cake with the name Nicole spelled out in purple. Michelle remembered asking Asia to order it. She clicked to the next blurry image, of Sasha posing by her makeup table in all her blond glory, hair cascading down the back of her hand-knit halter dress. This had to be from the set of the music video.

The fifth blurry image showed the band, young and scruffy, in hand-painted T-shirts. Like the one hanging in Nikki's closet.

Michelle clicked to the next shot, of Tyler on the pitcher's mound. He was frowning, the bill of his blue baseball hat shading his eyes. Michelle smiled, pleased that Nikki had not only come to a game, but appreciated her little brother enough to take this shot.

She clicked to the next frame and tilted her head back to focus on something sparkly, with bits of purple. It reminded Michelle of those cardboard toddler books with macro photos of everyday objects. You had to guess what they were. This was…a scarf. Michelle wished she could remember that day, knitting together at the field. She would give anything to go back.

The next picture showed half of Nikki's face—as if art and teenage vanity had collided. Michelle leaned closer. There was something different here than in the breakfast picture. It wasn't just that Nikki's brown hair was brushed and her cheeks were a pink contrast to the purple scarf at her neck. It was as if the cheekbones of a woman had erupted from the flesh of the child. And there were no tears.

The next image was dark. Michelle sat back, thinking the photos were a dead end, except for a scrapbook. She hid her face as a man got into a car a few spaces down and drove away. Then she clicked again, just in case.

Another image flashed on the small screen: Noah sitting astride a gleaming black motorcycle. Michelle recognized the chrome handlebars and the leather saddlebags immediately—this was the Harley in her garage. Noah's face looked harder than it had in the photo in the law office conference room. Dark stubble dotted his chin. His blue eyes were piercing, as if he had a plan, and he was looking directly at the lens. At the photographer. At Nikki.

Michelle tried to identify the background, to see where he was, but there was a blurred rim of pink at the corner. Nikki's finger, no doubt. Michelle clicked the button again.

Two faces appeared close-up, as if captured an arm's length away. Nikki and Noah, lips locked together in a kiss. Noah's eyes were closed, as if he was deep inside the moment. Nikki's brown eyes were open, wide open, and they were dancing. She seemed to be waltzing, in that one-two-three rise before sweeping across the floor in the arms of the one you…

Oh god. Nikki had been in love with Noah Butler.

The world stopped spinning; the parking lot was still. Michelle was slowly aware of her own breathing and the traffic outside. Someone was shouting. She looked up.

Victor approached, waving his arms. He saw her and shouted again, hurrying toward the car.

Michelle dropped the camera in her lap and reached across the steering wheel to crank the engine. She shifted clumsily. She heard banging on the window, but she didn't look up. She honked long and loud, then put her hand on the wheel. She hit the gas and sped away.

19

ICHELLE WAS STILL SHAKING forty-five minutes later, when she turned off the freeway into her tree-lined neighborhood. Every speed bump past the elementary school made her cringe with pain from her fall down the stairs. She was driving slowly to minimize the jostling when she saw a sleek black Porsche pull into her driveway.

A huddle of parents pulled their children away from the fallen fence as a tall figure with dark hair cut through the weeds to the front door. It was Victor.

Michelle braked and backed up to pull in Julie's driveway, which required a flurry of motion with one hand. She slunk down to watch from the rearview mirror. After knocking on the door a few times, Victor walked around the back of the house. Michelle looked in the side mirror and caught sight of a bruise blooming on her cheek. She climbed out of the car, leaned over to slip her arm through the camera strap and grab her purse, then bumped the door shut with her hip before running up to Julie's porch. She kicked the door. She had never appreciated the tall cypress trees bordering Julie's yard until now.

Julie opened the door in her work clothes.

"May I come in?" Michelle didn't wait for an answer. She

stepped over the yapping dog and around a headless Barbie into the messy hall.

Julie backed out of the way, then followed Michelle inside the living room to the bay window. "I was just heading to work. Are you okay?"

Michelle peeked outside between the chintz curtains. Victor was leaning against his Porsche, pulling his phone from his pocket. A ringing sound erupted inside Michelle's purse. She turned to Julie. "My boss wants his camera back."

Julie took the camera and eyed Michelle's cheek. "What happened?"

"I fell."

"That's what Rihanna said. You need to go to the hospital. You could have a concussion—or worse, after all you've been through."

"Seriously, I tripped on the stairs at my office."

"Let's get you some ice." Julie led Michelle to a shabby chic couch and set the camera by Michelle's purse. Michelle scooched away from some crayons and relaxed in the comfortable mess. It was so different than her empty living room. Julie returned and moved the camera aside to sit down and apply a mouse-shaped block to Michelle's cheek. "What's with the camera?"

"There are pictures of Nikki and Noah on the memory disc."

"So? I told you she was a fan."

"Big fan. They're kissing. As if no one else exists." She waited for a reaction, but Julie just sighed and repositioned the ice pack. "Did you know?"

"Of course not. It's just been a long time since anyone has kissed me like that. I was trying to remember how it feels."

Michelle saw the corner of Nikki's get well card peeking out from her purse. "I wonder if that's why she ran away."

"You mean, because she was angry that you...ruined it?"

"She said she felt awful—and she didn't want to see me." She nudged her purse with her foot. "Will you keep the memory card for me, just in case?"

"Just in case what?"

"In case anyone else gets the idea that my own daughter blames me."

"Doesn't everyone blame their mother for something?"

"Sure. But aren't some mothers to blame?" Michelle thought about Elyse, then shook it off and took over the dripping ice pack.

Julie went back to the window. "Still there. He's cute, your boss. Single?"

"Not worth your time. He's a player. Not to mention a traitor. He's waiting for me to come home so he can see the disk. He's making a documentary about Roadhouse."

"That's weird, but what does it have to do with the memory card?"

"Everything! If he includes the shot of Noah Butler kissing my daughter, I'll be cast as the avenging mother." She handed the ice pack back to Julie. "Would you let your daughter date a musician?"

"She's nine." They heard the old Mustang engine rev up and roar off. Julie peeked between the curtains. "Coast is clear, except for that white van, he's been parked there all day."

"You know what I mean. Even if Sophie was sixteen, I bet you'd say no."

Michelle struggled to pull the memory card out with one hand. "The lawyer from Orrin Motors wants to suggest the accident was my fault, that I didn't use normal precautions or some such thing. And Noah's parents could amend their lawsuit anytime to add something or other about intentional harm. I thought I could prove I didn't have a grudge after we found this skanky bartender from the Venice Bistro who claims she was his girlfriend. She's the one who gave me the memory card. Unfortunately, it doesn't prove anything about her. It only proves that Nikki and Noah really did have a relationship."

Julie returned and put a consoling hand on Michelle's knee. "That doesn't mean you were responsible for his death."

"Then why does it scare me so much?"

"Motherly concern?" Julie guessed.

"I hope that's all it is." Michelle offered Julie the disk. "In any case, if you have it, I can honestly say that I don't."

"Why can't you just say there's nothing on it?" Julie asked.

"We worked together for years. He'll know if I'm lying."

"I wish I could help you, Michelle. But, this divorce is taking forever and I could still lose custody of my kids. I can't harbor evidence." She pushed it away.

"You just said it's not evidence," Michelle pleaded.

"Saying and doing are two different things. That guy in the van watching your house might be a detective. Seeing him sit there all day reminds me of when Jack was on workers' comp and the insurance company watched to make sure he was really hurt. Why don't you send it to your husband?"

Michelle's eyes flashed. "Drew's been lying to me."

"Oh my god. Did he have an affair?"

"No, nothing like Jack. Turns out he never reported Nikki missing. And I understand why he lied, but…" She shrugged.

"I know what you mean," Julie said. "I don't even care all that much about Jack screwing around. It's the lying about it that hurt. Like he thought I was stupid."

"Exactly," Michelle said.

"Made me think I was the crazy one. My mother even bought me boobs, thinking if that didn't keep Jack home, at least it would make me feel better."

Michelle couldn't help but look at Julie's chest. "Did it?"

"It doesn't hurt," Julie admitted. "Sophie nursed so long I was embarrassed to wear a bathing suit. And now I get really fast service at the dry cleaner." They laughed together. "My mother isn't the class act that yours is, but it sure helps to have her on my side." She looked at the memory card. "What about your mother?"

Michelle shook her head. "She'll tell Drew, and he'll want to strap me to the bed so I can recuperate."

"Is there anyone you do trust?" Julie asked. "How about that cute care manager? You should have her take a look at you, anyway. There is something to be said about recuperating."

"Lexi? She's at work. I can't bear to go back to that hospital. Plus, I'll have to visit everybody and…" She pushed herself to a stand. "Ow."

"You really should see a doctor," Julie said.

Michelle thought for a moment. "You're right."

Dr. Palmer studied the X-ray film clipped to the light box on the wall of his clinic. Michelle tried to stay calm and focus on the colorful images that so captivated him, but they reminded her of Tyler's old Lite-Brite. She was tempted to go find the nurse who was printing out pictures from the memory card, but she didn't want to pass the patients at the weight machine. She was wearing little more than torn ribbons of pantyhose beneath her hospital gown. She shivered, guessing that the air conditioning was set to accommodate the shirt and tie Dr. Palmer wore beneath his lab coat.

Michelle smelled the half-eaten plate of jambalaya on his desk and felt her stomach growl. She spotted the bowl he kept chocolate

Kisses in, so she tiptoed around a few boxes of books. It was empty. "No chocolates?"

"Didn't know you were coming," he said. "Good thing you did, though. That must have been a nasty fall."

"Then why aren't you looking at my shoulder?"

He tore his eyes away from a pizza-shaped image. "Once you were in the MRI machine, it seemed prudent to do a brain series."

"No wonder it took so long in there." Michelle turned away so he couldn't see what she was really thinking. She didn't want him to know that she'd felt comforted by the immobility. There was nothing she could do in that white cylinder but rest. It felt safe, like the coma. Except for the screaming in her ears.

"You were lucky today. After the accident, it took months for the swelling to go down and your brain activity to return to normal. There may still be an increased risk of hemorrhaging."

"But how am I doing now?"

"You need to see me again in a few days. And you could benefit from more therapy."

"I tried that. Starting when I was a kid and my mom tried to kill herself, and again when Nikki got depressed and started crying at night. She refused to go, so I went. Didn't make me feel better, though."

Dr. Palmer pulled the scans down from the light boxes. "I meant physical therapy. More than once a week." He saw her blush at the misunderstanding. "Don't be embarrassed. You've been through a lot. People who avoid psychotherapy are often the crazy ones."

"What were you in for?"

He pointed at her in mock anger. "You didn't read my book?"

"I've been busy," Michelle said.

He gestured for her to sit, then flashed a penlight in her eyes. "So I gather. You could benefit from a bit more rest, Mrs. Mason."

"You sound like my husband."

"Is that good or bad?" Dr. Palmer looked up from his clipboard.

"I'm too tired to think about it," she admitted. "But do I really have to read the book to find out your secret?"

Dr. Palmer shook his head. "No secret. When I was a kid, my brother was jacking a car and his finger got torn off. I played lookout." Their eyes met, then he went on. "One of my mama's jobs was cleaning a building with a therapist's office, so—"

"Let me guess: after years of therapy, you channeled your guilt into fixing people?"

"That's what the book jacket says, but it wasn't so obvious at the time. Not until I did a stint at juvie hall and broke my mama's heart."

"What happened to your brother?" Michelle asked.

"I don't know. He's a trucker now. We don't talk much."

"I'm sorry."

Dr. Palmer slipped the pen back in the pocket of his lab coat and returned to the light boxes. "You can't control other people's actions. Only your reaction."

"And sometimes not even that," Michelle added, following him to the next film of her shoulder. On the image, ribbons of red nerves wrapped around her rotator cuff, then extended down the thin white bones of her arm. "So, what's the verdict, Dr. Palmer?"

He pointed his pen at the shoulder joint. "There's definitely an extension of nerve tissue here. You had a burst of motor movement prompted by the neurological regeneration. There was a cortisol release when you had to break your fall."

"Cortisol is the stress chemical, right?" Michelle knew the name from the research she'd done when Nikki started crying at night. Cortisol burned tracks in the brain, making people more sensitive to depression, more prone to reoccurrences of it.

Dr. Palmer aimed his pen back at the image of her brain. "See these nerve pathways here? Some are dormant, but some are just being built. When you had to protect yourself from the fall, your instincts kicked in—"

Michelle interrupted. "I was only protecting the memory card." He turned to look at her, but it was hard to explain, even to herself. When she was first pregnant, she made Drew promise that if they were ever on a sinking ship, they would save each other first. She could always have another baby, right? But as soon as Nikki was born, she felt differently. "I was protecting Nikki's privacy."

"Maternal instinct, then." Dr. Palmer said. "In any case, the nerve bundle in your arm was already under construction. Physical stimulation could aid the process." He began to knead her shoulders. "Your husband should massage you every night."

Michelle weakened beneath his touch before she could murmur a response. "He's in New York."

A ripple of concern washed across Dr. Palmer's face. "Well, your mother could do it. She's in town, isn't she?"

Michelle hesitated to answer. But it felt good to confide in him. Until now she hadn't realized how much she censored herself with Tyler. Before she could say anything more, the double doors swung open, and Bree brought in the folder with prints from Michelle's disk.

Music wafted in from the waiting room and overwhelmed the gurgle of air filters that echoed around the open room. When the doors closed, it faded.

Bree handed Michelle the folder with the memory card clipped to the outside. "We're out of matte paper, hope it's okay."

Michelle nodded, grateful to avoid talking about her mother. When the nurse went across the room to help patients using the weight and pulley machines, Michelle changed the subject. "Why don't you play music in here?"

"We do," Dr. Palmer said. "But we had strict orders to avoid the radio in the hospital, so I thought you preferred quiet."

"No. Maybe my husband didn't want me to hear Roadhouse. But my son blasts it in the car—and aside from his taste in music, it doesn't bother me."

"Good. Sensory information might help trigger your memory." Dr. Palmer looked up from massaging her shoulder and called to Bree as she checked on Robocop at the weights. When she left to put music on, he looked back down. His fingers hit a pressure point.

Michelle squirmed and dropped the folder. The color prints landed face up on the floor. They both squatted down to gather them. Michelle was panicked. "Please don't tell anyone about these."

He picked up the birthday picture and smiled. "Ah, your missing limb."

"That's not funny," Michelle said, stacking several on his desk.

"I wasn't joking. She's very beautiful, like her mother."

Michelle blushed and showed him the self-portrait of Nikki looking so grown-up. "Don't you want children?"

"Sure," he said. "But I think wanting the woman is more important. And after all the work my mother did, I couldn't waste time at singles bars. By the time I finished my residency, the good ones were all taken."

The way he smiled made Michelle wonder if that included her. She rushed to fill the silence. "I can't imagine you'd have trouble now: a handsome doctor with a book?"

"You sound like my mother. But she still cooks dinner whenever I want, so what's the rush? It'll happen when it happens." He set the first picture aside to look at the next one.

She reached to close the file, but he was on her right side and beat her to it. They both looked at the photo of Nikki and Noah kissing. Passion rose like a hologram from the glossy photo paper. Nikki looked straight at Michelle, her eyes glowing with innate knowledge. Noah looked blissed-out, with his neck stretched so that his lips reached hers, his black eyelashes curling from closed lids. Michelle turned to Dr. Palmer, who was mesmerized. "Do you believe in love at first sight?"

He looked up. "I believe in love at first smell. Pheromones are responsible."

Michelle looked back at the picture. "So you think this could be real? Not a fling? They only met a few weeks before the accident. Could they have fallen in love that quickly?"

Dr. Palmer shrugged. "What do I know about love?"

"What does anyone know?" Michelle said softly.

Smooth jazz rose in the background. The mood relaxed as patients using the weight machines across the room began to murmur to each other. Dr. Palmer led Michelle to the padded bench at the table with the electrical box, then attached electrodes to her arm. "Ready?"

She nodded, opening the folder to distract herself with the vivid prints.

"Your daughter has quite an eye."

"She took photography at school," Michelle said, then her mood darkened. She hoped Nikki was still taking pictures, somewhere. Something burned. "Ouch!"

"Sorry." Dr. Palmer turned the dial lower. He tipped his head at the picture of Noah on his Harley. "Bet his mother would like that. What's she like?"

"I have no idea. She looked like one of those sad women who lay in the dark all day watching reality TV."

"You haven't spoken with her?" He felt her wrist for her pulse, then adjusted the electrodes.

"She's suing me." She waited, but he didn't look up. "Her ex-husband called me a murderer. What would I say: I'm sorry?" She shut the folder. "I wonder if they even know about Nikki? What if she was just another notch on Noah Butler's guitar?"

He turned on the voltage again and started low. "You're judging a dead boy?"

"A dead man," Michelle corrected. "He was nineteen, legally an adult."

"What about your daughter?" He moved the motorcycle shot aside to the one framed around their kiss. "She looks confident there. As if this shot was proof."

"Of what?"

He scowled as if she was playing dumb. "That he loved her."

"Dr. Palmer—" Michelle started.

"Wes."

"Wes. What could I possibly say that would make his mother feel better?"

"I didn't suggest apologizing for her sake," he said quietly.

Michelle felt the tears coming. She reached for the voltage knob and cranked it higher. Let it burn. She liked this feeling. It distracted her from the heaviness in her heart. The sweet scent of burnt flesh tickled her nose.

Dr. Palmer switched off the power. "What are you afraid of?"

"Nothing," she answered. "It's not about me."

He yanked the electrodes from her arm. "You've been using that excuse for a long time, haven't you?"

Michelle held her singed arm protectively. "Excuse me?"

"You heard me." He called the nurse over.

Michelle stood up. Her knee caught the power cord, and the electrical box crashed to the floor. He didn't help her retrieve it, which made her more furious. She couldn't expect him to understand. He didn't have children. She slammed the box on the table. "Must be nice to know everything."

"I just want to help."

Michelle held her arm out. He was supposed to help—he was her doctor. Bree ran up with the first aid kit and set it on the table. She took out a cool pack and reached for Michelle's arm, but Dr. Palmer waved her away. Michelle winced as he cooled the burn, then patted salve on it, but it was clear by Bree's surprised expression that Michelle was wrong. He didn't have to help this much.

She pointed to the memory card clipped to the file. "If you really want to help, could you keep that until the trial?"

He looked at her for a moment, then unclipped the blue disk and dropped it in his pocket. "Of course," he said. "For your daughter's privacy."

Michelle waited, but he said nothing more. He went back to dressing her wounds with bandages. They would blister soon, then burst—painful reminders that he was right. This was about her, whether she'd killed Noah Butler or not.

20

A PUDDLE SPLASHED THE CURB as Cathy pulled her minivan to the front of Holy Cross Hospital. Between swipes of the windshield wipers, Michelle could see the Virgin Mary statue beckoning her toward the entrance of the small building. "Thanks for the ride."

"No problem," Cathy said. "But who's this doctor? I don't blame you for switching if that other guy burned your arm, but we had a deal. No more medical bills until my husband gets paid."

"It's just a consultation," Michelle said. A station wagon honked, then passed and turned into the mall entrance across the street. Michelle could see toddlers strapped into car seats, tiny fingers smearing Cheerios against the rain-streaked windows. She missed those days.

Michelle peered at the concrete building rising up in the clouds and pushed up her hood.

"Are you going to be okay?" Cathy asked.

"Good question," Michelle said. "See you in an hour?"

"Don't be late. I have a school committee after lunch." She leaned across to open the passenger door. "Good luck."

Holy Cross Hospital was as gray and dreary inside as the sky outside. Scarlet stained glass windows cast bloody shadows across the tile floors. Michelle stamped her wet shoes then submitted to the elderly volunteer in a wheelchair guarding the lobby with a pump of hand sanitizer. When the admitting nurse pointed to Dr. Braunstein's sign-in sheet, Michelle declined. "It's personal."

The nurse sat up, immediately alert. "Are you the one who called?" A woman at the desk in back looked up from the computer. Michelle heard whispering behind her as two nurses in green surgery caps looked up from the coffee stand. A sitcom star breezed past, but the nurses didn't flinch. Infamy trumped fame. The nurse pointed down the hall. "Second door on the left."

Michelle thanked her and started walking. Her heels echoed too loudly on the tile. She tried to keep the past separate from this moment, as if it hung on a lanyard around her neck, but with each step it tightened like a noose. She stopped at the door plaque that read: Laura Braunstein, MD. She felt faint. She had no idea how this woman felt.

Maybe she was being selfish, like Jack when he described his affair to his wife. The confession had made him feel better, but it broke Julie's heart. What if Michelle's presence made Noah's mother feel worse? She turned to leave.

A watercolor print next to the small office portrayed the sun shining on the ocean. Michelle studied the golden glow shimmering across the waves, and recognized it as a religious work symbolizing God's infinite power. She changed her mind. But the possibility of forgiveness wasn't the only thing that made her stay. The picture frame was the perfect size for the photograph of Noah. His good looks and high spirit would surely give his mother a moment of comfort. Michelle checked her reflection in the picture glass, counted to ten in French, and knocked.

Dr. Braunstein sat behind an enormous desk in the small, tidy room where she dictated patient notes into a tape recorder. Michelle stood in front of her, feigning interest in the diplomas from NYU and the plaque from the Women's Leadership Council hanging on the paneled wall behind her. She barely resembled the woman Michelle had seen sleepwalking out of the law office. Perhaps the other certificate, from the American Society of Anesthesiologists, explained it. Or maybe she was simply more at home here.

The woman had the kind of posture Michelle's mother would commend, and her broad shoulders filled her surgical scrubs with scalpel-sharp precision. Her graying ponytail was practical as opposed to lazy, and her face was as bare of makeup as it was of emotion when she finally looked up.

"Good morning. I'm Michelle—"

"I know who you are," Dr. Braunstein interrupted. She sipped coffee from a mug branded J&J, a pharmaceutical logo. "What I don't know is why you're here."

Michelle felt her pulse in her throat. "May I call you Laura?"

"No."

Michelle was pinned by the doctor's gaze. She wanted to wash off her lipstick, to pull up her sleeve and show her bandages. Most of all, she wanted to sit down. A leather armchair faced the desk, but she didn't dare ask. "I brought you a gift."

A nurse knocked and leaned in the open doorway. "Dr. Braunstein? You're due in the OR in five." Michelle turned and spotted the small bulletin board on the wall behind her, directly across from the desk. It was empty except for a baby picture and a photograph of a mother and son making a sandcastle on the beach. Michelle turned back. Better not to speculate. The nurse shut the office door, trapping her like prey.

Michelle pulled the folder from her purse and set it on the desk like an offering. "I'm truly sorry about—" She forced herself to say the name, to make him real. "About Noah." Dr. Braunstein said nothing, so Michelle rushed in to fill the silence. "I wish I could say something about how wonderful he was." She tried to remember Noah beyond the baseball field. "He was certainly handsome."

When Dr. Braunstein saw the photo of her son, her eyes softened. Her cheeks inflated slowly, melting her cool facade until her smile shone like the sun across the water in that seascape in the hall. She came out from behind the desk, then pinned his picture to the bulletin board. "Let me tell you about my son."

Michelle burst into tears. Dr. Braunstein gave her a Kleenex, then gestured toward the armchair. Michelle collapsed into it. This was the punishment, she knew. To learn what she had cost this woman.

Dr. Braunstein leaned against the desk, smiling at her son's image as she spoke. "Noah was a surprise. His father and I had already broken up when…the term Noah would apply is 'booty call.'" She chuckled.

Michelle sniffled. She liked this woman. In a different life they could have been friends. The thought squeezed her like an iron lung.

"I felt responsible for depriving him of a two-parent family, so I let him take his father's name. But they were never close—Guy Butler is a hard man to please. Do you remember him?"

Michelle nodded. If only she could forget his whisper. *Murderer.*

Noah's mother continued to reminisce. "He was always too quiet for his father. Preferred writing songs to surfing. When he was small, he played Little League while I studied for my boards, but he wasn't very competitive. Later, he got in a little trouble— like most boys do—and had to perform community service. His father accepted no responsibility, naturally, so Noah served his hours helping the League and stayed with me most of the time. He didn't feel comfortable at his dad's beach house once the new girlfriend moved in, regardless. Guy called him a mama's boy. So what if he was?"

She looked closely at the photo then pointed at the shadow of a scar by the cleft in Noah's chin. "That's from carving turkeys on Thanksgiving. Every year we volunteered at the Dinner for the Homeless at the Santa Monica Civic. He loved handing out cookies to the children. But that last year he was old enough to work in the kitchen. My sweet vegetarian was assigned to carve turkeys and he didn't say boo. By the time we got home for our own dinner, all he wanted was Lucky Charms."

Michelle perked up. She remembered the leprechaun T-shirt in Nikki's room. The two had marshmallow bits in common. That and the fact that they were both artistic—misfits to most kids their age. What did Tyler call his sister? A loser. Perhaps the video had changed that for both of them.

"He ate Lucky Charms for dinner when I worked nights, as well. I made him take a vitamin, but..." She tugged her stethoscope strap. "You just want their lives to be easier, you know?"

Michelle nodded. She knew very well.

"He wasn't serious about the band until his first semester at UCLA. I suppose I should thank you for making his dreams come true."

Michelle couldn't bear it anymore. "Did he have many girlfriends?"

Dr. Braunstein smiled at some private joke. "His father thought he was gay. That's why he bought the damned motorcycle."

"I'm sorry, I'm confused. I have a daughter named Nicole, who...I don't know what you've heard, but they knew each other. Did he ever mention a Nikki?"

"Nice girl," Dr. Braunstein said.

Michelle looked up. "You met her?"

"They brought me coffee. Noah was no saint, don't get me

wrong. He had plenty of girlfriends." She looked directly at Michelle. "But I know what you're asking. Nikki was the only girl he ever brought here. He wanted me to like her. And I did."

Michelle felt goose bumps. "You must hate me."

"No. I feel sorry for you."

Michelle tried to breathe. Anger would have been easier to deal with. "What about the lawsuit?"

"Peter Greenburg is my ex's half-brother. I plan to donate my share to a worthy cause. It took two Valiums to get through my deposition. Guy hired a publicist to cover the funeral. Can you imagine?"

Michelle was horrified, but not surprised. "Your son was very talented."

"It was only a matter of time until he left home," Dr. Braunstein mused. "The stack of apartment listings in his room was growing as high as the stack of songs he had written. If it wasn't your video, it would have been something else." Dr. Braunstein looked at the acoustical tiles on the ceiling.

Michelle imagined all the words left unsaid and felt grateful for every one.

The phone buzzed. Michelle waited for a chance to make a polite exit while Dr. Braunstein spoke to the caller. "Water is fine, but no food after midnight." When she looked up, her face was blank. She was done being Noah's mother for now. She had closed the door to her personal life and returned to the safe haven of work.

Michelle was envious, but only for a moment. "Thank you for seeing me."

The nurse opened the door and stood waiting. Dr. Braunstein opened her drawer and rustled about before retrieving a notepad. She rose and put her hand on Michelle's arm on her way out. "I hope you find her."

As Michelle watched her go, her eyes fell on the photograph of Noah pinned to the board. She called out. "Do you want Noah's motorcycle? It's still in my garage."

Dr. Braunstein turned back, her face red with rage. "Keep it or junk it, I don't care. Just don't let Guy get his greedy hands on it. With all the gruesome injuries I see in the emergency room, I begged him not to buy it for Noah. I know you stopped him from riding in the rain. But if it weren't for that two-wheeled death trap, my son would still be alive."

The nurse spoke up from the hall. "Dr. Braunstein?"

Noah's mother opened her mouth to say more, but only slapped her notepad against the doorframe. Then she disappeared from sight.

Michelle trembled. Now, every time Dr. Braunstein looked at her bulletin board, she would see that gleaming Harley and be reminded, not of how handsome her son was, but why he was in Michelle's car in the first place. She had to cut that part off. She scanned the desk for scissors. No luck. The side drawer was ajar, so she glanced at the empty hall outside the door, then went around and pulled it open. A postcard caught her eye.

Two sea turtles swam underwater across the glossy rectangle. They had emerald shells and enormous flippers, like the ones in Maui where Michelle bought the magnet that was on her refrigerator. She turned the card over. Sure enough, the print in the corner read: Turtle Town, Maui, Hawaii.

The postmark was smeared. Michelle's eyes automatically dropped to the handwritten message. It was written in purple ink, with small circles dotting the *i*'s. Michelle's breath caught. Nikki had used purple ink ever since she had graduated from pencils. Once upon a time, she made happy faces in those circles, or flower petals outside. But these letters were tiny and unadorned, like whispers between the white space.

Forget the fakes from Australia; there was a real postcard after all. It just hadn't been sent to Michelle. She looked up. No one was coming just yet, but she couldn't risk taking the time to get out her glasses. She squinted to read the first lines:

We chased our pleasures here, dug our treasures there,
But can you still recall, the time we cried...

There was a rap on the doorframe. Michelle shut the drawer. She made a show of clutching her arm as the nurse bored down. "Can I help you?" she asked, eyebrow raised.

"I hope so! Do you have scissors? The picture I brought for Dr. Braunstein has a motorcycle in it." Michelle pointed at the bulletin board. "She hates motorcycles."

"Most doctors do," the nurse said, unpinning the photograph. "We have scissors at the nurse's station."

Michelle followed the nurse out of the office, tempted to run back and read the rest. She was desperate to know when it had arrived.

She saw Dr. Braunstein turn the other corner. She ran after her to the operating room and peered through the small window. Doctors and nurses looked up. "Dr. Braunstein?" Michelle called. She felt a clamp on her arm. A security guard steered her back to the front, where the nurse who cut the photograph gave her the bottom half with the Harley on it. Michelle stuffed it in her purse as she was escorted to the elevator.

The rain had ebbed and the sky was bright when Michelle emerged from the hospital. Cathy's minivan was already parked in front. She pushed the door open for Michelle. "Howdy," she said, her cheeks flushed with anger below her dark shades.

Michelle hesitated. "Has it been more than an hour?"

"No, but it's been plenty long enough to figure out that Dr. Braunstein is not offering a consultation. Not about your health, anyway." She held up the Palmer Clinic card with Dr. Braunstein's name and address.

"Sorry, I must have dropped that."

"Sorry you dropped it, or sorry you lied to me?"

"Does it matter?"

"No, it doesn't, thank you very much. Either way, you counted on me to be stupid, to forget Noah's mother is a doctor. And you were right: I am stupid. Stupid to have trusted you. You've changed, Michelle. You used to screw up the team snack, but you were never a liar."

Michelle rubbed her bad arm. It had become a habit whenever she felt uncomfortable. "Please don't tell Kenny."

"I don't keep secrets from my husband." A shaft of errant sun through the skylight struck the sparkling *F* on the temple of Cathy's new sunglasses.

"So you'll tell him what you paid for the Fendi sunglasses?"

"They're knock-offs," Cathy said, avoiding her gaze.

"I may be a bit fuzzy, my friend, but I remember the difference between Swarovski crystal and glass beads. At least three hundred dollars."

Cathy shifted the minivan into gear and headed home. "Like the fine for taking a minor to a bar. A dive bar, no less."

Michelle looked at Cathy. "How do you know about that?"

"Boys will be boys, Michelle. Tyler bragged to Cody about playing detective, and now Cody thinks you're a cool mom. If Kenny finds out the case is compromised, he'll be livid. And it won't help you to be hanging around with that tacky divorcée neighbor of yours who struts around with her tits hanging out. Your reputation matters."

Michelle had to let the attack on Julie slide. "Why do you think I asked you for a ride? I didn't want to involve Tyler any more than I needed to."

"Michelle, it's common sense to avoid talking to someone who is suing you."

"That's her ex's doing."

"I don't care. She could use this little visit as proof that you feel responsible!"

"Cathy, if Cody died in my car, wouldn't you want to know that I was truly, eternally sorry?"

"Sure," Cathy said. "Then I'd strangle you."

Michelle shivered and let it go. She tried to recall the rest of the lyrics to that song on the postcard. Cathy interrupted. "So what did Noah's mother say?"

Michelle tried to push the postcard out of her mind for a moment. "She told me about her son. She did say he helped the baseball team for community service. Do you know anything about that?"

"I meant what did she say about the case?"

"Not much."

"Good," Cathy said. "Because I've made a decision. I'm not going to tell my husband about this."

"I thought you didn't keep secrets."

"These aren't secrets, Michelle, just extra details he doesn't need to worry about. He's got enough on his plate. And I don't mean Hamburger Helper. We'll just keep this little trip—and the price of my sunglasses—between us." She pulled the glasses off her head and shook them at Michelle. "But do not make contact with Noah's mother again unless your lawyer is present. Do you understand?"

Michelle didn't answer. She needed to ask Dr. Braunstein about the postcard.

"I'm serious. Promise you won't breathe word of this to anyone, ever! You could have a mistrial. I won't let Kenny start over. And since you're as broke as we are, you'll get some court-appointed attorney, some green kid who crammed for the bar exam listening to Roadhouse on his iPod. So, if anyone asks, we were out grocery shopping today—which we are, because I need some Chardonnay. Promise?"

Michelle nodded. Cathy had a point. Besides, Michelle could only make things worse by telling Dr. Braunstein she'd seen the postcard while searching through her drawer. Michelle raised her right hand, a tiny bit. The effort burned. "I promise."

Cathy eyed her arm. "Crap. I was going to ask you to stop physical therapy, too, but it looks like you've had a breakthrough."

Something clicked in Michelle's mind. "Break on Through," that was the song. Doors lyrics. Noah expressed himself in Doors lyrics and Nikki had picked up the habit. Michelle closed her eyes to remember the words.

At the next light, Cathy called in an excuse for missing the school meeting.

Michelle got out her new phone and turned toward the passenger window to try the voice command feature. She whispered the song title.

"Excuse me?" Cathy asked.

"Nothing," Michelle said, reading the rest of the lyrics on the screen.

Tried to run, tried to hide.
Break on through to the other side.
Everybody loves my baby.

The "other side" surely meant death, Michelle surmised. If this was meant as a condolence card, the song was a good choice. Wings of panic fluttered in Michelle's chest. Nikki didn't know about Elyse's history, but she'd studied *Romeo and Juliet* in English class, and Juliet was only thirteen when she'd killed herself.

Michelle read the lyrics again and relaxed at the last line. Everybody did love Dr. Braunstein's baby; according to Tyler, Noah had fans around the world. Why else would Victor be making a documentary? Nikki sent the card to Noah's mother, confessing that she loved him, too. That would mean more to Noah's mother than adulation from strangers. And it explained why Dr. Braunstein saved the postcard.

Michelle looked at the traffic. So many people! She was grateful that Nikki wasn't famous, that not everybody loved her baby. Drew and Tyler and Elyse did. But no one loved Nikki as much as Michelle. Every cell in her body ached with it. She didn't need to ask Dr. Braunstein about the postcard. The important thing was that it was written by her daughter. And at some point in the last eighteen months, Nikki had been in Maui.

Cathy hung up the phone and drove toward the grocery store.

"They really are stunning glasses," Michelle said.

"So we have a deal?" Cathy asked.

"Of course," Michelle said warmly. Cathy had given her the perfect alibi. Michelle would cooperate fully. She would smile and shop and go home.

Then she would go to Hawaii.

21

A LANDSCAPER'S TRUCK WAS PARKED at the curb when Cathy dropped Michelle off at home. She tightened her grip on the grocery bag and tiptoed around the muddy clumps of weeds splattered on the driveway next to the fresh-tilled soil. But something else was different. By the time she smelled the fertilizer around the pruned roses lining the porch, she knew: the picket fence was gone.

Pounding noise came from around back. Michelle headed around the side of the house, where the faint marks of graffiti could still be seen beneath a coat of fresh paint. She held her breath past the trash cans and Bella's travel crate, then circled around back. Across the muddy yard, workmen were tearing down the rickety trellis. Someone coughed. Michelle saw Tyler's open window. "Tyler? You getting sick?"

She shrugged off the silence and congratulated herself for splurging on the chicken soup cans with easy pull-off tabs, then headed back to the front porch. The door had been sanded in stripes. She balanced the bag on her knee, turned the knob, and nudged the door open with her hip. It swung open so quickly that her heel caught on the threshold. Michelle lost her balance and fell, her groceries spilling across plastic sheeting on the floor.

Footsteps pounded in the hallway, then Tyler appeared, his laptop still open in his arms. He helped her up. "You okay?"

She nodded. "Nice to see we're getting the house in shape."

"Painters, too. There were six men until an hour ago—and the guys outside only stopped for a few minutes when it rained."

"You were home all day? But I left you the car to go to the pier."

"I couldn't find the keys and Cody's truck is in the shop." He spotted the keys on the floor by an apple.

"Oops," Michelle said. "Guess they were in my purse when I left. Sorry."

"It's cool, the Internet guy finally came."

Michelle picked up a soup can and carried it to the kitchen. The sink was full of dishes from Tyler's day at home. Before she could complain, he picked up a small blue plastic plate decorated with a baseball and large *D*. "Look, I found my Dodgers plate," he said.

Michelle smiled, remembering. "You used to refuse to eat from anything else."

"Crazy, huh?" He pulled his inhaler from his back pocket, shook it and pressed it to his lips.

"We should get you out of here with all this dust," Michelle said.

Tyler put up his palm for her to wait. When he exhaled, his words came out in a rush. "I could stay at Cody's. His mom's making lasagna."

"His mother has already been generous today. I was thinking of a hotel."

"Cool. I heard the Hilton Courtyard across from the Commons has Wi-Fi and a breakfast buffet. All you can eat," he added, picking up another can.

"Sounds yummy, but I was thinking of somewhere more special. Like Hawaii."

"Yeah, right." Tyler laughed and crossed the hall to retrieve a cereal box. "What's with the Lucky Charms? You used to only buy whole grain."

"Couldn't resist," Michelle said. "Why don't you put the rest of these things in the kitchen while I talk to your dad? Can I use your phone to call him?"

"To invite him to Hawaii? Don't bother."

"Why not?" Michelle asked. "I bet he could use a vacation."

Tyler shook his head. A pained look crossed his face.

"What's wrong, Tyler?"

He shrugged. "Nothing."

"Look, if your father can't get away, we'll go without him. Phone, please?"

"Is your battery dead?" he asked.

"No, but he doesn't always pick up for me."

Tyler stood still for a moment. "I don't want to get in the middle of this."

"It's not a fight, honey. Your father is probably just sick of bad news. But this is good news, I promise."

Tyler reluctantly handed over his phone. Michelle kissed his cheek, took the phone to her bedroom, and kicked off her heels.

"Yo, dude," Drew said. Horns honked in the background.

"Mama dude here," Michelle said. "I have a question."

"Can it wait?"

"It's not about our argument when I was at the DMV." She heard him shush the people around him. A crowd of people. "Are you shooting?"

"No, just wrapped. Want to say hello? You remember my assistant, Travis?"

Before she could complain, the phone changed hands and another man's voice boomed across the country. "Hi, Michelle, how the hell are you?"

"Great," Michelle said. And for the first time in a long time, it almost felt true.

"Here's Sasha," Travis said. There was chatter as he handed the phone off.

"Sasha!" Michelle forgot everything for the split second she heard her friend's voice say hello. Even if Sasha was mostly a work friend, production crews spent so many hours together they felt like family. And she missed the social whirl. "Don't be mad, but someone else did my hair. Thanks for your card, by the way."

"It's the least I could do," Sasha said.

Michelle smiled and went to the window. The workmen were leaving, joking with each other in Spanish. It was good to have friends. "I miss you! Are you still knitting?"

"Yes," Sasha said. "But everyone I know has a scarf now, so I've moved on to blankets."

Michelle laughed. "I'm jealous. My doctor said to hang up my needles for good."

"You could crochet—that only takes one hand."

"So I've heard. Can you teach me?" Michelle asked.

"Are you coming to New York?"

"Not if I can help it. I hate cold weather. I'm thinking about Hawaii, though."

"Hawaii?" Sasha asked.

The phone rustled as Drew got back on the line. "What's this about Hawaii?"

"That was so rude, Drew! At least tell Sasha I said good-bye." She heard him mumble something, but she didn't care what it was. She was impatient, bursting with the news. Finally, she heard his breath on the line. "Drew, she was there!"

"Who?" Drew's voice echoed.

She looked at the phone as if he was crazy—or drunk, if they'd just wrapped. His voice did have a slight slur. If only she could see his face, she would know for sure. "Who do you think?"

"No way. Kenny says the car company has detectives looking for her. Professionals."

"Exactly—she's just a job to them. Anyway, it's a place to start."

"How do you know she was there?" Drew shushed people in the background, then a door shut three thousand miles away and all was quiet. He was about to grill her. "Michelle?"

She remembered her promise to Cathy. Shoot. She needed to come up with something fast. Think, think, think. She saw Nikki's self-portrait on top of the stack of photos printed from the memory card. "Mother's intuition?"

She bristled at the sound of his laugh. Even if it wasn't true this time, she believed in that sense of knowing, as sure as the leaden weight of her heart. When Tyler passed by with his laptop, she had a better idea. "It was posted on the band website."

"There've been sightings as far as China, honey. But she doesn't have a passport. And no one has claimed the reward."

"There's a reward?" Michelle asked.

"From one of the lawyers who wants her to testify. You didn't see it posted on the website?"

"Tyler's hogging the computer." That part was true, anyway.

"Are you in bed?" Drew asked.

"Yes," she said, leaning back on the bedspread. "I'm lying down. I understand if you have work, but why punish Tyler? He can be my chaperone."

"He's already missed a week of school," Drew said. "If you're weak enough to need a chaperone, you shouldn't be going at all."

"I was kidding about that—I need my family. You included. We'll do that snorkel trip to Turtle Town. Remember how much fun that was?"

Drew was quiet for a moment. She heard someone call his name, but he didn't answer. "I'm working, remember? And what about your physical therapy? I thought that was a big deal."

"Not as big as this."

"How are you going to pay for it?"

Michelle sat up. The floor was pockmarked with dirt from the landscaping that had stuck to her pumps. She'd thought the landscaping meant he had a new source of money, but apparently he'd simply gone further in debt. But soon the house would look perfect again. Even her mother would be impressed. Her mother! "I'll exchange the plane ticket my mother sent."

"Send Tyler home."

"What do you mean, send him home? This is his home."

"He needs to get back Saturday to study for midterms. If his grades drop, he'll lose his scholarship."

"He won't need one if he stays here and goes to public school. I can apologize to the dean."

"For what? No, don't tell me. It's not going to happen. I won't let him be dragged into this mess again and have to deal with all the paparazzi."

Finally, something that made sense, Michelle thought. Drew was protecting their son. "Why didn't you tell me that in the first place?"

"Other things were more important." He swallowed noisily, a slug of beer. "You almost died, Michelle. You're supposed to be resting."

"Actually, Wes—Dr. Palmer—said activity would be good for me."

"He didn't mean Hawaii," Drew said. "Take a few walks around the block. We'll see you during spring break."

"Stop telling me what to do! I have to find Nikki. I have to tell her I'm sorry."

"For what?" Drew asked.

Michelle felt a familiar catch in her throat. "For whatever made her run away."

"You can't change what happened, Michelle. And finding her won't make you a better mother."

"Go to hell."

"Too late," Drew said softly. "Already there."

Michelle hung up. She looked out the window at the moonlight. The yard was barren of grass.

A few minutes later, Tyler leaned in. "Mom? I tried to walk Bella, but some clown took a picture."

"That's it. Put her out back and get your toothbrush." Michelle shoved open the closet and found the suitcase from the hospital. She put the photos in first, then clothes for an overnight stay. When she opened the drawer of her vanity table, she saw the ticket from Elyse. She had meant to mail it back, but like Drew said, "Other things were more important." She needed her glasses from her purse to read it, so she pinned it under her arm and rolled the suitcase down the hall. Tyler was locking the back door.

"Can you read this?" Michelle gave him the ticket.

"What part? The flight number or the nonrefundable-nontransferable part?"

Michelle snatched the useless ticket back and shoved it in the drawer of the hall table. One last-minute round-trip flight to Maui seemed doable, but two would cost a fortune. She looked at the family portrait hanging above it.

"What's wrong?" he asked.

"You have to go back to school." She blinked back tears and put up her arm for a hug. Her right arm tried to follow. Fire shot through it, but that was far less painful than the burn in her chest.

Tyler hugged her back, engulfing her with warmth. "Why didn't you tell me you have to leave?"

"I dunno," Tyler said. "Everything is so complicated now. I hate it."

Michelle nodded. Things were as far beyond Tyler's control as they were hers. They went back to the kitchen to put the last groceries away. The orchid on the dinette was down to one blossom. She pinched a dead petal from the dirt. She decided to enjoy every moment—and to make sure he did, too. She could take him on the roller coaster at the Santa Monica Pier and to see the Van Goghs at the Getty Museum. Maybe he'd like the vintage stores on Melrose Avenue where Nikki shopped at his age.

"Is there anything special you'd like to do?"

"Sort of. The fan site says Roadhouse is filming in Hollywood tomorrow."

"Then, by all means, let's stop by," Michelle said. Victor had mentioned Henson Studios, the stage Michelle booked for the original video. He could beg for the memory card all he wanted—she didn't have it. And she certainly wouldn't tell him about the photos. But she needed money, so she could sell him the T-shirt for authenticity. It wasn't worth enough for a ticket to Hawaii, but she could sure spoil Tyler for a day or two.

"Can I invite Cody?"

Michelle nodded, hiding her disappointment at having to share him. When she pulled the keys from her purse, a scrap of paper came out with them. It was the bottom half of the photo she left for Dr. Braunstein: Noah's legs astride the Harley. That had to be worth more than a ruined T-shirt.

"Did you say Cody has a truck?"

"A pickup," Tyler said, pulling her suitcase through the kitchen.

"Perfect," Michelle said. "Let's go find that hotel with free Wi-Fi."

Tyler opened the door to the garage, and Michelle leaned in to turn on the light. The Harley was parked beyond the Volvo against the wall.

"Can we get the breakfast buffet?" Tyler asked.

Michelle smiled. "All you can eat."

22

ODY'S PICKUP TRUCK RATTLED as they waited for the traffic on
La Brea Avenue to thin out across from Jim Henson Studios.
"Now!" Michelle called. He turned left between a city bus and
a taco truck, then squealed to a stop in the driveway at the gate
blocking the small lot. Michelle had worked on her first commercials
after film school in these brick bungalows built by Charlie Chaplin.
Later, she rented the stages for Victor's shoots. Fortunately, the
guard watching telenovellas in the booth was a holdover from those
busy years. Michelle waved from the open window. "Salvatore,
long time no see! How's your grandson doing at Berkeley?"

"Graduates in June," he said, eyes flickering with recognition.
"How's your girl?"

"Working on her application now, I hope," Michelle said. She
leaned back to reveal the boys, who were distracted by the statue
of Kermit the Frog dressed as The Little Tramp. "This is my son,
Tyler—he has a few years yet. He and his friend are helping me load
in a picture vehicle. We're on stage four, right? Golden Hour?"

"Three," Salvatore said. He looked at the bulky tarp tied to the
flatbed, jotted the license number on his clipboard, and stuck a pass
inside the windshield. When the gate rose, he waved them past.

The chauffeur of the limo idling by the ramp looked up from

his *Daily Racing Form* as Cody pulled into the empty space between a camera truck and a cube van. Once parked, the boys climbed out. Michelle pulled down the mirror and brandished her red lipstick like a sword as she prepped for battle. When Tyler opened the door, she sheathed her lipstick, shook out her glossy hair, and climbed down to the cobblestones. Cody untied the motorcycle from the flatbed.

"Remind Cody that this is top secret: no bragging to Natalie, no blogging online, and especially no telling his parents."

"Don't worry. His dad would ground him for skipping school and Cathy wouldn't want him chilling in Hollywood. She's even more strict than you are."

Michelle ignored the irony and pointed to the red light glowing by the stage door. "After you open the door for me, wait for the light to go out. Then roll the bike in. You can get snacks at the craft service table, but remember it's called that because it serves the craftspeople, so don't be greedy. The crew works long hours. They might look lazy, but everyone has a specific job to do at exactly the right moment. Stay out of their way. Got it?"

The boys nodded, eyes so bright with anticipation that Michelle feared they might wet their pants. When was the last time she'd taken Tyler to the set? Maybe never. Then she spotted Victor's Porsche and remembered why. "If you smell anything funny in there, ignore it."

Michelle heard the hum escaping from beneath the door and smoothed her black linen dress. She felt more comfortable than she had for a long time, as if she was back in her element, at work. Whoever said home was a safe haven had it backward.

Tyler lugged the door open just enough for Michelle to slip through. Before, when she was in charge of payroll, Victor's crew had looked forward to her arrival and parted like the Red Sea.

Today, when the door clanked behind her, not one of the thirty people inside looked up. She peered through the haze from smoke machines as the drummer pounded out the last beat.

The barrel-sized Klieg lights clicked off, then the fluorescent house lights flickered on overhead, leaving the small stage in shadow. As the roadies unplugged the amplifiers, Michelle tiptoed past a man checking the lens of a handheld camera mounted inside a boxy image stabilizer. She picked up her heels to stay clear of the burly man coiling cable like a snake.

A clutch of executives in dark suits clapped one another on the back as they waited for playback on the video monitors. The engineer was busy matching digital time code above a mixing board that resembled spaceship control—editing shots together right there. Michelle looked away from the butt crack of the camera grip locking down the 35 mm film camera, the old kind with film reels shaped like Mickey Mouse ears. A scruffy guy with rolls of duct tape hanging from his belt sprayed the pebbly metal with Fantastic, which meant the camera was only a prop. When the dreadlock-haired drummer ran past in his hand-screened Roadhouse T-shirt, Michelle had a sinking feeling of déjà vu.

She spied the boys rolling the tarp-covered bike inside and parking it next to a forest of silver C-stands. They headed to a table laden with the same bucket of Red Vines and tiny bottles of Perrier she'd ordered for the original shoot. Michelle shook it off, chiding herself for being so sensitive. This was a documentary about the band, after all. She was bound to be reminded of that day. She wanted to be reminded, in fact. She needed to remember. Those missing weeks began right here.

Michelle felt a tug on her blazer and was immediately trapped by arms attached to a chest as hard as a brick wall. Her nose twitched at the scent of cinnamon. "Victor!"

He pulled her to the side of the stage and spoke quietly, as if they were still recording. "What a nice surprise. Asia didn't mention you'd be stopping by today."

She pulled away. "I didn't tell her."

"Ah. Sorry to hear about your nasty fall. I ran out to help."

"Did you? I must have been distracted."

He nodded. "Then I stopped by to check on you."

"How thoughtful," Michelle said. "I did get your messages. I brought you a present." She led him to the Harley and pulled off the tarp.

"Why would I want an old Roadster?"

Michelle faltered, noticing the cracked saddlebags for the first time. "Because it belonged to Noah Butler?"

"So sell it to Planet Hollywood, or the Rock and Roll Hall of Fame."

"Thought I'd give you first shot," Michelle said. "For the documentary. It's been in my garage since…Well, for some time now."

Victor nodded. "Do you need money?"

"Of course not. I mean, couldn't hurt, but that's not why I'm here."

Victor looked around before pulling out his money clip. "You should go before anyone recognizes you, doll. Your picture is on a dartboard in the band's dressing room. I'll call you later about your daughter's memory card."

"I wish I had a memory card," Michelle joked. "But there's nothing good on hers."

"You never know what might be helpful," he said, pressing two hundred dollars into her palm. That wouldn't even get her a red-eye flight to Honolulu. She looked up and saw the boys poking licorice in Perrier bottles like straws.

"Is that Tyler? He must have grown a foot since the last time I saw him."

Michelle nodded as a prop guy with clothespins on his belt set down a sheet cake that had melted under the lights. The craft service gal yanked out a birthday candle and gave it to Tyler before picking up a knife. Tyler loved cake, but when he turned and held the candle up to show Michelle, he was as pale as the icing.

Michelle dug in her purse for the extra inhaler she brought along. "That's him all right, maybe having an asthma attack." She hurried toward Tyler and nearly collided with a dark-haired musician deep in conversation with a slick silver-haired man with dual phone headsets. "Pardon me," she said, rushing past.

Tyler held out a piece of cake.

"No thanks, honey. Is the smoke bothering you?"

He shook his head and raised the cake into her line of sight. Across the white icing, purple letters spelled out *Nicole*. Confused, Michelle looked up at Victor, who had caught up to her side.

"How are you, kid? Look, buttercream, your mom's favorite." He reached out for a swipe of icing just as Tyler shook his head to disagree. He lost hold of the slice. It fell, smashing on the cement floor. Cody joined them, offering his slice as a replacement. On the top, frosted birthday balloons surrounded the number sixteen.

Michelle froze. Victor's voice was garbled on his walkie-talkie as the buzz in the room rose. A pimpled production assistant ran over to clean up. Michelle didn't move to make room. She didn't care if anyone slipped and fell and got injured. She didn't care about looking good or playing nice. Tyler was staring past her at the musician she had just bumped into, so she turned and took a closer look. He had blue eyes and long lashes, cheekbones slicing shadows across his pale skin. A dead ringer for Noah.

Michelle turned to question Victor, but her shoe slipped on the icing. He caught her just as a commotion rose in the makeup area.

They looked over to see the back of a petite blond with hair trailing to the hem of her knit halter dress. She was laughing with someone as she picked up a black La Knitterie Parisienne bag and jammed two pink knitting needles inside. Behind her, a girl was giggling in the makeup chair.

"Nikki?" Michelle whispered. Her heart pounded so hard it was painful. She rushed toward her daughter, marveling at her beautiful girl. She hadn't aged a day: still lanky and coltish, with dark brown eyes. Michelle took in the Goth costume, the hair gelled into submission between spray-on streaks and the black scrap of a Roadhouse T-shirt pinned together over her pale skin. A rip down from the collar exposed a hint of cleavage faked with a red push-up bra. Black eyeliner made her eyes pop and her lips were that same bloody shade of red she'd worn in the video. Michelle pulled away from Victor and ran toward her.

"Places, people!" the AD called.

Nikki stood up from the makeup chair. But she was tall—too tall. Her face was more oval, her eyes too small. And the purple high-tops she wore didn't have tiny black skulls or her name embroidered on the back.

Michelle slowed down, then stopped. Desire had clouded her vision. Desperation had filled her heart. But the day they shot the video was now clear in her mind. She had only been crunching numbers for a few minutes before she found her daughter in makeup.

"Mom. Say something," Nikki pleaded.

"Go wash your face!" Michelle pointed toward the restroom at the side of the stage. Stunned, she turned to Sasha. "Pack your kit. You're out of here!"

"Relax, it's just dress-up. Victor said she could be in the video."

"Victor wants you gone, too," Michelle said.

Sasha looked at Victor, who put up his collar and turned away. She swore and threw her brushes into the makeup chest. Michelle was halfway across the stage when she heard Sasha call after her. "What are you going to do, lock her up till she's legal?"

"Michelle?" Victor said gently, his hands on her arm. She peered through the fog of memory at his face. She wanted to punch it. She heard Dean Valentine's words in her head. *Every child is at risk.*

Victor grabbed her good arm. "It's a re-shoot. I thought you understood."

"Oh, I understand, all right," Michelle said, ripping her arm free. "But when Becca and I were in film school, a documentary meant actual footage of real people. Not actors, you lying piece of shit. Show me what you have so far."

When Victor hesitated, Michelle marched over to the monitor. The line producer looked up from signing a purchase order and scratched the gut straining from his windbreaker. An A&R executive with a bolo tie spilled a Rock Star drink on the mixing board. A PA scrambled to sop it up. Even the gaffer, the underarm of his T-shirt ringed in sweat, stopped halfway across the catwalk to peer down at her.

"Playback," she said to the man at the mixing board. "That means you, Carlos."

He looked up and saw Victor shrug behind her. This was the advantage of Victor's loyalty, of always hiring the same crew. She knew who they were. And vice versa. Carlos hit Play on the mixing board and pushed up a few levers. A heavy metal version of the Beatles's "Birthday Song" blasted from the speakers. "They say it's your birthday. We're gonna have a good time..." The large monitor lit up with the image of a clapboard spelling out the scene and shot number, then there was a close-up of the actress impersonating her daughter. Michelle curled the fingers of her left hand until the nails cut into the flesh of her palm. She felt nauseous, but she had to watch.

Victor tried to explain. "We wanted to be as accurate as possible, but we didn't film Nikki's entrance, so we had to recreate it. You had Asia send over the cake, remember? When you brought her inside, the band played for her."

Michelle studied the actress on the screen. She sulked convincingly, a grungy kid with blotchy skin and disco ball earrings. Then she pretended to recognize the band. Her face blossomed into a smile, just as Nikki's had.

When the band broke into the birthday song, she twirled her earring, shy, but happy. At least, that's how it played on the video monitor—it was a happy birthday. After the girl pulled a gleaming new camera up to her face, Michelle glared at Victor.

"You were right about one thing. I did fire Sasha, after she painted Nikki and pimped her out. Or was that your idea, Vic? Will you shoot that part? Your producer firing your girlfriend? And where are the purple balloons? And what about Nikki's grandmother calling about her sheepskin coat? Did you get that? How real are you going to make it?"

"That depends on you," Victor said. "We are missing a few things. Like the kiss."

Michelle felt goose bumps rise and turned back to the screen. "I have no idea what you're talking about."

"We've done the research, Michelle. People saw them hanging out together a week after the shoot. We need to set it up, establish eye contact between them on set."

"Wait a minute. You can't shoot this without my consent, can you? Or do you think I'm stupid enough to give it to you?"

"Golden Hour Productions owns the copyright for the video. That was your idea, doll, and a brilliant one." Victor switched to a new stick of gum, dropping the wrapper.

"That's for the final cut of the song—not outtakes of an unpaid extra who happened to be my daughter," Michelle said, picking up the wrapper. "But I'll take the compliment. Because we both know that without me you'd be a washed-up alcoholic on the verge of bankruptcy."

"God grant me the serenity," he muttered. "It's my work that made them famous."

"Not according to *Rolling Stone*," Michelle said.

"You agree with that scumbag reporter?" he asked. "*You* made Roadhouse famous by creating a martyr?"

"That's not what I meant," Michelle said, backpedaling. "I haven't actually read the article. I heard about it from Noah Butler's girlfriend."

Victor's eyes widened in surprise, then he noticed the crew watching. "Let's get the boys some souvenirs, shall we?"

"Let's get some for Celeste, too," Michelle said. "You've met her, right? The bartender at the Venice Bistro where the band played on Sundays? Or don't you bother with that kind of research? You know, the factual kind?"

Victor shoved the box back to Fletch. He leaned his face close. "Noah Butler died in your car, doll. What the hell happened in there?"

Michelle blinked. *She was strapped in the car, trapped by the steering wheel. Her vision clouded until she heard those raindrops thrumming just as they did against the windshield. She heard the tick-tick-tick of a clock and waited for the scream.* But there was nothing. Just the prickle of tiny hairs rising on the back of her neck.

A whooshing noise brought Michelle's attention back to the soundstage. She looked back beyond the wardrobe rack to the real hair and makeup area where the actress playing Sasha was taking off her hair extensions. She spotted the real stylist working a hair dryer on an older woman in a black suit. When she flipped her brown hair back, it was like looking in the mirror. She was the actress playing Michelle, overwhelmed and under pressure.

"Are we done here?" Victor asked.

"No," Michelle said, pulling her gaze from the actress. She didn't feel that way anymore. She had been through hell and come out stronger. "We're just getting started."

"You really want to profit from Noah Butler's death?" Victor asked.

"That's more your style, isn't it? But you have no idea what happened to Noah Butler—you can't just make it up. I'm the only witness. And one day, I'll remember and sue your ass. I want a thousand dollars for the Harley—or I'll call my lawyer and shut you down."

The color drained from Victor's face. "Could you do that?"

Michelle wasn't sure, but she pulled out her phone. "Two thousand."

There was a shift in the air as a side door opened and a sea of suits drifted in. Michelle was tall enough to spot a familiar head of red hair bobbing like a Man o' War in the center. She looked at Victor, who crossed his arms.

"You've got to be kidding me. This is Becca's project?"

"Oh, did I leave out that little detail?"

Michelle stormed across the soundstage until the sea parted for her.

The two women stared each other down. "I wanted to tell you," Becca said.

"Really?" Michelle scoffed. "Because you had plenty of chances. How dare you exploit this for your own interest! No wonder you got a studio deal, you lazy opportunist."

"Nothing lazy about it, Chelle. It's called business." She looked at Victor, who had just reached them. "Anything I should know?"

"She's holding us for ransom."

"Oh, phooey," Becca said, relaxing. "We're shutting down for rewrites. And look at you. I see the Wizard hasn't lost her touch." She reached in for a hug.

Michelle backed away. "Don't you kiss up to me, you traitor!"

Becca hustled Michelle away from Victor and the rest of the studio executives. "Chelle, you're taking this the wrong way. I meant it as a tribute to you. As much as I've seen of your long road to recovery, I'm still amazed you got out of that car alive. What was left was smashed like an accordion."

Michelle remembered how blurry the newspaper photographs looked. "You've seen the car?"

"Haven't you?" Becca waved two men out of their tall director's chairs so the women could speak privately.

"No. But why did you? Was this ever a documentary, like Victor said?"

"Studio funding for a documentary? No," Becca said, running her bitten nails through her hair. "Not that much has changed since you left the business. It's a biopic. We can tell a better story with dramatic license—and believe me, it's a better story now."

"What do you mean?"

"The tragedy of Noah Butler is practically Shakespearean. He's already a rock and roll legend being compared to his hero, Jim Morrison." She helped Michelle up to the canvas seat. Michelle sat, too angry to find the words to respond. "Look, somebody is going to make this movie. You should be glad it's me."

"Meaning what?"

"Meaning, stories are subjective. You can be the hero in this.

Tires slipping on the slick road, nearly dying trying to save your young star—you're the one who discovered him, right?"

Michelle shook her head. "I never wanted to be a hero, Becca, or I'd have gone to save that mess of a movie in Turkey instead of sending you. I wanted to have my baby. Now I just want to find her!"

"I get it," Becca said, opening her alligator messenger bag. "Look, there's something I need to show you." She pulled out her iPad and tapped the corner until a picture filled the screen. Twin babies covered with bubbles were giggling in a bathtub.

"You're expanding into soap commercials? Is that why you hired Victor?"

Becca laughed. "I'd never exploit them like that." She slid the image aside to show a closer shot of the girls. One reached for the photographer.

Michelle was dizzy with confusion. "Yours?"

Becca nodded. "Remember when I was trying in vitro?"

"Vaguely."

"Maybe because I gave up after two rounds. I was so moody from the hormone therapy—let alone broke—that it was starting to affect my work. Then, when I was wrapping a job in Guatemala, opportunity knocked." Becca rubbed her finger against their sweet faces.

"What are their names?"

"That's the thing," Becca said, sitting back. "The one biting her rubber duck is Milly."

"For your mom?"

Becca nodded. "She'd have been a wonderful granny."

Michelle pointed at the one with the bubble beard. "Who's this?"

Becca hesitated. "She goes by Chellie. Short for...Michelle."

Michelle burst into tears.

"I'm sorry I didn't tell you. I started to, in the hospital, but you were so messed up. What was I going to say: I named my baby after you because I didn't think you'd make it? Oh, Chelle, I missed you before you were even gone."

Michelle wiped her eyes and took a deep breath. "I don't know what to say." She spotted Victor speaking quietly to the actress playing Nikki. She was in full makeup now, a slutty Goth. Becca was an opportunist, but Michelle had created the opportunity. She should never have brought Nikki to the set.

"Why did you come, Michelle? Sounded to me like you need some money."

Michelle bit her lip.

Becca stood up and smoothed her leather pants back into her boots. Then she waved Fletch over. "How much cash do we have?"

"We haven't paid the caterer yet, or the stage, so...a little over eight thousand dollars." Becca held her hand out for the whole envelope. Fletch glanced back at Victor before offering a petty cash receipt and a pen to Michelle. "Can you make an X?"

"I can make more than an X, but I'm not signing a thing."

"I am," Becca said, grabbing the slip from Fletch. She signed it, then took the envelope and waved Fletch away. She put the money in Michelle's palm and let her hand linger. "I hope you do find Nikki. You deserve a happy ending."

She stepped down from the chair, then looked over to the set where the crew awaited direction for the next setup. She nodded at Victor.

"Thank you, people, that's a wrap!" he called.

The crew members looked around, then began breaking down the equipment. The stage went dark. The camera was shuttered, cables were coiled, and wardrobe was packed. "Don't forget your time cards," Fletch called. "We'll be in touch."

Michelle put her hand on the armrest to stand up. "After the rewrite?"

Becca helped her. "After the trial."

23

Four days later, Michelle was studying the postcards filling the wire stand by the Maui Charter Center desk. Similar shots graced every kiosk in Maalaea Harbor and she wasn't sure which one she'd seen in Dr. Braunstein's drawer. She was only sure of the words: *We chased our pleasures here, dug our treasures there…But can you still recall, the time we cried…* Was Nikki having fun here when she wrote that? Or thinking of the funeral where she had last seen Noah's mother? Michelle spun the rack so hard it wobbled. Nikki was here, or had been, but where?

Michelle scanned the boat slips, bustling with weekend activity. Suntanned crews were washing down fiberglass boat decks, rigging colorful sails, and fueling engines for today's excursions. She wished Tyler was here with her, enjoying the soft tropical air. But he was already in school back east, where the spring pollen was brutal.

Alone, Michelle was all business. Since Nikki's savings account was empty, surely she needed a job. When she showed Nikki's picture at personnel offices, Michelle learned that none of the hotels hired underage staff. So here she was, wearing an itchy straw hat and a long-sleeved cover-up, continuing her search outside.

Michelle joined the sleepy tourists clustered around the sales desk. She'd refused to waste time buying coffee, but now she salivated at the aroma of the Kona blend rising from their cups. A bell clanged and the crowd splintered into groups rushing toward the docks. Michelle turned to see the jumble of excited families on the boardwalk choosing between charters. Pale honeymooners strolled hand in hand to the sparkling white catamaran in the center berth. Michelle envisioned Nikki as one of the clean-cut tour guides in preppy shirts who welcomed the couple on board.

A jovial Hawaiian man waved a free postcard of the Maui sunset to Michelle from behind the desk. "Aloha, pretty lady! How can we make your holiday more enjoyable? Whale watching? Sunset cruise?"

She took the postcard to practice her signature for Wes and noted the tour manager's nametag. "Those do sound appealing, Reuben. I'll take whichever my daughter chooses, as soon as I find the boat she's crewing. I forgot the name—probably a snorkel cruise with a stop at Turtle Town."

Reuben reached stiffly for his thermos cup of coffee. "We have eight snorkel excursions in Maalaea Harbor."

"If I give you her social security number, can you look up her payroll and steer me in the right direction? I know that's bad to do, but—her name is Nicole Mason." Michelle flashed her sweetest smile.

He shook his head. "There's no one named Mason working for us." He beckoned the family in matching Hawaiian shirts behind Michelle. "Aloha!"

Michelle realized her mistake. "Excuse me, could you please try Deveraux?"

He dropped the smile. "Like I told your *Haole* friend, that *wahine* not here."

Michelle dropped the act, too. *Wahine* meant "woman" and *Haole* meant "someone from the mainland," but *friend*? That didn't translate. A chill rose up her spine.

"*Pau*—all set?" When Michelle didn't answer, Reuben welcomed a group of men in golf shirts. "Aloha! How can I make your holiday more enjoyable?"

A camera flashed. Michelle clutched the counter with her good hand and snuck a look behind her. She relaxed at the sight of tourists snapping pictures in every direction. The paparazzi hadn't followed her, but someone else had. Michelle felt someone's eyes on her and turned to see a pasty man in dark shades and a creased Maui Hilton T-shirt turn to a map of the islands posted on the parking lot fence. Michelle turned away and perused the postcards again. She picked one up, but her hand shook too much to hold it.

She ducked a few inches, leaning against the side counter to get her phone from the drawstring bag. "Husband," she commanded. The phone dialed and Drew picked up. Michelle panicked and clicked it shut. He'd ordered her not to be here. As if he could do that.

When the phone rang back, she snapped it open and rushed to explain. "I don't care if you're angry, Drew. I'm not the only one in Hawaii looking for Nikki. If money is the problem, get over it, because I got a loan from Becca, who, as it turns out, is working on a movie about Roadhouse. And don't be mad at Becca, because you know someone is bound to make this movie and I'd rather it be a friend, and she shut down production anyway, which means that Victor's audio engineer is out of work, so he's available to replace you in New York and you can meet me here in Maui." There was quiet on the other end as she caught her breath. "Okay?"

"Not okay," the man said. "This is your lawyer. Remember me? The one who advised you to stay home?"

Michelle swore to herself. "Hello, Kenny."

"Michelle, this case was hard enough without you sabotaging it. I was calling about Tyler's letter jacket. I found it in the truck.

If I didn't have so much time invested in this case already, I'd quit right now."

"I'm sorry, Kenny. I'll send you some money."

"From the producer of a movie that will be influenced by the case? Not a good idea."

Michelle spotted the man in the windbreaker a few slips away. The advantage of being tall was that she could spot him easily. The disadvantage was that he could spot her as well. "Kenny, I think someone's following me. Tell me I'm being paranoid."

"Paranoia is just a heightened state of awareness, Michelle. Any number of people could be following you. My bet is on the car company. They want to find your daughter as much as you do."

"That's not possible."

"Maybe not, but they'll pay more. They think her testimony about seeing the recall notice will absolve them of potential liability. I thought I'd explained this to you."

"I was a little foggy."

"But not too foggy to fly off to Hawaii?" Kenny covered the receiver and spoke to someone in his office far across the Pacific Ocean. She scanned the tourists until his voice returned. "Hang on, Michelle, that's Drew on the other line." He clicked off.

So did Michelle. She turned the ringer off her phone and buried it in her purse. For a moment, she wondered if she should work with the person following her, doubling their chances of finding Nikki. No, she decided, they might pull some legal shenanigans to keep them apart. She had to find Nikki first, even if it meant riding every boat in the harbor. She ran back to the Maui activity hut.

Reuben fanned several brochures. "What kind of boat for the pretty lady?"

"You pick," Michelle said. She looked behind her. The pasty man was gone.

Reuben tapped each brochure. "Tradewinds II is most popular. Five hours, pupu, mai tai, and BBQ. I offer special, one hundred twenty-five dollars, today only."

Michelle couldn't waste the day on one boat. She needed to check out all the crews. "Anything shorter?" She balanced herself against the counter to flip the brochure open. Her sleeve fell, exposing her forearm.

Reuben dropped the sales ploy. "My brah has an arm like that, from a sugar cane thresher."

"Nothing so exciting for me, I'm afraid. Car accident. That's why I'm a little fuzzy about which boat my daughter is working on. I've been in the hospital awhile. She's young, not an experienced sailor."

Reuben leaned close and lowered his voice. "There's one captain hires kids, pays cash." He pointed to a weathered gray fishing boat casting off from the dock at the far curve of the small harbor. "They snorkel at Molokini Crater, then make a quick stop for turtles. Maybe try that, yah? Only fifty bucks. All the poi rice you can eat. But you better hurry."

Michelle gave him three twenties and didn't wait for the change. What was an extra ten bucks in the scheme of things? She would pay anything to see her daughter's smile. Her flip-flops slapped against the wooden boardwalk as she hurried around the small harbor toward the last slip.

A red bandana waved at the end of the dock, where young families heeded the last call for the *Jolly Roger*. Despite the dented hull of the tour boat, the ragtag crew collecting tickets on the entry ramp was enthusiastic. They lacked proper deck shoes and pristine haircuts, but were easily identified by matching skull and bone T-shirts in assorted fades of black. Michelle slowed to study their faces.

"Ahoy there!" shouted a gravelly voice from above. High-pitched squeals were deafening as children spotted the spindly old man with an eye patch leaning over the crow's nest with a parrot on his shoulder. "Ahoy there," the parrot squawked as parents shoved past Michelle to secure spots at the railing.

A pretty Hawaiian girl passed out soiled orange life jackets. Michelle pushed up her gift shop sunglasses and peered into the portholes at the rest of the pirate crew setting up below. Once the first mate cast off, she would interrogate them one by one.

By the time the hotels lining the Kaanapali coast disappeared in the morning mist, Michelle was quelling her nausea with a macadamia nut muffin. Vomiting wouldn't endear her to anyone, so she was stuck outside on the deck until she could stand up between swells. The hearty couple sitting next to her clutched their coffees and pointed at the Hawaiian girl balancing the breakfast tray. They grinned at each other as their brood rushed to the rail where the girl flung crumbs to shrieking gulls. Michelle smiled at their matching yellow shirts. She and her kids had worn matching flowered prints when they were last here. Drew declined, but she didn't care how dorky they looked, they would never get lost. If only Nikki was wearing hers now.

When the seagulls flapped their wings and flew off in formation, the Hawaiian girl led the children back to the bench like baby ducklings. Michelle found the photo she had cropped of Nikki in her birthday crown and stood up. "Miss? Or should I say, Matey?"

The Hawaiian girl looked up. "Leilani. Can I help you?"

The boat lurched. Michelle grabbed the nearest pole and dropped the picture. She crouched to rescue it from water as dingy as Leilani's sneakers. Then she noticed a spot of color peeking through the grime. It was purple, dotted with tiny black skulls—like the Converse high tops Michelle had given Nikki for her birthday. Michelle hated the skulls, but Nikki had insisted. Michelle said a silent prayer and peered around Leilani's heel, but whatever name had been embroidered there had been blacked out. "Yes. You can tell me where you got these shoes."

"Lost and found," Leilani said, reaching to help Michelle up.

"When?" Michelle tried to keep the excitement out of her voice.

"Long time ago."

Michelle held up the sodden picture. "Ever seen this girl?"

Leilani's eyes glazed over like sea glass. "No. Is she in trouble?"

The music stopped and a voice called out on the tinny speakers. "Ahoy, me hearties! Time for snorkel orientation below deck. All landlubbers walk the plank!"

"No trouble," Michelle said, not sure what to reveal. A real friend would help a teenager hide, even from her mother. Especially from her mother.

Kimo, the buff first mate, approached, waving the crowd inside with his bullhorn. "Let's go!" He raked his blond locks and ripped off his shirt, like a Coppertone ad. There was something sad about the softening belly at the base of his V-shaped build, the tan line at the top of his board shorts, and the barest hint of ganja trailing him on the salty breeze.

"I'm not snorkeling," Michelle said.

"Bar's open," Kimo replied, pulling a tube of Chapstick from his pocket. Several tweens circled him like a sweet-smelling lei.

Michelle held her breath from the girls' cheap perfume as they asked for the loo. When Kimo corrected them and called it the "head," they giggled at the hint of sexual innuendo. Michelle watched them skip off. Tonight they would go to Cheeseburger in Paradise and sit at a picnic table on the top deck, giggling about this over milkshakes and fries. Nikki was never so silly. If only she had been, then maybe she'd have been on this boat for fun instead of food money.

Kimo waved them off then turned back to Michelle. "Piña colada?"

"Sold," Michelle said. She followed him down to the bar.

Halfway through her watery drink, Michelle heard her daughter's voice. At first she thought she was imagining it, or that she was already drunk, but no. That was Nikki. She dropped the plastic glass. She craned her neck over the sunhats and rose, oblivious to the complaints of tourists wiping sticky liquid from their shins. Michelle pushed through the crowd. Then she saw her, larger than life, an image of light projected on the fiberglass wall.

This suntanned young woman in the pirate hat was nothing like the gawky girl wearing disco earrings and a birthday crown, nor the blushing teenager in love. This was a stranger. Her cheeks were full and her eyes sparkled. She belonged more to the crowd of tourists than to Michelle.

And yet, none of them understood the irony of Nikki's beaded blond braids. They didn't recognize defiance in the way she tied her T-shirt above her black sarong. Nor could they translate the pierced navel into a message as clear as Morse code. Nikki had once prided herself on being intact, natural—she refused to pierce her ears. But at some point, she had severed the umbilical bond. Now, Michelle worried they might never be whole again.

"Pay now," Nikki was saying, "to appreciate the next two hours for the rest of your life." When she waved a henna-painted hand, Michelle caught her breath until her throat was so constricted that barely a speck of air flowed through. She swallowed hard and moved closer, one painful step at a time, until she was only inches away. She reached to touch her daughter's face. A hideous pain shot up her right arm. She bent over and cradled it tightly with her left hand, ignoring the crowd of witnesses who surely thought that she was crazy. But Michelle wasn't crazy for reaching out. She'd be crazy to ignore the heart heaving against her rib cage.

Nikki coughed on camera, then flashed her straight white teeth in a smile before resuming her speech. She knew she was being watched, but did she know that she'd been watched every day, twice a day, since she stood before the camera? The women longed for her freedom; the men lusted after her form. But only Michelle would love her long after they snorkeled and took their souvenirs home.

On-screen, Nikki flipped on a monitor and the darkness filled with dazzling fish. Giant turtles soon appeared on the wall like images of prehistoric ghosts floating past. The image popped, then a snorkeler swam into the frame. He waved until another snorkeler kicked into the picture, then a smaller figure paddled after them, like a family of seals. The camera froze on their facemasks. Letters typed in: *The Smith Family Vacation.* The screen went black.

Families rushed to the counter. Young couples stopped kissing to count their cash. Michelle stood like an island as they streamed around her. When a reggae beat flooded the air, Michelle began to move, but her steps were more frantic than festive.

Leilani pushed her mirrored glasses up, a shield against her gaze.

Kimo's voice boomed on the bullhorn. "Ahoy there! Once you've paid Leilani, help yourself to fins and masks. Anyone interested in a wet suit, follow me."

Michelle gave up on fighting the crowd and followed him to the storage locker on the aft deck. He flipped through the worn wetsuits hanging behind him. "Floatation belts are optional, but you'll want one."

"Just tell me about Nikki."

"Who?" He turned around, the small rubber suit in his hands.

"The girl in the video."

"Never met her," he said. "That recording is older than the turtles. Doing the new one myself, almost *pau*. Hi-def, 3-D—it'll be solid."

Beer-reeking boys with flippers tucked under their arms interrupted to rent wetsuits. Kimo set the small suit on the bench beside him, then pocketed the brothers' cash and pointed to the extra large suits. "Have fun, but stay off the reef or you'll get a ticket from the Coast Guard. And don't touch the fish! Seriously, brah, those scales are razor sharp. We'll have to sew you up with sailcloth thread."

Michelle waited until she had his attention. "Is the captain the owner? Would he remember her?"

Kimo looked up at the skinny old man who was steering them across the open sea. "Don't bother. I've been here since last summer and the dude has no idea what my name is. First mate is always Kimo. Photographer is always Leilani." He waved behind her at the next in line.

Michelle turned and peered back to the shaded area inside the cabin. There were still a few people surrounding Leilani. One of them looked like the pasty man outside the activity booth. Had he followed her? Michelle's legs felt wobbly.

She leaned against the bulkhead and took a deep breath, permeated by the scent of ganja. Snorkeling wasn't a bad idea if it would free her from being followed. She turned back to Kimo, and pulled a fifty dollar bill from her bag. "Keep the change. I hear weed is pricey these days."

"You a cop?"

"Just a mom," she said, tugging at her cover-up. Her rash of scars was exposed by her black tank suit.

"Fifty gets you personal service," Kimo said, stuffing the cash in the tip jar. When he opened the closet of wetsuits for the others, she saw the scar across his back. He caught her looking. "Hockey," he said. He helped her step into each leg of the wetsuit then pulled it up high to ease each arm in. He kept the back zipper open and showed her how to reach the pull tab. "My mom's freezing her ass back in Wisconsin, dusting my trophies. I keep asking her to visit."

"At least you talk to her. My daughter doesn't know I'm alive."

Kimo laughed, then saw that it wasn't a joke. "Talara—that's Leilani's real name—she might have gotten those shoes from a roommate."

Michelle gave Kimo a one-armed hug. "Thanks. I grew up in Buckeye country, so I know how important sports can be. But you're a good kid."

"Tell my mom," he called, as others surrounded him for help.

Michelle headed back where she had last seen Nikki. The wall was white and shiny, like a dream. Nikki had looked so confident in the snorkel video—so different from the scrawny girl she had reported to Detective Alvarez. Thank heaven for all that poi, Michelle thought. She wondered if she should call the detective—or whoever had taken over the case. Then she remembered there wasn't a case. It was up to her.

Perhaps Leilani would know what Nikki looked like now, but there was no sign of her amid the tourists milling about the boat. Michelle sat by the rail to wait.

A disposable camera dangled in front of her face as the young family beside her slathered on lotion. "Would you like me to take your picture?" she asked.

The young father grinned as if his crappy camera was too complicated for Michelle to handle. Then he displayed the ticket Leilani had given them. No offense, but here was proof they'd have plenty of pictures, moving pictures, the ultimate souvenir to show their friends. They were starring in a movie of Hawaii!

The young mother wearing a Hilo Hattie muumuu pointed at Michelle's zipper. "Would ya'll like some help?"

Michelle shook her head. In a world of helpers and helpless, she'd crossed the wrong line. When the woman finished rubbing lotion on the boy's face, he clambered up to the wooden bench. Michelle saw the Velcro closure on his red sneakers and chuckled. She missed those days of dressing her children. She'd dressed Tyler in sporty clothes, and he'd become a jock. She'd dressed Nikki in pink, and she'd become a pirate wench. Go figure.

Michelle clutched the rail and savored the last quiet moment of ocean mist. The sun burnt a hole in the clouds and the sky was a ceiling rising up and up and up. The day expanded on all sides, sharply real, as Michelle looked around. The surface of the deep green water lightened to a cool algae glow, then faded to a crystal sheen where the sunlight skimmed across.

The bench bounced when the boy started jumping and pointing at the yawning green patch ahead. Soon, the far side of the crater came into view with a ridge of scrubby trees clinging to steep rock. The horn wailed, the engine coughed, and gas fumes filled the air.

The deck soon resembled a country bar with couples dancing a rubber two-step. Families applied sunblock and adjusted masks as they prepared to snorkel. The young mother turned to chat. Michelle knew the kind of small talk to expect: children's names and ages and activities. She used to love to compare notes. But what would she say now that her daughter was a runaway and her son had followed his father? Michelle stepped away and pulled the leash from behind her neck. The zipper sealed up her sleek neoprene skin. No room for sympathy.

She looked out at the water, where yellow snorkel tubes sprouted like daffodils as the first group kicked past. A moment later, a flurry of violet fish flashed beneath the surface, then turned and swished from sight.

Michelle wandered back toward the empty cabin, taking deep breaths to stop herself from hyperventilating. A scuffling noise made her look around the counter. Leilani was kneeling in a bikini, with a wetsuit zipped up to her waist. She set a cigar box inside the cabinet, then lifted out the camera equipment.

"I know she lived with you," Michelle said. "Tell me where she is."

Leilani lifted the camera package up and set it on the table, avoiding Michelle's eyes. "Not me, my sister."

"She knew Nikki?"

Leilani slipped her arms into the sleeves of the wetsuit and zipped it over her bikini top. A fluorescent stripe rose up from each side. There was a hole in one armpit. She picked up the camera, and adjusted the shoulder harness.

Michelle blocked her way. "I'll give you fifty dollars to tell me how to find your sister."

"Forget it, I'm no snitch."

Michelle chased her to the edge of the cabin. "Hundred bucks," she said. "Tell her if she ever hears from Nikki, to please let her know—" she felt her throat closing up. This girl couldn't possibly express how much Michelle missed her daughter, how she had a hole in her heart that burned larger every day. Leilani shifted the camera and held out her hand. Michelle dug in the bag for her emergency cash. "Just tell her to be careful. I'm not the only one looking for her."

Leilani snatched the money and stuffed it in her fanny pack. "Okay. But if she's fencing drugs again my sister's no part of it."

"Excuse me?" Michelle said. This had a familiar ring.

"Word is, Cap'n found her stash in the camera hold. She split and stuck my sister with the rent." The boat horn wailed. "Believe me, if my sister could find her, she'd have gotten her money." She heaved the camera to her shoulder.

"Wait—if that's true about the drugs, then why didn't your boss call the police?"

"Cap'n keeps things on the down low. Plus, that girl had *da kine* eye. Cap'n says my underwater shots will go online soon, but I'm not holding my breath." She headed off.

The words echoed in the empty cabin. *Da kine* meant good. Nikki had a good eye? That meant she was good with the camera. But if that was true, then so was the part about selling drugs.

Marijuana was medically legal in California, probably Hawaii too, if Kimo could reek like that and still have a job. Michelle tried not to think of Colleen's son with his suburban heroin addiction. Nikki hated needles so much that it took three nurses to hold her down for her measles vaccine. Michelle couldn't imagine her shooting up. Then again, she couldn't imagine Nikki doing a lot of things that she'd apparently done. Were drugs the reason she couldn't come home?

Michelle wandered through a tunnel of confusion into the sunlight. Back when she was a rebellious teenager, her therapist had said that getting high was an escape, a distraction from counting Elyse's sleeping pills and checking that she was breathing. Michelle didn't let herself off that easily; she had been lucky nothing bad happened. And apparently, she'd lost enough brain cells to believe she could make her children happy. Now it seemed she was no better of a mother than Elyse had been.

A cold sensation startled Michelle awake. She saw bits of pink floating before her eyes and recognized her own polished toes, dangling in the dark water. She smelled coconut oil and ganja.

"All set?" Kimo asked, kneeling beside her at the ladder to

buckle a banana float around her waist. The parrot squawked. Michelle glanced up to see the captain surveying his domain. He reminded her of Dean Valentine. Maybe Nikki was selling pills. Michelle pushed the thought away and pulled her flipper on like a prophylactic. Kimo turned to calm a man who had slept through the snorkel video.

"No worries," Kimo said, taking a bite of a muffin. "You can still order online. Leilani takes pictures of everyone, just in case." He turned back to help Michelle with the other flipper.

"How can she take pictures of everyone?" Michelle asked.

"Everyone looks the same in a snorkel mask, yah?" He winked as he stuffed the rest of the muffin in the sleeve of her bad arm. "You want a good picture? Toss this in the water when Leilani comes close." As more snorkelers crowded the ladder, Kimo pushed her in.

The Pacific was clammy, so Michelle peed to warm up. Other snorkelers were a kazoo hum of voices beneath the surface, with the occasional toot as they converged on each glorious anchovy. Michelle kicked slowly over the mile-wide crater of igneous rock. A draft of warm water reminded Michelle of the lava vents below. She wondered whether this volcano was dormant or dead, how close she was to hell.

Above the surface, someone cranked the stereo until the tinkling ukulele tune gave way to Jimmy Buffet. Floating on her back, she could see Kimo's brawny arm pointing at another pirate to prep the galley for lunch. A loud splash interrupted the chorus of "Margaritaville." When Leilani floated her camera around from the other side of the boat, a dozen pairs of flippers turned and kicked like a school of barracudas. Those treading water adjusted their masks.

Leilani dove down deep to begin photographing the snorkelers. The white stripes glowing from the sides of her uniform wetsuit made her easy to track. The light attached to her camera shined a deep dusty path, like a searchlight exploring the *Titanic*. Twenty yards away, at the crusty lip of the crater, Leilani waved for paying customers to paddle by. Bubbles escaping from her ventilator rose directly above the red beam of the Record light.

Michelle kicked in circles above the others until her gums were sore from biting the mouthpiece. Far below, between the rocks, a long gray shadow rippled in the sand. Michelle didn't care if it was a shark or an eel or an octopus. She dove under, to the end of the picture parade. She was determined to make this special, not only to get it on the website, but also enough for Nikki to notice. Didn't all artists look in on their work? Michelle liked thinking of Nikki as an artist. It was so much nicer than thinking of her as a drug dealer.

Michelle kicked to stay upright and ripped off her mask. Then she pulled the sodden muffin from her right sleeve. An angelfish flitted across the expanse, then a flurry of fish surrounded her in a cloud of silver scales. A bright light glowed. Michelle held her clenched hand up like the Statue of Liberty with her torch. She kept kicking and opened her eyes. The strobe light flashed.

All was golden.

After a moment, Leilani kicked a cloud of bubbles between them. Michelle unclenched her hand. The fish turned and swished past, slicing the flesh of her wrist. Wisps of blood trailed as she swam up to the surface.

She floated in the amniotic sea, drifting over the depths. The sound of her breath eased until it matched the rhythm of her chest:

up and down and easy. She felt Nikki's presence, lurking like the fish so many fathoms below.

When the whistle blew, a snorkeler burst through the surface nearby. Another joined him and paddled past. Michelle flipped over and treaded water long enough to catch her breath. She heard music playing and smelled burgers grilling, as if it were just another day in paradise. She took one more look around, then kicked slowly toward the boat, her salty tears mixing with the sting of seawater.

Michelle didn't care what Nikki had done. She would do anything to let her daughter know she was here, that she would always be here, that she would never stop looking.

24

THE AIRPORT SHUTTLE DRIVER shouted Michelle's name as they jostled over the speed bumps on her street. The red-eye flight from Hawaii had been just as rough, so she hadn't slept much. The morning sun was so harsh that the houses looked like paper cutouts, with colors just as flat. They reminded Michelle of a movie she'd worked on when they shot "night for day." The location was only available after dark, so they blasted it with arc lights to make it look as if the sun were shining. Michelle peered out of the van window at her own house with the same sense of unreality.

"Is this it?" the driver asked, as he pulled to the curb. The new grass was lush and the flowerbeds were lined with pink impatiens, as if Victor's set decorator had been there. It looked so picture perfect that Michelle imagined walking up the cobblestone path, opening the freshly painted door, and finding nothing but sawdust behind it. When she realized that the old picket fence had been replaced with a perfect border of lacey white alyssum, she regretted her doubts about Drew.

Then she saw the For Sale sign.

Michelle shook her head to wake up. She knew she wasn't dreaming from the way her skin itched, from her sunburned shoulders down to the bandage wrapping her badly cut wrist. She rose stiffly after the long shuttle ride and lugged her carry-on down the stairs. Then she noticed that the porch mailbox had been scrubbed clean—not only of cobwebs, but also of the gold letters that spelled out *Mason*. A thick realtor's padlock hung from the door handle.

The other remaining shuttle passengers stared out the window at the realtor's sign; their questions filled the air. "How much are you asking?" called one. "How's the market?" asked another. "When are you moving?"

Michelle dug out her phone and pressed the On button, but it didn't light up. She pressed it again. Nothing. She moaned. "You okay, lady?" the driver called out.

"Jet lag," she said. The driver pulled the crank and the door squeaked shut. Michelle turned and watched the van drive out of sight. Then she left her suitcase and ran across the street down to Julie's house. She rushed past the BMW in the driveway and pounded on the door until her arm hurt. Then she kicked it. "Julie!"

Just as Michelle was about to give up, the door opened a few inches. Julie peeked out and took one look at Michelle's face. "Oh my god. You didn't know?"

"How could I know?" Michelle exclaimed. "My husband never answers the phone!" Then she remembered that she had turned her ringer off to avoid him. "Can I borrow your phone? I think my battery is dead."

Julie tied her silk bathrobe and ushered Michelle inside, where Sade's sultry voice wafted from the stereo. Michelle put her phone down on the whitewashed front table. "Can you believe this? All that landscaping was for curb appeal."

"Honey?" a man's voice called.

"Be right there!" Julie called, looking around for her purse. Michelle took it all in now: the seduction music on the stereo,

Julie's tapered nails tying the sash of her silken robe, the mascara smeared beneath her blowsy eyes. "I'm sorry, I didn't know you had company. Wait, isn't it ten o'clock in the morning here?"

Julie whispered. "Exactly. The kids are in school—it's perfect." She hurried down the hall to the bedroom door and opened it. Michelle heard a man's murmur. Then Julie reappeared with her cell phone in hand.

Michelle took the phone and stared at it. "I'm blanking on Drew's number."

Julie took the phone. "I have it for emergencies." She found it, clicked Send, and handed the phone back. "Want coffee? Let me get rid of my…"

"Friend?" Michelle asked. "Coffee would be great, but I don't want to intrude." Michelle waited for the call to go through. She prayed for a live voice to answer, then, miracle of miracles, one did.

"Hello?" The music couldn't hide the high pitch of a woman.

Michelle pressed the phone to her chest, as if to stall a heart attack. She looked at Julie as she returned. "A woman answered!"

Julie cringed.

Michelle put the phone back up to her ear. "Good morning," she said in a voice so sharp it cut through any pleasantry. There was a scuffling on the other end, then she heard Drew swearing. "Drew? Who was that? And what the—"

"Calm down, honey," Drew said.

Michelle stepped outside, away from the stereo. "Calm down? There's a For Sale sign in my yard! Who was that bimbo answering your phone? The realtor?" She marched past the BMW in the driveway, down the shady sidewalk and across the street, where she was momentarily blinded by the sun's glare. A car horn honked, then tires squealed around her on the asphalt. A jogger stopped on the sidewalk. Michelle was too intent to notice.

"The sign isn't supposed to be up yet. I tried to reach you yesterday to talk about it."

"About what, exactly? The house or the bimbo?"

"She's not a—you, of all people, used to bitch about how more women should get hired for production jobs. I finally hire a woman and—would you rather get my voice mail? She was doing me a favor. We've got enough problems as it is, Michelle; let's not start making up new ones."

"Fine," Michelle said, walking up the path through the front yard. "Let's start with the house. How can you sell it without my approval? Is that even legal?"

"Yes. I still have your power of attorney. And if you insist on staying in LA after the trial, we'll get you a smaller place."

"You're missing the point. How can Nikki come home if there's no home to come to?"

"She's not coming home," Drew said. "Stop talking crazy."

"Crazy? You have me mixed up with my mother." She was about to tell him that she'd found Nikki, then she realized she hadn't. She'd found a cold trail, littered with trouble. She took a breath and changed the subject.

"How is Tyler doing with midterms?"

"Not as well as he should be," Drew said. "He'll call you after basketball practice. The key to the lockbox is under the mat. I need you to find the home improvement records. The real estate agent needs to know when we put in the copper plumbing before the open house. And get some rest, will you?"

Michelle hung up. She dragged her rolling bag up to the door, then stooped to lift up the new welcome mat. Welcome, indeed. She was still struggling with the lockbox when Julie arrived with a steaming UCLA mug. A voice trilled from the pocket of her warm-up jacket. "*Bonjour.*"

Julie pulled Michelle's phone out. "Your battery was locked."

"Michelle, is that you?" Elyse's voice called out from the speakerphone. Julie clicked the speaker off and gave her the phone before opening the door.

"Yes, Mother, it's me." Michelle walked inside and looked through the French doors. Sure enough, the backyard had been beautified as well, with fresh sod and flowering bougainvillea climbing every fence.

"*Comment tu vas?*" Elyse asked on the phone.

"*Ça vas mal,* Mother. Drew put the house up for sale. Not only that, but when I called him, a woman answered!"

Elyse sighed. "*Je tel l'ai dit.*"

Michelle hung up and glared at the phone. She should have known not to confide in her mother.

Julie rolled Michelle's suitcase inside. "What did she say?"

"She said 'I told you so.' In French."

"About Drew, you mean?" She handed Michelle the coffee. "That's her own history talking. I know things weren't all rosy between you before the accident—we'd shared enough Chardonnay to be honest. But Drew's not the kind of guy who sleeps around."

"How do you know?" Michelle looked at her friend, with her makeup smeared, her honey-colored hair a mess, and her obvious lack of a brassiere.

Julie zipped her warm-up jacket higher. "I married that kind. Don't give up on your marriage. Divorce sucks."

Michelle pointed at the bruise on Julie's neck. "I can see that. Tyler had a hickey like that before he left for New York. Are you reliving your teenage years?"

"Me? I spent prom night at a Jane Austen convention," Julie said. She pushed Michelle's hand away, noting the bandage. "You didn't try anything stupid, did you?"

"I didn't slit my wrist, if that's what you mean." She looked at the wall of shelves, full of books and photo albums and audiotape boxes. She spotted the row of files and figured she might as well find the records Drew wanted and be done with it. She set her coffee on the shelf and pulled out a file of old tax receipts. She couldn't stuff it back into the narrow space, so she pulled it all the way out. Since there was no longer a couch nearby or even a coffee table, she simply dropped it to the floor. She pulled out another file, far enough to read the word *Furniture*, then dropped that one too.

Concerned, Julie took the coffee over to the dining room table. "What are you looking for? Can I help?"

"No, I've got it," Michelle said. Then she pulled out the next one and the next one and the next one, flinging them behind her until papers wafted through the air like giant snowflakes.

Julie watched, horrified.

Michelle turned and saw the mounds of tax forms and receipts and warranties. Her laugh was pinched. "On the bright side, I could leave it this way for the open house."

Julie tried to pick up a few papers and gave up. "I think you'd better cancel the open house. Maybe you should sit down. Can I get you something?"

Michelle's heart felt like it was going to escape from her chest. She clutched it and began to hyperventilate. She sunk to the floor.

Julie put her hand on Michelle's shoulder. "Breathe, okay? I think you're having a panic attack. I'm going to call Lexi. Do you have her number?"

Michelle nodded and pointed at her phone that had landed on the far side of the pile. Julie tiptoed between shiny strips of plastic running like worms across the mess, and looked up with a puzzled expression.

"Go ahead and step on it," Michelle said. "It's just old audiotape."

"Okay. Stay there and try to relax." Julie took the phone to the kitchen to make the call.

Michelle pulled a ribbon of audiotape from the spool that had fallen from a flat box labeled Cricketsong. She wondered if Drew needed this collection, whether she should rewind the tape and put the reels away. Michelle was afraid to call him to ask. If a woman answered, even a work associate, Michelle would feel like an idiot. It was sad how far they had drifted apart. He used to rig microphones under the eaves of the back porch to record the loud calling sounds, followed by quiet courting sounds of wings rubbing together. On warm nights, they would sit outside and share a bottle of wine until the concert began. Those days were but a distant memory now. She tossed the spool on the pile.

Julie returned and took the UCLA coffee cup.

"Hey!" Michelle said.

"Lexi said no coffee. She's busy today but wants to meet you in the morning. You can have coffee then. Right now, she suggested that you switch to water and get some sleep." She helped Michelle up.

"Fine, but it would be nice to make a little headway here. A lot of this is trash."

"I can help for a bit." She studied Michelle with concern. "You look a little better. Or that could be the suntan."

Michelle shrugged. "Did I mention that a man was following me in Maui?"

"No, but I'm not surprised. Were you wearing a bikini?"

Michelle couldn't help but laugh. "Thanks. You're a good friend."

"Seriously, if a pro was following you, he wouldn't have let you see him, right? Did you tell Drew about being followed?"

"No, he already wants me to stay with my mother. For a guy who wants to sell the house right out from under me, he's a bit overprotective."

"Maybe you do need protection."

Michelle felt a wave of jet lag as she surveyed the mess. "What I need is a shower."

Under the streaming hot water, Michelle relaxed. She grabbed the support bar and leaned against the tile. She closed her eyes. For a moment, she let it all wash over her as if she were back in her liquid coma dreams. That was tempting, a bit too tempting. She could fall asleep standing up if she wasn't careful. She cranked the spigot to cold.

When Michelle stepped out of the shower, the cuts on her wrist resembled a bright pink bracelet of broken skin. She pinned her towel with an elbow and yanked open a drawer in search of ointment. The whole drawer came out and crashed to the floor. It was empty, except for toothpaste and sunblock. She picked up the drawer, but couldn't quite fit it back into the opening with one hand, so she swung it up to the counter. A scrap of tin foil flashed from the corner joint. Michelle felt a wave of déjà vu as she stood there dripping wet, just as she had on another day, the day she first found that folded square of foil, like the kind that held cocaine.

Michelle shook the foil in Nikki's face. "Why do you have this?"

"It's pretty. Can I go now? I have homework."

Michelle wanted to believe her daughter, but Nikki had already lied about her algebra grade and her eyes were bloodshot. Maybe she was just tired, like Michelle. Tyler's game had gone an extra inning and there were pork chops to bake. Michelle's head pounded, so she reached for the Tylenol in the cabinet. "Go ahead."

Nikki knocked the bottle from her hand. Red and white capsules danced on the bathroom floor. "You're such a hypocrite."

"Nikki!" Michelle crouched down to pick up the pills.

Instead of helping, Nikki sniffed back tears and unzipped her father's toiletry kit on the counter. She pulled out two pill bottles and shook them like maracas. The thick white tablets were Vicodin, for pain in vertebra L5, known as the tall man's Achilles. The small white circles in the other bottle were Ambien. Nikki slammed a bottle of blue capsules on the counter next to the others. The lid was loose, so several bounced into the sink. Nikki pulled more bottles out like rabbits from a top hat. Michelle recognized the Zoloft sample from the commercial that paid for Tyler's summer camp. There were red anti-inflammatories, too, and yellow pills she had never seen, from a doctor whose name she didn't recognize.

"Voila," Nikki said, waving her graceful hand like a magician's assistant.

But there was no magic; Michelle couldn't snap her fingers and make them disappear. It resembled an old-fashioned candy store, or her mother's medicine cabinet long ago. She picked up the spilled pills and swept them together in her hands. This was crazy—they weren't pill people. That Grace Slick song came to mind, "One pill makes you larger/And one pill makes you small."

Nikki held the open prescription bottle. "Don't mix up the dope, Mom."

"It's not dope," Michelle said, dropping the matching pills in the bottle.

"So why does Daddy call this his dope kit?"

"That's a military acronym for Department of Personal Effects," Michelle said. "It's just a toiletry case. This is medicine, prescribed by doctors."

"Oh, is Daddy sick?" She raised an eyebrow as Drew's voice could be heard cheering for the Dodgers game along with Tyler and his friends.

"You know he has a bad back. He's getting a shot next week so he can keep working."

"Like the baseball players? And Lance Armstrong? What's the big deal, anyway? If you can take medicine to do your job better, why not? Don't pilots take NoDoz? Why is it okay that some people are born bigger and stronger, and if your parents are remotely artistic, you'll suck at algebra?"

"Don't say suck.*" Michelle zipped the dope kit. "Is that Noah's philosophy?"*

"It's a lot of people's philosophy. Tyler has an asthma inhaler in his backpack, allergy medicine in the cupboard, and two kinds of cough syrup under the sink. And what about you, Mom? Coffee in the morning, tea in the afternoon, and wine at night. What's the difference?"

Michelle lowered her voice. "The difference is that some drugs make your life better and some make you miss it entirely. If your life is that bad, let's change it. I want you to be happy, Nikki. I want you to experience the kind of joy you get from nature: a spectacular sunset or a beautiful flower or—"

"A pretty piece of foil?" Nikki asked. "Are you happy, Mom? Is it working for you?" She pulled a pack of Juicy Fruit from her jeans pocket and set it on the counter. Michelle saw the matching foil and regretted every word.

Julie was calling through the bathroom door. "Michelle? I brought you the jeans in Nikki's closet, if that's okay. I don't see any casual clothes here, unless you have some in your suitcase."

Michelle opened the door to the adjoining bedroom and took them. "I haven't even told you about Hawaii. Someone said that Nikki was dealing drugs."

"Oh my god! She babysat for my kids!"

"It wasn't until she got to Hawaii, as far as I know," Michelle said. "And it might have been prescription drugs."

Julie nodded. "A lot of students sell ADHD meds for studying. Wait a minute, didn't you say that Noah's mother is a doctor?"

Michelle shivered. How had she forgotten? "An anesthesiologist."

"Then maybe Noah stole samples. Or a prescription pad."

"I hope not," Michelle said. She remembered Dr. Braunstein admitting that Noah volunteered with Tyler's baseball league for community service. He had gotten in a little trouble, she had said, like "boys do." Michelle had been so distracted by finding the turtle postcard that it hadn't sunk in. But what if it was drug-related?

The jeans were too low for Michelle's taste, but they did fit, except for the lump in the back pocket. Once she was dressed, she went back to the living room where Julie was separating some of the paper into piles.

"They look good," Julie said.

Michelle turned around. "Can you get the other tag out, please?"

Julie pulled out an origami football. "It's a note. Want me to open it?"

"No. It probably reads: 'I hate my mother.' Sometimes Nikki was so sweet; other times she said 'Mother' like a swear word."

"Aren't all teenagers like that?" Julie unfolded the paper and held it up so the fading writing was visible. "Uh-oh. This looks like the writing in the Venice Bistro matchbook. That knitting yarn we found it in was a big hit with my daughter's Girl Scout troop, by the way."

"Glad to hear it. Is this another 'Hello I love you?'"

"Not exactly," Julie said. She read aloud: "The time to hesitate is through…" Julie hummed until the whole room swirled with the music. "Can't read the rest. Something about a funeral, right? That's a little creepy."

"It's from 'Light My Fire.'" Michelle felt woozy, but not

from jet lag. She knew she had seen it before, but where? She struggled to remember. "I think I found that in the laundry." The memory flashed in her head—it was the same laundry basket her mother had used. "I didn't mean to spy, but it was right there in her dirty clothes. And it sounded like a plea for sex, so I went to Nikki's room when she was getting ready for bed and asked her about it. She turned on me, all red-cheeked and angry. She told me to not worry. Nothing had happened, except—Noah called her a baby."

"You're remembering a lot more lately. That's good."

Michelle nodded at Julie. "I don't remember her words exactly, I just remember this huge feeling of relief. Even though she was upset. I thought it meant she was still a virgin. She still had panties with turtles on them."

"You're lucky. My kid is nine and she's already swiped my lace booty shorts."

"Nikki wanted lace panties, too. This was after her birthday, about the time we bought the jeans, I guess. The cheerleaders were teasing her in PE class."

Julie folded the note back into a football and gave it to Michelle. "My son did mention that our babysitter beat up a cheerleader. He was very impressed."

"She didn't beat her up," Michelle said, but she didn't bother explaining. It didn't matter. She had reached out to comfort Nikki that night, and Nikki had pulled away. She hadn't mentioned being suspended. Michelle pressed the edge of the football against her thigh. "I figured it was puppy love—that it would pass."

"That picture of them kissing didn't look like puppy love. It reminded me of when Jack and I were starting out. You know, that first rush when you can talk all night and your heart feels like it's taking wing. Nothing compares to it, until—"

"The birth of your first baby," Michelle finished. They were both quiet for a moment. "I'm glad Drew didn't find this when he packed her things. If he showed it to Kenny, it would look bad. I remember that now—that feeling of anger. First I give the kid this big break with the video, then he goes after my daughter?" She looked at Julie. "I think I hated Noah Butler."

"Why didn't you call his mother?" Julie asked.

"He was over eighteen, for chrissakes. Plus…I did business with his father, Guy Butler. He did A&R for the album and promised that Victor would get a credit on everything related to the video. I guess I had a vested interest in Noah's success."

"Why didn't you forbid Nikki from seeing him?"

"Ha." Michelle stood up. "I can't wait until your kids are teenagers. Seriously."

Michelle jammed the note back in the jeans pocket where she found it. "Just what I needed—something else to worry about."

"Why, can they get a search warrant?"

"Only if they know about it. But Kenny said they can amend the lawsuit anytime. That's why I didn't want anyone seeing Nikki's pictures, remember? I even took the prints with me." Michelle looked around at the rest of the mess. For once she was glad the living room was so bare. A few piles had been sorted, but it would take forever to organize the rest, especially with one arm. A full trash bag already leaned against the front door. "Thanks for your help today."

Julie smiled. "I just hope no one asks me about it. I don't want to lie under oath."

"Of course not," Michelle said. "No one should lie under oath." After a quick hug, Michelle let Julie out and shut the door. Then she tucked the note into the trash bag.

She leaned against the door and looked up at the family portrait before surveying the mess in the living room. This whole thing was crazy-making. Michelle looked longingly at the empty coffee mug. She needed more. She wished she could inject it directly into her veins. She looked for veins on her limp right arm and thought of Wes. She'd like his opinion on what to do next. But he'd already put himself out by hiding the memory disk in his safe, and she was reluctant to call and take time away from another patient. That's all she was to him, she reminded herself. Even though they had been on a first-name basis since the day she showed him Nikki's pictures, she was still a patient. She would talk to him soon enough, at her next appointment.

"Hey!" Julie peeked her head back in. "Forgot my mug."

Michelle went back to the living room and stepped over a stack of automotive records to get it. When she came back to the hallway, she noticed something that had slid into view. She handed Julie the mug and picked up a white postcard. The Orrin Motors logo was printed above "Recall Notice #5175, Potential Seat Belt Malfunction."

Julie snatched it. "This is proof that you're innocent. Or not liable or whatever. The rain caused the accident and the seat belt is the reason that it got ugly."

Michelle saw the back, where purple doodles filled the corner. "Nikki definitely saw it."

"So maybe that's why she ran away. Not drugs or blaming you for her boyfriend's death. Let's stop worrying about this legal stuff. They're not accusing you of murder, right? Even if you hated Noah Butler, why would you drive dangerously, if you could get hurt, too?"

Michelle thought of her mother but didn't answer. She walked Julie outside to where the realtor sign violated the pristine lawn.

"Besides, right now you have other things to deal with." Julie hugged her good-bye again, then crossed the street. She called back. "Don't worry, once this blows over, Nikki will come home."

Michelle kicked the For Sale sign over. These days, *home* was a four-letter word.

25

L EXI ADJUSTED THE BANDAGE on Michelle's wrist and looked for an empty table among the laptop crowd in Starbucks at the corner of Ventura and Topanga Canyon Boulevard. No such luck. She held the door to the patio open for Michelle.

Michelle picked up her latte, wondering what drink Nikki and Noah brought his mother at work. She saw Lexi waiting and hurried out.

They shooed pigeons away from an empty table and sat down. "So, how have you been since I last saw you?" Lexi waved at Michelle's auburn hair and the blouse draping the designer jeans. "You look healthy. Stylish as ever."

"After twelve hours of sleep, I feel pretty good," Michelle said. "Except for a few minor concerns about killing a rock star, driving my daughter to deal drugs, alienating my husband to the point of selling our house, and trying to keep my mother from driving me crazy."

"That is a lot to deal with. But why did you say, 'killing a rock star'?"

Michelle sipped her latte. "It's easier than explaining the negligence charge."

"Funny how it's easier to blame yourself than to accept all

these things that are out of your control." Lexi grinned and unbuttoned the aqua sweater over her scrubs. "Although during one of the therapy sessions I sat in on, I do recall some mention of control issues."

"True, but there's reason to feel blame about some things," Michelle said. "During the last month, I've lied, stolen, hidden things…I used to think of myself as a good person. Maybe I was wrong about that, too."

"I doubt it. I warned you about adjustment issues. Plus, good people can do bad things, right? But if you feel bad…" A car alarm went off, so they waited until it stopped.

"I don't feel bad so much as clueless. One of the lawyers suggested hypnosis. Do you know anyone who does that?" Michelle asked. "Besides the shrink who kept asking about my mother? That's so cliché. I just need to remember the accident."

"You need to?"

"I want to."

"That could be dangerous," Lexi said. "Memories are mutable—you could create a false one. Have you seen the accident site? The senses can be a strong trigger to recall actual events."

Michelle finished her latte. "Drew thinks it will upset me."

"He didn't think you'd be upset about the house?"

"Thank you!" Michelle tossed her cup in the wastebasket nearby.

"Two points," Lexi said. She checked her Mickey Mouse watch. "Let's do it."

"What?"

"You don't think I'm going to let you drive one-handed through Topanga, do you?"

Lexi drove straight out of the parking lot up Topanga before Michelle had time to chicken out. An ancient oak tree still guarded the corner where the road crossed Mulholland Drive and headed up over the Santa Monica Mountains. The gnarled branches seemed to poke the air in protest of the cactus garden now tucked like a patchwork quilt around it. Michelle could only imagine the other changes the tree had witnessed over the centuries, from horseback riders to hitchhikers, hippies to Hollywood actors, all the people who had come and gone.

Lexi pressed the gas with her tennis shoe until her Jetta zipped up the first rise of the coastal range. Michelle found herself clutching the strap of her seat belt so hard that her knuckles went white.

"Okay so far?" Lexi asked.

"Nervous," Michelle admitted. The truth was that she was scared. Not just of going back to the scene of the horrifying crash, but of what she would learn there.

They inhaled the eucalyptus and pine as the car rounded the first set of horseshoe curves. A new wooden sign announced the entrance of the Santa Monica Mountains Park. Michelle turned to read it. "They paved over the gravel lookout?"

"You mean the make-out spot?"

Michelle smiled. She and Drew used to park here and search for their street in the grid of lights below. As the stars rose over the valley, against the backdrop of snowcapped mountains, they pointed out constellations and dreamed of the future. According to the sign, the view could only be seen during park hours now. The future felt just as limited.

Despite the sun flooding the two-lane road, Michelle shivered. She gripped the edge of her seat as Lexi drove slowly up and around the mountain. Volcanic rock jutted out above the bushy tree line to the left. Bright mustard plants lined the edge of the road like caution tape as the canyon yawned to the right.

The road switched back like a figure eight around the mountain until it crested again. Michelle took a deep breath and noticed several cars trailing them in the rearview mirror. The Mercedes behind them honked. Lexi looked back and waved at the driver. He ignored the double line and sped past, barely missing an oncoming car.

"That guy has a death wish," Lexi said. She caught herself and changed the subject by pointing across the road to the pole topped with a pink plaster pig. "Who do you think put that flying pig up there? Some local artist?"

"Probably my old boss," Michelle said. Pigs were sure flying now. They approached the concrete ruins of the infamous road-house ahead. She didn't point it out. Her phone rang and she checked the number. "Where's three-oh-five?"

"I think that's a Florida exchange," Lexi said. "My grandparents live there."

"Must be a wrong number," Michelle said, relieved that it wasn't her husband. She felt a familiar pang of guilt. Then something else tugged at her. She did know someone in Florida—her stepbrother. She answered, but it was too late. If it was him, he'd leave a message. She was too distracted to deal with it.

A mile farther, as the narrow lane hugged the mountain, dented signs warned about falling rocks. Michelle longed to look down to see the creek, but the curves were closer now, treacherous and tight. There was no place to pull over, no shoulder to lean on. The metal girder ended just ahead. "How could they run out of guardrail? This used to drive me crazy, when my kids rode on the camp bus."

"I guess it's a spot that doesn't seem risky."

"It's all risky—too tempting. You know, that urge to just yank the wheel?" She saw Lexi shrug. "Oh come on, everyone gets that urge."

"No, Michelle. Flying is a popular fantasy. Yanking the wheel is not."

"Don't worry, I'm not suicidal," Michelle said, slouching lower in the seat. "I'd never risk being crippled, or leaving my kids without a mother."

Lexi looked at her, concerned. "But that's just what happened."

"No, look: the edge of this road is so close you could sneeze and drive off." Michelle imagined how soft the air would feel when flying, how sweet the moment of freedom before the blood and broken bones. Why not yank the damn wheel and get it over with? To end all the questions, once and for all. "Maybe I'm cursed with a vivid imagination." Or was it memory, she wondered.

Lexi was watching now. "Didn't you tell the doctor that your mother was suicidal?"

"Yes, but not like this—she wasn't impulsive. She planned ahead. Shouldn't you keep your eyes on the road?"

Lexi chuckled as they passed the rainbow-colored peace sign staked in the side of the road, up where the Mercedes now waited behind a line of cars. There was always traffic at the driveway descending to the Theatricum Botanicum where Shakespeare was performed every weekend. A Jeep bursting with tie-dye-clad teenagers led a train of cars coming the other way. A dented blue van with surfboards tied to the roof rack raced ahead of a Jag. A Star Tours van rumbled past, packed with tourists snapping photos from the windows.

A motorcycle cop zoomed up behind the Jetta. The red light flashed just long enough for perspiration to prickle beneath Michelle's blouse. He steered slowly around Michelle's window and nodded his aviator glasses at her as he passed. He was young and good-looking, like the cop who fetched her from biology class the day they found her mother.

The theater was noisy. The young dancers were aflutter, worrying over their fallen idol. A security guard had found her unconscious, without even a pulse. Michelle was escorted past the yellow tape to identify her mother's duct-taped toe shoes, the blue ribbon from her favorite corset, and the green stem of a plastic daisy with all the petals plucked. The police thought it was an accidental overdose, from the cheese and crackers and the bottle of wine. But Michelle knew that her mother had planned it. She found her empty pillbox by the stage curtain when they tore down the tape.

When she had already missed her afternoon classes, Michelle talked the detective into dropping her off at the hospital. She was too young to be admitted to the intensive care wing, so when the nurse wandered away, she snuck in.

Elyse's name was posted outside of a private room, but Michelle barely recognized the wisp of a woman sleeping beneath her sheet. Elyse's high cheekbones looked like they were wrapped in rice paper; her pallor was tinged yellow, like an old, painful bruise. She was a broken doll of a ballerina, fractured and frail. Machines mimicked life by pumping liquid through thin tubes stabbed into her blue-veined skin and by forcing air through the plastic worming into her nose. The worst part was that she was absolutely still. So still that Michelle wondered if she would ever wake up.

Michelle breathed in time with the compressor, as if her own free will had died along with her mother. After what felt like hours of humming silence, Elyse lifted her crepe-paper lids like a curtain before the show. Her eyes bulged from her sunken face. Her faded irises floated in a bloodstained sea as she stared at Michelle without surprise.

Michelle wanted to shout and break the spell. But she was afraid. If she was too loud, too pushy, her mother might close her eyes again and shut her out forever.

Elyse licked her scabby lips and whispered with all her might. "Three minutes…so peaceful." She turned her head away from the noise of the nurses in the hall, the machines in the room, the girl by her bed. "I wish I was dead."

Michelle made herself sit. She watched herself wait. For what, a sign? Would her mother take it all back? Elyse had been gone for three minutes. One hundred eighty seconds of oblivion. Michelle could sing the national anthem in that amount of time, recite the pledge of allegiance in pig Latin, run away and not be missed. Could she hold her breath that long? One, Mississippi, two Mississippi, three Mississippi…Michelle swung her leg back and forth. Eight, Mississippi, nine Mississippi…she felt woozy. Where was she, twenty-seven or twenty-eight Mississippi? She let the air go and gasped for breath. Three minutes was a long time.

Elyse didn't care if Michelle earned an A in biology or wore a sundress in the snow. She didn't care if she got to see her grow up or get married or have children. She didn't care about her at all.

"Michelle?" Lexi's voice cut through the past. They had passed the traffic and were riding the curves once more. "I just asked how much farther it is."

"Oh, sorry." Michelle shrugged. "I have no idea. That's the point, right?"

"What were you thinking? Anything helpful? You sound annoyed."

"I am. I was thinking of my mother. After all those nights I counted her pills, how did I not know she snuck out? To do it when I wasn't watching?"

"It wasn't your job to protect her," Lexi said.

"Maybe not. But it was my job to protect Nikki. And I know I would have done anything. It would have been so easy, just to—"

"Yank the wheel?" There was a moment of stillness, then Lexi saw the tall cross by the road a hundred yards ahead. She pulled over and parked behind a few other cars. They climbed out slowly and hiked over.

Michelle felt wobbly as her heels sunk in the soft dirt. "Please don't tell any of this to the lawyers."

"I'm not a shrink, Michelle. As far as I'm concerned, this is emotion running amok. And with good cause." They passed a few teenagers heading back to their cars before seeing the picture of Noah nailed to the cross above a column of shiny CDs. Flowers wilted at the base next to a pair of pink panties and a pile of guitar picks.

They stepped past the shrine to the edge of the cliff behind it. "The only thing I could possibly testify to is the fact that you have a very strong will to live. Or you would not have survived. And we wouldn't be standing here now."

Michelle clutched Lexi's arm and took one more step closer. She had to see the cradle of the canyon where Noah Butler had died.

Nothing was there. A meadow grew, fed by the creek. There was no sign of a life lost or others changed forever. Michelle forgot to breathe, and darkness enveloped her for the slightest of moments.

A hawk cawed as it flew over them.

Lexi nudged her back to the car. "Shall we keep going toward the beach?"

Michelle nodded. She longed to see the ocean, put some space between her and this wooden cross.

They drove slowly through the small town of Topanga in the center of the canyon. Bicycles were locked up outside the organic café. Michelle was tempted to stop for coffee as if this was a regular day. But there were too many people out, from gauze-skirted women holding hands outside the antique barn to art lovers flocking the gallery and wine bistro. She used to love the sequined mermaid statue at the vintage clothing store. Today, she couldn't even smile at the gray-haired protesters waving Honk for Peace signs by the post office.

A Harley-Davidson howled past. Michelle shuddered. She should have let Noah ride his damn bike home, then she wouldn't feel responsible. Or maybe she still would. She remembered the sound of the rain, his shouts of protest as she closed her hand around his keys. Now, he was part of the local legend and her name was a rock 'n' roll footnote.

The car crept across the creek bridge then emerged on the ocean side, where the cliff edged the opposite lane. They drove down, down, down until her ears popped. Michelle's heart slowed to a steadier beat as they rounded a few more curves, farther and farther from where Noah had died.

Lexi pointed at the puffy tail of a deer bouncing up the mountain beside them. Michelle felt the pressure lifting as they reached the flatland, where lacy ferns lined the creek bed. And there it was, the shimmering sea. Seagulls cawed as they dive-bombed the deep blue water. Barely a whitecap was visible from here to the horizon. Michelle smelled the salt air and felt a sweet rush of relief.

Lexi coasted toward the intersection. "Which way?"

Michelle smiled at the simple choice of turning left or right at the sand. The Pacific Ocean was the ultimate guardrail. They could drive along the edge of the continent and never fall off.

26

COMMUTER PLANES FLASHED LIKE sardines swimming across the sky above the Key West airport. Michelle pressed her nose to the steamy window and watched until her eyes burned. Ten hours after leaving California, she could smell sweat through the layer of baby powder she'd shaken down her back, but she didn't dare find the ladies' room to freshen up. Drew's flight from Miami was an hour late and every minute mattered.

She fanned herself with the postcard she'd written to Wes, wondering if she dare call him for moral support. Here she was, following a hunch that felt crazier by the minute. That missed call from Florida lingered in her mind long after her drive through Malibu with Lexi. When she got home and found the disco ball earring, she could no longer resist calling back. An electronic recording answered, but it was the same exchange as the bed and breakfast run by her stepbrother. It had to be him. When she reached him, he denied making the call. But she couldn't let it go. They were rarely in touch beyond birthday cards, so why wouldn't he simply ask how she was doing? And if it wasn't him, then who was it?

For three days, Michelle had done her husband's bidding and compiled information for the real estate agent. She wanted to go through the motions of cooperating until she could see Drew in person and talk him out of selling the house. That's when she realized she could talk to him here. If there was nothing to her suspicion about Nikki, they could at least have a family vacation and no one would be the wiser. But that call couldn't be a coincidence. Michelle knew in her bones, there was more.

Michelle fanned herself one last time. Wes wouldn't get the message until she had already missed her next appointment, so phoning was the polite thing to do. Then again, Kenny had warned her about cell phones. The GPS signal could be tracked so far that she had used a gum-encrusted payphone to call Frank. She dropped the postcard in the mailbox.

Michelle looked past the display of shell horns used by ancient sailors, then rolled her suitcase under the bright Welcome to the Conch Republic banner. A map of southern Florida hung on the wall next to the window of blinding blue sky. Michelle imagined Drew pointing out the airplane window, showing Tyler the white ribbon of road winding from island to island over the mint-colored sea.

On their honeymoon, Michelle and Drew had rented a convertible in Miami and sped the entire 113 miles south on the Overseas Highway. They'd imagined moving to a house hugging the shore and fishing for dinner from a rowboat. Drew would quit the film biz to sell bait. "Crickets?" she'd teased. He'd worn a Dodgers cap over a full head of hair, but his face was fried by the time they reached the Seven Mile Bridge. Michelle remembered falling silent as the car climbed high above the sea. The endless pool of aquamarine seemed to seep right into the sky with no horizon. It felt like their love would last forever.

No doubt Tyler would be more impressed by the marvel of engineering than any romantic stories she might share. But there was a toll on every road, so many turns you never took, then you found yourself here, alone in a tiny airport, watching happy families come and go. Soon, Michelle prayed, the Masons would be among them.

Flight 117 was finally announced on the tinny loudspeakers. She pulled the collar of her silk blouse away from her slick skin and tugged down her long sleeve. Then she fluffed out her hair and rolled her suitcase outside where lush palms lined the runway.

When the aircraft door clanked open, Tyler was first to appear. His hair hung below his Yankees cap and he seemed to have grown another inch since she'd last seen him. When the wave of heat hit, he whipped off his letter jacket, tightened his grip on his duffel bag, and rambled down the rollaway stairs.

Michelle put her arm around his shoulder and kissed his cheek. Passengers bunched up behind them until she pulled him aside. "Where's your father?"

"He couldn't get away," Tyler said. "It's lucky I made it. I was about to go on a school camping trip."

Michelle's heart felt as if it had fallen and stuck to the soft tarmac. "I'm sorry it was so last minute. I wasn't sure Frank had room during high season." She led him toward the taxi line.

Tyler steered both bags to the end. "Is he really your stepbrother?"

"Technically no, but he still sends birthday presents," she said. "Nana was only married to Frank's dad for a few months, but he was a good guy. He came to her rescue once upon a time, like a fairy tale." Funny how infrequently Michelle thought about that period of time after she left for college. Elyse had eventually married the handsome detective who visited her in the hospital. Michelle shrugged it off and smiled at her son. "Frank is the one who sends disco ball earrings and—"

"Salt water taffy," Tyler finished. "You said our dentist loves him."

Michelle laughed. "Which reminds me, I have something for you."

"I have something for you, too," Tyler said, "but you go first."

Michelle pulled his old Dodgers plate from her suitcase. "It's silly, but I thought you might get a kick out of it."

Tyler grinned and took the plate. "This makes me hungry for a Happy Meal."

"Will you settle for a shrimp taco?" Michelle asked.

They climbed into a sweltering cab with a Rastafarian driver. Tyler stuck his face in the bleating air vent, then turned to Michelle and shouted over the reggae blasting from the radio. "Dad says if you watch the sunset toward Cuba, you'll see a green flash. Can we do that?"

"Absolutely," Michelle said. She peered out the window between ships' masts at the marina where the afternoon sun glowed like a burning fuse across the Atlantic. They slowed for a clutch of chickens on a road lined with pastel houses, then turned up Duval Street, the main drag in Old Town. The street was clogged with tourists trawling between bars.

"What's the drinking age here?" Tyler asked.

"Older than you," Michelle said. She smiled as the taxi careened around the Conch Train Trolley on the cobblestone street. She scanned the sun-burnt families until Tyler noticed and put his arm around her.

"Don't be sad. We'll have a good time even without Dad. Just the two of us."

Michelle couldn't bring herself to tell him the real reason they were there. He deserved her full attention. She saw several cats lounging in a patch of sun by a patio restaurant and remembered his allergies. "Did you bring your inhaler?" she asked.

"Of course. I'm not a baby," Tyler said.

Michelle was about to say he would always be her baby when they pulled into the circular driveway at the historic Curry Mansion. Tyler whistled at the sight of the gracious white Victorian. From the New England widow's walk to the Southern columns, the inn was a testament to the treasures plundered from turn-of-the-century shipwrecks. Ragtime music was playing from the grand piano on the wraparound veranda, and a bear of a man growled from the porch.

"Mademoiselle Michelle!"

She waved, then let Tyler help her from the taxi.

Frank finished pouring a pitcher of mojitos into cups for hotel guests, then hurried down the wide stairs to welcome them. "And Master Tyler! So grown up!" He paid the cabdriver, then carried their luggage up. "Where's hubby?"

"Stuck in New York," Michelle said, following Tyler up to the porch.

"What a shame."

She nodded, grateful that Frank hadn't mentioned her bad arm or how bedraggled she must look. She surveyed the tables ringed with hotel guests enjoying the daily happy hour. Had any of them seen her daughter?

Frank poked at the albino cat sleeping on the porch rail until she stretched out a six-toed paw. "See the toes? Descendent of Hemingway's cat, Snowball."

Tyler petted the cat, then sneezed. "Dad said to make sure to see the Hemingway House. There's a jillion cats there, right?"

"At least—and we'll see them all." Michelle gave him a smile, then glanced over his shoulder at the old man in a tuxedo playing ragtime at the piano by the serve-yourself bar. His Afro was now a cap of white curls, but his keyboard style was unmistakable. "Is that Bojangles?"

"Who else? He'll outlast us all." Frank opened the glass door to the house, where a welcome blast of cold air met them in the dark maple entry. Tyler whistled at the eighteenth-century furniture in the roped-off parlor. The dining table was set with so much crystal and gilded china that it seemed dinner would be served any moment.

"It'll be a few minutes until the Madame Deveraux Suite is ready, but if you're hungry, there are peanuts on the veranda."

"Deveraux?" Tyler asked. "As in Nana? She comes here?"

"A few weeks every winter. She's very popular." Frank led them through the narrow hallway lined with framed sepia photographs of the historic building. "Especially with my dad."

Michelle hadn't known, but it made sense. He pointed to a newspaper clipping of her mother wearing a cape and a crown as she rode in the annual bed race, being pushed by a royal court of drag queens. "She didn't come until April last year and everybody missed her so much, she was appointed Queen of the Conch Festival. She judged the Key Lime Pie Contest." Frank tapped the top button of his bowling shirt. "I won."

Michelle pointed at a photo of a burly man on a live-aboard sailboat. "Is that your dad?"

He nodded. "He retired from the force and moved down here—about the same time your mom started visiting. He still does a bit of surveillance on the side." Frank grinned, then opened the door of the office. "Even checked out my partner here, before I took him on. Sterling, this is Madame Deveraux's daughter."

"Ah, VIPs," he said, pushing a stack of proof sheets aside to reach for her limp hand. Michelle startled as he pressed his lips against it.

"Nice to meet you, Sterling." Michelle pointed to the proof sheet with shots of the Curry Mansion. "You're not changing the postcard, are you? That watercolor is classic."

Frank nodded. "Unfortunately, *classic* means 'outdated' in the tourist trade. While our guests enjoy our escape from modern life, they do make reservations online. We need to keep the website current." He handed her a postcard from the shelf of discount fliers by the office door. "Collector's item."

Michelle smiled and surveyed the tourist attractions. "Tyler, why don't you take some brochures out to the veranda and plan our week while I check in. Which do you recommend, Frank? Aquarium? Cheap cruise ship connection to Miami?"

Frank shook his head and gave a few fliers to Tyler. "Deep sea fishing, that's the ticket."

Michelle smiled. "Tyler, get yourself a cold drink and I'll meet you out there." Michelle waited until Tyler was out of sight, then addressed Frank directly. "Thanks for having us on such short notice. The truth is, I'm looking for my daughter. After that call—I was hoping there was more to it.

Frank rubbed his beard. "Nikki's the one who sends thank-you notes written with purple ink?"

Michelle smiled. "That's her. Has my mother mentioned anything...amiss?"

"She's been worried about you, of course, but she hides it under that regal bearing. She seemed a bit tired this year, but I figured it was the arthritis. What's up with Nikki?"

"I haven't seen her since I got out of the hospital. Since you know everybody in town, maybe you could call around? I'm hoping she called home, then just got nervous. If she is here, I don't want to scare her off. I just want to see her."

He nodded and shut the office door so Sterling could get back to work.

Michelle headed out to the front porch where she scanned the couples sipping rum drinks. Tyler was sipping a sweaty beer from his perch on the wooden railing by the cat. She swiped the bottle. "Get a couple of sodas, will you? Request a song, if you want."

Tyler frowned. "Like what?"

Michelle rubbed her arm absentmindedly and spotted the pile of cocktail napkins by the tip jar. "Let's see what other people requested." She dug out some cash and walked over to the piano. Tyler stopped halfway at the self-serve bar. Michelle made sure Tyler was pouring soda into his cup before turning to Bojangles. "How are you, Mr. B? Holding down the fort?"

"You got that right, Miss Michelle."

"How'd you remember my name?"

"I'd recognize those eyes anywhere. The windows to your soul."

"So I've heard." She stuffed a twenty in his tip jar. "What's your favorite song?"

"Happy Birthday." His long fingers trilled up the keyboard. "Every time I hear it, I know I'm still here."

Michelle smiled, but the song no longer made her think of celebrations. It reminded her of the Roadhouse video, of the band singing the song to Nikki. She flipped through the soggy pile of napkins with requests written on them. The first was "Girl from Ipanema." Michelle held it up, but Mr. B shook his head. He'd played it enough. The next song, "Margaritaville," was so popular that she didn't even ask. The next title was more unusual. And it was written in purple ink.

All at once, Michelle felt the oppressive heat, heard the drunken laughter, and smelled the too-sweet drinks. She wondered if she was having a heart attack. She squeezed her eyes shut, then focused on the words printed on the napkin. This was Nikki's handwriting, complete with circles dotting the *i*'s. Michelle held it up to Bojangles.

He tapped the keyboard, as if the song was right there waiting for him to play. She didn't recognize the jazzy Jose Feliciano introduction, but soon the music settled into the familiar melody of "Light My Fire." A drunken woman behind the piano garbled the first line: "You know that it would be untrue..." Michelle's entire body flushed. She ran inside, letting the screen door slam behind her.

"Mom?" Tyler called after her.

Michelle ran through the lobby toward the office. "Frank?" She ran down the paneled hallway past the office to the homey kitchen, where a drunken game of Marco Polo echoed from the pool area in back, and found Frank standing at the back door.

"Where is she, Frank?" Michelle held the napkin up.

He waved it away to see a chubby girl in a bikini do a sloppy cannonball. "I'm liable if someone gets hurt." The goons in the pool were splashing each other now, nearly soaking an elderly couple retiring to their room. "*Amigos!*" Frank called. "*Por favor!*"

Michelle shouted. "Hey, asshole! Knock it off or you're out of here!"

The guy gave her the finger.

Frank pulled Michelle back into the kitchen. "Very effective, thanks. Especially since every room in town is booked and there aren't any more flights out." He poured himself a glass of water from a frosty pitcher. "Now they'll write bad Internet reviews."

"Not as bad as the ones I'll write," Michelle said.

He rolled the cool glass against his forehead. "Nikki's not here."

"Don't give me that bullshit."

"I swear—she called last week out of the blue. She needed a place to chill, so I put her up in the annex and paid her to take a few pictures. No good deed goes unpunished."

"Tell me about it," Michelle said, thinking about Noah's motorcycle.

"Look, she made me promise. By the time I got your new number and dialed—I thought better of it. I'm not taking sides."

"I don't want there to be sides!" Michelle waved the napkin in his face. "She's my daughter. You should have told me!"

"I figured you knew. When she said someone was looking for her, I thought it was an old boyfriend, not you."

"Her old boyfriend is—nevermind. You didn't hear anything on the news? You weren't curious?"

"We don't have television or Wi-Fi for a reason. Folks come here to get away."

Michelle was skeptical. "My mother didn't mention it, either?"

"She likes her privacy. We respect that—the lifestyle here is about privacy. That's why she's so popular. That, and her fabulous mambo." He struck a dance pose.

Michelle didn't have time to hold a grudge. She needed his help. "Okay, I believe you. Maybe I'm the only one who tracked Nikki here. Hope so. But the last thing I want to do is worry Tyler. When is the last time you saw her?"

"This morning," Frank admitted. "Sterling held on to her check until she turned in all the proofs. She needed money to leave." He handed Michelle a glass of water.

Michelle took a sip. "Are there really no more planes out?"

"Not tonight," Frank said.

"Good. I'll look for her at the bus depot. What does she look like now?" Michelle was too upset to drink any more. She threw her glass in the sink, and it shattered. "I don't even know what my daughter looks like!" She burst into tears.

Frank grabbed her shoulders with both hands. "She looks beautiful. She looks like you." He wiped her tears, then unpinned a business card from the bulletin board.

"Take Tyler to Louie's Backyard. Their pie is actually better than mine. Whatever happened between you and Nikki, let it be."

"Let it be what?" Michelle asked, pulling away.

Tyler appeared at the door with the room key. "Room's ready. You okay, Mom?"

"Just tired," she said, narrowing her eyes at Frank to warn him to keep mum. "A shower will wake me up." She followed Tyler up the grand stairway to the Deveraux Suite.

Inside the large room, piano music drifted in from the open balcony. Tyler set his duffel bag on the quilt and looked up through the hanging fringe of the antique canopy. "I need a shower, too. You want first dibs or do you want Dad's letter?" He pulled a Polo shirt out of his duffel, then handed her a manila envelope.

"You," Michelle said, waving him off. She struggled with the clasp, then gave up. Why work so hard for real estate papers or some bullshit apology? Michelle needed to focus, to figure out where her daughter could be. She was too close to let her slip away. She pulled the cord for the fan hanging from the pressed tin ceiling, but the blades merely sliced through the air.

She unpacked a few things, then stepped out to the small balcony and looked down at the pool. The guests had gone to dinner now; the water was crystal blue. Beyond the piano, the squeals of tourists rose on the warm breeze from Duval Street. Smoke stacks from a cruise ship towered over the rooftops blocking her view of the harbor. The horn blasted, long and loud. Michelle stiffened. She felt her daughter's presence, as sure as the lump in her throat. Without a car, that ship was the only sure way off the island tonight. Nikki was on that ship.

"Tyler!" she shouted. "Let's go!"

She grabbed the key and careened around the bed, yanking the door open to the hall. "Hurry," she called, stumbling down the staircase.

Tyler's hair was still wet as he bounded down behind her. "Did I take too long?"

"No, honey, I—forgot about the green flash." She grabbed his hand and pulled him out. "Come on!"

They hurried through the happy hour crowd on the porch, down the steps and out to the sidewalk where they joined the tourists streaming to Duval Street.

Tyler pointed to the daiquiri machines lining an open-air bar like dryers at a Laundromat. "Look, Mom, just like Baskin-Robbins: thirty-one flavors." Michelle nodded as if she cared, then stepped into the street to avoid a cluster of college students. A trolley clanged for room, so they leapt back on the curb. Michelle wove between women browsing racks of batik sarongs and children jostling to see the blue toucans squawking from the shoulder of a jester on stilts. She waited in front of an art gallery for Tyler to catch up.

They crossed to Mallory Square and raced through rows of coconut purses to the waterfront. She pulled Tyler past the tourists applauding a fire-eating savage, but paused at a hanging display of disco ball earrings.

The crowd was claustrophobic, so Michelle looked up to get her bearings. The sun was huge, a flat yellow circle hanging like a painting in the sky. It appeared to drop lower as she watched. She pulled her gaze away and locked eyes with a gypsy fortune-teller with kerchiefs wrapping her leathery face. She beckoned Michelle to her shawl-covered table, but Michelle shook her head.

She called to Tyler, who had stopped to watch a magician. He saw her and blessed her with the barest of smiles. Michelle's heart leapt to her throat so fast, she felt like she was choking. Once you created life, love was beyond your control. A grin could lift you to the heavens; a frown could smash you flat. She waved for him to hurry.

Tyler caught up and pointed at the taco bar on the boardwalk.

"I'll meet you on the dock," she cried, racing ahead until her heel caught between bricks. She staggered forward, then caught herself. She looked back for her broken heel amid the flurry of tourists.

"You're looking for Nikki, aren't you?" Tyler asked, when he reached her.

She pointed at his taco. "Do you need to stop to eat that?"

"No. But if I were Nikki, I bet you'd chew my food and regurgitate it into my mouth." He took a big bite of his taco.

Michelle shook her head and shoved her broken shoes into her purse. She looked up to see how much time was left. The sun was rolling across the horizon like a bruised orange. The sky was so golden that it looked as if juice had leaked out. Except to the left of them. There, the ship's hull blocked the view like a great black wall. The ship gave another honk. Steam rose against the blushing sky.

"Wait!" Michelle murmured. She ran down the boardwalk through pockets of tourists staring straight up at the wailing ship. Michelle ran across the open cement toward the water, in the dark shadow of the ship. The dock vibrated beneath them. She reached the edge and stopped. The mooring hook was empty.

"Nikki!"

With a great groan, the ship motored sideways ten yards, then fifty, then five hundred. Black water roiled between the hull and the enormous tires nailed to the dock. Rows of cabin windows glowed like full moons above. The dock stopped quaking, but Michelle didn't. The ship was out of reach, and so was her daughter.

Tyler caught up and pointed at the glowing horizon. Michelle blinked and followed his gaze. The fiery globe sunk in jerks, the curved edges dropping line by line until it was gone. A green tint flashed across the horizon line, then vanished.

"Did you see that? The green flash?" he asked. "We made it!"

"No, we didn't." She watched the cruise ship shrinking in the distance, then looked up. The sky was periwinkle blue, then deep violet, easing into indigo. But Michelle didn't care about pretty views.

Tyler tossed his trash toward the garbage can and missed. "I want to go home."

Michelle closed her eyes for a second and took a deep breath. She wanted to disappear and start over. But when she opened her eyes, Tyler was the one who had disappeared. For a moment, it seemed that the earth stopped spinning, and everyone was still. From the corner of her eye, Michelle saw a silver statue move. When she looked over, his eyes locked on hers. Then he covered his mouth with a silver hand…and froze.

She threw Tyler's trash into the garbage can and limped back, scanning the crowd. In the next row, a fire-eater sipped a bottle of water and a clown pulled off his nose. The fortune-teller looked up, then away. Michelle was the freak now, the unfit mother.

By the time Michelle got back to the Curry Mansion, Tyler was in their room stuffing clothes back into his duffel. "I'm sorry," she said, reaching to touch him.

He brushed her off. "Sorry is just a word."

"If you want, we can tour the Hemingway House in the morning."

"I'm going to the airport in the morning."

"Fine, I'll take you, but let's at least have dinner. Give me a minute to wash up."

"No more minutes," he said, dragging his duffel to the door. "Dad's right. You're sick."

"I hope you mean sick in a good way."

"Sick as in crazy." He shut the door.

Michelle stood there a moment. She didn't think anything could be worse than losing a child. Now she knew better: it was losing them both.

A jazz trumpet wailed from Duval Street. Michelle picked up the Dodgers plate that Tyler left on the bed and fanned herself, but it was no use. She stepped out on the balcony again. The air was too steamy, the music too loud, the tourists too goddamned happy. She whipped the plate over the pool, like a Frisbee. It cut through the sticky air until it dropped into the water with barely a splash, then sashayed to the bottom, a dark polka dot in the glow of the underwater light.

Michelle went inside and sat down on the bed. She tore open the envelope with her teeth and dumped the papers beside her. She gasped. She'd seen a lot of legal documents over the past six weeks, but this one was new: Petition for Dissolution of Marriage.

She felt the lure of the liquor downstairs, but her foot throbbed too much to walk. She pictured her mother curled up here, eating bonbons beneath the canopy, a monogrammed bed jacket draped around her shoulders. Madame Deveraux, Frank had called her. Michelle wondered if his father had told him that it was a miracle that he ever met Elyse, a miracle that she had survived. Michelle reached for the gilded phone on the bedside table and lifted the handle to her ear. Then she dialed her mother.

That was the funny thing about mothers. How you still wanted them, even when they'd shown time and again that they couldn't help you. It was enough to drive anyone crazy. Michelle laid back and watched the fan whirring above her.

Surely her mother had lain here. Had she noticed how the blades slashed through the air like a guillotine?

Michelle hung up. If her mother said that she was crazy, it just might be true. And she wasn't ready to face that possibility. Not while Nikki was still missing.

27

THE DOORBELL RANG REPEATEDLY in Michelle's dream. She pulled the pillow over her head to block out the noise. The crickets had kept her awake with their mating calls since her return from Key West, and she needed rest to clear up this divorce thing with Drew. It had to be some kind of legal maneuver. Or was he lying about the woman who answered the phone? Maybe it didn't matter. Maybe that was him pounding on the door.

Michelle blinked until she could see beyond her wrinkled nightgown. The floor was littered with papers and plane tickets, lists of places Nikki might go. There were stale pizza crusts and a box of Lucky Charms with the marshmallows gone. There were also photographs of Nikki that she had been keeping under the mattress.

Michelle reached for her phone in the charger, to see if Drew had called, but her elbow knocked over the nesting doll on the nightstand. The shooting pain reminded her that her hand was useless. She rubbed it and ignored the clatter of the wooden dolls spilling to the floor. She squinted at the blank phone screen, then looked under the nightstand. Sure enough, the power cord dangled above the dolls.

The doorbell rang again.

"Coming!" She jammed the plug into the wall and cranked the volume on the phone before staggering through the mess to the bathroom. She recoiled at the unkempt woman in the mirror and scooped up her robe from the floor where she must have dropped it in a melancholy daze.

By the time Michelle reached the foyer, the tang of lemon sliced through her stupor. Cathy wasn't the last person she wanted to see, but she was high on the list. Michelle opened the front door and saw Kenny. Damn. He was on top of that list.

"Welcome home," he said, already headed to the dining room table.

Cathy set her plate of lemon bars next to the dried out plant. "I thought orchids last forever."

"Nothing lasts forever," Michelle said. "Did Drew send you?"

"No," Kenny said, shuffling documents. "Ms. Rodriguez from Pacific Auto Insurance has been trying to reach you."

"You look thin," Cathy said.

"Thanks," Michelle said.

"I didn't mean it as a compliment. Eat something." Cathy nudged the plate forward. "Kenny insisted," she said.

Michelle started to object, but Kenny interrupted. "She's just trying to help."

"Me?" Michelle asked.

"No, me," Kenny said, kissing his wife's hand. They exchanged looks, then he turned back to Michelle. "Something has come up. Rodriguez is having complications with her pregnancy. She's on bed rest."

"How scary," Michelle said.

Kenny nodded. "For both of you. She won't be available to defend the insurance company for the civil trial in June. Her second chair is preparing a motion to continue the trial—to move it back."

"Good. That is good, right? More time for me to remember?"

"Not exactly," Kenny said. He looked at his wife, who gave him an encouraging squeeze. "I got a call from my buddy in the DA's office this morning. There's a rumor they'll file criminal negligence charges against you. And possibly vehicular manslaughter."

Cathy covered the plate. "That's almost the same as murder in the second degree."

Kenny winced at the harsh comparison.

Cathy looked at him. "Isn't that what you said? That there are varying degrees of manslaughter charges? Including gross negligence based on being 'reckless, with disregard for human life'?"

Kenny shrugged. "Close enough."

"What happened?"

"Dillenger's team has dug up forensic evidence that looks damaging." He set a document in front of her.

Michelle didn't even bother trying to decipher the legalese. "And?"

"They scavenged the wreck. Tests show that the locking pin was never secured. That means Noah Butler was not wearing his seat belt."

"Maybe he couldn't get it to work and gave up."

"That's plausible. But they also collected tire remnants that are nearly intact. Not the kind of rubber loss that results from a skid. Now they can include punitive damages, alleging 'conscious disregard' for passenger safety. They'll have experts to testify that you didn't brake at all."

"But why go to all that trouble?"

"More money—that you would pay, not the insurance company. Plus, it would set things up nicely for the DA to bring a criminal charge. According to my buddy, the DA needs the eighteen- to twenty-four-year-old vote in the next election, and he's not above avenging a rock star's death to get it."

Michelle rubbed her eyes. "Am I going to jail, Kenny?"

"Not if I can help it," he said. "The civil claim against you now is essentially about financial liability. You could get fines and maybe a year in county. But a criminal charge is a felony, that's the big leagues. Then we're talking about state prison."

Cathy saw Michelle trembling and put her hand on her husband's arm. "That's enough, honey."

"She needs to know." Kenny turned back to Michelle. "We don't want to give the DA time to build up the case. With Rodriguez out, I could take over as the main trial lawyer. It's unusual to have one lawyer represent both the insurance company and the defendant, but in special circumstances like this, it's in the best interest of the client. The judge will allow it."

"How will this keep me out of jail?"

"If we win a defense verdict—meaning you are found to be 'not liable' in the civil trial, then the DA will be less inclined to file a criminal charge. He'd need all twelve jurors to disagree with the civil ruling and find you guilty beyond a reasonable doubt. It would look like he was a celebrity ambulance chaser, trying to keep his name in the news."

"So the whole thing would blow over?"

"It could. If we win."

"Then go for it. I just want this to be over."

"So does the Butler estate, trust me," Kenny said. "My guess is that Noah's father initially had Greenburg file the civil charges because he wanted someone to blame. And between you, me, and the wall, the Killer Mom mystique is good publicity for album sales. It pumps up his son's legend. But the man is well aware that your policy limits and personal assets won't offer a big payday.

Especially if the jury doesn't find a preponderance of evidence against you."

"It was raining," Cathy offered. "Maybe your stiletto slipped." She raised an eyebrow at Michelle then went to the kitchen. "Anyone else for tea?"

Michelle ignored the dig and turned back to Kenny. "Thank you."

"You're welcome. I'll reconfirm our trial date in Santa Monica." He closed his briefcase, but didn't get up. "So long as there's no new evidence to delay the proceedings, we'll be fine."

"What do you mean?"

"I mean, mind your own business. Sit tight and try to remember what happened. The more detailed your knowledge, the less there is to be left to the jury's imagination. And depending on how the seat belt argument goes, the issue of character may arise. No matter what the facts are, the jury decides the verdict. And juries can be swayed by unconscious bias. Anything that implies you had reason to dislike Noah Butler could influence them to think your personal feelings affected your reactions in the heat of the moment."

Michelle thought of the photographs of her daughter scattered by her bed, but said nothing. When Cathy leaned around the doorway from the kitchen to give her a hard look, she recalled what Noah's mother had said about his "trouble." She also recalled her pact with Cathy. She looked back at Kenny and played dumb. "You mean like Nikki dancing in his video?"

"Good Lord, everyone's already seen that," Cathy called from the kitchen.

"I'd argue it's circumstantial. Either way, Nikki's testimony might help you. Have you heard from her?" Kenny watched her shake her head no. "If you had, would you tell me?"

Michelle leaned her head in her hand.

The teakettle whistled, but Cathy's voice was sharper. "Kenny, give me a hand? Now!"

Michelle heard him go to the kitchen. Fervent whispers of their daughter Emily's name followed, then Kenny's protest. But the strident tones softened, and Michelle recognized the sounds of a marriage that worked. She was embarrassed by the intimacy. And more than a little jealous.

Michelle's cell phone rang from the bedroom. She sat up and called to the kitchen. "You know Drew wants a divorce, right?"

Kenny emerged carrying a cup of tea. "I was sorry to hear that. The timing isn't ideal, but it shouldn't hurt the case."

Michelle had nothing to say that wouldn't sound pathetic. She'd dared to hope that Kenny would explain some legal advantage. She was suddenly conscious of how naked she was beneath her robe. She heard her phone ring again and wondered if it was him. Except now she wasn't so eager to answer. "Does Drew know about the new evidence?"

"Yes," he said, setting the tea down. "We've spoken about having you examine the wreck. A visit might jog your memory."

"No, thanks," Michelle said, warming her hand around the teacup. "I went to Topanga Canyon, and that didn't do much good."

Kenny nodded. "I know it sounds frightening, but now that there's new evidence, we need something to contradict it. Any little detail will help your credibility. Thanks to county budget cuts, the wreckage is still in a junkyard downtown." He pulled a paper with the address from his pocket.

Michelle took it reluctantly. "Isn't there something else I can do?"

"Plenty. Get me a list of character witnesses—people without so much as a parking ticket who would testify on your behalf. Get me records of your volunteer work, donations to charity, that sort of thing."

"PTA meetings count," Cathy said, returning from the kitchen.

Michelle rose and walked them out. As the door closed, she heard the phone click over to voice mail. She trudged back to the bedroom and read Wes's name on the caller ID. Michelle relaxed. He would be a character witness for her, she was sure of it.

Her stomach growled, but there was no food in the house. She wandered back to the dining room and dipped a lemon bar in her tea. It wasn't so bad, she decided. There would be a lot worse food in jail.

28

A FEW DAYS LATER, JULIE was driving them in circles, lost in an industrial area downtown. When Michelle read the address Kenny had given her, Julie jammed her foot on the brake of her Acura. The cement truck behind them shuddered and stopped inches from the back bumper. The driver laid on the horn until Julie stuck her arm out the window, her bracelets jangling as she waved him around. The trucker's mouth opened, but a tanker lumbering across the freeway above them drowned out his angry words. Michelle coughed at the exhaust fumes. "Sorry."

Julie backed the car to the dirt-covered sign for the LA County Impound and pulled into the gravel lot. Barking Dobermans lunged against a fence topped with barbed wire. Julie freshened her lip gloss in the mirror.

"Why bother?" Michelle asked.

"Because you catch more flies with honey than with vinegar," Julie said. She came around to help Michelle out. "And they close in five minutes. If you notice anything about the car, even the tiniest thing, tell me." She pulled a notepad and pencil from her purse. "This legal stuff can come back around and bite you in the tush. The judge in my custody case wouldn't take my word for anything, but Jack had his lies all typed up, so he was golden. Ready?"

A stringy man with a five o'clock shadow unlocked the gate and beckoned them to sign in at his trailer. Michelle followed Julie in a wide berth around the snarling dogs, and slipped her new driver's license under the plexiglass window. The man—Gus, according to the name on the pocket of his short-sleeved shirt—turned to the faux wood paneling and lifted a grimy clipboard off a hook.

Michelle was distracted by the calendar posted near the hook. Miss May wore leather chaps astride a gleaming motorcycle. Michelle wondered if Nikki would ever shoot a picture like that, or worse, pose for one. She signed her name slowly, as if to make it perfect, until Gus cleared his throat. Michelle put the pen down. She could delay all she wanted, but it wouldn't get her out of this.

A hush fell over the group as Gus led them back between the rows of wreckage. They tiptoed past the mangled metal corpses as if it were a real cemetery. The steel bodies were coated with dust, making each wreck look like a member of the same doomed family. Michelle shivered, as if spirits lingered in the air around them. But the only signs of life were the cars flashing like a strobe light as they sped across the concrete overpass and blocked the blue sky above. What was it Cathy had said so long ago? "There but for the grace of God," that was it. And the grace of brakes, and seat belts, and good intent.

Gus stopped at Lot 709. They stood before the hollow frame of Drew's SUV. What little remained after the wheels had been removed and the seats torn out did resemble an accordion, just as Becca had said. The hood was nonexistent; the brackets were bent like bobby pins. Michelle stood anchored to the ground. She was too terrified to move any closer.

Julie flashed another smile at Gus and wandered around to the dented tailgate—the only part that still suggested a vehicle. "Are we allowed to touch it?"

"Suit yourself," Gus said, crouching in the dirt. "Every time the Santa Ana's blow, more shit falls off." He whistled and the dogs snarled in the distance. They bounded through the wrecks to nuzzle at his touch.

Julie poked a metal shard and black chips flaked off. "Not even car paint lasts out here."

"Naw, that's just blood," Gus said.

Julie blanched, then turned to Michelle. "Yours?"

Michelle felt Gus's scrutiny as he scratched the mongrels behind their ears. She stepped toward the gaping hole in the frame on the passenger side. She pretended to be oblivious, as if it wasn't such a miracle she got out of this alive. Then again, maybe it was a curse.

When she tugged idly at a scrap of cloth beneath a metal joint, it cracked like a potato chip. Despite two rainy winters, a hot summer, and constant diesel fumes, the crackled grain of black leather was apparent. But it wasn't a remnant of the upholstery—the seats had been covered in the patterned fabric now coating the doorjambs like a melted web. Her finger caught the edge of a small rusted circle, and she rubbed it until she could see an outline of wings, like the Harley-Davidson shield. It was a metal snap from Noah's jacket. She dropped it in the dirt.

A shadow flickered over them, then dust rose like a ghost as a police helicopter whirred past. Michelle heard the familiar thwack-thwack-thwack just as Gus warned them to cover their eyes. Too late. She was already blinded by the swirl of soot, like the blanket of fog that had coated Topanga Canyon that morning.

Steam rose from the narrow strip of pavement that Michelle spied through the flailing windshield wipers. The bordering trees and mountains were hidden in the low-lying cloud. It looked as if she and Noah were alone, tunneling through heaven.

He was raving mad as he punched the radio buttons, shouting about

Morrison and Manzanek, Timothy Leary and psychedelic drugs. Rebuttal points buzzed in her brain, but mostly she wanted to end that head-banging beat, to brush his hand from the buttons, to make him put his goddamned seat belt on...

"Anything?" Julie's voice broke in, dissolving the cloud of memory.

Michelle startled. Her heart was pounding so loudly that Julie must have heard it. What about Noah's seat belt? She was furious with him, she remembered that much—and that alone could incriminate her.

"Nope," she said. "At least nothing you should write down." Michelle took a deep breath and kicked the frame in frustration. A small object fell out and bobbled across the dirt. A bolt or a washer, Michelle didn't care. But Julie leaned over and snatched it.

"No souvenirs," Gus warned. "Police won't even let me use scraps for a sculpture. Fucking cops."

"That's awful," Julie said, making a show of leaning over to adjust her ankle strap before standing up. Michelle saw her stuff something in her bra before turning around. "So you're an artist?"

Gus lifted a metal blob on the bike chain beneath his soiled collar. "I dabble."

"Sweet," Julie said, asking about his art as he led them back through the rows of carnage.

Michelle trailed, trembling from the magnetic pull of memory. She heard only barking and the sound of her own breath until they were outside the gates and Gus was locking up.

Once buckled into the car, Julie punched on her CD player and pulled out of the parking lot. The soothing voice of a self-help guru enveloped them as they merged into traffic. Julie cast curious looks at Michelle as they joined the line of cars waiting at the on-ramp to the Santa Monica Freeway. When the light turned green, Julie wove over toward the far lanes heading west. Rush hour traffic bunched up as they approached the 405 North to the Valley.

"You mind if I take the coastal route?"

"No. But can we stop by the clinic first? It's on the way."

"Dr. Palmer's clinic? Office hours are probably over by now." They cruised under the congested overpass and sped toward Santa Monica.

"I'm sure Wes will wait if I call."

"You call him Wes?"

"Why not? He calls me Michelle. And he's leaving for Pittsburgh tomorrow for a meeting. I need to talk to him."

"About your therapy? Can't you call the nurse tomorrow?"

"It's not about my arm."

"Then what's it about?" Julie asked. "Oh no, you went to see him after your fall at the office, didn't you? Please don't tell me he's the one hiding that memory card."

Michelle sighed. "I trust him, Julie. You've been so generous with all you have going on, but you're busy. I spend hours with him every week."

"He gets paid for it," Julie said.

"No, it's more than that. He really seems to care."

Julie didn't bother to look up from the road. "That's called projection, Michelle. Everybody falls for their doctors. It will pass."

"He was going to give me balls today—manipulatives, he calls them, to strengthen my hand."

Julie wove her way to the carpool lane on the left. "Don't you have plastic cups or something to use at home? I could lend you some old sandbox toys."

"I guess I could work with the nesting dolls," Michelle said. "They're small."

"Hate to see one crack, though. That design is unique, right?"

"Yes, but I doubt they're worth anything, except to my mother. It's not a complete set."

"That makes them perfect to practice small motor movement. Forget the clinic."

"Please, Julie. I want to ask Wes to be a character witness."

"I'll be a character witness," Julie said.

Michelle flipped the visor down to block the glare from the sun. "Thanks, but you're a divorcée fighting a custody battle." Michelle pointed at the 26th Street exit.

Julie jammed her foot on the gas pedal and swerved around another car. Michelle watched the Santa Monica Airport and St. John's Hospital whiz past. "If you think being divorced will make me look bad as a character witness, how do you think you'll look, confiding in your celebrity doctor?"

"He's not a celebrity."

"Really? He has a book. There's probably a Dr. Wesley Palmer fan club on Facebook."

"He only wrote that to help win a research grant," Michelle protested. "He's a hardworking guy who grew up riding the bus across town to go to a decent school and earn scholarships to college."

"That's exactly the kind of information that you shouldn't know. And don't call him by his proper name or you sure as hell won't look like a loyal wife. It might work if he was fat and ugly, but I met him at your house. He's gorgeous! This friendship is dangerous, Michelle. I've read every book on divorce in the LA library system, and with this hot bachelor in the picture, Drew could sue for alienation of affection. You'd end up with nothing."

"Calm down, Julie. The divorce papers say irreconcilable differences. Besides, Drew left right after I got home from the hospital."

"To work. To support you," Julie said, slowing with the traffic by the 4th Street exit to the courthouse. "Leaving LA is not the same thing as leaving your marriage."

It sure felt that way, Michelle thought. The granite courthouse loomed south of the freeway. The orange sunlight reflected in the windows was the color of prison overalls. "You really think I need to be married to avoid jail?"

"No. You might even get a sympathy vote for getting dumped. But not if you're dating your doctor before anyone's even signed the papers." Julie glanced over. "Seriously, Michelle, you're educated and pretty and have a nice house in the Valley. And you used to work in Hollywood. The only people who can't get out of jury duty in LA are hardworking blue-collar folks or the unemployed. They'll associate you with the celebrities who get away with murder. So to speak."

Michelle turned to glare at Julie. "You think I'm guilty?"

"No, I think you're naive." Julie reached in her bra and fished out a mangled ring. "And I think this is a sign."

Goosebumps rose behind Michelle's neck at the sight of her lost wedding ring. She took it and rubbed enough tarnish off on her pants to uncover a glint of gold beneath. She tried to put it on, but with one hand, it was like playing ring toss.

"What makes you such a marriage expert, with all the lovers and the Sade CD in the morning?"

"For Pete's sake, Michelle. I don't have a pack of lovers. It's Jack. We're getting back together."

"Your ex? But he had an affair! You kicked him out!"

"What happened before doesn't matter. It's what happens next that counts." Julie focused on the tunnel to the coast highway. Cars honked past. "I still love Jack, and it's better for the kids. I don't want to be a poster child for divorce. I want to be happy."

"Why didn't you tell me?" Michelle asked.

"I didn't want you to feel bad, with Drew being so far away." Julie slowed along the coast highway. When she stopped behind the line of luxury cars waiting at the light between the beach and the bluffs, she put the car in park and reached over. She tried to jam the ring on Michelle's finger, but it was too bent.

"You think I should go to New York?" Michelle asked.

"Now you're talking."

"But I hate New York."

"Bullshit, you're scared," Julie said. "You were brave enough to face the wreck of that death trap back there. Be brave enough to face the wreck of your relationship…before there's nothing left to salvage."

Michelle opened the window for some air. She glanced over at her friend, but the reflection of the Ferris wheel on the pier caught her eye in the rearview mirror. It spun behind them, the neon spokes flashing blue then fading to purple, like a bruise. Next to the Ferris wheel, the yellow cars of the roller coaster were clanking up, up, up. Children screamed around the curves as if they were hanging on for dear life. She wanted to scream along with them.

"I can't afford to go to New York."

"You can't afford not to." They watched the last bicyclists ride off the beach path to their cars in the parking lot. Beyond them, in the water, figures floating on wake boards stood sentry with saber-like paddles.

"Didn't you say your mom sent you a plane ticket?"

"Nontransferable."

A biplane buzzed overhead, pulling a banner across the fading sky. The rose-tinged light shimmered across the wings.

"Know anyone with a private plane?" Julie asked. "Anyone from work?"

Michelle spied the Welcome to Malibu sign up ahead. If she was going to be blamed for having celebrity connections, she might as well try to come up with one.

The last rays of light ran across the cresting waves, glowing like the stained glass window of a church. The sky was lavender now, pierced with starlight and a rising moon. Michelle tried to relax as Julie turned right on Topanga Canyon Boulevard and headed through to the Valley. There was no way to avoid driving past the wooden cross marking Noah's grave. Michelle raised her ring like an offering to the heavens.

29

MICHELLE WASN'T KIDDING ABOUT how much she hated New York, but if braving the big city helped get her marriage back on track, it would be worth it. Yet, after four hours in the studio jet, agonizing over what to say, all she had to show was a Paramount Pictures notepad smeared with lobster salad. She recalled neither the plot of the film Becca had screened, nor the names of the stars Victor had gossiped about. When she heard the unmistakable explosion of a champagne cork, she flipped her pad over on the mahogany tray table and gave up.

Bubbles fizzed so close to Michelle's nose that she sneezed.

"Bless you," Becca sang from the aisle, where she was holding a flute of champagne out over the empty seat.

"Thanks." Michelle reached across the leather armrest for it. "And thanks for letting me stow away. Here's to your success at the Tribeca Film Festival."

"I don't have anything in competition this year, it's too soon." Becca shook her spiky red hair and took another flute from the assistant in the Ivy League tie. "The champagne is in honor of you." She clinked her crystal flute against Michelle's. Victor came up from behind her to join in the toast with his bottle of vitamin water.

"Why? It wasn't enough that you named your daughter after me?"

"Did you see the necklace she made me for Mother's Day?" Becca lifted the yarn strung with painted macaroni out from the collar of her red suede jacket. "Of course the nanny did most of the work, and I'm sure both girls will hate me when they're teenagers, but for now..." Becca took the bottle of Dom Pérignon and shooed her assistant away. He returned to the lounge area, where several executives spooned caviar from martini glasses. "Victor is presenting his trailer of *The Noah Butler Story* tomorrow—and we have a great offer for you."

Michelle tried not to burp. "What do you mean?"

"How does a million dollars sound? For story rights?"

"Good." Almost too good, she realized. She set the champagne down. After getting loaded on two shots of Kahlua in that bar on the beach in Venice, she knew better than to negotiate drunk. Or at all. "I'd better talk to an agent."

Victor pointed his fancy water bottle at Becca. "Told you."

Becca turned to Michelle. "You don't need an agent. I put my ass on the line for this number to cut out that bullshit. You've been in the business forever, Michelle. You know how this works. Why waste months haggling over a price then pay some hotshot fifteen percent to justify his existence and a lawyer another fifteen to play with the punctuation? By that time you could have donated ten percent of your earnings to charity and become a legend." She snapped her fingers and held her hand out. Her assistant appeared and slapped a check in it. Becca held it up.

Michelle counted the zeroes. A million dollars was tempting, all right. She could take the cash and run. But how far would she get? She imagined paying off her attorney, her medical bills, creating a college fund for Tyler, and getting Drew to stop working out of town. Then, if Orrin Motors offered a settlement...Oops.

Michelle shook her head. "I don't think this will look good at the trial. It might not even be legal. And if I'm found liable, there may be another trial—an even bigger one. I doubt I could keep the money then—even for charity."

Becca scoffed and poured more champagne. "You're not guilty. And you'll be the best real-life hero we've seen on the big screen in years. First, you give a scrawny kid from a broken home a break in the business, then you try to save his life in a rainstorm and you nearly lose your own life in the process. It's an Oscar-winning role. Actresses will fight over it. Who do you like?"

Michelle blushed. The bubbles burst like miniature fireworks. "I don't know."

"Come on, we used to play this game all the time."

"But it's not a game anymore, is it?" Michelle said.

Victor pointed his glass at her. "An actress with attitude."

"And humor," Becca argued.

Michelle looked up. "Then be sure to write a scene in a private jet, where she's offered a million bucks."

Becca laughed as a slick-haired executive joined them and chimed in. "Maybe an unknown blond, so she doesn't play guilty."

"Blonds played guilty for Hitchcock," Victor said.

Michelle pointed her flute at Victor's bowling shirt. "The actress would have to play what you write, wouldn't she, Victor? And you have to abide by my testimony?"

"Of course, doll. 'The truth and nothing but.'"

"Still, casting an unknown might be best," Becca said. "An A-list actress would pull focus from Noah—and it is his story. With a softer look, we sell a morality tale: the sensitive artist, the love story, the wounded mother against the man. Corporate greed and all that. Tate, have you met our leading lady? Michelle Mason, Tate Collins, vice president of distribution."

"Pleasure," he said, studying Michelle. "You're pretty enough to play yourself." He toasted her with his tumbler of scotch just as the plane hit an air pocket.

Becca used Tate's silk pocket square to dab at the wet spot on his Armani jacket. "Excuse my maternal instinct." She winked at Michelle. "That's what inspires our hero, right? A universal theme."

The plane hit another air pocket, and they all clung to the closest seat back. Michelle held her notepad to keep it from sliding off the tray table.

"I'll leave you a festival pass for tomorrow so you can see the trailer on a big screen," Becca continued. "You know how most videos either cut the song to a story or the live concert? Not Victor. He cross-cut the concert footage with a close-up of tires on a rain-slicked road. It's genius. We're sure to lock financing."

Tate nodded at Michelle. "You know the real casting challenge? The daughter."

Michelle's giddy mood popped like the bubbles in her flute. With a million dollars on the line for story rights alone, this was no art house film. Nikki's part would be cast with an eye on Best Supporting Actress. And if they didn't know the true story, Victor would make it up. Michelle could run from the accident, but she couldn't hide from the movie. She had forgotten how slick these people were, how seductive the spotlight could be, how she had used it herself to close deals. Friends or not, the moment Michelle gave in, she gave up her power. She looked up from the bubbles. "Becca? Tell you what—I'll sell you exclusive rights if you make me a producer."

Becca toyed with her macaroni necklace. "You want producer credit?"

"No, I want the job: script approval, casting approval, and a veto on ancillary rights so there's never a Nikki doll sold at Target." She looked sideways at Victor. "And Victor gets final cut."

Victor stood up a little straighter.

"Stop kidding around," Becca said. "This is business. You know I can't get a green light with all that. Think about it, Michelle. Most people sell their rights for fifty grand. This is a very generous offer." Her voice rose until you could hear the concern in it. "And it might be your only chance to make a deal."

"You mean, before the judge finds me guilty?" Michelle put her flute down. "I'll take that chance. Because if I'm not guilty, I can sell my soul to the highest bidder."

"But we're friends," Becca protested. "I'll protect you."

Michelle laughed. "You said it yourself: this is business. All you have now is a two-minute trailer. And without the juicy details from my side of the story, all you'll ever have is a making-of-the-band video."

The call buttons dinged, signaling the initial descent. Becca glanced back at all the eavesdropping executives. She leaned forward and dangled the check in front of Michelle. "C'mon, Chelle. Take the money and run."

Michelle took it. Then she stuffed it in her flute and thrust the soggy mess at Becca.

When Becca stomped away, Victor slumped in his seat. He stared into his bottle of vitamin water as if he could see the future.

Michelle's skin prickled as she realized that they had never spoken about the accident. Something was wrong. "Is there anything you know—something I said in the office, maybe—that makes you think I was responsible?"

"That's not it," Victor said, sipping his drink. "That took a lot of balls."

"Balls?" Michelle repeated. That's what Becca once said she lacked.

"Thing is, if you don't do this thing, I'm screwed. I already spent the advance. Now I'm stuck with the bitch."

"She's not a bitch. That's just what it takes to get a studio deal."

"Ha. This movie is how she got her deal. Without it, she won't let me direct traffic." He finally looked up. "But no, doll, I don't think you're guilty of anything. It would be more fun to write the script if you were, but you're a good person."

Michelle smiled. "Would you say that under oath?"

"Sure," he said. "But you're practically a fugitive. I've helped transport you across state lines, and I've colluded to buy you off for a million bucks. You want to go to jail, I'm your man."

"Nevermind," Michelle said. She lifted the window shade to check out the vast metropolis. Drew was down there somewhere. The thought parched her mouth, so she reached for the call button to ask for a drink of water. Her arm knocked her notepad to the carpet. "Can you help me with something else?"

Victor retrieved the pad.

"Thanks," Michelle said, "but there's more. How are you at love scenes? I'm working on a romantic reunion between a handicapped woman and the estranged husband who served divorce papers via their teenage son."

Victor shook his head. "Fucking asshole. He doesn't deserve you."

"Don't be petty. I know you and Drew don't always get along, but that's my fault. I spent more time with you than with him, so of course he didn't kiss your ass like the rest of your crew. But he's an upright guy. I don't want to get divorced."

When the seat belt light dinged, the uniformed steward hurried over and asked them to put up their tray tables. He pointed at Victor's near-empty glass. "All done?"

"Wait," Michelle said. She reached for his glass and took a slug before he could stop her. The taste was bitter. Michelle spit it out.

She mopped up the spill with the towel the steward handed her, then she shook her head at Victor.

"Wake up and smell the vodka, doll." He stood to go back to his seat.

"See you at the trial?" she asked, her throat constricting.

"Wouldn't miss it," he said. "Can't."

Michelle nodded and watched him amble off. She appreciated his frankness. He did have to write the script, but the story was in Michelle's hands now.

The pilot's voice oozed from the cabin speakers, announcing their initial descent into New York. When he advised the passengers to fasten their seat belts, Michelle couldn't help but look at her lap. Sure enough, hers was already fastened.

She unbuckled it and stood up. Peering out over Victor, she could see the lights of the city. Spotlights scanned the sky, as if searching for remorse. And Michelle had plenty. She looked closer, guessing which lights were from the film festival, where the trailer would be shown to promote a movie that might never get made, not without her blessing. Michelle considered her options, not just for now, but for her future. She spotted Becca's red hair, like a stop sign, a few rows up. She took a few tentative steps, tagging the seat backs for balance, until she towered over her old friend.

Becca looked up. "Shouldn't you be in your seat? You could fall."

Michelle chuckled—how much lower could she go? "I wanted to let you know that you were right. I trust you more than I would a stranger."

"That's great news," Becca said, smiling.

"Here's the thing. If I win—proven not liable—I can write my own check. But since your friendship means so much to me, I'll offer you a preemptive deal. I don't want anything now. But if I do win…it's double or nothing."

"Two million?" The plane lurched. Michelle held her ground as Becca tightened her seat belt. "You've become quite the gambler."

"Take it or leave it, my friend."

Becca fiddled with her necklace until it broke. Macaroni chips spilled to her lap. She picked up a few colored pieces, then looked up. "Deal."

The pilot's warning light dinged.

Michelle made her way back to her seat and buckled in for the descent. She closed her eyes until the whispering of studio executives turned to white noise. Then she looked out the window past the flashing red light on the shuddering wing. As the jet made a slow turn, she caught a glimpse of dark water. She imagined herself floating on the smooth surface, out to the sea. Oh, to dive under, into a world where she was a mermaid with long flowing hair and a neck ringed with pearls. She rubbed the anniversary pearls around her neck and thought about her husband.

30

BUDDING TREES GREW BETWEEN the apartment buildings in Drew's Upper West Side neighborhood. Michelle had heard how lovely springtime was in New York, but until her taxi circled Central Park, she thought that was only in comparison to winter. Today, she appreciated the delicate scent of the dogwood trees and the laughter of families strolling slowly to brunch. And who knew the locals were so friendly! The concierge at her midtown hotel pinned a corsage to her silk sweater and promised to mail her postcard to Wes without even asking her room number. Had she not been so eager to see Drew, she would have strolled through Central Park, or splurged on a horse-drawn carriage.

Michelle signaled for the taxi to stop a few blocks shy of Drew's apartment. She wanted to walk the last few blocks and pin down her opening words. When her cell phone rang and she saw Elyse's number, she was tempted to look for a hidden camera. Michelle shrugged off the impeccable timing to mother's intuition. "Happy Mother's Day."

"The same to you, *ma chérie*. What are we doing to celebrate?"

"Taking a little walk," Michelle said, "*a vous?*"

"We are dancing, of course."

"Of course," Michelle said. She heard the hesitation in her

mother's breath and spoke quickly to cut her off. "Do you mind if I call you back when I get home?"

"Not at all," Elyse said and hung up.

Michelle smiled, pleased that her excuse had been honest. She had said *home* automatically, but if Drew kept working here, she might as well give it a shot. The film industry was here, too, and the women appreciated stylish shoes. She put her phone away and bought an I ♥ NY pennant from the newsstand on the corner. Elyse might not approve of her black dress and bare legs, or traveling when she was ordered to stay put, but she would certainly agree with this mission to win back her husband.

Michelle spied Drew's address on a small stone building and took a deep breath. She smoothed her hair in the reflection of the glass walled lobby, then circled her smile with red lipstick. She practiced posing with the pennant, until the doorman opened the door. Then she took a breath big enough to fly into the future. At that moment, with her life waiting seven floors above, it was true. She could live here. She loved New York!

When the elevator doors groaned open, Michelle's mouth went dry from nerves. She recognized the muffled music of Coldplay seeping from apartment 7B and gave herself a pep talk. If Drew's taste in music hadn't changed, maybe nothing else had either. Their problem was circumstantial, she decided, like the grounds for any manslaughter charge that might be brought against her. Marriage was like religion: a matter of faith. Michelle gathered her courage and knocked.

A deadbolt clicked, then Drew's face appeared in the crack. His eyes widened.

Michelle waved her pennant. "Happy Mother's Day."

His eyes fell to her corsage. "We sent you flowers."

"Thanks. Missed you in Key West."

Bella's muzzle pushed through the crack. Drew slipped past the dog into the hall and shut the door, ignoring the barking that followed. He wiped his hands on the dishtowel tucked in his jeans and pounded the door to quiet Bella. The scent of cinnamon clung to him, or maybe she was just giddy from the sight of his gray T-shirt spilling over his beloved rodeo belt. The bandana on his head added a hip touch.

Michelle smiled. "What's for brunch? I'm starving."

"What are you doing here?" he asked.

"I love you," she said. It had just occurred to her—the perfect start. She waited for him to respond, feeling the weight of the world hang from her aching shoulder: the legal documents, the lipstick, the long nights alone.

Drew nodded to the couple passing behind her to the elevator, then locked his eyes on hers. But he didn't say "I love you" back.

"Please, Drew. I don't want a divorce. I'll move here."

"Does Kenny know you're here?"

She shook her head.

"Your mother sent you, right? You wouldn't just show up here after—"

"After what?" Michelle cried. "Where the hell have you been?"

"Making a living!" he said, and the years rewound as if not a day had passed, as if he'd hit Play on the tape recorder in her head.

"Right, there are no TV shows in LA, no movies, no union jobs—"

"You don't need me. You never needed me."

"That's not true!" Michelle said.

"You look beautiful," he said, like a swear word.

Michelle followed his gaze down from her red lipstick to her chic sundress and high-heeled sandals, and finally she understood. Once, he had been attracted to her strength. Now, he held it against her. Yet it was all a glittering lie, a sparkling facade. How could he not recognize her Oscar-worthy act? She stared at the straps pinching her toes. Her head ached, and her body throbbed from exhaustion. She felt tears on her cheeks, but if she looked up he would see them. He had never seen them.

"I couldn't let myself need you," she said quietly. "How would I have endured all the months you were gone if I did?" She took a deep breath and looked up. He saw her tears and looked away.

"The batter's going to burn."

"Since when do you cook?" Michelle asked.

An old woman reeking of roses faltered by on a cane. "Morning, Mr. Mason."

Drew saluted. "Happy Mother's Day, Mrs. Gottfried."

Michelle wiped her tears and smiled at the old woman. "Yes, have a wonderful day. So sorry we haven't met. I'm Mrs. Mason."

The woman sniffed, then shuffled past to the elevator.

"For chrissakes, Drew, aren't you going to invite me in?"

He held the door open and Bella barreled at her. At least someone missed me, Michelle thought, squatting to pet the slobbery beast as she looked around. The wooden floors were scratched from Bella's nails, and Drew's John Wayne movie posters hung above their old leather couch. But a knit blanket was crumpled on the end, and on the coffee table were pictures of people Michelle didn't recognize, a life she knew nothing about. To the right, a round table was set for two. Michelle felt a flutter of relief. She stood up and called out. "Tyler?"

"He's at school."

Then she heard a woman's voice. "Honey?"

Michelle froze. She was tempted to take a swing at him with her purse. "You fucking liar!"

"Michelle?" The voice was familiar now, and not just from the phone call.

"Is that Sasha?" She let her purse slip to the floor. "My friend? Who used to do my hair? And taught me to knit? Did you know she's the one who made Nikki up like a slut for the video? Is this revenge for me firing her? Or do you just like fucking my boss's old girlfriend?" Michelle looked around. "Sasha! Come out from wherever you're hiding."

"Michelle, it's not like that. We're not just sleeping together."

"Gee, that makes me feel so much better." Michelle tried to make sense of it all. No wonder her husband couldn't make love to her. He didn't love her anymore. "Nevermind, I was supposed to die, right? Sorry to disappoint you."

Sasha tiptoed out from the other direction in a cotton bathrobe. A knit cap hugged her head. Then Michelle's rage dissolved like smoke and she could see more clearly. Sasha's slow approach wasn't fearful; it was feverish. Her pallor was gray, and her frame was skeletal. There were no blond tufts peeking from the cap, no silken strands hanging below. Sasha began sobbing. "I'm so, so sorry."

Michelle started crying, too. The tears were so close, they came easily. Only the breathing was hard. Michelle leaned to embrace the fragile woman, but she could only raise the one arm. Then Drew stepped between them, and Michelle remembered where they were. And why. He stood a few inches in front of Sasha, blocking her like human armor. He turned and took Sasha's bony hand. He was best at playing the hero, and from the way Sasha winced as he steered her away, Michelle could see that she needed one. She wondered how much time he got to enjoy when Sasha was a stunner. Where was the line between hero and martyr?

"Goddamn it, Drew!" Michelle punched his arm as he passed, but he caught it easily. His eyes noted her gleaming gold band, newly repaired for the occasion. He let go.

Michelle tiptoed after them until she saw the dark bedroom

and spied the side table laden with medicine and magazines and a mess of Kleenex. Pillows were piled against the headboard above the wrinkled sheets. The plaid bedspread was smooth on the other side, balancing a lap table with knitting needles and burgundy yarn. A book titled *Meditations for Cancer* lay beside it.

Michelle ran back to the living room, past the tiny kitchen, searching for a place to cry. The first door opened to a bedroom with a Yankees pennant pinned to the wall above rumpled twin beds. Michelle backed out and found the bathroom, with towels on the floor and toothpaste on the sink. She looked at herself in the mirror, at her perfect mask of makeup. Then she turned on the faucet and scrubbed it all off.

Her head was pounding, so she opened the medicine cabinet. She recognized Drew's silver razor and Tyler's can of Axe. An asthma inhaler stood next to a near-empty prescription bottle, and she couldn't help but check the label to see if her son still took the same allergy pills. Without her glasses, she had to hold it close to read the patient's name. Antianxiety pills. For Drew. She wondered if Drew's anxiety was better or worse now, whether he could sleep at night. Then she saw the physician's name: *Dr. Braunstein.*

"Drew!" Michelle stormed out. "How do you know Noah Butler's mother?"

"We met at his funeral. Nikki introduced us."

"Did she prescribe drugs to Nikki, too?"

"Michelle, please. She was doing me a favor. We didn't get a chance to speak that morning, as you can imagine, but she called a few months later as a courtesy, to see how you were doing and— she was nice enough to help me out. She was taking a leave of absence, so she gave me a few refills."

"Ever notice a bottle missing?" That would explain the drugs that Nikki had sold in Hawaii. Drew's dope kit had to be Nikki's source. Why had Michelle not thought of that when she remembered the fight over that pretty piece of foil? Instead, she'd thought the worst. Nikki had called Michelle a hypocrite. She was right.

The smoke detector sounded. Michelle followed Drew to the cramped kitchen, where he chucked a burnt pancake and heaved the window open. The smell was overwhelming, so she went to the open window where she could breathe. The traffic reminded her of Drew's recordings of city sounds: rumbling engines and honking horns and screeching brakes. But there were no crickets calling out to lovers in the night.

He spooned a few small circles of batter onto the frying pan. Michelle watched the bubbles rise. No wonder Tyler liked boarding school. There were fewer secrets to keep. Then she realized how awful that must have been. "I can't believe you made our son lie to his own mother! Why didn't you just tell me?"

"You had enough to worry about," Drew said. "It didn't seem fair."

"Fair?" She watched him flip the pancakes and called up his oldest line. "The fair comes once a year." They smiled at each other, not because the line was so funny, but because it was such a relief to do something—anything—together.

"I'm sorry, Michelle."

She tried not to cry. "Is she the reason you're in such a hurry to get rid of me?"

Drew put the pancakes on a plate. "You and I were drifting apart well before the accident. Sasha hasn't worked in months, Michelle, and she just started chemo. I wouldn't have rushed this, but a divorce takes six months, minimum. If I marry Sasha, she can be added to my insurance policy. You'll be fine after the trial."

He meant the settlement. Michelle didn't tell him about her

deal with the redheaded devil. She rubbed her temple. "Not if I go to jail."

Drew looked up. "Why would you?"

"If I'm found guilty—or liable for negligence—whatever they call it. What if the jury hates me?" She felt a pang and hurried on. "You'll probably come off like a saint: hardworking dad, wife in a coma, falls for a sick friend. Fuck you, Drew."

Michelle turned to leave, but her eyes caught on Tyler's report card clipped to the refrigerator door. Drew put the plate down to yank a photo from beneath it. But Michelle was quick with her left hand now. She snatched it back.

In the photo, Tyler and Nikki were bundled up on a horse-drawn carriage in Central Park. The harness was adorned with Christmas holly. Nikki was red-cheeked and healthy in her sheepskin coat and her purple scarf, with snowflakes dotting her eyelashes as she hugged her little brother.

Michelle looked up at Drew. "You made Tyler lie about his sister, too? He said she ran away after being suspended."

"She did—just not right away," Drew protested. "We already had airline tickets, remember? You wanted us to have a white Christmas? I thought you'd still want that."

"Of course, but…I thought Tyler meant it was just the two of you." Michelle looked up. "Nikki's school records show that she didn't return after Thanksgiving. You let her stay home? Did you give her the Vicodin, too?"

Drew shook his head. "She was a mess, Michelle. We had to keep the blinds closed from reporters. A bootleg video went viral even before Victor's cut was on VH1." He cocked his head at her. "I never pressed Tyler about it, but I suspect he uploaded the video after getting it from you." Michelle shrugged, so he continued. "Noah had already recorded a dozen songs with the band and leaked them as downloads. His father formed Butler Music to release the first album and cut a distribution deal with Sanddollar Records. *Rolling Stone* did a cover, the album went platinum, and fans started loitering on the sidewalk and pounding on the door all night."

"So Nikki ran away."

"When you had trouble pulling out of that last surgery in November, she couldn't take it. Eating Thanksgiving dinner in the hospital cafeteria was depressing enough, but having instant potatoes instead of your garlic mashed…" He hesitated, then turned away to get his coffee cup. "Once the doctor induced the coma a few days later, there was nothing to do but wait."

Michelle pressed the photo to her heart. "She needed me."

"I think she felt responsible," Drew said.

"For the rain? The accident wasn't her fault. Didn't you tell her that?"

"Of course. You don't think I blame myself?"

Drew dumped his cold coffee and poured another cup. He offered it to her, but she wasn't about to put the photo down to take it. Drew took a gulp, thinking back.

"I should have known something was up that day we came to say good-bye to you. Just in case, you know…Nikki was jumpy as hell, kept fiddling with those wooden nesting dolls she brought from her room."

Michelle looked up. "I thought my mother brought those."

"You're missing the point, as usual. When Nikki said good-bye, she meant it."

A truck beep-beep-beeped seven floors down. The echo was so loud in the tiny kitchen that Michelle felt like she was the one backing up. Did she really love this man, or did she love the idea of him? Was this painful longing one of loss, or just plain loneliness? She was too tired to tell the difference.

She started to put the photo back, then decided to keep it. "I'll sign the divorce papers, Drew. But you have to tell me where Nikki is."

"I swear to you, I don't know!" Drew shouted. "Every night I'm afraid she's eating out of trash cans. When you came back from Florida, Kenny gave me hell. Those fucking lawyers—Dillenger and his henchmen—were sniffing around here like a pack of coyotes. If I knew where she was, of course I'd tell you. And I'd send her money even if it cost us. And it would cost us plenty, because if I sent her so much as a dime, Dillenger would trace it and haul her in to testify. She knew you saw that seat belt recall—she brought the mail in every day, and I should have remembered and not let you drive the damn car. But Nikki was also the last person to see Noah Butler alive before he got in the car with you. Do you really want her to relive that day?"

Michelle shivered. "It must have been horrible."

He nodded. "It's better for you, too, Michelle. No matter what happened that morning, Nikki's words will be used against you. Do you understand? She's an emotional girl. There are hundreds of millions of dollars at stake for the car company. One of us could go down."

He took off his apron and tossed it on the counter. "But none of that would matter if I knew she wanted to come home. She went to a lot of trouble to get that Internet voice mail I couldn't trace. And to use prepaid burner phones to leave us messages. And to mail you bogus postcards of Australia. So the only thing I do know—and you know it, too, from the recording on the get well card—is that she doesn't want to see you."

Michelle's chest clutched. "She's young. She doesn't know what she wants."

Drew went to the doorway with the pancakes. "Then give her time."

"Time?" Michelle shouted after him. "It's been forever!" She grabbed the spatula and threw it at him. It clattered to the linoleum floor as he left.

After a moment, Michelle picked up the spatula and tossed it in the sink. She drifted out to the dinner table and pulled the divorce papers from her purse. She signed her name perfectly, then waited for Drew.

"Do you think I'm guilty?"

He met her eyes and hesitated. "Does it matter?"

Michelle realized that it didn't. And that hurt more than any answer. She tore off her Mother's Day corsage and left a trail of white petals all the way to the door. Drew picked up the I ♥ NY pennant and caught up with her.

"That's for Tyler," Michelle said. She took a long, last look at her husband, who no longer fit that description. "I hate New York."

Floor numbers flashed in the elevator like the bright lights of a migraine. Michelle could barely breathe. She rushed out of the building into the blast of exhaust fumes and humanity, then collapsed on a grimy bench where the world blurred into colors around her. Buses screeched, horns honked, and people shouted until her ears split. For the first time, she understood her mother's craving for white light and the numb promise of peace. Instead, sirens screamed past. They were calling her name.

31

Workmen removing the Palmer Clinic sign from the building whistled as Michelle emerged from her car. She waved her bottle of champagne, then hurried across the parking lot past Wes's nurse, who carried out a box of pictures and potted plants.

"Am I too late?" Michelle asked.

"Only if you wanted a cupcake," Bree said. She waved good-bye.

Wes was on the phone when Michelle banged through the swinging doors of the treatment room. The weight machines were gone, but a few examination tables remained between storage boxes, and the aquariums still gurgled against the wall. The doctor's jacket was off, his sleeves were rolled up, and his tie hung loose from his neck. While she waited for the call to end, Michelle walked over to the creatures that inspired his research.

The spiny arms of the coral starfish stuck out at odd angles in the aquarium. Michelle leaned over the top to see it clinging to a large rock. She held her own arm in commiseration, wondering if Wes would notice how her first laser treatment had begun to lighten her scars. She heard him promise someone he'd be home for dinner, then he hung up.

"Congratulations," she called.

"Thanks. This grant was such a long shot, I can't believe I got it."

"I can. Shall I put on a smock for my last exam?"

He surveyed the boxes and shrugged. "How about a quickie with your clothes on? So to speak."

Michelle blushed. "So what's the deal with your starfish?"

Wes turned the music back up and met her at the tank. "First of all, it's a sea star, part of the same echinoderm family as starfish, but in the asteroidean genus."

"I'm starting to believe the whole geek thing. No wonder you got beat up."

Wes looked up and grinned.

Michelle realized she was flirting and focused back on the sea star. A hard shell covered the top as well as the soft underbelly. She watched Wes poke at the creature, until it edged out from behind the rock. The hidden arm ended in a stump.

"Is this the one you showed me a few months ago? That lost its arm?"

"Even better," Wes said. "This is the arm. It regenerated an entire body."

"Creepy," Michelle said.

"No, genetic genius. Got to love a survivor." He turned to face Michelle. "Speaking of which, have you practiced with the manipulatives?"

She nodded, afraid to admit how many days she'd languished in bed doing little else since returning from New York.

"Let's have a look," he said, opening her file. Michelle spied the postcards she'd sent taped inside: the Maui sunset, the Key West sunrise, and Central Park in New York. "If I knew you were going to save those, I'd have written more than a weather report."

"No need," Wes said, pointing his *Star Trek* pen at her signatures. "Plenty here to track your progress."

Michelle dug the nesting dolls out of her purse and set them on the closest table. The head of the outer doll was wide enough to hold easily now, so she set it aside. She slowly grasped the second doll, heavy with the smaller dolls inside, and raised it up out of the larger base. Then, finally, she joined the large head to the painted tutu to make one complete doll.

"Nice work," Wes said, jotting a note in her file.

Michelle tackled the second doll by pretending her hand was the steel claw in the stuffed toy machine at Denny's where Tyler had lost so many quarters over the years. Her arm shook as she lifted the head off and set it down, then pulled out the inner doll and set it aside. Wes nodded. She took a deep breath, rubbed her sore arm, and looked at the third one. She used her left arm to support her weak right arm so she could aim her hand better. After a few tries, she managed to knock it over so that her right hand could at least scoop up the inside doll and set it down beside the others. She turned to him, her arm shaking.

"Keep going."

Michelle wiped her damp forehead with her arm, then considered the fourth doll. This one was thinner, more proportionate to Elyse, the real-life model. And with its yellow chignon, blue eyes, and blue tutu, it really did resemble her. Michelle shook her head no.

Wes traced the seam that cut across the smaller ballerina's painted corset. "Come on. There's another inside."

"Not anymore," she said. "Must have gotten lost at the hospital."

He looked inside the empty doll. "Okay, then, put them back together."

"Didn't you say on the phone you were on your way out?"

"That can wait. This is for your insurance company. Your radial dexterity is impressive." He looked underneath the large doll. "Who makes these?"

"Russian artisans. This one was painted for my mother before I was born."

"She's a ballerina?"

"Was," Michelle said, rubbing her arm.

"The blue dress is from the tragic Giselle, right? I saw the Bolshoi at UCLA a few weeks ago."

"Hot date?" Michelle asked.

"Smoking," he chuckled. "Mother's Day."

"That is tragic," she teased.

"That was her on the phone tempting me with her famous pot roast."

Michelle began putting the dolls back together. "My mother doesn't cook, but in the ballet world, she was famous for her Giselle. She was Giselle. Even at home."

"At home?"

Michelle shrugged. "Except at home, she used pills instead of a sword."

"I thought Giselle died of a broken heart."

"Suicide." Michelle tried to put the third doll back into the bottom, but it slipped. "Giselle would have gotten over it if there hadn't been a sword handy. Didn't you see the male dancers bury her *outside* the church walls?"

"I was watching the maidens," Wes admitted. "But I met your mother in the hospital. She seemed charming...And very much alive."

"Purely by accident," Michelle said.

"Didn't you once tell me you don't believe in accidents?"

"Did I?" Michelle's face clouded at the thought.

"In any case, if I'd known, I'd have invited you, to explain the story. But I gathered from the New York postmark that you were busy."

"Yes. Signing divorce papers." Michelle set the doll's head down properly. "It's been a horrible month. But I finally understand what my mother went through."

Wes stacked the rest of the dolls for her. "How are you feeling now?"

"I could use a drink," Michelle admitted, nodding at the champagne. He retrieved the bottle she brought and twisted the cork out with a pop. He filled two leftover party cups.

"To your grant," she toasted.

"To a full recovery," he said. They both drank.

"That's a good word for it," Michelle said. "Even with the trial coming up, I have this odd sense of relief about the end of my marriage. Drew traveled so much it was hard to feel connected. I really wanted us to make it, but…maybe only to prove we could." She took a bigger sip.

"To closure, then," Wes said. "And a taxi ride home."

She smiled, noticing the shadow of his beard and the weary droop of his shoulders. His musky smell had burned through his Irish Spring scent like a top note of cologne. She felt awkward for noticing and hotly aware of being alone with him. Now he was looking at her. She pushed her hair behind her shoulder and realized how much it had grown in two months. "What?"

"You look good," he said.

She blushed. "You, too."

"Thanks, but I meant—beautiful." Then he seemed to catch himself and nodded at the white silk blouse tucked into her pencil skirt. "You've gained some weight back."

Michelle nodded. The room shrunk around them. They

looked away from each other, as if surveying the space. Wes fumbled with the stethoscope beneath his loosened tie. "We should finish your exam."

"Your mother's waiting," Michelle agreed. She had goose bumps, but it wasn't from the air conditioning.

Wes pressed the stethoscope against her back. The cool disk tickled through the thin silk of her blouse, but warmed quickly. She felt his moist breath and smelled his perspiration as he leaned close to listen. He tilted his head, brows furrowed in concentration as he moved the stethoscope around in circles. She felt her heart pound, but apparently he didn't. He dropped the stethoscope and wrapped his fingers around her wrist.

Michelle was nervous. She fought the urge to kiss him. "Mind if I sit down? My legs feel like noodles—probably from the champagne."

He helped her up to the padded table to sit facing him. Her long legs made it hard for him to reach, so she tugged her skirt up just enough to spread her legs and let him lean between them.

"This is awkward."

"I'm still a doctor, Michelle."

"Am I still your patient?"

"For a few minutes, until I finish your file." He slid two fingers to the side of her neck.

He was so close she could see the tuft of hair erupting from his collar, the bristles on his chin, and the intensity in his eyes as they widened. "What's wrong?"

She followed his gaze to the lace band of her thigh high stockings.

"Do you have any idea how hard it is to put on pantyhose with one hand? These are easier."

"I don't mind; it's just making my pulse sound louder than yours," he said, chuckling. He looked around. "No idea where we packed the thermometer."

318

She couldn't resist. "When my kids were little, I used to kiss their foreheads to check it."

"My mother did that too," he said. "But it's not professional."

"Maybe not." She looked up at him and held her breath.

He traced the small scar on her forehead, then pressed his lips against it. "You are a little warm," he said, standing back up and placing the stethoscope against her silk-covered back. "Breathe."

She tried. But as he leaned forward, his belt buckle dug into her belly. She could feel the hardness beneath it and sat up. Now, she could barely breathe at all. Every light in the room seemed to flicker and die. Her skin prickled with heat. It wasn't until the music came to an abrupt stop that she realized the power had shut off. She looked around. "What was that?"

"The end of our lease," he said. "Utilities were included." He turned and looked at the silent aquariums with concern. A loud boom sounded, then bubbles rose against the glass as they hummed back to life. The lights remained off. Wes apologized to Michelle. "I only have the one generator."

Michelle smiled as the late sun streamed in through the window, basking the room in a warm glow. The music, on the same electrical circuit as the aquariums, created a soothing background. "At least you have your priorities straight."

"Shall we finish before it gets too dark?" He placed the stethoscope inside her wrist. Then, he placed it just under her pearls, against her breastbone. The top button of her blouse was in the way, so she reached up to unbutton it. She felt the metal slide against her skin as the silky fabric slipped, revealing the red lace edge of her bra. He cleared his throat. "Your scars are fading nicely."

"Thank you," Michelle said, looking down at the vivid contrast of her pale skin against her lingerie. She'd worn red to help her feel bold enough to ask him to be her character witness. Whatever else it got her was icing on the cake. Michelle smiled, surprised at her own daring thoughts. When she looked up, he was still staring at the red lace cupping her breast. "I mean, yes, the scars are lighter. Are you going to make a note?"

He did. "Need help buttoning up?"

"No." She fiddled with a button, then looked up slowly. "You were right, I'm feeling quite warm."

"Is that so?" he asked, eyes twinkling.

Hallelujah, Michelle thought. She'd never acted so brazenly before, but what did she have to lose? Julie had been wrong, not only about Drew, but about the fact that this man—this handsome, brilliant, total babe of a doctor—cared about her. And not just as a patient.

Michelle unbuttoned the next button, and the next, until his eyes widened at the full bloom of her breast. "Do you want to make another note?"

He put his pen down. "I'm done making notes."

"So you're not officially my doctor anymore?"

"No," he said. Then he kissed her. Tentatively at first, then deeply. He pulled back and raised his eyebrows, giving voice to the question hovering between them.

Michelle felt moisture behind her neck, beneath her arms, between her legs. "Go on," she whispered.

He pushed her blouse from her shoulders and swept his lips across her neck. He slid the red satin strap off her left shoulder, looked down at her breast, then looked up slowly and smiled. "You're absolutely gorgeous." Then he licked her nipple.

Michelle whimpered. After a moment, she lifted his chin back up and kissed around his lips until she could feel the ridge of whiskers. Then she bit him. He kept kissing her, sucking her tongue into his mouth. She pulled away in surprise. Then she reached out and ripped his shirt open, until she could see his chest muscles etched by the streaming moonlight. She wanted to see more.

She wrapped her legs around him, then traced the buckle of his belt until he yanked it open. He kissed her again. She felt his strong grip around her thighs, his kisses on her neck, and his breath in her ear until she couldn't bear it any longer. She arched back and pulled his hips closer. He looked into her eyes and pulled off her panties achingly slow.

She felt the cold rush of air, then the heat of the moment, the world gone dark, as he pushed her back on the table and pressed himself inside her with one strong plunge. She moaned at the shock of it. His strong hands clamped her hips, and for a moment he held himself still, pressed all the way up inside her. He began moving above her, slowly at first, then faster, until he was driving himself into her like he was out of his mind. She cried out, wanting more, but not wanting it to end. She placed her hand on his hips and locked her eyes with his.

Then she pushed him away. He dove toward her for a kiss, but she slipped sideways and tapped her stiletto heel against his calf until he rolled onto his back. She swung her leg over and climbed up on top.

When she smiled, he sat up just enough to kiss her and hold her bottom in both hands. She pushed his shirt back and dragged it from his shoulders, then unclasped her bra with one hand and flung it away. She leaned forward, pressing her bare breasts against his slick skin, her lips clinging with each kiss as she rode him, harder and harder until she tingled where she had been numb, burned where she had tingled, and still they kept rocking, until she blacked out and saw fireflies, and they cried out together.

When their heat had cooled, she lay trembling on top of him.

He rolled her sideways and held her. She was full of feeling, but empty of words, as she fell asleep in his arms.

When she awoke, she didn't know how much time had passed. He was naked, with his arms still locked tightly around her. His eyes fluttered, then he kissed her on the forehead. Michelle nodded; it was easier than forming words as Wes's strong fingers massaged her neck. When her muscles relaxed, he flattened his palms and rubbed them along her shoulders and down her arms, then walked his fingers back up to knead the muscles in her back. Next, his hands traced her hip, then stretched down to caress her thighs as if spreading the warm glow of the orgasm through every inch of her skin. Michelle's entire being was in a blissful oblivion. She barely had enough breath to speak. "What kind of therapy are you doing now?"

"PCR," he said with a straight face. "Postcoital rub."

"Very effective," Michelle said, laughing. Then she pushed to a seated position and winced. She saw the empty champagne bottle on the floor. "That explains a bit."

"No excuses, Michelle. You blew my mind. Want some water?"

Michelle suppressed a giggle and nodded. He may have woken Sleeping Beauty from her slumber, but he looked just as shaky as she did. It took a few moments for him to gather the strength to rise and stumble, naked, across the room.

She watched her dark Adonis, his muscles twitching across his shoulder blades, his bare ass flexing as he circled back to the cooler by his desk. She averted her eyes as he returned with water, but couldn't help but peek as he pulled his trousers on. She covered by glancing at the first rays of morning light streaming beneath the blinds. "When do the movers come?"

Wes handed her the water. "In a few hours," he said. "But don't rush off."

She took a sip, then set it down to pull her stockings back up. She was still wearing the stilettos, but when she stood up from the table, she wobbled upright. She pulled her blouse on one arm at a time. "Want me to pick up some breakfast?"

"No thanks. I still have to pack the books. If you're hungry, I have protein bars with my running gear. Maybe some chocolate."

"Perfect." As he searched his desk, she remembered what she needed to ask. "I know you'll be busy setting up the new office for a few weeks, but is there any chance you can stop by the courthouse to testify for me?"

"I wish I could."

She buttoned her blouse slowly with her left hand. "Should we not have done this?"

"No, that's not what I mean. I've been subpoenaed by an attorney involved in your case. If I have to testify about the camera disk, I could lose my grant—not to mention my license. I had to hire my own lawyer to avoid testifying at all. Doctor-patient privilege."

"I'm sorry about that," Michelle said.

"It's not your fault." He went to a safe behind his desk and unlocked it. "I wanted to help. And no one can search private property without a warrant, so I logged this into Lost and Found. You need to sign for it." He returned with the memory card.

Michelle closed her weak hand around it. As the plastic pressed into her palm, the images on the disk flickered like a slideshow in her mind. Nikki's birthday, Noah's motorcycle, their kiss...Nikki had lifted the camera, locked her eyes on the lens, and captured the moment—a triumph of bliss. At this moment, she could almost understand how it felt.

Wes set the property release down with his *Star Trek* pen. She put the disk in her purse and signed the form. Then she watched as the tiny *Enterprise* flew up the barrel of space.

"One of my patients gave me another as a going-away gift," he said. "You can keep it. And 'may the Force be with you.' At least until I'm back in town."

"Very funny, but I know that's not from *Star Trek*." She put the file aside. "Wait—what do you mean 'back in town'?"

"My grant is for a residency at the Carnegie Institute in Pittsburgh. I thought you knew. They have the best facility for tissue regeneration."

Michelle clapped her hand on her heart. "What about this tissue?"

"That's a muscle. It just needs exercise." He reached for her, and she rested her head against his chest. The gurgle of air filters filled the silence.

"Everybody leaves."

He straightened her collar around her pearls. "Visit me."

She slapped his hand away. "It's cold there. I grew up in the Midwest, I know."

The voltage meter would rise until it burst if she were hooked up to it now. He had cured her, all right. She could feel everything. And it hurt.

She pulled away and snatched her panties from the floor. "You collect souvenirs from all your warm-blooded specimens, Doctor?" She stuffed the panties in his pocket, then pulled her skirt on. "You like us sick and helpless? Is that it?"

Wes stood there a moment, then he went to the aquarium and tapped fish food into the tanks. When he looked back, Michelle was struggling to zip her skirt.

"Want some help?"

"No!" She didn't want help—not from him, or Drew, or her mother. She could do this by herself if she had to. She just wished she didn't have to. She gave up on the zipper and hooked the waistband.

Wes's chuckle broke the quiet. "I knew it."

She scooped her red brassiere from the floor and turned on him. "What?"

He stopped laughing. "That I could love you."

Michelle stepped toward the tank but didn't dare look him in the eye. She was afraid he'd be able to see right into her. Instead, she crouched down to take a better look at the sea star, at how the spindly new arms sprouted from the center. The creature undulated sideways, then wrapped its tentacles around the rock. "Does that mean that you do love me?"

"Only if you'll let me." He held a Hershey's Kiss out to her right. "Last one."

Michelle looked up, exhausted by this game. His eyes caught hers and softened, as steady as the gaze of her daughter in the photograph. He'd never felt that way before, she remembered him admitting. He'd saved her arm, risked his career to protect her, and now he was offering her his very last Kiss. He unwrapped the foil slowly, until she could smell nothing else, until her mouth filled with liquid and her tongue swam with desire. Then he popped it in his mouth.

"Bastard," she said and stood up.

He lifted her chin and kissed her slowly, sucking on her tongue until every trace of chocolate melted away. She clung to him and kissed him back, surrendering to the blend of sweet and salty, pleasure and pain, innocence and fear.

32

THE JUNE FOG BURNED off like wisps of steam from the pie slice of ocean visible from the courthouse. Michelle clutched the second-floor railing and rose to her toes in *éléve*. The ballet position allowed her to peek between the royal palms and see the pier. When Tracy, the court officer, beckoned her back inside, Michelle followed, no longer interested in the Ferris wheel. After weeks of searching for jurors who swore they'd never seen the Roadhouse video, Michelle was sick of Santa Monica.

Flashbulbs popped as she steeled herself for the daily gauntlet of reporters in the hallway. A correspondent in a suede miniskirt smiled for the KTLA camera. "The Hollywood producer accused of reckless endangerment already faces huge penalties—even the possibility of jail time. The district attorney is expected to make an announcement today about filing a criminal charge of vehicular manslaughter for the death of rock legend—wait! Here she is now! A comment, Mrs. Mason?"

Michelle focused on the speckled tile beneath her practical pumps and veered toward the drinking fountain.

Kenny's brown loafers padded into view, followed by Greenburg's black wing tips. Someone grabbed her left elbow and hustled her through the forest of flip-flops and sneakers. She recognized the beloved Louboutin heels she'd traded for the camera disk and looked up at Celeste. She couldn't help but smile at the Venice Bistro bartender who claimed to be Noah's girlfriend.

As the news stories spread over the past few months, Michelle had been deluged with interview requests. She was forbidden to respond. Who would have guessed that she would end up *MOS*? That was the German term for recording silent films, known in film school as mit-out sound. *MOF* described Michelle better: mit-out family.

A few fans in Killer Mom T-shirts called her name, then the courtroom door clanked shut behind her.

Lexi was waiting inside with a comforting hug. Michelle had never seen her out of her nurse's uniform, but her flowered sundress had won hearts on the witness stand.

Julie was there too, apologizing for sending Michelle to New York. Michelle didn't blame her—it was better to know. "I can be a character witness if you need another," she said. "Married, if that helps. That's why I've been out of touch. Jack and I stopped the divorce and took a second honeymoon. Come to our party next week?"

"Sure," Michelle said. "If I'm not in jail."

Cathy overheard and stepped to her side. "Nonsense, I already splurged on a steak to celebrate."

She led Michelle down the aisle past a *Rolling Stone* reporter in a Hawaiian shirt and a preppy columnist from *Variety*. Michelle used to love being in *Variety*, but not anymore, not like this. A sketch artist made strokes with his charcoal as he stared at her little black dress. She still refused to wear beige, but she had compromised with Cathy by wearing the pale lipstick her mother left at her house.

The sketch artist nudged his neighbor, a fellow parasite with a press pass. The reporter awoke with a snort. His story had only one line left to fill: "Butler Music Scores $_____ for Tragic Death of CEO's Son."

Michelle heard the stamp of Becca's boots then a whisper in her ear. "I brought the check. Double or nothing. Good luck, my friend." Becca gave her shoulder an encouraging squeeze before Cathy pulled her away.

Kenny opened the low gate behind the counselor's table. Cathy kissed him for luck and handed Michelle off like a relay baton. Kenny nodded at Greenburg and Guy Butler, resuming their positions at the plaintiff's table before escorting Michelle to her chair.

Once the spectators settled in, the jurors were ushered back to their seats as if the curtain was about to go up. Michelle heard Drew's whistle amid the hubbub and felt for her pearls. She'd expected a thud in her chest at the sight of him, but felt only sadness. She wore the pearls with pleasure today, not because she was sentimental that he'd given them to her, nor because she was proud to have worn them with Wes, but because they were hers and they were pretty and she liked them.

When a figure with a duffel bag squeezed past Drew to sit down, Michelle nearly looked away before recognizing her son. He must have come directly from the airport, after final exams. She hadn't wanted Tyler to see her like this, or to relive the day he lost her. But when he looked up and caught her eye, she let go of her necklace to wave.

Kenny nudged her to turn around and clasp her hands in her lap.

The courtroom door banged open, and they both looked back. Young men the age Noah would be now slunk in wearing UCLA T-shirts. Tracy marched back with all the authority of her silver badge, then pointed to an empty row and shut the door behind them. Kenny scowled, as if he was expecting someone else. Michelle prayed it would be Nikki.

"All rise," the bailiff said.

Judge Vaughan, a tall, middle-aged woman with yellow cuffs protruding from her crisp black robe, carried her own gavel to the gleaming bench. She explained the alleged causes of action to the jury, reminding them that attorneys representing all parties were permitted to question the witnesses. The jurors needed to pay close attention. Then she faced front and invited Greenburg to make his opening remarks.

He unveiled Noah's picture on the easel and began slowly, his quiet intensity making up for his short stature. In this room, the only size that mattered was the space between your ears. Or in your wallet, which was clearly the case when Mr. Dillenger, representing Orrin Motors, took his place on the floor.

Good ole boy Kenny could only smile when he rose to pay respects in his wrinkled brown suit. When Michelle frowned, he gave her a capped pen and a legal pad as if she were a child who could be kept busy with doodling. If she wanted to write anything, she'd have to bite off the top with her teeth. Michelle dug Wes's silly pen from her purse and watched the tiny USS *Enterprise* float down the barrel through space. She wished she were on it.

When Greenburg introduced Guy Butler, Noah's father swaggered to the witness stand as if he'd won a game show. He paused at the easel to replace his dead son's photograph with a band poster and a pie chart of projected earnings. Then he strutted over to sit in the spotlight. As he cocked the microphone closer to his suntanned face, his leather jacket opened enough to reveal a Roadhouse RIP T-shirt.

Greenburg smoothed the silk tie beneath his razor-sharp lapels until the whispers died down and the only sound in the room was the tick-tick-tick of the clock on the wall above the jury box. He bowed to the judge, apologized, and sent Noah's father back to his seat without asking any questions.

Then he called Dr. Laura Braunstein to the stand.

Noah's gray-haired mother walked slowly to the front. Dr. Braunstein looked just as sharp as she had in her surgery scrubs, but today she was draped in the black caftan that billowed down the aisle like a tent. Greenburg helped her up to the witness stand, where she put one hand on the Bible and the other on the Star of David pendant choking her neck. Her voice shook as she took the oath, but her eyes were clear. And they never strayed toward Michelle.

Michelle wondered if Dr. Braunstein liked the photo of Noah that she'd posted on the bulletin board or if she'd noticed that the postcard in her drawer was askew. Michelle glanced back at Cathy behind them, but her accomplice looked pointedly away. No one else in the courtroom knew that Michelle had apologized. She felt like a pariah.

Greenburg confirmed that Noah's mother was a physician who had taken a leave of absence to deal with her grief. He removed the spreadsheet from the wooden easel, then asked her to identify the photograph behind it. She confirmed that the smiling image was her son's student UCLA ID picture. Greenburg then showed a picture of Noah dressed in a turkey costume serving cookies to sloppy children sitting at a table in an auditorium.

"Can you identify this picture?"

She laughed. "Yes, that's Noah under all those feathers at the Thanksgiving Dinner for the Homeless a few years ago. When he turned eighteen, they asked him to work in the kitchen, but he missed giving cookies to the kids. He asked me about doing a benefit concert for the children's shelter the year he…" She looked down, unable to finish.

Kenny called out. "Objection, Your Honor. While I grant you that Noah Butler was an upstanding citizen, the estate is not suing for America's loss."

"Sustained," the judge said.

Kenny patted Michelle's hand. Then he grabbed his handkerchief from the table to wipe his forehead.

Greenberg bowed in obedience and replaced the picture with a sentimental shot of Noah in a sports jacket, leaning down to hug his mother in front of Holy Cross Hospital. She held a sprinkle-covered cupcake with a candle.

"My birthday," she said with a smile in her voice. "That last fall, when he wasn't at band practice, he spent most of his nights with me in Tarzana instead of in Malibu with his dad. He was surprising me here to see the Herb Ritts photography exhibit at the Getty Center."

Greenburg smiled. "Sounds like the perfect son."

"Oh, no. He couldn't get his dirty bowls in the dishwasher for the life of him."

The audience snickered. For a moment, Michelle couldn't remember whom she was rooting for.

"He wasn't perfect, but he was a good boy."

"Objection," Kenny called.

The judge shook her head at him. "You're going to accuse Dr. Braunstein of hearsay in her opinion of her son?"

"Bingo. Noah Butler may have been a good son, but he was not a 'good boy.' Not in the eyes of the law."

"I'm listening," the judge said.

"We all like to think the best of our children, don't we?" Kenny turned and smiled at the jury. "And I know firsthand that Noah Butler's heart was in the right place. He helped out with my son's baseball team."

Mr. Dillenger rose. "With all due respect, Your Honor, Mr. Kazan is not a witness."

"Quite so." She turned back to Kenny. "Is this relevant?"

"It is, Your Honor. Noah Butler couldn't have been described as a good boy, because he was arrested for possession and sale of cocaine when he was a juvenile. His volunteer hours with the baseball league satisfied community service requirements. I know, because I signed his log."

The jury gasped.

"Objection!" cried Mr. Greenburg. "Those records were sealed and are inadmissible."

"You're out of order, counselor," the judge called. "You pull that kind of stunt again and I'll hold you in contempt." She waved all the lawyers to the bench. Dillenger marched up with Greenburg, but Kenny made a show of tucking in his shirt and ambling up behind them, as if confused by his mistake.

Michelle smiled, knowing that he was trying to protect her. For once, she was grateful that her ears were so sensitive. Between the titters of the gallery behind her, she could make out enough from the lawyer's conversation to understand that as long as Noah stayed out of trouble, the record was to be destroyed after five years. Now, there was no need.

Michelle had enough experience with the music industry to guess that Noah's dad had been the source of the cocaine. That's what Noah's mother had meant when she mentioned that her son got in a "little trouble." Something flashed in Michelle's memory as Kenny ambled back. But it wasn't the silver foil that Nikki had passed off as a gum wrapper. It was something about Noah. Something she couldn't quite place.

Kenny gave an aw-shucks shrug, then sat down. The other attorneys were still whispering vehemently with the judge.

"Kenny," Michelle whispered. "Why bring that up? Wouldn't his arrest give me more reason to want him to stay away from my daughter?"

"Only if you were aware of it. And since it's unlikely he would have told you, how would you have known about the arrest before today?"

Michelle watched him, wondering if Cathy had told him about her visit to Holy Cross after all.

Judge Vaughan instructed the jury to disregard the last question. They looked at each other with eyebrows raised. Kenny clicked his pen and reviewed his notes.

The judge ordered the stenographer to repeat the last bit of testimony. "He was a good boy," she read aloud.

No, Michelle thought. Her arm jerked. She cried out, wincing in pain.

Kenny put his arm around her, shielding her from the curious glances cast her way. Unbidden, he helped her remove the prim white cardigan she'd borrowed from his wife. The air conditioning chilled Michelle's arms, making her fading scars raise and redden. He poured her a glass of water and set it down out of reach on her right. She stretched her left arm out to clasp it. Michelle felt the glare of the fluorescent lights, the attention of the audience, and did as Kenny directed.

"Is everything all right, Mr. Kazan?" the judge asked.

Kenny nodded for them to continue, so Mr. Greenburg straightened his cuffs and stood once more, looking pressed and polished as he played his part. Michelle wanted to believe this scene had been written in stone, that there was nothing she'd change, no reason for regret. Kenny saw her shiver and placed his hand on her elbow. Michelle looked at his rough skin and thick knuckles, and remembered another time when Kenny had reached out to her.

It was a rainy morning at the ball field and the game had just been called off. She could see the sopping wet boys piling into Kenny's van with the muddy ball bags. Michelle offered to take the team banner so it wouldn't be ruined. Kenny gave her elbow a squeeze, grateful for her good nature. He had no idea how quickly her mood would change.

The courtroom was gone now, Kenny's hand was gone, and all she saw was that damn motorcycle dripping in her driveway.

Tyler spotted the black Harley through the splash of the windshield wipers. Michelle parked the SUV, pressed the garage door opener, then climbed out into the rain. The engine tick-tick-ticked as Michelle circled the hood. She heaved the motorcycle off its kickstand and rolled it into the garage.

"Don't forget your bag," she called to Tyler.

It took two hard jerks to park the Harley, then she hurried inside. A football game raged on the television, but Bella was the only one watching. Michelle unzipped her wet jacket and surveyed the empty room.

Tyler tugged on her arm. "Where's Noah? Can he catch for me?"

"Not in this rain. Go put on dry clothes."

"Make me a sandwich?" Tyler asked.

"Make it yourself," she snapped, looking around for his sister. Tyler tracked mud across to the kitchen and took a bag of chicken leftovers from the fridge. Michelle felt bad; she followed him to apologize. She corralled Bella, who was pestering him for scraps. Then she heard muffled music over the thrumming rain.

Michelle's stomach seized with every step down the hall, closer to the sound flooding from beneath Nikki's door. She knocked, but there was no answer. She twisted the doorknob. It was locked. Michelle ran down to Tyler's room, but the shared bathroom was locked as well. She opened Nikki's drawer and rifled through toothbrushes and tampons. Still no change in the music, but now she recognized a Roadhouse song from the video shoot. Under a half-squeezed toothpaste tube, she found *a flowered hair clip. She ran back to the hall door, bent it open, and went to work.*

The lock clicked and the door swung open. Noah's ass confronted her, his bare legs banging against Nikki's as he fucked her on all fours. That was Michelle's voice screaming, her baby jumping naked from the bed, her eyes bloodshot and vacant, and her hand throwing the hair clip at his head. "Get out!"

Noah pulled his jeans up, trying to focus his bloodshot eyes as he fumbled with the zipper. "Sorry."

Sorry? She wanted to reach over and zip his balls off then yank off his shriveled penis and grind it in the kitchen disposal. She picked up his motorcycle boot and threw it at him. It slammed against the buttercup wall. Nikki shrieked. She clutched the sheet and sunk to the floor in a shivering mess.

When Noah snatched his keys from beside the CD case on the dresser, Michelle changed her mind. She couldn't let him leave without punishment. She should tell his parents or call the police.

Beneath the bass beat, rain still clattered against the rock roof. Michelle hurried back to the kitchen. Tyler was on the couch across the room, glued to the game on TV. She grabbed the open bag of chicken. She ran back to Nikki's room with Bella barking at her heels.

Noah emerged in the doorway, fully dressed. "Later, babe," he called back.

"You're not going anywhere," Michelle cried. She pitched him the chicken. Without thinking, he caught it. Bella jumped him and he dropped the keys. Michelle snatched them.

Nikki shrieked from the bed. Michelle kicked Nikki's stereo. It went silent, but so did Nikki. She hid under the sheet.

"Nikki!" Michelle shouted, but there was no response, no movement at all. Michelle tore the sheet away. She didn't want to see if there was blood on her daughter's thigh or tracks on her arm—but she had to be sure she was breathing.

When the front door slammed, Michelle looked up. Nikki grabbed the covers back. Michelle reached for her. Nikki twisted and batted her away, clawing through the air with both hands. Michelle kept trying to grasp the moving targets of fingers and hair. She felt a sharp scratch on her forehead as Nikki lunged and fell out of her bed. Michelle sat on the hysterical girl, wrapping the fallen quilt around her as she writhed on the floor.

Noah appeared, dripping rain in the doorway. "Where's my bike?"

"Michelle!" Kenny's sharp voice woke her up. She looked at him, then ran her fingers across the scar on her forehead. The medics had assumed it was from the accident, and in a way, that was true. She caught her breath and clasped her hands in her lap.

Greenburg was still questioning Dr. Braunstein. "Can you describe for us, Laura, the last time you saw your son alive?"

"I scolded him," she said. "He left his bowl of Lucky Charms in the sink, and he'd only eaten the marshmallow bits." Someone chuckled, so she looked up. "I gave him a multivitamin and offered him a ride to the field on my way to work. He said no, he was staying home to study."

Greenburg spoke gently. "What happened next?"

"I received a call during a gall bladder operation. Just after ten."

"Do you remember the exact words?"

"There's been an accident," she said.

Necks swiveled in Michelle's direction. The heat of a hundred eyes bored into her. Kenny slipped her his handkerchief and she cried right on cue.

Noah's mother continued. "My first thought was of that motorcycle his father gave him for his birthday. I wanted to get rid of that two-wheeled death trap, but he threatened to move out. He was already in college, so I didn't have much time left with him…" Her voice trailed off.

"No, you didn't," Greenburg agreed. "Were you aware of any relationship between your son and the defendant's daughter?"

"Objection!" Kenny called. "Hearsay."

"Overruled," the judge said. "Answer the question, please."

Noah's mother nodded. "Yes. They brought me coffee at work. They were friends."

"You're certain of that?"

"His lovers tended to be more voluptuous. Like Celeste, who tended bar where his band played. He was quite aware of the advantages of being a musician."

Greenburg ignored chuckles from the gallery and pressed on. "Are you aware that Nicole Mason ran away after the accident?"

"Yes. Her father was in touch after the funeral. He offered condolences."

"Do you have any idea why she might have run off?" Greenburg asked.

Kenny jumped up. "Objection! Calls for speculation."

"I'm going to allow it," the judge said, waving at Noah's mother to continue.

She considered the question. "Her mother was gravely injured. I imagine she was confused and upset."

"Fair enough. But be honest: don't you hold her mother accountable?"

"For giving my son a ride in the rain?" Noah's mother asked.

"Let me rephrase," Greenburg said. "When you visit your son's grave, do you think about how he died?"

"I don't visit my son's grave." Gasps filled the room, but she continued. "He isn't there. There wasn't enough left of him to bury. Do you know what it's like to have your child vanish into thin air?"

Michelle looked up. Yes, she thought. Yes! Kenny saw Michelle tearing up and pointed at the pad in front of her. She picked up her pen and drew circles.

Greenburg tipped his head at Dillenger. "Your witness."

Dillenger tucked his watch into the pocket of his pinstriped suit and strutted to the witness stand. "If I'm not mistaken, isn't there an eight foot tall crucifix on the roadside where Mrs. Mason's car drove off the cliff? A memorial?"

Noah's mother shrugged. "That has nothing to do with my son. Noah was Jewish. And he wasn't a rock star when he was alive."

Dillenger was silent for a moment. Then he held his hand to his heart. "I know I speak for everyone, Dr. Braunstein, when I tell you how sorry I am for your terrible loss. It's especially tragic in light of his success. You don't get a penny. In fact, according to public record, disability payments provided by the state of California were your only source of income during your leave of absence. Isn't it true, Dr. Braunstein, that financial concerns forced you to return to work, despite the fact that you were still being treated for depression due to grief over the death of your only son?"

"I'll be grieving forever," she said. "But I missed my work."

"You're under oath, Dr. Braunstein. Didn't financial concerns play a part in your decision to return to work?"

"A part," Dr. Braunstein admitted.

Judge Vaughan cut in. "Let's get to the point, counselor. It's no secret that this plaintiff does not profit from licenses and related copyright owned by Butler Music, Inc."

"Thank you, Your Honor," Dillenger said. "Dr. Braunstein, are you aware that you can obtain damages from either Michelle Mason or the Orrin Motor Company, one or the other, or both?"

"Yes," Dr. Braunstein answered.

"Then isn't it true that you are also aware that you would

benefit the most from the ample resources of a Detroit automotive manufacturer? Why, you could erect a shrine to your son and top it with a solid gold Star of David!"

Appalled spectators gasped from all sections of the gallery.

"Objection," Greenburg called. "Badgering the witness."

The judge rapped her gavel. "Sustained. Shame on you, Mr. Dillenger. Dr. Braunstein is a respected member of the community and deserves to be treated as such."

Dillenger bowed his head. "My apologies. In fact, you strike me as the kind of woman who could never put a price on the relationship between mother and child. Wouldn't you agree that no amount would be sufficient for the loss of your son?"

"Yes, I would. That's why I've set up the Noah Butler Trust for the children's shelter."

"Even so. A verdict against Orrin Motors would provide a generous contribution."

Noah's mother rose slowly, like a tank cresting the field of battle. She aimed and fired, every word charged with ammo. "You don't have children, do you, Mr. Dillenger?"

"Sadly, no," he said. "That's why I need you to explain why, if it isn't for the money, you would defend the very woman who drove your son to his death."

"I'm not defending anyone. If you want to find out if Mrs. Mason is responsible for the accident in which my son died, then you'll have to ask her. Frankly, I don't care why that car crashed. My son is dead. And I blame myself. If I hadn't let him keep that damn motorcycle…" Defeated, she sat down and looked at her son's picture on the easel. "And if by some miracle, God gave me another chance…" Her voice faltered as she finally, and for the first time, looked at Michelle. She caught her eyes and didn't let go, pronouncing each word like a pledge. "I would do anything to protect that child."

The room fell silent, except for the voice in Michelle's head. She blinked and saw nothing but white.

A thick swirl of white, like the blanket of fog in Topanga Canyon. The road blurred between each slash of the windshield wipers. Beyond the headlights, there was nothing but a black hole, an abyss. It looked as if she and Noah were alone in the world, tunneling through heaven, straight down to hell.

Static raged from the radio until Michelle slapped it off. The kid kept shouting. Now he was quoting William Blake. His argument was irrelevant. The only thing that mattered was removing him from her daughter's life. Noah jammed his demo CD into the dashboard player. The old speakers strained under the beat. He sang along. She hated this song, this rain, this boy. Michelle leaned over the steering wheel to see through the mist.

A truck horn shattered the quiet.

Michelle stomped on the brake. The softball banner banged against her seat back. Noah was thrown forward. He thudded against the glove compartment.

"Didn't your mother teach you to wear a seat belt?" she asked.

"Leave my mother out of this."

Michelle nodded, but if his mother had been home, they wouldn't be on this godforsaken road to meet his father in Malibu. Headlights blinked, then faded past. The SUV jolted, then bounced over gravel.

Noah laughed.

A sign flashed out of the mist. Michelle swerved. The headlights streaked across the scrubby brush and lit the jagged mountain where it dropped off, crumbled from erosion above the canyon cut by glaciers. She slowed. They couldn't be too far from the little downtown area, with all of its stores. If she could make it that far, she could pull over at the coffee shop and wait out the storm. Her knuckles were white as she peered blindly at the fog.

The music kept blasting: "Eyes on the road, your hands upon the wheel..." Noah sang along to his recorded voice, then shrieked with laughter.

Michelle did as the lyric suggested and stared straight ahead. Anything to avoid the sight of his mocking grin, his bloodshot eyes, his naked body slamming into her baby girl. He cranked the volume knob up until her head throbbed with the beat. "Just wait until I talk to your father."

He burst into laughter again. "You kidding? He thinks I'm gay. He'll be thrilled."

"About statutory rape?"

"Any publicity is good publicity."

"No, it's not, you little shit. What did you give her?"

He sang over her—"Going to the roadhouse. We're gonna have a real good time." He put his hand around his mouth like a megaphone to shout between choruses. He punctuated the beat with his pelvis and added an extra line to the lyric. "Let it roll, baby roll, in Ec-sta-sy."

Michelle glared at him. She saw his seat belt, still hanging loose, and reached over to his lap to try and fasten it herself.

He batted her hand away. "Like mother, like daughter, eh?"

"You stay the hell away from Nikki!" she shouted, as the tires caught the edge of the curve.

"You can't protect her forever," he said, taunting her with those long lashes and that leering grin. He was writhing now, dancing, wouldn't sit still.

"I can try."

"Fuck you, I'm out of here," he said, opening the car door. He leaned out and lifted his leg. Michelle lunged to reach him, to pull him back in.

The steering wheel turned without traction. The tires crunched over gravel, the bumper bounced against dirt, branches scraped and pine needles sprayed rat-a-tat like shrapnel through the white cloud. The bass note beat to a whoosh of airborne bliss, like flying. Then the air whistled. Noah screamed in perfect pitch, the key of C to silence.

"Michelle?" Kenny asked.

She blinked and saw him standing in front of her. He glanced at the jurors a few yards away, their faces upturned and expectant. She was on the witness stand, her legs neatly crossed at the ankle. He had promised he wouldn't make her testify unless it was absolutely necessary. So, how did she get there? What had she said?

"Are you all right?" Kenny asked. "According to your medical records, you suffered a traumatic brain injury in the accident, resulting in memory loss. Is that true, Mrs. Mason?"

She heard the name, but it wasn't hers anymore. It was a person from a past life, a stranger. She shook her head.

Kenny exchanged concerned looks with the judge. "The defendant is obviously in a state of confusion. We may need a recess."

"Are you able to continue, Mrs. Mason?" the judge asked. "Speak up for the record."

The record? Michelle nodded along to the music, that song in her head. "Yes."

Kenny raised his voice. "Fine. Can you tell us anything about the events on the morning of October 8? Anything at all?"

Could she? Michelle could barely speak, she was so tongue-tied with the truth. Could she tell him that she'd killed Noah Butler? She knew now, without question, that it was true. He had done his part by taking his seat belt off, but she was angry and she couldn't see through the rain and they argued and he opened the door and she panicked. She had let go of the wheel to grab him. Only for a moment, but a moment was all it took. She would be led away in handcuffs to await a criminal trial.

Michelle cleared her fuzzy throat, struggling to free herself from this straitjacket of guilt. She was ready to accept punishment. She looked at the faces of others who would pay: Kenny, who had sacrificed so much time to help her; Cathy, who splurged on a celebration steak; Drew, the father of her children—and then she saw Tyler. Her son was the most innocent among them. He would suffer most.

Tick, tick, tick.

The door in the back of the gallery squeaked open. When Kenny turned to look, so did everyone else in the courtroom. But it wasn't Nikki. It was Elyse.

Kenny turned back to Michelle and spoke slowly, carefully, so that she understood every word. "Once again. Can you explain what happened the day that Noah Butler died?"

"No," Michelle said. "I can't."

The courtroom was still for a moment, then there was a flash of light from the back. When darkness resumed, the door was closed and Michelle's mother was gone.

"Michelle Mason may be liable for many things," Kenny said as he stood before the jury box and began his closing argument. "But negligence isn't one of them." He glanced back at her, then faced the jurors once more. "This is a confusing case; at least, it is to me. Did the car hit a puddle of oily rainwater that caused the fatal turn? Did the seat belt stop working, or had Noah Butler failed to fasten it in the first place? How long does the owner of an automobile have to repair a potential malfunction? Why did Nicole Mason run away? Who gets all the money that Noah Butler's songs have earned? And yet, few of those questions have anything to do with Michelle Mason.

"My esteemed adversaries want you to believe that Mrs. Mason is a typical Hollywood player who thinks she is above the law and who wanted this young man to stay away from her daughter at any cost. They have told you that she has a family history of depression and that her daughter is, in so many words, a runaway. A video slut. They have implied that Mrs. Mason neglected her children and drove her husband away, that she enjoyed working in an environment of casual drug use, and that the tabloids are correct to call her 'Killer Mom.' How crazy is that? These fancy lawyers deserve their high salaries. Mr. Greenburg is helping his own family find closure. And Mr. Dillenger is legendary for his success in protecting wealthy stockholders.

"But neither one has provided evidence proving that Michelle Mason got in that vehicle with any conscious disregard for passenger safety, nor malice aforethought, nor a history of improper driving. We have only seen evidence that her daughter was a lucky kid who got to dress up on her birthday and be in a low-budget video—a project that her mom talked her boss into making as a favor to a teenager who helped out her son's baseball team. Turns out that Noah Butler did have talent, the kind that comes with tattooed groupies and postmortem fame. But even if Noah Butler turned out not to be so typical, Michelle Mason surely is.

"She is a typical working mom, trying to do all the right things. The evidence presented shows that she often raced straight from work during rush hour to her son Tyler's baseball practice, talking to her husband long-distance when he could only find work out of town, and knitting with her daughter on the sidelines while planning the evening meal. On the day of the accident, evidence shows that her son's baseball game was called off due to rain. It shows that Noah Butler, the assistant pitching coach, rode his motorcycle to Tyler Mason's house. It shows that Tyler's mom was giving him a ride to his dad's house while it was still raining. And it shows that she nearly died doing it.

"By some miracle, Tyler's mom is sitting before us today, scarred inside and out. She will never forget that a young man's life ended when he was thrown out of her car. If anyone wants to profit off this tragic accident, or fight about the particulars, so be it. Make no mistake: this is a terrible tragedy. Nobody should ever lose a child. But it's not my client's fault!"

Kenny took a deep breath to collect himself, then continued. "Michelle Mason is only responsible for being a typical mother who gave another mother's child a ride home in the rain. This could have happened to any of us. Like it says in the Bible, 'There but for the grace of God, go I.'"

The courtroom was quiet as Kenny's closing words filled the room. They echoed in Michelle's head, and she recalled when Cathy had first spoken them to her. But when she glanced behind her, Cathy looked away. Maybe Cathy hadn't meant that it was simply bad luck. Maybe she'd meant what she had said about strangling someone. Maybe that's what Noah's mother meant when she said she would do anything to protect her child. And maybe the knowledge that she would do anything to protect her child was the very thing that made Michelle so typical.

Kenny patted her hand as he sat down, but he avoided her eyes, as if it was all for show. And at that moment she realized that Cathy hadn't bothered him with extra details for a reason. Like she'd said at the ballpark, Kenny knew *exactly* what he was doing.

33

WHEN THE JURY LEFT to deliberate, spectators strolled to the lobby as if it were a theater intermission. Kenny made Michelle wait, restless with guilt, in her seat. Greenburg and Dillenger could be heard debating tee times for the Riviera Country Club as the aisle began to clear. Noah's father ran up to catch Becca and Victor, who were adjourning to the hotel bar across the street. Finally, Kenny escorted Michelle out of the courtroom and past gossiping fans. Reporters looked up from their handheld devices, alert for the district attorney. Kenny didn't stop until they reached the drinking fountain. Then he stood uncomfortably close, like a human handcuff.

Tyler ran over and gave her a big hug. Michelle smoothed a lock of hair from his forehead. "Thanks for being here. I'm sorry about Key West."

"Me too," he said, cutting her off before things turned maudlin. He turned to shake hands with Kenny. "Nice play, Coach."

"Brilliant," Cathy agreed. She shooed Tyler toward the snack machine, then lowered her voice. "How do you feel?"

"Not sure," he admitted. "I still don't believe that none of those jurors have ever heard of Roadhouse or Killer Mom. It was probably a mistake to mention the bartender. And the jury foreman's eyes widened when I mentioned Hollywood, as if he could see his name in lights. Undermines all that crap about being typical." He rubbed his temple. "Damn it, I should have kept it about the car. How you put your trust in a vehicle and look what happens. These cars are known for rollovers—I could have made a case for unreliability." He shook his head in misery.

"He's just nervous," Cathy told Michelle. They both looked at Kenny, the coach who never broke a sweat at the league championships, even when his team was down two runs at the bottom of the ninth. He wasn't nervous; he was scared, and not just for Michelle. They'd go bankrupt if he lost the case.

Cathy pointed at a court clerk watching the Dodgers game on some portable device. "Honey, why don't you go see how the Dodgers are doing? I'll take Michelle to the ladies' room."

When Kenny wandered off, Cathy put her arm around Michelle to protect her from Roadhouse fans. Yet, there was no need for protection now. Michelle repelled everyone equally, as if she glowed with radiation. She felt like a bomb about to blow. But it wasn't the jury's deliberation or the plutonium guilt that weighed so heavily in her chest. Michelle had judged herself already. It was her mother's verdict that she feared the most.

Michelle spotted Elyse across the lobby, deep in conversation with Drew. Elyse's silver hair flamed like a lit match on a long fuse.

Michelle and Cathy ducked into the ladies' room. Cathy was chattering as she wandered back to find an empty stall, but Michelle wasn't listening. She washed her hands at the closest sink. She wanted to powder her nose and pull herself together, but she didn't dare look at herself in the mirror. She was afraid a murderer would look back.

When a toilet flushed and footsteps approached, Michelle kept her head down and dug out her mother's Chanel lipstick.

Cathy's voice called out. "Michelle, did I tell you that Julie offered to write Cody a recommendation for UCLA? That's all a mother can hope for, right?"

Michelle looked up slowly and saw Noah's mother in the mirror. Their eyes locked, but neither said a word. Then Noah's mother slid something across the countertop. It was the postcard of Turtle Town.

The stall clanged open and Cathy called out. "Michelle?"

Michelle jammed the postcard in her purse. When she looked up, the hem of the black caftan was sweeping out through the door.

"Was that Dr. Braunstein?" Cathy asked. "How awkward. Are you all right?"

Michelle nodded, then escaped outside to wait by the windows. Her fingers itched to feel the paper her daughter had touched, to read the lyrics she'd written, but she didn't dare. She stared out to sea. A frothy set of waves was rolling in. She breathed deeply, but all she could smell was Chanel No. 5.

Elyse's reflection loomed in the window. A shank of hair hung loose from her chignon, and where was her signature silk flower? Even the lacy scarf ringing her neck looked out of place against her tired St. John's suit. Time had taken a toll on them both.

"I wanted to come sooner," Elyse said. "But we had our spring recital."

"Let me guess: *Giselle*?" Michelle kept her eyes on the ocean. The horizon was clear now, a narrow strip of blue dividing the earth and sky, like the fine line that Michelle danced on. When she heard the angry click of her mother's compact, she turned around.

"I fly clear across the country, squeezed between a drunken letch and a fat slob who sneezed all over me, but everything I do is wrong!" Elyse flung the compact back in her purse as if it was burning her fingers. "I might as well be dead."

"Is that a threat?"

"It's just an expression. Stop being so melodramatic." Elyse clasped the railing like a ballet barre and stretched by force of habit. "All that was long ago."

"True, but now we have something in common," Michelle said. "Almost dying, I mean. Although I didn't have the pleasure of seeing your pretty white light."

"Ah, but your memory remains faulty, *oui*?" Elyse's glance was as sharp as a dart until she recognized the pink on Michelle's bitten lips. Then she released the barre and almost smiled. "I knew that shade would become you."

"It's just for today; you can have it back." Michelle set her purse on the floor to retrieve her mother's lipstick, then held it in her outstretched palm.

Elyse reached toward the black tube, then her eyes widened and she clutched Michelle's hand. She raised it higher in the light to see the razor thin scars on Michelle's slashed wrist. The lipstick clattered to the floor.

"It's not what you think," Michelle said, yanking her hand away. "It's just a cut." She saw Elyse drop her chin as if to chide her for a lie. "I'm not like you, mother!"

Elyse spun away. She sat on a nearby bench and adjusted the Ace bandage wrapped around her thin ankle.

Michelle tried not to care, but it was a losing battle. She'd always been her mother's protector. Why stop now? "Are you hurt?"

"*Mes enfants*," Elyse said, waving the topic away. "Where shall we dine? They don't feed you on the plane anymore."

"I could add plus one to my reservation at the jail cafeteria," Michelle said.

Elyse frowned as she finished wrapping her ankle. "Is that what you want? To be a martyr? To leave everyone else to clean up your mess?"

"My mess?" Michelle asked.

Elyse stood up. "If you have something to say, Michelle, say it now. As much as I abhor your husband's behavior, I will not return if you don't invite me back. *Comprenez-vous?*"

Michelle nodded. For once, her mother was on her side. Too bad it was now, when she had given up on being good. She turned toward the ocean and hoped her mother would wait for her to find the right words. There was a question that had lingered all of her life, the one she'd never known how to ask. Until now.

Michelle took a deep breath and concentrated as if this was a game show. *This is Your Life—and Mine!* She watched the Ferris wheel spin and felt her heart race as if she were at the carnival, crossing a cakewalk of shifting ground, as her mother stepped to the railing beside her.

When Michelle finally spoke, she pushed the words out of her mouth one by one, focusing on the syllables instead of the meaning behind them. "When you swallowed those pills, it was never a cry for help like the doctors said, was it?"

Elyse tucked the loose hair into her chignon. "*Non, pas du tout.* I wanted to be dead."

Michelle nodded. "But, why?"

Elyse shrugged, as if this game was too easy. "I couldn't under-stand why your father didn't want me. *J'étais dévastée.*"

There was a rush of activity behind them, an announcement on the loudspeaker that they both ignored. "Didn't you love me?"

Elyse pressed her eyes closed.

Michelle wanted to smooth the lavender powder smudged across her mother's crepe lids, but she was afraid to touch her, afraid she would be pushed away.

Elyse finally looked up but refused to meet Michelle's eyes. It seemed like she was staring into the past, watching an old movie.

"I loved you so much, *ma chérie*. When Alexander left, I was devastated, but that's not why I did it. I gave up dancing, everything I knew, to make up for not giving you a family—and it was a mistake. I burned your soup and left you backstage alone all day. I was a horrible mother. And you knew, always watching me with those big brown eyes…" Elyse turned to face Michelle. Her accent went flat. "I thought you'd be better off."

"Without you?" Michelle asked.

Elyse nodded.

They stood in stunned silence for a moment. Then the years melted away and the wall between them crumbled. "Oh, Mother," Michelle cried, her tears flooding from a lifetime of feeling alone. "How could you be so wrong?"

Elyse wrapped her arms around her baby and hugged her, rocking gently as Michelle sobbed. They clung together until a man's voice echoed across the lobby.

"All rise," the bailiff called from inside the courtroom.

Kenny tapped Michelle's shoulder. She pulled away from Elyse and tripped over her purse on the floor. Her pen spilled out. She looked down and spied the edge of the postcard. She leaned down to hide it but lost her balance. She reached out, catching her fingers in Elyse's scarf. The woven yarn stretched until a hole gaped open. Kenny caught her by the elbow and steadied her feet.

Michelle looked back at her mother's ruined scarf. "I'm sorry. About everything."

Elyse shook her head. She pulled the scarf free and took it off. She wrapped it around Michelle's neck as if for luck. Then she reached out for one more hug. She held Michelle close and whispered in her ear. "*Je suis désolée aussi.*"

"Ladies?" Kenny took Michelle's arm. He pulled her across the lobby, away from her mother. Elyse watched the whole way.

Michelle reached the open door and looked back. "Mother!" she cried, afraid she might not return. The courtroom door clanked behind her for the last time. Kenny escorted her inside the dark courtroom and down the aisle. She felt the eyes of the judge, the jury, and everyone in the gallery. She blinked in the darkness as Kenny steered her limp body through the wooden gate. He sat her down at the defense table. The room was dead quiet.

She looked back again, but her mother was gone. Kenny tapped her knee and reminded her to look down, look sad, look innocent.

Michelle fingered the scarf nervously, studying the loose strands of purple yarn shimmering under the harsh light. It was the kind of yarn Nikki had used, the kind Michelle had found in her bedroom. Where had her mother gotten it? Then Michelle knew. She started shaking.

Je suis désolée, her mother had said. But she didn't mean she was sorry about the scarf or even about the trial. Elyse was sorry about Nikki. And Nikki had made the scarf that hung like a noose around Michelle's neck.

Kenny patted her knee, as if calming her for the verdict. Michelle took a deep breath and fought to put the facts together, to avoid showing the grief that could give her away. Elyse had said something else that rang true: she'd thought Michelle would be better off without her.

The judge was speaking now, but Michelle couldn't hear a word. Her head was crowded with the testimony written all over her mother's face, the secret message in sparkling yarn. The bailiff took an envelope from the head juror and walked it back to the bench. Michelle felt a tap on her shoulder and turned around.

Tracy offered the *Star Trek* pen that had rolled out of Michelle's purse in the lobby. Michelle nodded thanks. She studied the tiny starship floating inside the barrel. Then she remembered the plane ticket her mother had sent. The one stuffed in the drawer of the hall table.

All at once, she was surrounded. Light bulbs flashed and shouts rang out. Strangers were hugging her and shaking Kenny's hand.

"It's over?" she asked him.

He spotted the district attorney slipping out quietly past the reporters, then nodded. "Congratulations. You can go home."

34

TOWERING COLUMNS OF CORN flashed past the old Mercedes in hypnotic stripes of green. Elyse's knuckles were clamped white on the wheel, but not a word was wasted between them. An hour had passed since Michelle stepped down from the airplane stairs and stuck her heels in the soft tarmac. Each breath still held a familiar torture, as if she'd never escaped this iron lung of heat. Fifty miles outside Columbus, the land was still as flat as when she was a kid, cruising all day on her ten-speed. Now, night was falling and the devil had caught up. She was at her mother's mercy.

They sped past a cluster of spotted cows, then the unmistakable aroma of fertilizer whooshed in with the hot air. Michelle rolled the window up and peeled her white T-shirt away from her chest. She jiggled the lever of the broken air conditioning vent, then opened the purse on her lap for something to fan herself with.

The envelope that Becca had given her after the trial was right on top. She pulled out the check and read her name above the dollar amount: $2,000,000. Michelle couldn't help smiling. She'd never seen so many zeroes. She waved it a few times, but the flush of shame only made her feel hotter. She pulled out her pen and signed it: *deposit to the Children's Shelter c/o The Noah Butler Trust.*

"What do you have there?" Elyse asked.

"Just something I need to mail," Michelle said. She put it back in her purse, then unlatched the glove compartment. When the door swung down, spilling the contents, Elyse stiffened beside her. "Sorry. I was looking for something to wedge the vent open."

"We're almost there."

"No, I can reach," Michelle said.

"Have it your way," Elyse said with a sigh. "There's mail for you, too—a reminder for a PCR appointment with Dr. Palmer. What is that?"

"A kind of therapy," Michelle said, stifling a smile. She spotted her name on the reminder card printed with the address of a "clinic" at the Columbus Hilton where they'd planned to meet. She leaned down against the seat belt and extended her right arm just enough to pick it up between her fingers.

"Must be effective," Elyse observed.

Michelle nodded. She saw Elyse's furtive glance and followed it down to the mess. She leaned forward and spied a postcard of the Great Barrier Reef in a plastic sleeve labeled Australia. Michelle raised her eyes slowly toward her mother. "You sent the postcards?"

Elyse kept her eyes on the road. Michelle knew by the firm line of her mother's lips not to press further in this prickly heat. She hoped to find out soon enough. The last fallen item was a brochure for the Elyse Deveraux School of Dance. Michelle fanned herself for a moment. "Mind if I use this?"

Elyse glanced over. "*Non.*"

Michelle winced at how she'd dismissed the sample Elyse had brought to show her in California, when she'd just returned home from the hospital. She could apologize, but it was time to start fresh. Even her mother was looking ahead, her eyes fixed on the vaporous mirage rising from the road before them.

Michelle studied her mother's Degas-style portrait on the cover. For the first time, it inspired pride instead of anger. When Michelle opened it, she looked more closely at the glossy pictures. The collage of children caught her eye, especially one brown-eyed baby in a tutu.

"Is this a picture of me?" Michelle asked.

Elyse smiled. She slowed at the next corner where a cloud of mosquitoes circled the cottontails, then turned right past Kern's, the general store where Michelle used to stop for apple cider. The wooden fence along the parking lot was skirted with a banner of red, white, and blue.

"Any of this look familiar?" Elyse asked.

"All of it," Michelle said, fanning her damp face with the brochure. Independence Day was huge in Ohio. Police vans with bullhorns prowled the riverside at dawn to wake the sleepy neighborhoods. Children dressed like Betsy Ross and Abe Lincoln rode on crepe paper–covered floats pulled by tractors in the parade. There wasn't a whole lot else to do when the heat hit 100 besides swim, catch crawdads, or hitch a ride down the Scioto River on a ski boat.

Michelle marveled as they passed an empty fireworks stand and tunneled into a shady road of maples. Before leaving for college, she'd helped wire the skinny saplings to tall sticks. The middle-class houses looked like mansions now, especially the brick colonial where she grew up. She wondered about the real estate value but could barely think beyond her throbbing heart.

Elyse parked on the circular driveway, then walked around to open the passenger door. Michelle peeled herself off the leather seat and climbed out. She tugged her damp shirt from her dark jeans and smoothed her frizzy hair. She was so nervous it felt like her brain was buzzing. Then the sound rose until she recognized it as the cricket's summer song. Not Drew's crickets—hers. Drew's obsession had seduced her from the beginning, with the familiar sound of home.

Elyse popped the trunk to get the suitcases, but Michelle heard music drifting from the backyard and didn't wait. She slapped a gnat on her neck, then followed the path past the trellis of scarlet roses climbing up the side of the house. The lawns joined without fences into a common carpet of green. A cluster of fir trees filtered the shouts of children playing down by the creek. Michelle rounded the corner and spied red and green balloons tied to the porch rail.

Nikki stood by a picnic table, a backlit dream come to life. She turned down the tune on the CD player, a love song Michelle recognized from the Roadhouse album. Then she picked up her camera from beside the silver Christmas tree on the table and tossed the strap over her head before stepping down the wooden stairs. Michelle started to run. She wanted to sweep her daughter off her feet, just like in the commercials she used to produce. But Nikki held her camera up like a shield between them, click-click-clicking with each step closer.

The sound made Michelle pause. Panic overwhelmed the impulse and her stomach cramped with regret. She spoke as loudly as she could over the lump in her throat. "Looks like a party."

The sun dove for cover behind the house. Loss flickered in the dusk between them, along with the first real fireflies Michelle had seen in many years. When the porch light clicked on, she could see Nikki more clearly, dressed in an Ohio State tank top and a denim skirt. Her brown hair was cut short without care.

"You look good," Michelle said, instantly aware of how little her opinion mattered, how silly her words must sound.

Nikki stopped a few feet away and lowered her camera. "So do you."

Michelle reached her with her good arm, inhaling the rancid scent of bug spray, her favorite perfume as of right now. Nikki was an inch taller, and she'd lost more than the weight she gained in Hawaii. Michelle would fatten her up with potato salad and peanut butter Buckeyes—all the local delicacies. She studied her daughter's face, but for the first time, Nikki's eyes were unreadable.

"I missed you," Michelle said, or thought she said. Her voice sounded strange, because the lump in her throat had grown to feel like a concrete dam choking back her words. She heard children whooping like Indians and wondered if they still used that term for the Wyandotte—or if they were Native Americans now—but frankly she didn't care. There were a million other thoughts stacked in her head and if she pulled one out they would scatter like pickup sticks and she might lose hold of her baby, finally back in her embrace.

"Mama!" a little girl cried.

Michelle answered in her head, like when a child calls across a toy store and every nursing mother's milk bursts in sticky circles beneath her blouse. A moment later, a ragtag parade of children in party hats scampered over the rise, followed by a matronly woman in a housedress.

Nikki broke away to snap pictures like a babysitter on duty. Michelle couldn't tear her eyes from Nikki's face, her confidence with the camera aimed at the children skipping across the lawn. Nikki scooped up a crawler in a pink tutu and straightened her birthday crown. She gave the squirming child a squeeze, then spun her around and lowered her slowly, until she could stand by herself on the soft grass. "There's someone I want you to meet. Mother, this is Noelle."

Michelle blinked at the girl's brown eyes, framed by long lashes, familiar from the brochure—and beyond. She collapsed to her knees and knelt at eye level, steadying herself with her good hand. Noelle. After a moment, she found her voice and glanced up. "Christmas in July?"

Nikki nodded. She held her daughter against her knees and removed the birthday crown to finger-comb her hair.

"Happy birthday, Noelle," Michelle said. "I like your tutu."

"Mine!" Noelle cried. Nikki laughed.

The porch light blinked on. The sliding door opened, and Elyse appeared with a pile of gifts.

"Nana!" Noelle tried to pull away from her mother.

"This is your Nana Michelle," Nikki said, holding her there. "She's a present, too. The one we've been waiting for."

Noelle stopped wiggling and scrunched her eyes at Michelle.

"Happy birthday," Michelle said again, blinking back tears.

Noelle rubbed her tiny fist against Michelle's right hand. Her sparkly pink nails were clenched around a toy.

Nikki nodded for Michelle to take it. "I think it's a present for you."

"Thank you," Michelle said, but her reach was slow. Something fell and rolled a foot away. She clenched her teeth against the pain to reach farther, finally closing her weak fingers around the muddy figurine. She rubbed the dirt away to see a painted ballerina in the blue tutu. It was the smallest nesting doll.

Noelle put her arms around Michelle's neck in a stranglehold, her warm breath tickling her ear. Michelle's arm tingled as she lifted it up inch by inch, reaching to wrap both arms around Noelle's tiny back. She hugged her so tightly that she forgot to breathe; she could inhale this child instead.

Noelle broke away and toddled a few steps toward her mother. Nikki immediately adjusted her camera and aimed like an expert. Click-click-click.

Michelle ignored the noise. "You shot the brochures?"

"And portraits. You'd be amazed how much parents will pay."

"No, I wouldn't," Michelle said.

After a dozen steps, Noelle fell down. She looked up at her mother, ready to cry. Instead, she broke out giggling. Nikki grasped her tiny hand and pulled her back up to a stand. She twirled her slowly, like the ballerina in her music box.

"You used to twirl like that," Michelle called to her daughter.

Elyse stepped up quietly behind Michelle and helped her up. "So did you."

The woman in a housedress emerged from the porch with a tray. "Who wants cake?" she called.

The children squealed and scrambled to the stairs leading up to Elyse's deck. After the woman set the lopsided cake on the picnic table, she looked up and waved. It was Noah's mother. Michelle had never seen the woman smile, but it was a beautiful sight. She waved back.

Elyse picked up the birthday girl and carried her over to the garden hose, calling the other children to join them and wash their hands.

Michelle caught up to Nikki, confused. "My mother knew the whole time?"

"No, not until after Hawaii. I didn't show for a while, and I ate so much poi on that pirate boat that I convinced myself I was just getting fat. But after a few more months, it got too hard to zip the wetsuit and keep those stripes straight. I knew I had to find a doctor. I got desperate."

"So you sold drugs?"

"It's not like it sounds. When I saw you that last time in the hospital, it was awful. Nana told me to say good-bye. I had to get away from it all. I swiped some of Daddy's pills to feel better, but I was throwing up so much in Hawaii, pretending to be seasick, that I knew I shouldn't take them, so…"

"You're lucky you weren't arrested." Michelle scolded herself for the tone.

"I know. And by the time I was ready to deal with being pregnant, it was too late to do anything but wonder if the baby would look like Noah."

This time, Michelle was more careful. "Did you love him?"

"Not like I love her," Nikki said, glancing back at Noelle.

Michelle understood exactly.

"I wanted to tell you first, but as soon as I heard you woke up, I read about the lawsuit online and I was afraid."

"So you called Nana?"

"I was afraid Daddy would be furious. I had the baby here, but…" She fiddled with her camera strap. "When he kept calling about your rehabilitation, Nana's boyfriend warned her to be careful about other people nosing around. I had to make myself scarce."

Michelle noted the stickers from San Francisco and Chicago on Nikki's camera strap, cities where the echo of Elyse's name would still rate a bunk backstage. "That must have been rough."

Nikki shrugged. "One of the ballet teachers helped out. And Noah's mother. I'd hinted about being pregnant in a postcard, but I didn't get in touch again until Noelle was born and I got desperate. She sent money as soon as she could. She has a vested interest."

"So do I!" Michelle heard her voice rise with frustration, but she couldn't stop the volcano of emotions from erupting. "You must have heard that I was out of the hospital. Why didn't you at least call? And I don't mean to leave a message."

"Because you would have found me!" Nikki tried to hold back her tears. "People have been searching for me almost from the beginning—Dad and Noah's father and lawyers and reporters and fans—my own brother has no idea that I follow him as a school friend on Facebook. Then you learned I was missing—and within weeks, you were so close I could hear you calling my name!"

"In Key West?"

Nikki nodded, then lowered her voice and continued. "I wanted to answer, I really did. But all those people were keeping tabs on you. If you'd found me, everyone else would have found me too, then they would have found Noelle. And I couldn't let that happen." She looked up and met Michelle's eyes. "I'm sorry."

It was in the card all along: *Hello, Mother. I feel awful about what happened. But I can't see you like this. I hope you understand. Love, me.*

Michelle wiped her daughter's tears. "I'm sorry too—about Noah."

"No one is innocent here. Except…" Nikki pointed at Noelle. "I want her to grow up away from all the fuss. When the legal stuff is settled, Laura can set up a trust and Noelle will be safe." They watched as the little girl climbed up on the picnic table and plunged her hands in the cake.

Laura laughed and braced Noelle from a fall, then leaned in to give her a kiss. *I would do anything to protect that child.* She hadn't been referring to Noah on the witness stand. She meant his daughter, Noelle. That turtle postcard was left exposed in her drawer at the office on purpose. She wanted to lure Michelle off the trail. But it was also a gift of hope.

Michelle watched Elyse turn off the hose and run to stop Noelle. She picked up a birthday napkin and tried to wipe Noelle's face, then gave up and wiped frosting off her white pantsuit. "So she wore your scarf to the trial on purpose? That explains why her outfit didn't match."

Nikki giggled in agreement.

Michelle smiled and turned back to her. "But what if I hadn't recognized that yarn? What if I hadn't understood the message?"

Nikki stopped giggling. "Then I would know for sure that the mother I knew was gone. Losing Noah was bad enough. But losing you?"

She could no longer speak for crying. Michelle took her in her arms, both arms, and held her close.

After a moment, Nikki spoke up. "Will you help me call Daddy later? She was—an accident. But I need him to understand."

"Of course," Michelle murmured. There was no such thing as an accident.

Elyse's exasperated voice rang out from the porch as she passed plates out to the other children. "Nikki, it's time to cut what's left of the cake!"

Nikki giggled again and wiped her tears as she pulled away. She looped her arm around Michelle's waist and led her toward the deck. "Would you like a piece? It's chocolate."

"I love chocolate," Michelle said.

"I know," Nikki replied. She skipped up the stairs to do the honors.

Michelle set the tiny painted doll on the wooden railing. She was tempted to line up all five of them, but there was no need; they were all here. Elyse lit the candle, and they sang the birthday song. Nikki's voice was full with forgiveness and regret, hopes and dreams, and all the plans that paled in the light of the moon.

Michelle plucked a dandelion. She waved it around until the cottony seeds drifted like fluffy parachutes to the ground. They dotted the summer rye rolling down the hill to the creek that connected to the river beyond. Michelle thought of the blue lines on the map, how they connected the dots of the cities she searched in, the states that separated them, the oceans she swam in her dreams. Not one of them was alone for a moment, not on this tiny ball of Earth spinning below the heavens, sparkling with stars like a mirrored ball.

It was a wonder she didn't fall off.

Reading Group Guide

1. This story takes place in Hollywood, the origin of our celebrity culture. Michelle loves her work, yet keeps her children "as far away as possible." Do you think this is a realistic objective?

2. Michelle has compromised her career for her family and her family for her career. Are women wrong to want to have it all? Do you think women *can* have it all?

3. If parents experimented with drugs at some point in their life, should they share this information with their children? How do you think this could affect their relationship with their children?

4. Michelle was worried that Nikki was suicidal. Do you believe that suicide is prompted by mental illness or is a deliberate act? Is it preventable?

5. Why was it so hard for Michelle to forgive her mother? How did Michelle's history with her mother influence her when it came to being a mother to Nikki?

6. Michelle's hopes for her daughter changed from wanting her to be wildly successful to just wanting her to be happy. How do you think this compares with other parents? Do you think she was wrong?

7. Why did the author include Michelle's run-in at the DMV with a "perfect mother" whose tennis champ son became a junkie?

8. When Michelle wonders who she is without her daughter, she is talking about a large part of her identity. How do you think our identities are linked to our familial relationships?

9. Becca knows that the reason Michelle can't reach her friend Sasha is because Sasha is with Michelle's husband. Is she being a good friend by not telling her—or a bad one? What would you do?

10. How were Julie and Cathy both allies to Michelle? How did they also hurt her?

11. Many parents travel for business, but the film business is known for location affairs. How does this change the character of the mothers at home? Do you think it contributed to the weakening of Michelle's marriage?

12. When Michelle says she "couldn't afford to miss" Drew, what did she mean?

13. Why did Dr. Palmer value the very qualities in Michelle that threatened Drew?

14. Lexi notes that Michelle finds it "easier to blame" herself than to accept all the things that are out of her control. Why is this true for Michelle? Have you ever felt this way?

15. Elyse tells Michelle that Nikki is "a mystery," but she offers hints as to her whereabouts. Why doesn't she tell Michelle the truth?

16. The mothers in this story—Michelle, Elyse, Julie, Cathy, and Noah's mother—all took unethical actions to protect their families. What do these women have in common? How do they differ?

17. Do you believe what Elyse says, that "there are no accidents"?

18. How did Michelle's relationship with her son end up being the turning point in her testimony?

19. What is Michelle's true need? How is it different from her desire in this story? How are they related?

20. When Nikki ran away, the places where she spent time tended to be places where her family had vacationed. What does this say about Nikki?

21. Noah's mother was Jewish but worked at a Catholic hospital. What does this tell us about her character, and how is it reflected later by her actions?

22. How do the symbols of the turtle and the starfish represent Michelle's character growth?

23. Cake is a symbol that even the author was unaware of until the story was complete. The confection is featured at both the beginning, the end, and in a different but significant event in the middle. Why does cake enhance such moments?

24. Which character do you most identify with and why?

25. How far would you go to protect your child?

Acknowledgments

THANKS TO MOLLIE GLICK, for believing in this story from its dark beginning, and to her excellent assistant, Kathleen Hamblin, as well as Stephanie Abou and Rachel Hecht at Foundry Literary & Media. Thanks to my insightful editor, Shana Drehs, and the rest of the team at Sourcebooks, including Beth Pehlke, Heather Hall, Danielle Jackson, Valerie Pierce, and Nicole Villeneuve.

A big hug for my brilliant husband, John Truby, who pointed out the detective story beneath my fancy prose. I'm so lucky to have found someone who enjoys discussing the possibilities of a single sentence as much as I do.

Medical expertise was provided by Dr. Robert M. Bilder, Ph.D., Tennenbaum Professor of Psychiatry and Biobehavioral Sciences and Psychology at UCLA's Semel Institute—whose full title is so much longer that I'm honored he found time to help. Legal aspects were honed by the real Kenneth Kazan, an attorney far more sophisticated than the fictional character on these pages. Any medical or legal mistakes that remain are mine.

A special note of appreciation goes to my aunt, Edith Amsterdam, the true proprietor of the fabulous Curry Mansion in Key West, Florida. Scenes in Santa Monica and Maui evolved from work with Nancy Zafris and Jim Krusoe of the MFA program at Antioch University.

Thanks to my readers who were game from the first draft: my sister Tracy Lehr, who will appreciate the angst even more when her girls are teenagers; the real Cathy Kazan, a friend since our daughters were in preschool and who is far hotter than her fictional counterpart; Janet Orloff, who also served as my psychology expert; Karen J. Rinehart, Sandwich Generation blogger; and the real Michelle M., the hairstylist who made me feel so pretty at my wedding that her name became a touchstone.

This story was inspired by love for my sweet daughters, Juliette and Catherine Spirson, and serves as an ode to my mother, Dr. Claire Lehr.

Finally, I'm grateful to everyone who understands how our children's happiness is often the key to our own.

About the Author

Megan Stark Photography

*L*ESLIE LEHR IS THE award-winning author of the novels *66 Laps* and *Wife Goes On*, and humorous parenting books including *Welcome to Club Mom*. Her essays have appeared in the anthology *Mommy Wars*, *The Honeymoon's Over*, and Arianna Huffington's *On Becoming Fearless*. She was the screenwriter for the romantic thriller *Heartless* and sold the script *Club Divorce* to Lifetime. She has a BA from the USC School of Cinematic Arts and an MFA from Antioch. She has two daughters and lives with her husband in Santa Monica.

Please visit Leslie at www.leslielehr.com.